THE NETHERGRIM

BOOK 1

MATTHEW JOBIN

PHILOMEL BOOKS • An Imprint of Penguin Group (USA).

PHILOMEL BOOKS
Published by the Penguin Group
Penguin Group (USA) LLC
375 Hudson Street, New York, NY 10014

USA | Canada | UK | Ireland | Australia | New Zealand | India | South Africa | China
penguin.com
A Penguin Random House Company

Library of Congress Cataloging-in-Publication Data
Jobin, Matthew.
The Nethergrim / Matthew Jobin.   pages cm.—(The Nethergrim ; book 1)
Summary: An evil force has been awakened from years of sleep and it is up to fourteen-
year-old Edmund, an aspiring sorcerer, and his friends to stop it.   [1. Fantasy.] I. Title.
PZ7.J5784Net 2014   [Fic]—dc23   2013005309
Printed in the United States of America.
ISBN 978-0-399-15998-5
1 3 5 7 9 10 8 6 4 2

Edited by Michael Green.   Design by Semadar Megged and Amy Wu.
Text set in 12.5-point Fiesole Text.

For Tina

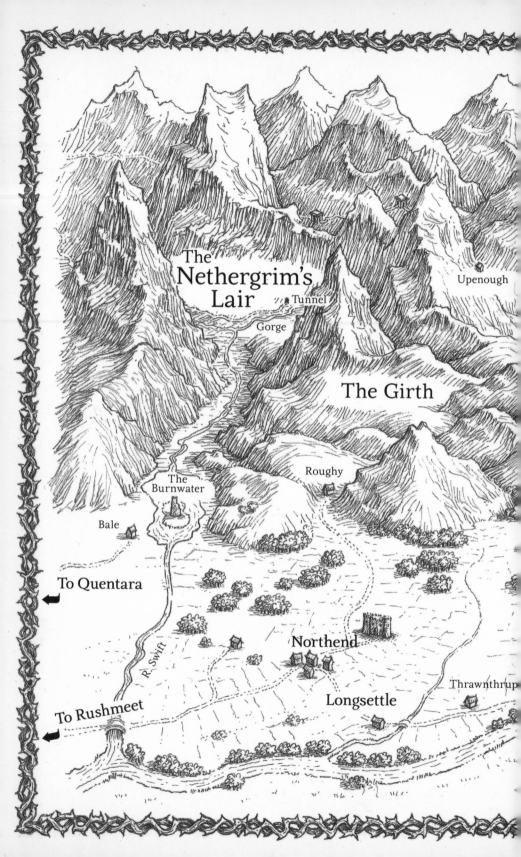

Prologue

The best horse I ever knew was a bay stallion with a white star on his face. His name was Juniper—a strange name for a steed of war, but that's what he was called when he was born, and his rider never changed it. The rider was the fourth son of the lord of a little place far away south. This boy had heard every tale of every grand old hero ever told, and when each of them was finished, he asked to hear it again, long after the other boys had started sneering at them. His father gave him Juniper on his sixteenth birthday because he had no land left to give, and so this boy—his name was Tristan—thanked his father for the horse and the armor and the sword he was given, and rode away from home. He had too many brothers for anyone to miss him much.

Tristan and Juniper wandered the roads for many months, looking for good deeds that needed doing, and after a while they found some—lonely things, quiet things in little hamlets and manors at the edges of the land. Tristan's shield was often dented and often mended. His sword grew notched, but he kept it carefully keen. Juniper grew as fearless as any horse ever born, and the rumor of their coming sent awful things scurrying into their holes.

But the world is not a story, or if it is, the plot is very strange. The people Tristan helped were mostly poor, and though they were grateful when he killed a quiggan or caught an outlaw, it was hard to live on what they gave in thanks. He and Juniper grew both tough and wild, and in safer places where there were no such troubles, he found that people had no use for him. After a while he found himself dreaming of a different life, with warm fires, good food and cheerful friends.

One day, as Tristan traveled through a land south and west of us near a great curve in the mountains, he was met on the road by a lord and his household knights, well-fed men in polished mail astride great horses of war. They commanded that Tristan stop, for they had heard stories of this youth who roved the marches, doing the bravest of deeds for the least of men. The lord bade Tristan attend him at court, where Tristan spoke of his adventures with the grace of perfect truth. The court sat up listening long into the night, and when Tristan was finished, the lord raised his cup and welcomed him as a knight of his household. Tristan was overcome with joy, and swore a sacred oath to serve the lord all his days.

All seemed well at last. Tristan was a gallant young knight in service to a mighty lord, riding at the head of his vanguard in gleaming armor. As the months went by, though, Tristan

MATTHEW JOBIN

began to discover something he did not like. He would hear stories of trouble out on the borderlands, just as before: boggans in the millponds, thieves and cutthroats on the roads—the sort of things he would always go and try to fix when he was on his own. But now he was an oathbound knight, and his lord would never allow him to go help anyone. Tristan's lord wanted very badly to have more land, even though he already had so much that you could not ride across it all in a week. He plotted and schemed for months, drawing up his plans in secret and buying allies with coffers full of gold. Other lords came and went from the castle—some fearful, some angry, and some with terrible hungry smiles.

Soon enough, war came, a war that was happening only because Tristan's lord wished to rule more of the world. Tristan had sworn an oath, and that meant he would not leave no matter how unhappy he became, for he had been raised to keep his word, especially when those words were sacred oaths. His lord led an attack through a nearby land, fighting all the way. Instead of monsters, Tristan found himself in the thick of battles against other men with whom he had no quarrel. He tried to be merciful whenever he could, but people died on his sword—perfectly decent people who did not deserve it. Sometimes he would lie awake at night, and a little voice in him would ask if it would be better if it was he who died.

At last they laid siege to one of their enemy's great castles. Tristan's lord thought he could win if he struck fast and hard, so on a hot night in summer some of the men were ordered to throw ladders up the sides of the walls and try to take the castle by storm. They scaled the gatehouse and let down the drawbridge under a rain of arrows. Thinking victory was his for the taking, Tristan's lord charged in, leading Tristan and the other knights far ahead of the footsoldiers. He made an awful mistake, for the enemy within the castle was much stronger than he had guessed. They sprang in a mass from every tower, trapping the knights in the courtyard below. Tristan tried to protect his lord, throwing himself in front of every enemy who came near, but it was no use. An arrow struck the lord in the neck and he fell off his horse, dead.

The attack had failed. The courtyard was strewn with the dead and the dying. Tristan lowered his sword and stared about him like a man in a dream, and it was only Juniper, weaving this way and that through the fray, who saved both himself and his rider. Tristan let his sword fall with a clatter to the stones, and then his shield. He grasped the reins and rode from that courtyard through a hail of arrows, past his own army and into the night. He was never seen in that country again.

Seasons turned in their weary round. Tristan and Juniper became lonely, wandering creatures again, but this time Tristan was afraid and ashamed, and did not try to be a hero. Juniper's saddle was sold for food, and so was Tristan's ring that was given him by his mother, and still they had hardly enough to eat. For many months they roamed, a ragged young man with his big shaggy horse, until they came into the north in the middle of a winter just like this one.

In that winter, in a place not far from here, there was a little

MATTHEW JOBIN

village in terrible trouble. It stood at the very edge of the kingdom, far out and alone on a road so old that no one knew who
had built it. Tristan rode Juniper into the village just as it was
getting dark. They crept along from house to house, finding
no one anywhere, until they came to a crossroad where stood
a tiny inn. No sound came from within, but firelight flickered
through the shuttered windows. Tristan threw a blanket over
Juniper and led him to the empty stables in the back, then
opened the inn's front door.

"There's a draft," spoke a voice. Its owner was the only person inside. He sat with his feet propped up before the fire and
the cowl of his fine dark cloak over his head. He seemed—of
all things on such a night—to be reading something.

"Why are you not at the hall with the others?" The cloaked
figure spoke without turning.

"Please." Tristan stepped in and shut the door. "I am just a
traveler. I do not know where I am supposed to be. It is very
cold outside."

The other man turned to look at him. "You, friend, must be
the most luckless traveler in all the world."

Tristan came closer to the light and warmth of the fire. He
could see that the other man took him for a beggar or a run-
away slave. He certainly looked it; his tattered old tunic had
been made for a much shorter man, and he had sold his shoes
months before. His feet were bound with rags, and in his long
wandering grief, his beard had grown tangled and his eyes
sunken.

The other man bent to throw a log on the fire. "The innkeeper is at the hall with the rest. Your best chance for survival is with them."

Tristan held out his hands to the flames. "What is happening here?"

The other man looked up at Tristan with an expression both searching and amused. "Tell me, traveler, where were you going?"

"I do not know. I was following the road."

"You could not follow it much farther. Past here there once stood a few farms; they are nothing now but ashes. The road then rises into the mountains, but you would never reach them. The Nethergrim has come. He has found these people living on his doorstep, and he is angry."

"The Nethergrim?" Tristan sat next to him and warmed himself by the fire. "I thought that was just a story."

"Would that it were." The other man flipped to the end of his book, searching page after page. He closed it with a sigh. "Nothing. No help at all."

"What were you reading?" asked Tristan.

"My master's journals, for the third time," said the other man. "I was looking for some secret knowledge of the Nethergrim, some weakness I could use against him."

"Where then is your master?"

"Dead—along with his guards, servants, mounts, guides and all of his apprentices save me. I was the only one who got back here alive." The cloaked man laughed, short and bitter.

"We were exploring the pass, you see, searching for some sign of the fabled Nethergrim."

Tristan stood and looked through a crack in the shutters. He saw nothing but the snow-dusted road and dark houses. "And he is coming here?"

"He is," said the other man. "There are records of such things from long ago. The villagers know much less than I, but their legends are enough to feed their fears. They meet now in the hall to decide their course."

"Why are you not with them?"

The other man looked around him at the shadows on the walls of the tavern. "I don't like crowds, and this seems as good a place to die as any."

Tristan felt a chill, for he knew despair when he saw it. "You are sure there is no hope?"

The man looked Tristan up and down again. "What is your name?"

Tristan hesitated, for it had been long since he had used his right name—first from fear, then from shame, and after a while from simple hopelessness. There was something, though, in the way the other man looked at him that made him want to speak truly. "I am Tristan."

"You may call me Vithric," said the other man. "Give me your counsel, Tristan. The Nethergrim has arisen and slain my master, a wizard of no small power. Foul things of many orders obey his will. Tonight they will enter this village and harrow it—tomorrow I doubt any of us will be left alive. There are perhaps a hundred folk holed up in the hall, forty of them children, and maybe a dozen old or sick. Few of them are armed, and none are well armed. What would you have them do?"

Tristan was surprised, as it had been some time since anyone had looked on him as someone to be heeded. "The village hall—how is it constructed?"

"Timber over a stone foundation, with a high roof of thatching."

Tristan shook his head. "It cannot hold." He pondered for a moment. "Perhaps the villagers can buy their freedom. If they put together all their possessions and offer them as tribute, maybe the Nethergrim will let them go."

"Here in the north the Nethergrim has many names," said Vithric. "The Old Man of the Mountains, they name him, the Thief at the Cradle, Mother's Bane. They say the flesh of children is the only thing he truly prizes."

The thought of those poor children trapped in the hall and awaiting such a fate was more than Tristan could bear. "We must do something!"

"There is nothing to do," said Vithric. "The villagers might as well pass the time digging their own graves. Perhaps the Nethergrim will be so kind as to toss in their bones when he is done with them."

"They can run." Tristan stood. "They can run! If they hold together—"

"It is forty miles to the nearest village, and sixty to the castle at Northend," said Vithric. "They are all as good as dead—so are we."

Tristan paced across the room and back. "How many horses do they have?"

"None. My master hired them all, and they are all now eaten or fled into the mountains." Vithric raised his hands and let them drop again. "Were it morning, and the fast did not wait for the slow, some of these folk might reach safety—but it is night, and mothers will carry children, sons will prop their aged fathers on their shoulders and they will all of them die upon the road. Some of these creatures can move through the shadows at great speed."

"I know that."

A somber smile crossed Vithric's face. "Then you no longer wish to play the wandering pilgrim? You were not at all convincing—sir knight."

"What use is there in hiding, if this is truly my last night in the world?" Tristan stared into the fire. Vithric watched with him. Neither man looked at the other.

"Tell me," said Vithric. "When you did fight, for what were you fighting?"

"I once served a great lord," said Tristan. "I thought I fought for honor, but in truth I fought for his greed. I killed good men; I made widows of their wives, I made orphans of their children so that I might hear my master say that I had done well."

"You score above the other knights I have known in your honesty, at least," said Vithric. "There is nothing else?"

"Once," said Tristan, "long ago it seems, I wandered from village to village, throwing my shield over poor folk with no other hope. I never asked for more than they gave, and they never could give much. I had my sword, my shield, my horse and my honor."

"And you had their thanks," said Vithric. "Their praise and their love. And in time, as you saved the lives of more of these poor, decent folk, you began to wonder . . ."

Tristan looked up to the rafters. "I began to wonder if I was doing it because they needed me or because they praised me."

Vithric nodded just once. "That is indeed the question. I would have liked to spend some days discussing it, for the currents of your thought run deeper than most men's. I fear, however, that we have no time."

"You speak truth." Tristan roused himself from his place by the fire. "Come with me."

"What do you mean?" Vithric spoke in a snap. "We have already discussed it. There is no way out."

Tristan opened the door. "I have lost my sword and shield. I may have lost my honor, too—but I did not lose my horse. Come."

He led a dumbfounded Vithric to the stable. "You will have to ride without a saddle." He touched Juniper's face. "Goodbye, dear friend. Bear this man to safety."

Vithric gaped at Tristan. "You could have run. You could have gotten on this horse and galloped for your life as soon as you knew you were in danger."

"His name is Juniper." Tristan walked them out to the road. "I ask only that you treat him well."

"You grant me the hope of life," said Vithric. "How do you know that I am worthy of the gift?"

Tristan helped him onto Juniper's back. "Make yourself worthy."

Vithric took the reins. He stared down at Tristan, then off into the distance. "Then—what will you do?"

"Help the folk of this village escape their fate if I can, or die at their side if I cannot." Tristan slapped Juniper's flank. "Now ride, and do not look back."

Juniper sprang off at a gallop down the cold and empty road. Tristan turned to walk to the hall alone, but before he had gotten much closer, he felt a chill down his back. He looked around; creeping from paddock to garden to byre, the servants of the Nethergrim had shadowed him, and now they drew in. He would never reach the hall alive.

Even though he knew it was useless, he took a fighting stance. "I know what you are—I have killed your kind before. You cannot scare me to death. Come and take me, if you can."

The creatures closed in, emerging from the shadows under cottage and haystack. Just before they crept onto the road and their forms became more than awful suggestions, Tristan heard the sound of hoofbeats approaching at a gallop. At first he thought he was dreaming, and then he thought it was the villagers, but it came from the other way. He looked down the road and could scarcely believe what he saw.

Yes. It was Juniper—and Vithric, too. They rode in at a thunder, a heartbeat ahead of the Nethergrim's creatures.

"I come to return your gift!" Vithric reached down for Tristan's hand, and so the greatest knight and the greatest wizard this world has ever known became friends. You see, before they could save that little village, and then the kingdom and all the world, first they had to save each other.

Chapter 1

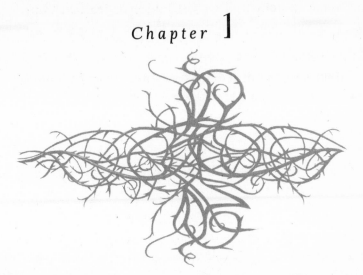

Edmund Bale came last to breakfast, too bleary to note the curious silence until it was too late. He descended the rickety steps into the tavern at a sleepy shuffle, yawning all the way down. His family ate their morning meal at the best table by the fire. The rest of the room was a jumble of benches left as they were when the last guest stumbled out the night before.

"Horsa left his fiddle here again." Edmund kicked it aside. He had reached his chair before he came to understand that his family was neither talking nor eating. Between them on the table, amongst the loaves and leeks and bowls of porridge, lay a pile of parchment—bound scrolls and loose leaves thrown carelessly over a pair of worn old books.

Edmund felt the blood drain from his face. "Where—"

"Where you hid them," said his father. "Sit down."

His mother fixed him with a wounded look. "Son, we told

you about this, we told you and told you. What does it take, Edmund? What does it take to get through to you?"

"Mum—"

"Sleepy, are you?" Edmund's father ground his teeth. "Up late?"

"No, I—no, it's not—" Edmund could not find a good lie. "I just—"

His father grabbed him by the arm. "Sit. Down!"

Edmund sat, reeling. He had been so careful, so sure to pick his moments, stealthy almost beyond reason with his secret stores of books. His mother sighed, looked away, shook her head and sighed again. His little brother, Geoffrey, curled his snub-nosed, freckled face into a smirk from across the table.

"You're in it now." Geoffrey mouthed the words.

Edmund responded in kind, moving his lips slowly so that his brother could not mistake him. "If you did this—" He curled a fist. He was by no means big—something less than average height for his age and rather underdeveloped compared with the beefy apprentices and farmers' sons who lived in the village. He was, however, more than a match for his twelve-year-old brother, and he felt a tiny moment of pleasure at the death of Geoffrey's smile.

Their father reached into the pile and pulled out a thin pamphlet, no more than a few dog-eared pages folded over and bound with string. He opened it and read: "The Song of Ingomer."

"It's just a story, Father." Edmund tried to catch a glimpse of which books lay beneath the parchments; if they had found only the songbook and the one on old legends, he might escape the worst. "Ingomer was a famous wizard from away south, and that's just the story of his life, all his travels and—"

"I know who he is." His father set down the pamphlet and picked up a scroll. He unrolled it. "The Discovery of the East, being the account of Plegmund of Sparrock on his journey beyond the White Sea." He tossed the scroll aside and shook his head.

"Edmund, how many times have we had this talk now?" His mother had a face made for grievance. "How many? Why must you act this way?"

"The Fume or the Flicker." His father read from another scroll. "The debates of Tancred of Overstoke and Carloman the Short on the subject of Fire, transformation and the magical union of opposites."

"The waste, Edmund, the utter waste." His mother threw up her hands. "I argued with your father, I told him letting you keep your tips would let you get some savings started, teach you the value of a penny. You've made a fool of your mother, a right fool. Are you happy, son? Are you?"

"Beasts of the Western Girth," read Edmund's father from the top of a scroll. He tossed it aside and read another, and another. "The Circulation of Harmonies, The Illuminations of Thodebert."

"He's always reading, Father." Geoffrey bounced in his chair but could not draw their father's eye. He gave up and turned the other way. "Always reading, Mum, reading stupid things when you're not looking."

"Now what's this?" Edmund's father had uncovered a flat sheet of parchment, much scraped, upon which was written a number of verses filled with edits and crossings-out. Edmund let out a gasp and tried to seize the page, but his father snatched it up and stood him off with a glare.

"Looks like our boy's been doing some scribbling of his own." Edmund's father scanned the parchment. He staged a cough and held it up to read aloud:

> Katherine, Katherine, ever fair,
> A waterfall of lustrous hair,
> Two eyes whose gaze fill me with bliss,
> And lips I dream each night to kiss.
> Katherine, Katherine, perfect girl,
> Before you I am but a churl,
> Look down to me from far above,
> And tell me how to win your love.

Edmund felt a flush run up his neck and out to the tips of his ears. Geoffrey broke into hoots of nasty laughter and made taunting signs with his fingers.

"Just let that go, Harman," said his mother. "That's normal."

"I doubt you could say the same for this." Edmund's father picked up the heavier of the two books. The last of Edmund's hopes fell to bits. They had found both of his hiding places.

Harman Bale pulled open the soft cover of the book, paying little heed to the new crack he gave its spine. He held it down flat to the table and thumbed through its pages; closely written passages flipped past, followed by pages filled with geometric shapes, then drawings of lutes, flutes and fiddles surrounded by notes and words of song. Then a set of numbers and symbols, then a series of chords across circles, then a long list of words and then more passages of writing. Anger grew on his face with every page he turned. He set the book down with a thump in front of Edmund. "What is this?"

Edmund glanced up at his father, then away. "It's called *The Seven Roads*."

Harman leaned closer. "The Seven Roads to what?"

"It's—" Edmund swallowed. "It's a preparatory course."

"And what's it preparing you for?"

Edmund's stomach flipped and churned. He made no answer.

His father came closer still. "Say it."

"Magic," muttered Edmund.

Harman picked up the smaller book and brandished it as though he were readying to smack it across Edmund's face. "And this one? The same?"

"Yes, Father."

Harman reached out and tapped a finger hard, again and again, at Edmund's temple. "Like a hole in your head. Everything I say, in one ear and out the other. Makes me sick."

Edmund sat still, swaying with every strike of his father's fingertip to his head. The look of sneering triumph began to fade from Geoffrey's face.

His father slammed down the second book. "That's it, Sarra. Tips go back to me until he's grown up enough to deserve them."

"You were right, dear." Edmund's mother shook her head. "Still a silly little boy."

"This book alone is worth nearly a mark," said Harman. He turned to Edmund. "If I found out you stole this—"

"I paid for it," said Edmund. "I bought it with my own money."

"Son, this pile must have cost you every single coin you earned in the last year!" said Sarra. "What were you thinking of? What were you thinking of to do this?"

"I like it, that's what I was thinking!"

Harman brought up the back of his hand. "Don't you dare raise your voice to your mother!"

Edmund flinched away. His father started in on one of his favorite themes—even through his fright Edmund found himself mouthing along with the too-familiar words:

"Do you think I moved this family to this backwater, this sleepy little patch of nowhere for the good of my own health?" Harman punctuated his speech with a slam of his fist onto *The Song of Ingomer,* so hard that Edmund heard the parchment rip. "Do you think I put up with those stinking drunks every day because I like their company? I moved us here to set you up in a place you could inherit, to found something that will last—and this is what I get in return."

"I didn't ask for us to move here." Edmund could not raise his voice above a mutter. His brother looked down and away— their father never said a word about what Geoffrey was meant to inherit.

Harman drummed his fingers on the table, scowling out

the window at the rising day. He reached for his ale, took a swig, then glared at Edmund's mother over the rim of his mug. "This is your fault."

"My fault?" said Sarra. "How is it my fault?"

"You treat that boy like a baby. You let him do as he likes, and see what comes of it!"

"He's only fourteen."

"Fourteen is old enough to start acting like a man!"

"Well, maybe if you paid more attention to them, they'd know what you wanted!"

"Don't you start with me, woman! That boy is old enough to know what's expected of him, but what does he do? He doodles funny symbols all over the ledger book. He daydreams by the fireplace. He plays about with an orphan slave and moons over that great ox of a girl."

Edmund gripped the table hard.

"There's nothing wrong with Katherine Marshal," said Edmund's mother. "A little tall, maybe, but a nice figure. Good hips on her."

Harman snorted.

"She's just a tomboy—most tall girls are," said Sarra. "She'll grow out of it."

"Well, she'll have a good dowry, at least, so if he likes her so much, he should be asking to marry her." Edmund's father rounded back on him. "And do you know what you need for that, boy? You know what you need to persuade John Marshal to give away his only daughter? You need a living, you need a future, you need the coin you had before you tossed it away on this nonsense. You try finding yourself a wife with a pile of parchment, see where you get. You like that orphan boy, too? Then earn some money, save it up and buy him off his master. It'll teach you to drive a bargain."

Edmund stood up, his fists balled tight and trembling. "Don't talk about my friends like that."

Harman rose from his chair. Edmund quailed, but the blow never landed. His father looked down at the table, then in one swift motion snatched up the books and scrolls and threw them onto the fire. He might as well have thrown Edmund on, too, for the way it felt. The parchment caught at once, sending up a roll of sickening smoke.

"Harman!" Sarra coughed and waved her hand before her face.

Edmund's father stepped around the table, caught Edmund by the ear and dragged him over to the washpot that sat above the fuming fire. He bent Edmund's head over the pot until Edmund could see himself in the water, his eyes streaming from the smoke that came from his burning books below.

"Take a look," he said. "What do you see? What are you?"

Edmund looked at the reflection of his face, then at the reflection of his father above him. He saw that their noses were alike and their chins unlike, that he had his father's eyes but lacked his brow. His own hair stuck up all about like a messy bale of yellow straw—his father's had begun to thin into a dark lace across his crown.

A rippled Harman stared up at Edmund from the water. "Are you noble?"

"No, Father."

"Are you rich?"

"No, Father."

"Do you live in the city with the other rich nobs?"

"No, Father."

"Are you going off to study with some great fancy wizard and fiddle about with books all your days?"

A tear struck the water. "No, Father."

"No, boy." Harman let go of Edmund's neck and shoved him away from the fire. "You know what you are? You're an ungrateful brat who has no idea how good he's got it. You have a roof over your head, good solid meals and a trade to inherit, and still you act like it's not good enough for you. You are the son of innkeepers. You fetch ale. You count kegs. You cook and you serve. You are a peasant, and you'd do well to remember that you're better off than most."

Edmund stumbled back a few paces, clutching at his throbbing ear. Harman took his place at the table and resumed his morning meal.

"Grow up." He said it through a mouthful of porridge. "I'm not going to tell you again."

"Come to the table, Edmund," said his mother. "Eat your breakfast."

"I'm not very hungry this morning, Mum."

His father turned a look upon him. Edmund sat.

Chapter 2

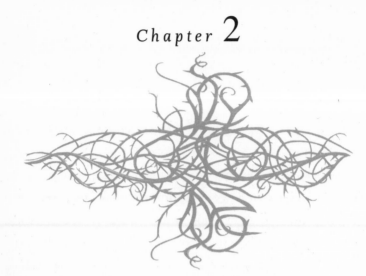

"You there—boy! More ale this way!"

Edmund topped off the mug of the man seated before him and peered through the smoke-laced light. A grubby hand rose and beckoned from the table in the far corner. Several others rose with it: "That's six ales, now, and hurry it up!"

Edmund wiped the beaded sweat from his forehead. He looked into his pitcher—down to the dregs once again.

"Right away!" he shouted back. "I just need to get some more!"

He had never seen a night like this. The tavern bustled and swung; folk laughed and rubbed elbows, talking endless nonsense. Nicky Bird and Horsa Blackcalf played back and forth on flute and fiddle by the fire, and it seemed that Wat and Bella Cooper were having better days, for they danced and spun together through the middle of the room.

Edmund elbowed past and hurried down the narrow steps

into the cellar, a cramped and clammy place that smelled of ale and must. Three kegs lined one wall, opposite shelves that would have held the inn's store of mugs had they not all been in use upstairs.

"This one's almost done." Geoffrey bent at the tap of the middle keg and watched the thin, slow stream of ale fill his pitcher. He blinked and rubbed at half-lidded eyes.

Edmund pressed his back against the cool plaster of the cellar wall. He let out a weary breath. "Where's Father?"

Geoffrey shrugged. Another shout for ale resounded from above.

"That's the second-to-last keg," said Edmund. "If this keeps up, we'll have to tap the dark stuff."

"No one likes drinking that in hot weather."

"You watch. If they finish this keg, they'll be so drunk we could serve them ditchwater."

Geoffrey snorted and stomped upstairs, holding his brimming pitcher in both hands. Edmund replaced him at the tap. He let the cool brown ale fill his pitcher to the brim, wiped the foam and then rushed back up to the tavern before the shouts for service could grow too loud.

"I tell you, they're gone! Bossy, Bessy, Buttercup—all of 'em, gone!" Hugh Jocelyn sat hunched over his mug at the end of the table by the stairs. Hugh always wore a battered old cap jammed down over his ears, save only for those times when he was particularly worried. "It's not right, I tell you it's not right." When he was worried, he removed the cap from his spear-bald head and wrung it round and round by the brim.

"Did you look in the sty?" Hob Hollows leaned next to Hugh on the bench. He swung his fingers out in Edmund's face, then tapped his mug.

"Of course I looked in the sty—they're pigs!" Hugh raised his voice to a reedy chirp. "I've looked everywhere, everywhere! And Bossy's to farrow soon, good fat piglets, she always gives good'uns—oh, what'll I do?"

"Sure you didn't slaughter 'em and then forget you did it? Eaten any bacon lately?" Hob looked down to find his mug still empty, then up at Edmund.

Edmund held his pitcher in close at his chest. "Who's paying?"

Hob made a show of reaching at his belt. He looked across at his brother Bob, who shrugged with an amiable smirk.

"Alas, we left all our coin at the house," said Hob. "But you wouldn't let us run dry, would you? Not tonight of all nights!"

Edmund sighed and topped his mug.

"There's a lad." Hob slapped Edmund's shoulder. "I'll bring a good chicken by tomorrow, settle it up proper."

Edmund took a look at Hugh's drawn old face and decided that Hob was buying his ale. "How long have they been gone?"

"Oh, days now, days." Hugh sighed. "I took them out for pannage in the wood, you know, out for acorns. Bossy loves acorns. I always let them have a run of it, let them come back on their own. Bossy knows the way, she's a wise one. She always comes home."

He put his face in his cap. "I can't find them anywhere—oh, what have I done?"

Hob winked up at Edmund and tapped a finger to his temple. He knocked full mugs with his brother. "To Bossy! Hey? Wherever she is."

"Boy! You there!" The shout from across the room was repeated more loudly. "I said ale!"

"Just a moment!" Edmund raised his pitcher over his head and dodged around the dancers, taking the long route past the door and making to hop in front of the fire on his way toward the far table. He did his best not to meet eyes with anyone who looked thirsty. He caught odd, disjointed bits of conversations as he pushed along:

". . . and folk out that way still don't go above the foothills. They say them shrikes aren't all gone by any stretch—"

"Oh, just shut it, will you? There's not been shrike nor bolgug nor any other such thing seen around here in thirty years, and you'd think that tonight of all nights you'd know to keep your tall tales . . ."

". . . and they were just gone the next day. That's what they said, just gone, the whole herd. Folk were looking high and low for 'em but couldn't find hide nor hair. If you ask me . . ."

". . . drove the shipment out of town, put it in a cave, waited a week, and brought it right back in. Sold the lot for five each! Shrewd, was our Bill . . ."

". . . well, I couldn't do that, could I? Was already married, you see, so . . ."

"This is undrinkable."

A goblet was thrust out in front of Edmund—a real, proper goblet made of pewter or maybe even silver. Its owner was younger than he sounded, with thick short hair just starting to turn gray and a strong chin shaved smooth like a city dweller.

"Worst wine I have ever tasted." The stranger waved the goblet back and forth under Edmund's nose. "The very worst. A singular achievement, considering the wide and multifarious competition. I very much hope the ale is better."

Edmund could not help but stare. Scrolls, books and parchments covered the whole surface of the stranger's table—a trove ten times the size, and he could not guess how many times the worth, of the paltry collection his father had sent into the fire that morning. A script of round and sweeping elegance graced the pages of the book in the stranger's hands, adorned with capital letters worked in whorls of color upon color and gilded with leaf of gold. A pair of eyes seemed to watch everywhere, inked with cunning craft above the figure of a star, upon which lay seven men—no, seven children, each laid out upon one of the rays. Symbols wound ox-turns around them, each changed by the one before and after, not one of them repeated on the whole of the page. Edmund knew just enough to read a small piece: *Bring a blade for He-That-Speaks -From-The-Mountain—*

The stranger placed a firm hand over the book and shot a barbed glance up at Edmund. It felt exactly like a slap.

"I'm very sorry." Edmund took the goblet and poured out the wine in the straw. "It's just that I've never seen anyone doing that in here—reading, I mean."

"Indeed? I would never have guessed." The stranger licked a finger to turn the page—then he coughed. He coughed again, then bent over and retched into a square of fine cloth. He left the pages of his book exposed, and Edmund could not restrain himself from sneaking another look. A creature made all of thorns had been inked with chilling art into an upper corner, its tendrils curled around the first letter of a neatly written passage: *As the quiggan serves the Nethergrim in fouled water, and the stonewight in his—*

The man placed both hands across the page. "I said ale."

Edmund filled the goblet, reading as he did the symbols incised around the rim: *Wind, Thunder, Ten Thousand Seasons.* He shot a closer look at the stranger—the man was not old, but neither did he look at all healthy. His skin looked as though it had been cured like his parchments, yellow at the edges and with a sickly, translucent gloss. He had missed a fleck of blood on his lips, and another on his chin.

Edmund turned to look out across his neighbors and the travelers in the tavern. The stranger's coughing fit had rung to the rafters, his clothes could buy everyone else's in the room all together in a bundle—and yet no one so much as glanced at the man.

It struck him in a flash: "No one else can see you."

A thin smile curled the stranger's lips. "They can see me perfectly well." He turned a page. "But they cannot perceive me. They cannot think about me—they cannot remember me from one moment to the next. When you walk away from this table, neither will you."

He held out a hand without looking up. Edmund gave him back his goblet foaming with ale.

Another bellowing cry sounded from the far corner: "By all thunder, boy, what is keeping you over there? Ale, curse it all!"

"Yes, yes, all right! Just a moment!" Edmund turned and pushed his way between the crowded benches, making sure to fix the stranger's face and voice in his memory as firmly as he possibly could. Anna Maybell tried to pull him into the dance, but he shrugged her off and shouldered through the last few feet of chattering locals to the gang of traveling merchants in the far corner.

"About time." Grubby Hands pushed his empty mug across the table.

"So sorry." Edmund picked it up and poured. "Busy night."

"We've got some fish coming our way, too. I thought that surly redheaded boy would have brought it out by now."

Edmund searched through the crowd. "Mum, where's Geoffrey gone?"

"He must be down in the cellar." His mother passed him with a tray of griddled rabbit, her mousy braid swinging out like a rope as she turned her head his way. "Can you go serve the Twintrees when you're done?"

Edmund reached out for the next of the mugs, muttering curses at his lazy little brat of a brother under his breath. Weariness sprang on him in mid-pour, a yawn that sent the world to gray for a moment. He could not remember how long it had been since he last sat down. He wondered if this was how old people felt all the time.

"That's the word going round, Father." The young merchant who spoke could be no one's son but Grubby Hand's, right down to the fat gut and gaudy shirt. "They say Lord Tristan's not coming to the fair."

"What? Now why isn't Tristan coming?" The woman seated between the two men drained her mug to the dregs, then held it out for Edmund to refill. "Isn't this whole thing done half for him?"

"Lord Tristan's getting on in years," said Grubby Hands with a sagacious nod. "Must be sixty by now—probably just wants to live quiet-like."

The woman pursed her lips. "He's alive, isn't he? It's just good manners to show up at a feast in your honor."

Edmund cast a glance around the room. The news spread from guest to guest, deadening the frolic in the tavern. Horsa Blackcalf left Nicky Bird hanging at the chorus of a jig and drew a long, slow air on his fiddle.

"It's a bad lookout for us, Father, no mistaking it," said the younger merchant. "Bad for business. No Vithric, and now no Tristan."

The woman looked from son to father in unhappy surprise. "You mean Vithric's not coming, either?"

"Oh, you never heard?" Grubby Hands scraped at the remains of his porridge. "Vithric's been dead for years."

"A shame, really," said the younger merchant. "Best wizard of his time—of any time, some would say."

"Well, it's a bit late in the year for a fair, anniversary or no," said the woman. "It'll be a thin one, you mark me, and we'll be out a fair handful for the trip."

Grubby Hands made a fat, self-satisfied smile. "And that,

my sweet, is why I'm the one to set our course." He turned to Edmund. "This village—what's it called—"

"Moorvale," said Edmund.

"Right, Moorvale. This little spot's as near as any other to the Girth. I'll wager more than half of these folk lost a father or a brother on that mountain, battling their way up to the Nethergrim all those years back. They're drinking to them as much as to Tristan, and tomorrow they'll bring every coin they've managed to scrape—and, oh yes, they'll spend it, they'll trade bulls for goats for a chance to mark the day. You heed me— heroes or no, we'll not see a better haul all year."

"Oh, quit your blather, I'm not a customer." The woman turned away. "We've come all the way up here to trade at an anniversary fair in honor of two old heroes, but one of them's been dead for years and now the other's not going to bother turning up. What a fool's errand—why I listen to you, I'll never know."

"She may be right, Father." The younger merchant scratched his jowls. "What's the point of it without Tristan and Vithric? They're the grand heroes—the only ones who even came back."

"Three came back." Edmund spoke before thinking. *Never gainsay a guest*—one of his father's many rules. *Let them say the sky is green so long as they pay.*

Grubby Hands squinted at him. "What was that?"

"Three came back, begging your pardon." Edmund took up the last mug at the table. "Sixty men went up the mountain, but only three came down again. Tristan and Vithric, and John Marshal."

"Hadn't heard that." Grubby Hands said the words in a manner that meant that since he had not heard it, it must not be so. "So where is this John Marshal now, then?"

"He lives in the village—well, on a farm just outside." Edmund poured a little steep to make some extra foam and hide the fact that he was half a mug short. "He's marshal of Lord Aelfric's stables, raises and trains his warhorses."

"Hmm. Well." Grubby Hands shrugged at his son. "Better than nothing, I suppose."

"He must be quite a hero to you folk." The woman did not seem quite so pompous as her companions. "Bet he tells some grand stories!"

Edmund shook his head. "No. He doesn't."

"My friends! A round for this house on me!" Henry Twintree stood and slapped a large silver coin to the table. "And when you drink, drink to the memory of Vithric, the great and the wise, who saved us all from the Nethergrim in years gone by!"

The answering shout belled in Edmund's ears. He cast a frantic look around for Geoffrey, hoping against hope for some help, but instead caught sight of his father glaring his way from across the room. Harman Bale turned from his cheery conversation with the elders of the village and made a significant jerk of his head in the direction of the cellar.

"Drink, my friends and neighbors, to Vithric, to Lord Tristan and to our own John Marshal." Henry Twintree's eyes shone dewy and soft—he seemed to be making his speech to a corner of the ceiling. "But most of all, drink to those who gave all, for you stand upon the ground their courage gave you!"

His neighbors gave throat to their agreement. Mugs were thrust up in firelight on all sides, dozens and dozens, to acclaim and to signal.

"Go on!" Edmund's mother nudged his back. "That's half a mark!" She picked up the coin and thrust it in her apron. Edmund hurried down the cellar stairs to find his brother's pitcher lying empty on the floor. He kicked it against the wall with a curse and set his own under the tap.

A noisy, stamping dance had gotten underway by the time he came back up, making the trip to every table a whirling gantlet of arms and legs. It took seven weaving, ducking trips down to the cellar and back to serve the whole of the tavern—it would have taken only six if Wat Cooper had not chosen that particular moment to swing his wife right around in Edmund's path. No dodging that one—and of course Father saw it all.

"Everyone got your round? Got it? Then here's to 'em!" Nicky Bird leapt onto a table. "Raise 'em, come on, raise 'em up. Here's to Tristan and John, to the Ten and the fifty, to Vithric!"

Edmund stopped, seized with the sick and flailing sensation that there was something he wanted very much to remember but could not. He glanced around the tavern room, thinking that maybe he had missed serving one of the corners. For a moment something slipped in and out of his thoughts, leaving only the memory of a pair of eyes watching him in cold disdain. He shrugged—or shuddered—then poured out the foamy bottom of his pitcher into the mug of old Robert Windlee, who had so far managed to sleep through all the din.

"To Tristan and Vithric!" Everyone raised his voice, even Grubby Hands. It was the loudest sound Edmund had ever heard: "To the Ten and the fifty, the men who slew the Nethergrim!"

Chapter 3

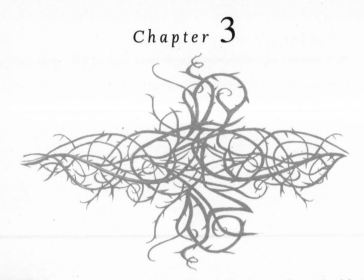

Edmund lay upon his pallet, fully dressed. He had been drifting off to the sound of distant, rumbling conversation and drunken singing for as long as he could remember, and by rights should be so weary as to sleep for a week—yet he had never felt so awake, so quick with anticipation. He passed the time by watching the shafts of firelight that shot up through the many gaps in the floorboards to play on the sharply angled ceiling of his bedroom, winking off and on as the shadow of a reveler passed near the fire in the hearth of the tavern below. They were still at it, long after his father would usually have kicked out all the locals and shut the taps for the night. Horsa Blackcalf scraped the tune of a bawdy drinking song; villager and traveler slurred and shouted their way through the chorus, bashing their mugs on the tables in clumsy rhythm. Edmund could hear his father circling the room, holding them all to the tune in his fine, round baritone, pausing only to urge them to louder choruses, greater joy, and most of all the purchasing of more of his ale.

There came a restless rustle from the pallet next to Edmund's. He shut his eyes and breathed in through his nose, deep and even as though lost in sleep.

"Edmund? Edmund!" Geoffrey leaned across the gap between their beds. His breath reeked of the onions Edmund had avoided at dinner. "Why have you got your clothes on?"

Horsa drew out the last note of the song into an uneven tremolo, after which there came a raucous cheer and the dull clack of coins being tossed into a hat. Edmund savored the familiar, happy tension in his belly. He ran back and forth over the things he had been practicing to say.

Geoffrey grasped his shoulder. "I know you're awake!"

"Get off." Edmund shoved his brother back with one arm and gained his feet.

Geoffrey followed him over to the window. "Where are you going?"

Edmund opened the shutters. The moonlight shone in at a slant. Nothing moved amongst the shadows in the yard below. He turned from the window and opened the trunk at the foot of his bed.

Geoffrey crossed his arms over his hand-me-down nightshirt. "I'll tell Mum."

Edmund favored his brother with a look of withering scorn. He pulled out a belt, then dropped it and felt around for the other.

"I'll tell Father!"

"Think it through for a moment." Edmund fastened the belt around his waist. "I've heard that you actually have some friends now—Miles Twintree, Emma Russet, that kid from across the river, what's-his-name."

"I have lots of friends. More than you!"

Edmund moved a bowl of water to the window. "You and I share a room. We have since we moved here four years ago, and we will until one of us runs away or Father dies. Must I go on?" He examined his wavering reflection in the moonlight and tried to smooth down a few jutting strands of his hair. Folk carried on downstairs as though that night was all there was or ever would be.

"So—I think we understand each other." Edmund ruffled his brother on the top of his head. "Yes?"

Geoffrey slapped his hand away. "Are you waiting for that girl?"

"No." Edmund reached down to fuss with his boots. "What girl?"

"You know—the big one!"

"She's not big!" Edmund caught himself before his voice rose too loudly. "She's just tall."

"She's a head taller than you, and she could pick you up and toss you like a sack of apples." Geoffrey stuck out his chin. "Father's right, she's an ox!"

"Who's an ox?"

Edmund jumped. A head thrust itself up over the sill of the window beside him. Katherine's eyes were so dark a brown that in moonlight they were wells, endlessly deep but sparked with mirth.

"Evening." She leaned crossed arms on the wooden sill, as though she were twelve feet tall and just passing by the window. "Lovely weather we've been having." All the smooth, clever things Edmund had been meaning to say simply melted.

Geoffrey scrunched up his freckles. "How did you get up here?"

"This is hurting some." A boy's voice floated softly from the yard below. "Don't know how long I can hold you."

"Sorry, Tom." Katherine disappeared from the window. Edmund leaned out to see her jumping down off a pair of skinny shoulders, landing in the stack of hay beside the empty kegs and rolling back into the yard with a whoop. Wat Cooper's dogs set to barking from the next croft over, but they barked at everything.

"Is that Tom?" Geoffrey pushed up next to Edmund. "Oh, ho, he's not supposed to be out!"

Tom slipped back into the shadows under the grain shed. Edmund sighed to himself. Just once he would like to ask Katherine to sneak out with him and have her come alone— just once.

"If Tom gets caught, I bet his master whips him good," said Geoffrey. "Emma Russet says his master whips him all the time!"

Edmund seized his brother by the shirt. "And if Tom gets caught, we'll know who tattled, won't we?"

Geoffrey shrugged him off. He leaned out the window. "Hey, Katherine? Katherine!"

"Yes, Geoffrey, hello." Katherine beat bits of chaff from her cloak. "Edmund, are you coming down?"

"Katherine, I saw what Edmund wrote about you!" Geoffrey leaned out. "He said—"

"You little toad!" Edmund ripped his brother back from the window. Geoffrey squirmed from his grip and dodged giggling around the tiny room.

"He wrote a poem!" Geoffrey raised his voice dangerously high, almost as loud as the singing from the tavern below. "He said that your hair was like a—"

"Shut your face! Shut your face!" Edmund got a grip on Geoffrey's collar. He threw his brother hard onto the cot and raised a fist.

Geoffrey sneered at him. "Go on. I'll scream."

"Edmund? Tell Geoffrey I saw him playing down in the creek with Miles Twintree and Peter Overbourne this evening." Katherine spoke just loud enough to be heard over the noise. "I thought it was a bit odd since the tavern was so busy. My papa saw it too, and thought the same."

Geoffrey's face twisted into the sort of scowl that spoke of unquestionable guilt.

Edmund smiled. He let go of Geoffrey's shirt and tweaked his nose. "Sleep tight, little toad." He swung a leg over the sill and hung from it to drop into the hay.

Geoffrey sat up on the pallet. "Why can't I come, too?"

Edmund pretended not to hear. He shifted over, trying to angle his fall into the soft middle of the haystack.

"Come on." Katherine beckoned smiling. "It's not far."

Edmund let go—and knew at once that he had missed his mark. He landed one foot hard on a tight-wound bale and stumbled backward through the yard to flop at Katherine's feet.

"Whoops." She stooped over him. "You're not hurt?" Her long hair swung down across his face—it smelled of spice and apples. He wanted to lie there forever.

"There you go." Katherine grabbed his hand and hauled him standing. She wore breeches under boots, and a shirt cut for a man but embroidered with roses at the collar. "Come on, let's get moving before we're caught. Tom?"

"Here." Tom stepped out from the gloom—taller still than Katherine, half a head over most grown men, but where Katherine had gained grace in proportion to her reach, his height had seemed to come by stretching him into a raw, rangy spindle. There were moments, especially in poor light, when they could almost be brother and sister, but the illusion disappeared when they moved or spoke. Katherine always led, and Tom followed, stuck to her like a burr on her shirt.

Katherine listened at the corner of the inn, then shook her head and pointed north. She crept off in front of her friends, leading them in between Wat's looming kennels and Knocky Turner's ramshackle garden, then up between the cottages to the edge of the village square. She leaned out to peer around, then crooked in a finger. "Looks clear."

Edmund followed her out into the square, which was really no more than a bulge in the wide West Road where it met the roads to Dorham and Longsettle. A statue of some old knight stood between the sweeps of wagon ruts, facing east across the bridge toward the dark and empty moors. No one knew who he was, or even whether he was meant to be saluting or shaking a sword in that direction, for his head and right arm were long gone.

Katherine looped them around behind the statue, creeping under the yew trees that flanked the grand silent entrance to the village hall. Edmund shot a glance down the Longsettle road toward the inn as they passed west, and spied the dim outlines of men talking on the steps. Nicky Bird was in the middle of one of his shambling stories, from the sounds of it, and no one seemed to take note of the three friends before they slipped safely out of view.

Tom wore a ragged tunic cut for a man his height but twice his weight, which made him look something like a running scarecrow. Absurd as he appeared, he had the practiced, economical gait of someone who traveled long distances on foot, and Edmund had to break into a sprint from time to time just to keep him in sight. The sound of their footfalls seemed to carry an uncomfortable distance across the open fields around them, but they were free of the village by then, and there was no one to mark their passing.

"All right, Tom, we're not running all the way there." Katherine let herself drop back next to Edmund. She shot him a smile that raced his heart. "What is it about sneaking out that's so much fun?"

Edmund looked up at the stars. A few fat clouds slid past the moon. The breeze was just cool enough to tingle on the skin. He had the unaccountable feeling that marvelous things were possible.

"Your father must be excited for tomorrow." He had rehearsed it ten ways, and judged this opening the best.

"Papa? No, he hates the whole idea. If it weren't for me, I'm not sure he'd even go, though I guess Lord Aelfric would likely make him." Katherine stopped, looking ahead, then south into the trees that lined the road. "Tom?"

"Over here." Tom's voice came from somewhere past the first few trunks. "It's the short way."

Katherine felt out before her and plunged off the road. Edmund followed at her heels, breathing in the trail of her scent, blessing the darkness for an excuse to keep so close. He could see his hands well enough, and the occasional flash of movement from Katherine, but all else was shadow and suggestion. Their clothes made rounds of creak, hiss and whip as they fumbled on, deep in gloom on a rising course up the side of Wishing Hill.

"But you'll be going to the whole thing? The reason I ask is, well, you see—I heard there was a feast afterward—and a dance—" Edmund failed to catch a branch Katherine bent back before him. He did his best to splutter and gasp without making too much noise.

"That was not the short way, Tom." Katherine pushed out onto a space of open trail that wound toward the summit of the hill. She drew up level with her friend, then leapt abruptly past him and pelted up the track. "Race you to the top!"

Tom watched her go, then turned to Edmund. "You don't want me here."

"That's not true." Edmund tried to face his way through the lie, but Tom just stared at him until he shrugged and looked away.

"You can go on ahead of me if you like," said Tom.

"She would only believe I really beat you if you broke your leg."

Tom nodded, then seemed to disappear into the dark, so rapid and silent was his ascent up the path after Katherine. Edmund set his feet and put on his best turn of speed, determined at least to come in a respectable third, even if third was last.

The earth of the slope on the north face of the hill had long ago been fashioned into sharply twisting ramparts, forcing any who ascended it to switch back and forth on his climb. The ramparts had sunk into gentle, waist-high rolls of ground, covered with a vigorous growth of spruce and maple, yet they still preserved the blurring form of a trail with only a few downed trunks to be vaulted on its course. At every puffing switchback Edmund spied a little more of the broken-down ruin of the old keep at the summit, first the tallest standing tower, then the snaggled top of a wall. Tom stood on a rock at the edge of the hilltop, looking out over the valley that surrounded their home.

"Are you two coming in here?" Katherine's voice carried out through the tumbled gap of what once had been the gatehouse, her voice folded onto itself in close echo.

Tom's face had that expression he sometimes got, a blank and faraway stare that most folk took for evidence he was a little soft in the head. "Just looking at the trees."

"Oh, you can look at trees anytime!"

Edmund picked his way past Tom, over the waist-high jumble of stones that choked the entrance. He found Katherine in the courtyard beyond, seated on the tall dark stone that stood in the center, at the very tip of Wishing Hill.

"I love it here." She swung her legs back and forth, kicking her heels into the stone.

"So do I." Edmund jumped down to solid ground. Beyond the ruined gates the courtyard lay nearly bare, too deep in the shadows of the walls to let much of anything grow. "Did you win?"

"The race?" She laughed—two notes at even pitch. The moonlight lit her silver, glinting down the spill of her long dark hair.

"Come on, Tom!" She leapt down from the stone, then turned and placed her hand on it. "Make a wish!"

"I don't need a stone to make a wish." Tom answered from somewhere over the wall to the north.

"Fine, then!" Katherine looked at Edmund. "But you'll do it?"

"Oh, yes." Edmund put his hand to the cold, blue-gray stone—it was so old that whatever had once been carved on it had weathered away to the mere suggestions of shapes, though he always thought he could trace the outlines of some of the oldest and strangest symbols he knew.

"My father burned all my books this morning." He spoke it in a blurt, then cursed himself. The last thing he wanted was to seem like a sap in front of a girl who trained warhorses, a weedy little boy who cared only for books—and just then the sting of Father's punishment seemed blunted to nothing.

"Oh, Edmund, that's awful! I wish he understood you—oh, no!" Katherine let go of the stone. "I just made my wish!"

"I still have one."

"Go on, then."

Edmund shut his eyes. It might not be strictly fair to relate exactly what it was that he wished for.

"And I hope you get it." Katherine stepped away from the stone, looking up at the tallest tower—a grand, imposing structure twice as wide as the shattered ruins of the other three. "I forgot—I was going to bring some rope this time. I want to climb that someday."

Edmund drew in a breath. He rolled back his shoulders and stood as tall as he could.

"Katherine—" His voice came out as a squeak.

"Though we'll have to be careful. That's how Nicky Bird got his name, you know, back when he was our age. They say it's a miracle he survived the fall." Katherine picked up a rain-worn shard of wall. She flipped it over in her hand, then hauled back and tossed it on a high, sailing arc. The rock struck what was left of the battlements—the impact smacked and resounded between the walls.

"The feast tomorrow, after the fair." Edmund got control of his voice. "Since Father's on the village council now, he got invited—so I can go, too."

"Oh, good." Katherine reached down in the straggled grass and plucked up another rock. "I was afraid I'd get bored."

"And there's a dance."

"You know we're supposed to get all dressed up?" Katherine took aim at the tallest tower.

Edmund approached at her side. He shot a glance back at the Wishing Stone. "And so I was wondering, when we're there—"

Katherine judged her mark and threw, striking the tower a few feet from the top. "Ha! Close!" She reached down. "I'm aiming for the arrow slit. Want to try?"

"When we're there—" Edmund wrung his hands, then thrust them behind his back. "If I could have the honor—the great honor of asking you—"

"Katherine." Tom's voice cut across Edmund's words, not least because it came as near a shout as Tom ever got and carried with it a tremble of fright. "Edmund, please come here. Please hurry."

"What is it?" Katherine turned to dash for the entrance. She was over the scrabbled stones and gone before she said, "Tom, where are you?"

Edmund shut his fists—for a moment he wanted Tom to just go jump off a cliff. He hurried after Katherine, clambering over the stones, but found neither of his friends on the other side. He looked about him, at a loss. The trail dropped away before a view of their home that was half the reason they risked so much trouble to come up there. The course of the broad river Tamber could just be guessed by the folds of the silver-lit valley around it, but that deep in the night there was no sign that anyone lived down there—not a light, not a sound. The river bent just before it reached the village, turning from its western rush down from the grand far peaks of the Girth to a more stately flow south, almost but not quite navigable by boat. Eastward the moon sat on a throne of cloud above the flat nothing of the moors. North, past the last of the fields, the broad line of the Dorwood bounded the world to the horizon and over. The sight had always filled Edmund with the urge to pack a store of provisions and walk, to see what lay beyond the edges of the world he knew—but just then it made him feel exposed, a foolish little mouse in sight of owls. The breeze blew up stronger, and rather too cold.

"Over here." Katherine spoke from somewhere west along the wall. "Have you got a knife?"

"Why?" Edmund drew his work knife from his belt. He felt his way in near-blackness along the shadowed strip between the foot of the wall and the eaves of the nearest trees. He found his friends crouched by the crumbled ruin of the northeastern tower over a pile of something nearly white.

"Bones." Katherine held one up. "Pig bones."

Edmund knelt at her side. "Not a wild boar?"

Tom shook his head. "Pigs."

"So a dead pig." Edmund shrugged. "A long-dead pig."

"Pigs—three of them. And piglets—they weren't born yet." Tom placed a bone in his hand. "Feel that."

Edmund rubbed a thumb on the surface of the bone. "What am I supposed to be feeling?"

"It's greasy, not dry," said Tom. "This pig was alive yesterday."

Edmund took a closer look down at the pile. Even in the feeble light the bones had the yellowish tinge of a freshly dead animal—but there was not a speck of flesh on any of them.

"Bossy," he said. "Bessy and Buttercup."

Katherine glanced at him. "Hugh Jocelyn's pigs?"

"He was looking for them, said he'd lost them." Edmund gripped his knife and looked around him. "There must be wolves!"

"Not wolves," said Tom. "These teeth marks are too long for wolves—and wolves don't make a pile after the kill. They like to drag bits away."

The last tingle of thrill left Edmund, replaced by a true and present fear. "What are you saying?"

"Look at this skull." Katherine held it up. "Broken right in half and the brains scooped out. Those are hack marks—an axe or a sword."

"Cracked every bone to get at the marrow." Tom dropped the bones in his hands. "Crunched the piglets to bits."

Edmund swallowed hard. His friends looked just as frightened as he felt.

Katherine stood up first. "We should go."

Chapter 4

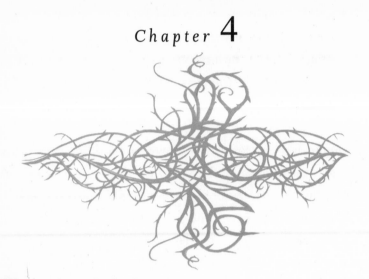

*L*ook inside the flame.

Edmund stared. He tried. The candle before him flickered back and forth. It fizzed and guttered, its light drowned in the sunshine flooding through the opened window of his bedroom.

Look inside the flame. Somehow he had to see the flame and know it. Somehow a wizard could know, just by looking, exactly what the flame would do, how it would move with every moment. Somehow a real wizard could ask it to change, and it would obey.

He strained to remember what his books had taught him: *Fire is the right hand of the Wheel of Substance. Its color is red, it is both dry and hot. In its true form it is entirely red, entirely dry and hot—only in the lost and muddy world in which we live can it be any less than its perfect self. Do not see the flame before you. See Fire.*

"See Fire. See Fire." Edmund gazed at the candle until it hurt his eyes. "See Fire and see Light. Fire makes light, but it is not Light."

The rickety stair outside the bedroom creaked. Edmund let the sound come and go in his thoughts.

Bits and pieces of the next lesson returned, things he had read in the last pages of *The Seven Roads*: *Light, in its true form, is a crack in the darkness. It is the flaw in the tyrant's perfect plan. It is hope flowing in with a dying man's last breath. It is a sound, a harmony. When you wish to call on Light, do not see what meets your eyes. See Light, the crowning Sign of the Wheel of Essence.*

Wait—maybe that worked. The flame seemed to move the way he guessed. He raised his right hand in the Sign of Fire, his left in the Sign of Light.

The stair creaked again. Edmund glanced aside.

No! He snapped back. He had it—he almost had it! He could feel it, his mind moved with the dance of the flame. He had to get it right this time—good tallow candles cost a whole penny for a pound, and there were only so many he could sneak from the cellar before his father noticed the loss.

One more sign: Quickening. *The first kick of a baby in her mother's womb. To be surprised by joy. The world flows past in a ceaseless rush—Quickening, the right-hand sign of the Wheel of Change.*

He almost had it! He was sure—now all he needed were some words. The words would seal it, make it his own.

"Fire is a quickness. Fire—" Edmund paused to think. "Fire within makes—"

A hand snaked into the room. Edmund caught the sight from the corner of his eye. He could not help but look.

The hand seized Edmund's longbow from the wall, then his quiver of arrows.

Edmund jumped up. "Hey!" He doused the candle and sprang from his bedroom, taking the stairs in threes. "Where do you think you're going with that?"

Geoffrey rounded at the front door of the inn. He scowled, defiant. He reached out to open the door a crack.

"That's mine!" Edmund knew better than to simply stand and shout. He stepped quick across the tavern. "Give it back."

"I'm a better shot than you!" Geoffrey held Edmund's un-strung longbow like a sword, and wore Edmund's quiver of arrows on his back. "You stink at archery—you don't even practice! Why should you get to have it?"

"Because you're a kid." Edmund advanced to charging range. "You want your own longbow, go buy one when you're older."

Geoffrey shook the whippy shaft in Edmund's face. "You didn't buy this! Father gave it to you!"

"Which means it's mine, so hand it over."

"He gives you everything." Geoffrey threw the bow and quiver at Edmund's feet, then flung back the door to stomp outside. Sharp white sunlight cut through the middle of the tavern.

"Shut that, will you?" Wat Cooper raised a hand to shade his eyes. He sat with Hob Hollows by the fire, their feet up on benches, ales in hand.

Edmund pulled the door to, muffling the happy chatter and the tramp of feet on the Longsettle road. He bent to gather spilled arrows back into the quiver and laid it on the tavern's best table. He considered giving the spell one more try, then changed his mind and reached for his best new shoes by the door, the ones he had haggled hard for at market. The last thing he wanted was to keep Katherine waiting.

"It's burning low." Hob waved a hand at the fire. "Fetch us some wood, there's a lad."

Edmund raised the lid of the pot that hung over the hearth. An odor of garlic and onions stung his nose. "Mum!" He aimed his shout at the closed door to the kitchen. "I'm going early!"

"Edmund, did you do the threshing?" His mother's voice rose from somewhere out back. "Your father said you have to get the threshing done before you go."

"Geoffrey hasn't done anything, and he already left!" Edmund took up a spare bowl and spooned out a few globs of barley porridge from the pot. The new shoes pinched his toes painfully tight, but he supposed that was the fashion.

"You can't just leave it sitting on the stalks, Edmund!" His mother spoke over a swirl of clucks. "You get that threshing done or you'll catch it from your father when he gets back!"

"All right, all right." Edmund ate standing by the pot, scooping down the porridge as fast as he could. He nudged a bit of charred leather with his foot—the binding from one of his books. It had fallen off onto the hearth, preserving with it the torn, burnt corner of a single page.

Hob Hollows shouldered him aside and reached for the

ladle. "So then, Edmund." He slopped himself a huge helping of porridge. "Going in the archery tourney today?"

Edmund eyed up at him. "Maybe I am."

Hob looked over at Wat. They broke out in peals of drunken laughter.

Edmund chewed at his gummy porridge. He pointed at Hob with his spoon. "Are you going to pay for that?"

Hob dug out one last spoonful, put it in his mouth and belched. "I'm good for it, lad, no problems." He regained his seat by the fire. "I'll bring a good chicken by tomorrow, settle it all up proper."

"That's what you said last night."

"Did I?"

"Edmund!" His mother sounded louder and closer amidst the clack of bowls being stacked for the wash. "Did you hear me?"

Edmund thunked down his breakfast and reached for bow and quiver. "Yes, Mum!"

"The threshing, Edmund, you see that done before your father gets back. If he catches you—"

"Just going now!" Edmund did not stay to hear the rest. He thrust back the door and leapt into the sunshine. Almost everyone was going south, dressed up in their humble finest, but Edmund turned north up through the square. Short and shaggy Nicky Bird lounged at his ease on the steps of the hall. Martin Upfield leaned against one of the yew trees—Katherine's cousin on her mother's side, a great bush-bearded hulk of a man almost twice Nicky's size.

"No, he's just sitting up there with his head in his hands." Nicky whittled at a stick of wood. "No helping him."

Martin looked up over Baldwin Tailor's roof toward the distant top of Wishing Hill. "So who found 'em, then?"

"Your cousin Katherine. Says she was giving one of the horses a run about this morning, and—Edmund! Did you hear about the pigs?"

"No." Edmund kept moving, unwilling to stop in case he betrayed too much of what he knew. The day promised to be fine, as fine as anyone could ask so late in the year, and he would not waste a moment more.

By the time he had gone half a mile up the Dorham road, he had come to regret his choice of shoes in bitter earnest. He jogged awhile, then loped, then walked. The country north of the village broke up into hills, banded rows of crops rolling eastward to the river and pasture rising west into the foothills of the Girth. The village was halfway through harvest, half the fields cut to stubble but the rest still bursting with growth— acre after acre of wheat, oats and barley mixed in the furrows with beans and pulse. Tomorrow they would all be back to it hard, bent first in the lord's fields, then their own, trying with all their might to reap and bind and thresh enough to last them through to spring. Knowing it gave the day a special shine— for the sheer stupid joy of it he nocked and loosed an arrow. It shanked and spiraled in the wind, landing sideways in the pasture. The cattle nearest by spared him a look, then got back to grazing.

Edmund followed the inside wind of the road, between a pair

of pasture hills crowned with oaks going scarlet with the dying days. He caught a blur of motion just beyond them—Katherine hurtling at a full driving gallop through a strip of open pasture on the back of a dark gray horse. Her hair streamed out behind her, nearly the same shade as the horse's mane and tail, a triple banner giving full account of their speed. She held a lance couched in the crook of her arm, which she lowered in one smooth action to point at the cross-shaped device at the near end of the pasture. From one arm of the cross there hung a weighted sack; a round shield had been bolted to the other with a red dot painted on the boss. She leaned into a crouch, bracing herself in the stirrups—and struck the target square in the middle, swinging the weight out, up and over her ducked head as she thundered past.

The horse saw Edmund coming first. He twitched his ears and snorted, thumping one great hoof into the turf.

Katherine raised her free hand. "Edmund! Sorry—I suppose I must be late." She tightened the rein and rode over to the railing.

Edmund looked over at the device, still spinning from the impact. "What happens if you miss?"

"I don't miss." She handed him the lance butt-first. "You remember Indigo, don't you?"

Indigo's massive flanks heaved in and out. His mane hung damp with sweat down his hard-muscled neck. In full sun his coat had a sheen like blue slate from the white hairs that grew amongst the black. Edmund was no more a horseman than most peasants, but he knew perfection when he saw it. He

MATTHEW JOBIN

considered reaching out to stroke Indigo's long, straight nose, but one look into the stallion's eyes told him how very bad an idea that would be.

Katherine leapt down. "I like your shoes." She hooked a finger in the reins and led Indigo back across the pastures, to the stables and cottage at the heart of the farm. Edmund walked alongside, savoring the feeling of carrying her lance, still warm on the end from her grip.

"Papa, Edmund's here!" Katherine pushed back the stable door.

"Over here, child." Katherine's father, John, the Marshal of Elverain, stood in the middle of a paddock, walking a very young horse in a wide circle on a lunge line. He twitched a whip, no more than a touch, and the horse changed his gait, bringing his hooves up high in a handsome trot.

"Papa." Katherine sighed. "You are still not dressed for the fair."

"Not yet. You go on ahead with Edmund."

"It's in your honor, Papa!"

"Yes, yes." John clicked his tongue. The horse on the lead reversed his course, stepping back around the circle in the opposite direction.

Indigo whickered and stamped. He pricked his ears toward the stable, then ducked his head and walked in on his own.

"Well, don't be too long." Katherine followed Indigo inside. "Stay here a moment, Edmund. I'll be right back."

Edmund leaned Katherine's lance by the door, his mind racing through grown-up and manly things to discuss. As lost for words as he got around Katherine, he had an even harder time with her father, a real and proper hero from his younger days, though you could never tell by looking.

"Good morning to you, Edmund." John Marshal flicked the whip behind his horse to correct the stride. "I see that you are entering the tourney."

"Oh. Well—I'd been thinking about it." Edmund had thought only to keep his longbow from his brother's greedy clutches. He had not considered what carrying it with him would mean.

"I wish I had time to watch, but I'm sure Lord Aelfric will be dragging me about all day, trying to press my hand with every noble guest in the hall." John gathered up the whip and brought the young horse to a stop. He looked down at Edmund's shoes. "I must say I don't agree with these new fashions you young folk wear. You could take out someone's eye with those things."

Edmund shifted from foot to foot. "I liked that horse Katherine was riding, Master Marshal. He looks ready to be given as a warhorse any day."

"Oh, he is." John Marshal led his horse to the paddock gate. "I've only seen his like once before in my life. He's only four, though, and we usually pass them on to Lord Aelfric when they turn five."

He reached down for a canvas bag and fed his horse a carrot. "Between you and me, it will be hard on Katherine when the day comes. That horse loves her and cares nothing for anyone else in the world. My only fear is that the knight who finally gets him will find he's got himself a steed who will resent him all his life."

Katherine came around the side of the stable, on the path that led down from the cottage. "I had no time to do much with my hair. Do I look all right?"

She had woven a bright blue ribbon into her braid that matched the color of her dress. Edmund tried to speak. He thought for a moment he would find the right words, some compliment that would not come out a blurting jumble. The moment dragged.

Katherine smoothed down her dress. "I don't?"

"You look lovely, child." John led the yearling to the stables. "You two go on ahead and enjoy yourselves."

"Lovely." Edmund seized on the word. "Lovely, no question."

Relief tinged Katherine's smile. "Oh, good, thank you. I was afraid I looked a fool." She turned and made to hop the fence, then changed course and used the gate. "Papa, I laid out your good shirt and breeches. You wear them, and don't be long!"

"Yes, child." John shut the door. Katherine flashed Edmund a long-suffering smile and skipped onto the road, as high as her skirts would allow. Edmund wanted to skip right along beside her, but men should not skip, and he had never felt more nearly a man in his life.

Katherine spoke over her shoulder. "I have a surprise!"

"You do?" Any surprise seemed a happy wonder, whatever it might be. "What is it?"

"Tom! He's coming with us!"

"Oh." No—some surprises were not happy at all. "But—how? Why?"

"His master threw out his back again, so he's sending Tom

to sell his fleece. Isn't that wonderful? It's the very first time he's ever even seen a fair!"

"It's—" Edmund did not trust himself to say anything Katherine might want to hear.

"We have to make sure to show him a good time." Katherine pointed. "Oh, there he is!"

Tom stood at the juncture of the road with a path that ran off into the western pastures. At his feet lay a pair of sacks, each of them larger than himself. Even from a distance he looked exhausted—but then, he usually did.

"I heard the story going round about how you said you found Hugh's pigs." Tom struggled one of the sacks over his skinny shoulders. "Everyone seems to believe it. Thank you."

"Poor old Hugh—he loved those pigs, especially Bossy." Katherine heaved up the other sack before Edmund had a chance to offer. "But let's not think of it today. Let's have us some fun!"

They walked the Dorham road around the hills and down into the village. By then the moving crowd had swelled until Edmund could see at least half the people he knew in the world ranged out in a stream going south—some on carts, a few riding, but most of them walking the seven miles down to Longsettle and then over to the castle.

"I really could take one." Edmund could not bear the thought of being seen by his neighbors walking empty-handed while Katherine hauled a sack in her finest dress.

"Take Tom's then. He's been carrying longer."

Edmund sighed. He dropped behind Katherine's back and held out his longbow to Tom in exchange.

"Sorry about this." Tom shifted his load onto Edmund's shoulders. "I didn't know I'd be coming."

Staying angry with Tom was like kicking a starving puppy. Edmund bore up under the weight as best he could. "You know, I suppose it makes some sort of sense that your master takes you for granted. What I object to is the thought that he takes us for granted, too."

"I have to sell all this for two marks at the least." Tom leaned back to stretch as he walked. "But I can't remember how many pennies to the mark."

"We'll help." Katherine nodded back over her shoulder. "Edmund's good with money."

The weight, in truth, was not so very much. "Of course I will."

They turned through the square, joining the West Road for a few yards and then south past the step of the inn. Edmund held his breath, but saw no sign of his mother.

Wat and Hob seemed to have decided that they had better things to do than drink in the tavern all day—they ambled up ahead, passing a wineskin between them. The Longsettle road wound up against Lord Aelfric's private hunting chase, then down between the fields in the broad basket of the valley. The Swanborne stream made its silly music under the footbridge, giggling all the way down to meet the Tamber. On such a day even the distant moors had a kind of cold majesty.

"Katherine—Katherine!" The voice came shrill from behind them. Edmund moved aside to let a wagon pass, and found his brother sitting with his stupid little friends on the back, their legs all dangling in a row.

"Have you decided, Katherine?" Emma Russet was far too pretty to be only thirteen, and mean as a badger because of it.

Katherine muttered something under her breath. She unbent her back to look up. "Good morning, Emma. Decided what?"

"Well, who it's to be, of course." Emma stretched a hand to point at Tom and Edmund. "The slave or the runt?"

Katherine flushed dark. She opened her mouth, but nothing came out. She looked down again.

"Oh, it's Bony Tom, it must be!" Tilly Miller tittered in her hand—Emma's best friend, her shadow, her echo. "He trades her a kiss for every hot meal!" She was the youngest of Geoffrey's gang of friends by some years, and had been following Emma around for as long as Edmund could remember.

Geoffrey nudged his own best friend, mouse-brown little Miles Twintree, then flung the soggy core of a half-eaten apple at Edmund's feet. Miles did the same, though he looked somewhat guilty. The kid from across the river—Peter Overbourne, that was his name—did not bother to aim wide, nor was it only a core that he threw.

"Ow!" Edmund dropped Tom's sack in surprise, spilling a pile of fleece onto the road.

"That's a lovely dress, Katherine." Miles's big sister, Luilda, passed on a following cart, holding hands with Lefric Green. "Did you inherit it?"

"What? You—" Katherine balled up her fists, glaring at the back of Luilda's head. Wagon and cart trundled on into the trees.

Katherine sighed. "Why is it I can never think of anything to say back?" She knelt to help Tom pack everything in again.

"That kid Peter's the worst of them." Edmund rubbed at his chest where the apple had struck. "Geoffrey's turned into an utter brat since they started running about together."

Tom beat some dust from a fleece. "I know why folk make fun of me, but I can't see why they do it to the two of you."

"I'm too big, and Edmund's too small," said Katherine. "I run about dressed like a man most of the time. He likes books a bit too much for a village where hardly anyone can read."

"We don't fit." Edmund heaved up his sack. "We never will."

"So long as we're all together, I don't care." Katherine led them onward down the road. Her words hung in the air, and after a while "all together" was all that seemed to matter.

Chapter 5

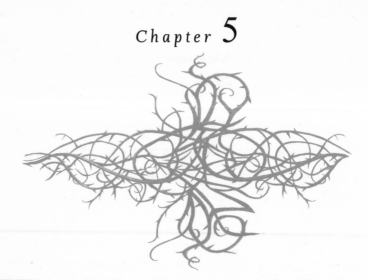

Edmund had learned since moving to the village that everyone resented the town that had sprung up around the castle. That's how they said it—"sprung up," though from all he knew, the town was more than a hundred years old. People had long memories in Elverain, long enough to tell muddy stories of a time when things were different, though there was no one left alive who had ever seen it. What seemed to bother them most was the name—the town was called Northend, which gave the idea that it was somehow the north end of everything, though of course any number of villages were yet farther north, off the king's highway and up the old roads. Edmund did not dislike Northend at all, a well-kept and prosperous place made of tall, narrow houses of wood and plaster clustered tight and bounded by even narrower alleys and cross streets. At its center was the large cobbled square where the highway came north out of the flat, fertile fields of

Quail to end where it met the Longsettle road. Bright banners and pennants had been hung about the square in the baronial colors, dark green and silver-white, above a noisy crowd that milled to and fro amongst the many stalls that had been raised there. Lord Aelfric's castle stood north of the town, old and massive and squatting lonely on the crest of a treeless hill.

Tom stopped abruptly by the first of the houses. Edmund took the pause to let his sack down to the road. "You all right?"

Tom did not look all right in the least. "I've never seen so many people."

"You'll be fine—we'll look after you." Katherine took him by the arm. They followed the road in between the best-made houses in Elverain. They were soon surrounded by hawkers and merchants of all descriptions.

"Fine linens!" A short man with a braided beard bellowed from his stall. "Shifts, dresses, and headpieces, or buy it by the bolt! The finest Westry flax, spun into linen light as a feather. Approved by the renowned Weavers' Guild of Tambridge! Step right in!"

"Candles!" called a young woman, pointing to a stall full of elegant tapers. "Lovely white wax, brilliant light! Made in the famous beehives of Anster. Come get your candles!"

"Honey cakes!" cried the man from the next stall, who looked like the young woman's father. "Delicious pastries covered in sweet Anster honey! Nothing so delicious in all this world!"

Katherine stopped and reached into her belt. "Oh, I love those!"

"I'll get them!" Edmund dug out a tiny wedge of silver—one piece of a penny that had been cut into fourths. He bought two cakes and—a stroke of genius!—gave the first to Tom. Katherine beamed at him as he held up the other before her.

"Potions!" shouted a man as he came between them, carrying a box full of all manner of vials and jars. "Potions of all descriptions and efficacies! Potions to help you sleep, potions to keep you up all night! You, my lad!" He looked Edmund up and down, then over at Katherine. He drew Edmund aside.

"I've just the thing for you—you look like you could use the help." He swirled a crystal vial full of rich red liquid. "A few drops of this in her wine and before you know it, she'll be waiting for your hand. Just six pennies, but a whole lifetime of joy! What do you say?"

Katherine stomped over and led Edmund away by the sleeve. "Whatever it is, he doesn't need it!"

The man gave Katherine a dark look. "You mind that one, my boy. More trouble than she's worth." He turned his back before Edmund could think of a retort.

Tom stared around him as though looking for some path of escape. "What do I do?"

"The first thing you do is keep your hand on your purse." Edmund pulled him out of the worst of the bustle.

"Why? I don't have any money yet."

"It's just a good habit." Edmund cast about him for a likely-looking merchant. They had laid things out in a different pattern than they did for the regular fair in the spring. This fair had a wild, haphazard character, more ale tents and makeshift gambling halls than proper merchants, and far too many folk who just seemed to loiter and look, neither buying nor selling and so quite likely there for a less savory purpose.

"That one looks promising." Katherine stood up on her toes. "Over here." She shouldered up a sack and pushed them off toward the corner of the square in the fullest sun.

Tom craned around him, his green eyes wide. He pointed. "What's that?"

Edmund glanced across. "That's a play. People acting, you know. That one's about the making of the kingdom. It's a bore."

"Oh." Tom nodded. "I didn't know they had singing. What's that, then, over there? Is that a play, too?"

"Those are two men arguing over the price of a barrel of salted herring. I suppose you could treat it as entertainment if you wanted."

"And that?"

Edmund tried to catch Katherine's eye to smirk at her, but she seemed intent on finding their way through the crowd. He turned to follow Tom's direction. "What are you looking at?"

"That big tent where the woman is shouting inside."

"Oh, that? That's the court." Edmund stopped—he thought he felt something brush at his side. He clapped his hand at his belt and glared around him, but it was only an ox being driven past for sale. He looked back at Tom. "The Court of Dusty Feet—Lord Aelfric sets one up for every fair. There's more trouble for him to hear about in one day than he usually gets all year."

"—stole my pigs!" The shouting woman could be seen

through the opening of the tent, but the person she jabbed her finger at could not. "I swear to you, my lord, and I bring ten solid folk to swear on my name that I am no liar! My pigs, good porkers, stolen and gone!"

Edmund laughed. "Oh, no—more missing pigs!"

"So Lord Aelfric's in there?" Tom bent down to peer beneath the flap. "I've never seen him before. Does he leave the castle very much?"

"I must remind you, good woman, that I merely sit in my father's name." The answering voice had a highborn accent but sounded clear and young. "I judge for your lord, but I am not your lord. I would ask you again to address me as a squire for the sake of propriety. Clerk of the court, you will note her claim and take the names of those who swear for her."

Edmund looked inside the tent. A ring of angry relatives surrounded the woman, all of them glaring at a cringing, road-dusted man with the look of a traveling tinker about him. A platform stood at the opposite end, upon which had been set a thick oaken chair. Its occupant could be called boy as easily as man, sixteen and sandy fair, with what Edmund thought to be an ill-advised attempt at a beard.

Edmund shook his head at Tom. "No, that's his son, Harold. Aelfric must be training him at law by letting him sit as judge for the day, so he knows how it works when he inherits."

Katherine dropped her sack into Edmund's arms without so much as a warning. "Oh, let's go in for a while!"

"What? What for?" Edmund staggered under the unexpected weight. "Why on earth would you want to stand around in a court? There's a whole fair to see!"

"Let's go in—just for a bit! Let's go in! How do I look? Do I look all right?"

"I can't see you right now, I've got a sack in front of my face." Edmund managed to maneuver the sack to the ground without spilling it. "Why don't we sell Tom's things first so we don't have to carry them around?"

"Good idea. You do that—you're good with money, no one better." Katherine arranged her skirts and tossed her hair back over her shoulder. "I just want to know about the pigs. Could be important. See you soon!" She plunged into the tent.

Edmund shrugged at Tom. "I don't understand. Pigs? Who cares?"

"I truly am sorry," said Tom. "I know you wanted to come alone with her."

"There's still the feast and the dance." Edmund heaved up his load, and took his longbow back from Tom. "I thought I handled all that with the honey cakes rather well, don't you?"

"I wouldn't know, but the cake was very good. Thank you, by the way."

It did not take long to sell the fleece, once Edmund had prevailed on Tom to let him pretend that they were his and go stand somewhere out of view. Tom had the disturbing tendency to agree with anything every haggling fat-face of a merchant said to him, nodding like a yielding little lamb and saying that yes, they did look a bit off, now you mention, and no,

I suppose it's not fair of me to foist such junk on a man of your elder years at such a price. Edmund gently shoved his friend aside and got to business, and by the time he heard the fanfare of trumpets from the field north of town, he had two marks, three pennies and a farthing to press in Tom's hand, along with a pair of empty sacks.

He saw Katherine coming, and made a point of letting the money clink into Tom's open palm at just the right moment. "So, what of the missing pigs?"

"More than just pigs. Cattle and cats, goats, favorite dogs." Katherine walked with them out on the lane that led from the town up to the castle. "There's even a man from Roughy saying he's missing a daughter and both his sons."

"Well, that's just a jumble." Edmund shrugged. "Nothing to connect them."

"That's not what Harry said."

Edmund shot her a look. "Harry?"

Katherine fidgeted with the tassel of her belt. "I heard that his friends call him Harry."

"I can't think of anything that would eat both cattle and dogs, let alone children," said Tom. "What did folk say about it?"

"Well, someone said the Nethergrim, but everybody laughed." Katherine sounded odd—unlike herself, with a giddy, girly trill in her voice Edmund had never heard before. "Harry got angry about it—said it was wrong to speak of such a thing today of all days, when we have gathered to honor the men who slew the Nethergrim and made the north safe for us all. I think he even looked at me when he said it. You should have seen him—he handled it so well, put it all together as clever as you like. He's going to tell his father all about it, told everyone he would make sure that the land was safe, and not to worry. You should have seen him!"

Edmund had to look to make sure that clouds had not come in. The sun shone as bright as before, the sky the same full blue and the world around him dancing in high holiday, but he could no longer feel the joy of it.

"Oh, look, there's Papa!" Katherine waved. Her father did not seem to see her. He stood beneath a brightly colored canopy next to the stern, stooped figure of Lord Aelfric of Elverain, looking obviously uncomfortable amongst the crowd of noble guests gathered to soak in his unwanted glory. Lord Aelfric was making a speech, but his creaky old voice did not carry far.

"We should go and watch." Katherine grabbed for Tom and turned to push into the crowd. "And then when Harry comes to join them, we can tell him all about what we found up on the hill last night. I could even lead him up there myself, and—"

"No, no!" Edmund wanted more than anything to avoid another brush with Harry. "We should take Tom to see the archery tourney. He's never seen one before!" He tugged Tom the other way, off toward the dozen targets that had been raised on open ground below the castle.

Tom looked from one friend to the other, his long arms stretched out wide in both directions. He did not seem to care which way they dragged him.

"Well—all right, then." Katherine let go. "For Tom."

They turned back across the field, finding a place along the strip of trees beside the archery lists. A crowd of men, none of them rich or noble, stood at the other end with longbows in hand. A few at a time stepped up to the mark, shot three arrows at the butts and earned the praise or joking scorn of their fellows.

"A good day for it, I suppose." Katherine fluffed out her skirts to sit in the grass. "Not much of a crosswind." Tom lay back against a walnut tree. He reached out to pluck a blade of grass and started chewing on it. Edmund found a spot on a boulder that had soaked up some heat from the day, and sat atop it with his longbow laid across his lap. One of his neighbors stepped up to shoot—Jordan Dyer took his stance, drew back and hit within a hair of the bull's-eye.

"Good one, Jordan!" Edmund clapped along with the crowd. He felt an idle wish that he practiced more himself, enough at least that he could enter the tourney without looking a fool. The trouble was that just about everyone in the village was a crack shot—they started drilling at the targets once a week as little kids, and the men were bound by Lord Aelfric's laws to keep at it until they were sixty. There were no such laws in Bale, the town where Edmund had lived until he was ten. By the time Edmund had moved to Moorvale with his family, the boys his own age were so good that there seemed no point in trying to catch up.

"You're right—better than a speech." Katherine settled back

MATTHEW JOBIN

against the boulder, her shoulder resting just near Edmund's foot. "You're coming to the feast for sure, then?"

"I wouldn't miss it." Not for all the world.

"I'm a little afraid of it, to be honest. The dance, I mean."

"Why?"

"There are going to be rich girls there, noble girls with their dainty little hands, wearing gowns that cost as much as Papa's house." Katherine looked down at her own hands, then tried to hide them up the sleeves of her dress. "I know what people say about me. I'm afraid I'll just stand by the wall all night."

Edmund could not have asked, could not have dreamed in a thousand nights for a better moment. He nearly let it slip by, so amazed he was at its perfection. He took a breath. "Well, if you want, I would be happy—no, I would be honored, deeply honored, if you—"

She looked up at him. His mouth went dry.

"Ah—Katherine, isn't it?"

Katherine gasped and leapt to her feet. She curtsied. "My lord!"

"Not a lord yet." Harry waved a hand through the air. "I was just speaking to your father, Katherine. What a day this must be for him!"

Edmund sat staring at the space where Katherine had just been. Tom awoke, blinked up at Harry and scrambled out of the way without being noticed.

"I have not seen you in some time, Katherine—it must be years, I think." Harry stood Katherine's height, or perhaps slightly taller. His bright hazel eyes seemed to flash golden in the sun. "Was it at a winter feast?"

Katherine stammered, and curtsied again at his side. "I was eleven, good squire."

"Yes, that's right, we had your father up for that, and you came along." Harry's boots were fashioned of fine kid leather, and his clothes seemed made to mold to his frame. "We played a game of chase-about behind the hall with some other children. I seem to recall you played a little trick on me that day."

"I'd hoped you'd forgotten, good squire." Katherine flushed bright red.

"How could I forget? It took me days to get that gunk out of my hair!" Harry laughed—Edmund would have liked to pretend it was false and snobbish, but it was neither. "You were such a little imp back then. You've grown."

Katherine stared at the ground. "Everyone says that."

"I wonder if they mean it the way I do."

Katherine looked up at Harry. The mooning look on her face made Edmund sick.

Harry seemed to notice Edmund only then. "Oh." He arched one elegant brow. "And who is this? Your friend?"

"Yes, good squire," said Katherine. "This is Edmund Bale. My friend."

Edmund scrambled off the boulder and bowed. "Good squire."

"Ah, yes, from up in Moorvale, are you not? The innkeeper's son." Harry leaned down to smile over Edmund with his

MATTHEW JOBIN

hands behind his back, acting for all the world like Edmund was a child who wanted a pat on the head. "Do you know, I was just telling our noble guests that we have the best archers in the kingdom right here in Elverain, and the best archers in Elverain hail from the village of Moorvale."

Edmund nodded. "The best, good squire, no question."

"And so, young Edmund," said Harry, "when is your turn?"

Edmund blinked. "Turn?"

"In the archery tourney!" Harry tapped the longbow in Edmund's hands.

Edmund gaped—first at the bow, then at Harry. "Oh. I wasn't—"

"Come, come," said Harry. "Let us have a sample of your deadly skill."

"My deadly—?" Edmund swallowed hard. "Yes, good squire." He turned and shuffled out onto the field. He took his place in line, shooting looks across at Harry and Katherine whenever he could.

"You must be proud of your father, Katherine." Harry's voice carried across the open field. "And we are all grateful for the work you do—John often says that the horses he sends us are as much your handiwork as his." Katherine seemed to be turning pink at his side.

Edmund stepped up to the mark and gauged the wind. He looked around him at the gathered crowd, and saw almost every one of the neighbors who stood next to him week after week at archery practice. He tried to remember all that they had shown him. The stance comes first. Plant your feet shoulder width apart and stand with equal weight on each leg. Your toes should line up to the bull's-eye. Nock the arrow between your first two fingers, but don't pinch it or you'll throw off your aim. He sighted down to the target—maybe he could do this after all.

"Miss! Miss, miss, miss!"

Edmund glanced over to find Geoffrey and his stupid little friends lined up along the trees. They passed along the chant to children Edmund did not know, who took it up without knowing or caring why it was right and good that Edmund should miss the target.

"I saw you earlier, when I was holding court down in the square." Harry drew in at Katherine's shoulder. "I'm glad I found you again."

If Katherine made a reply, it was too breathless for Edmund to hear. He gauged the distance—one good shot would draw a cheer, draw Katherine's eye. One good shot.

"Tonight we do honor to your father, so I think you should sit in a place of honor as well." The nervous, hopeful tone of Harry's voice made it grate all the worse in Edmund's ear. "I will arrange for you to sit with the nobles, at the high table."

Edmund did his best to pretend he was deaf. Put your other hand on the bow with the grip right at the base of your thumb—that was next. He drew back. A bull's-eye—please, just once.

"You won't be out of place at all, I promise. Sit next to me; we can talk about horses. It will be such fun—and, later, if you like—" Harry moved in for the killing stroke. "Katherine, may I have the honor of asking you to the first dance at the feast tonight?"

Edmund loosed his arrow. He had already sunk his head before it landed in the dirt, yards away from the target.

"Me?" Katherine sounded near to losing her voice. "I would—that would—yes, please, good squire!"

"Ha!" Geoffrey hopped up and down from the sidelines. "Good one, Edmund!" His friends laughed long and loud.

No one else said much—most grown-ups were not so cruel. It all had the feeling of a bad dream, though Edmund could not remember a particular dream so perfectly bad. He thought for a moment that he might as well strip off all his clothes and stand naked in the field, just to make it all as horrible as possible.

Harry looked out to the archery field. "Oh." He turned to Katherine. "Your friend is not a very good shot, is he?"

Edmund felt a nudge at his back. "Er, you do have another go."

"Forget it." Edmund slumped off the field. He looked up at Katherine and found her still turned to Harry, her eyes shining wide, a spot of flush on each of her cheeks. The ache was more than he could bear.

He found Tom on the other side of the walnut tree. "I'll walk home with you if you like."

"What about the feast, though?" Tom turned as he passed. "Aren't you going to the dance?"

Edmund could not bring himself to answer. He watched the ground at his feet, nudging through the crowd without seeing them, and it was only by the sound of following footsteps that he knew that Tom had come along to walk home at his side.

Chapter 6

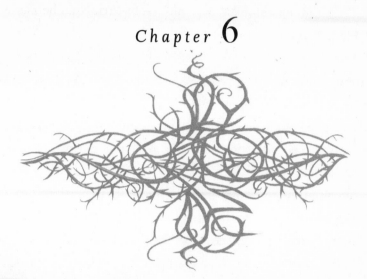

"P apa, your guard is low." Katherine twisted up her arm to take a strike on the edge of her shield.

Her father parried her counter. "Have mercy on an old man!" He sprang back a step and switched his stance.

It was too late in the year and in the day to be warm, but the sun had broken bright above the clouds. The dull thwack of wooden sword on sword returned in echo from the wide country all around. The horses grazing down in the pasture had long ceased to pay the noise any mind. The longer Katherine sparred, the deeper she got into the shift of stances, lunges and blocks, the closer she came to forgetting for a moment the horror of the night before.

"You're getting sweaty, Papa." She jammed a thrust down her father's sword to the crossguard. "Would you like a rest?"

John knocked her blade wide. "That's odd, child. I was just

about to ask you the same thing. Arm straight, now—you're falling out of stance."

"Ha! As you like, then." Katherine came on, swinging high across the shoulders, meeting each parry and driving her father back over the top of the hill. John gave ground past the splay-limbed oak at the summit, stumbling over the roots and seeming barely able to stave her off—but never losing his smile.

She read the trick a moment too late.

Her father drew her in, then planted his foot and broke her advance, stumbling no more. "Out of stance, child. Too eager for the kill." He did not fake his hard breathing, though—she had gotten very close. She wove and ducked, giving ground in return until she found her balance.

"Hello up there!" The voice floated up the hill from afar.

Katherine and her father stepped apart, then dropped their guards. Two figures rode proud horses up the Dorham road— the first of them young and straight of carriage, the second riding sidesaddle in long skirts. The first rider dismounted to open the pasture gate—Katherine gasped and threw her sword aside.

John shaded his eyes to squint at the approaching figures. "Who's that?"

"Harry—Harold, Papa." Katherine unbuckled her shield and let it drop in the grass.

"With his father?"

"No, his mother." Katherine tried to brush the dust and bits of grass from her tunic, then looked herself over. No good, no good—sweat stains on her breeches, mud on her boots. She reached up to push errant strands of hair into her braid. A little voice in her asked her why she bothered, but she could not help herself.

John set his sword against the trunk of the oak. "Don't worry so, child. We raise and train their horses for them—they do not expect us to be so very clean."

Harry came first up the hill, astride a dun stallion Katherine had helped to birth six years before. He turned to call behind him. "Here they are, Mother!" He slipped down from the saddle. Katherine kept her head inclined, watching the grass at his feet. A silence yawned and dawdled past.

"You are most welcome here." Her father filled the gap. "I trust you enjoyed the feast?"

"I did—very much," said Harry. "Did you also?"

"It was an honor, good squire."

"Oh, good. That is very good. And—your daughter?"

Katherine could not bring herself to say a word. Her dreams had died far too hard.

"There was no need to come up so far, Harold." Lady Isabeau crested the summit on the back of a pure white palfrey. "If you wish for a tour of your father's stables, you need only command our servants to come down and show you them." She was neither young nor old, neither fat nor thin. She wore her hair bound in an elaborate headpiece ten years out of date.

"My lady." John bowed low. Katherine curtsied behind him, her hands held out to lift imaginary skirts.

"John Marshal." Lady Isabeau glanced around her at the

weapons lying scattered in the grass. Her face pinched in disapproval. "How long have you been training your daughter in swordplay?"

"Since she was eight, my lady."

"For what purpose?"

John Marshal looked up at her, then down. He made no answer. A pained look crossed Harry's face. Katherine flushed in hot misery.

"Well, Harold, here you are. Your father's training stables—your stables, one day." Lady Isabeau wheeled her horse around. "John, walk with me. I want your advice on a few small matters."

"My lady." John stepped out to follow down the hill. Lady Isabeau made him jog a bit to catch up to her horse.

"I'll just stay here, Mother." Harry turned to call after them. "To take in the view. Shall I just stay here?"

"Do as you like, son. Have the girl fetch us some refreshment."

"Yes, Mother." Harry watched them go, then looked at Katherine, once and again. She could not bring herself to fake a smile in return.

Harry shifted away under the oak. He picked up the practice sword that leaned against the trunk. "So—are you good?"

"We just pass the time this way, me and Papa—when we're done our work for your noble father, of course." Katherine wanted him to go. She would never have dreamed that she could wish for such a thing, but she did.

"Come, then." Harry motioned that she should retrieve the other sword. "Let us see."

Katherine could think of no excuse. She picked up her sword, but held it limp at her side, her fingers curled loose around the hilt.

Harry laughed. "You can't fool me—I saw you up here. I know you are better than that!" He made a playful lunge. Katherine turned the blow by reflex despite her surprise.

"That's more like it!" Harry tried again, coming forward with a series of slow, lazy swings placed deliberately off target, followed by a single close swipe aimed to just brush Katherine's side. Katherine parried each strike with ease, batting the last one wide and returning with a checked riposte. She found herself in stance, up on the balls of her feet and treading light. She found Harry smiling at her over the guard of his sword.

"Now—shall I tell you why I came here today?" Harry tried for a backhand stroke, but led the move so far ahead with his foot that Katherine saw it coming all the way in.

The proper counter would have had her blade up in his face. She settled for a simple parry. "Why, good squire?"

"Call me Harry." He advanced, dodging to jab along her side. "I came today to offer my apologies. I am a bad dancer, you see."

"But it was my fault." Katherine blocked across the center. "I'm the one who stepped on your foot. I'm the one who knocked Lady Tand into the minstrels."

Harry leaned in across their pressed blades. "It was my lead, and my fault." His eyes were the color of a field of summer wheat. "I was nervous."

"Nervous? Of me?" Katherine leapt back and took up her stance. "Then you don't find me—strange?"

"I find your guard very hard to get through." Harry tucked a strand of hair behind his ear. The flush of action made him even more handsome, if such a thing were possible. Katherine searched his face for some sign of mistaken intent or cruel jest, but found only hopeful intensity. She had much less trouble reading his style of swordplay. He knew most of the basic stances and strokes, but did not know how to move between them. He played it all so much by rote that she could almost count out his swings for him. She could not help but guess that the knights who trained him must have let him off easy.

"But I'll bet you don't know this move!" Harry tried another lunge, more direct than the last. Before Katherine knew what she was doing, she had wound her blade over his and jerked it hard aside, ripping the sword from his hand to send it spinning off the top of the hill.

Her stomach sank.

She had beaten the boy that she adored—not just beaten him, but disarmed him and shamed him. She had made him look like a clumsy oaf—again. He turned to watch his sword land halfway down the slope.

"That was an accident." Katherine dropped her sword, then made a fool, an utter fool of herself trying to curtsy again. "Just bad luck, that's all." Wisps of hair fell messy around her face—she breathed like a cow. The urge to turn and run into the woods consumed her.

"That—" Harry turned to her agape. "That was wonderful!"

Katherine looked up under her lashes. "It was?"

"We should have you training Father's knights!" Harry's face showed not a trace of bitterness. "I've never seen such a move!"

"Papa taught it to me. He learned it from Tristan."

"Of course he did! Well—" Harry bowed. "I am squarely beaten, and cry mercy! Will you come down with me? My dear mother grows cranky if she goes too long without her wine."

· · ·

Katherine threw on a dress and pulled a brush through her hair in the wood-and-thatch cottage she shared with her father, then poured out his whole store of wine into a flagon. She dug three goblets from the trunk by the door and left the house, rounding the stables to find Harry alone by the paddock, leaning on the fence to watch the yearlings at play just beyond.

He beckoned her over. "Now, you must tell me, what is the name of that horse over there?"

Katherine poured a goblet full of wine. "He doesn't have a proper name yet. We just call him Indigo."

Indigo cocked up his head at the sound of his name. He chewed a mouthful of hay, then dropped down for another.

"I have never seen his like." Harry leaned on the rail to watch. "Who is the sire?"

"Break-spear, out of Sir Ranulf's stables at Thicket."

"The dapple gray with the black mane? About sixteen hands—white on his lower legs?"

"Yes, that's him. One of Ranulf's favorites. We've had him

out once or twice for some new blood." Katherine held out the goblet. Their fingers drew across each other as he took it, leaving warm shocks that ran up her wrist.

"A fine match, if I am any judge." Harry turned his gaze across the eastern pasture to the mares with their foals and then the older colts—each in his own paddock, each on his way to becoming a horse of war. "It must be a good life, here. So simple." The wind touched across his brow, ruffling his hair as though it loved him, as though it meant to caress. She tried as hard as she could not to simply stare.

Indigo ambled near, munching on some grain. Katherine reached out to stroke his neck, to bring herself back to earth while she still could.

"Look at that stride." Harry dropped his voice in awe. "Such a horse comes once in a lifetime, if that."

"I'm training him for you." Katherine blurted it out.

Harry turned in surprise.

Katherine had no choice but to go on. "When we pass the warhorses on to the castle—I know we don't get to choose where they go, but I've been hoping you would be the one to take him."

Harry looked long at Katherine, then at Indigo. "Do you know—that's the kindest thing anyone has ever done for me."

"It is?" Katherine could not hide the note of disbelief in her voice.

"I know you might laugh to hear it, but it is not always so grand being the only son and heir. Sometimes I—" Harry shook his head. "No. I have no right to complain."

"You could visit us here, to get away from things." Katherine hugged the flagon to her chest. "You could visit anytime!"

He relaxed into a smile that pierced her through. "I would like that. Very much."

They stood inches apart, eyes to eyes. Words tumbled in Katherine's head, but nothing came out. The ground seemed very far away.

He reached out. She let a hand slip from the flagon and laced her fingers into his.

"Harold!"

They jumped apart. Lady Isabeau stooped through the doorway of the stable behind them.

"Oh—Mother. Hello." Harry bobbed his head. "We were just looking at the horses."

"Were you." Lady Isabeau approached the rail. Katherine offered her a goblet of wine and retreated with a fumbling curtsy.

"Katherine Marshal." Lady Isabeau sipped, then grimaced. "It grieves me to learn that you are yet unmarried."

Katherine felt relieved that it was not her place to answer back. She kept her gaze averted.

Harry coughed. "Mother—you might know that peasant girls often marry somewhat older than ladies of noble blood."

"A shameful practice. Dangerous to a woman's virtue." Lady Isabeau turned on Katherine. "We hold your father in high esteem. He is a good marshal—we have had no complaints about our stables these twenty years. The horses he breeds and raises are superior. He is never out of account. Such a man deserves a daughter who honors him."

Katherine made a strangled noise. "Yes, my lady."

"Have you a suitor?"

"No, my lady."

"Time passes. Think on your father's love."

"I do, my lady." Katherine raised her face. "Every day."

"Harold is a good son." Isabeau bored a look into Katherine. "Our only son. We have great plans for him."

Katherine felt the urge to stare her down—but then her father stepped from the stables with Harry's saddle in his arms. She remembered her station in life, and who owned the farm where she lived. She curtsied. "My lady. Please forgive me if I gave offense."

Lady Isabeau dropped the goblet in her hands. "Come, Harold. I think we have seen enough of this place." She passed on toward her waiting horse.

"Mother." Harry turned with an outstretched hand. "Mother, we were only talking!" Katherine took the saddle from her father and hurried over to Harry's horse, grateful for something to do besides stand in misery.

"Mind how you raise her, John." Lady Isabeau drew on her gloves. "You will need to get her married off someday."

"My lady?" Katherine's father brought her saddle cushion and strapped it around the girth of her horse. He kept his face a careful mask.

Lady Isabeau allowed him to help her up into her seat. "The fences of this farm will not shield your daughter much longer." She arranged her skirts to flow aside. "She must know her place in the world by the time she leaves it."

John stared up at Lady Isabeau. His brow darkened—he very nearly glared—then he broke. "Yes, my lady. I thank you for your kind advice."

"I say it for her good, John." Lady Isabeau took the reins. "You must shape her into a woman while you still can." She kicked in her heels and left the farm at a canter. Harry shot a stricken look at Katherine, then leapt into the saddle and swung his horse around to chase.

Katherine hung her head. Tears pricked out along her lashes.

Her father let his face fall into a scowl at Lady Isabeau's retreating form. He turned to Katherine. "Are you all right, child? What did she say to you?"

"Am I an embarrassment, Papa? Are you ashamed of me?"

"No, child." Her father took her by the shoulder. "No. You are my joy."

Katherine wiped her face. She looked at her father and tried to return his smile.

"There now. Let's forget all about it." Her father took up the goblets and started off toward the house. "Tell you what, I'll make supper tonight."

"Papa." Katherine tried, but could not keep the question down. "Would you have liked it better if I'd been a boy?"

"What? No!" He spun back to face her. "Never think that, child. Promise me."

"I won't, Papa." Katherine felt some small relief when he turned to go inside. She hated lying to him.

Chapter 7

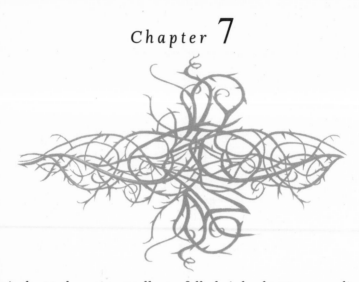

I t's the Nethergrim. I tell you folk, he's back! He never died!"

"Oh, will you shut it?" Katherine's cousin Martin Upfield turned around on one thick arm to glare at Grubby Hands from across the tavern. He shook his head and proffered his mug again. "Sorry, Edmund."

The anniversary fair was already a distant memory, lost in the desperate rush of the harvest. Like everyone else Edmund had to work the fields from dawn to dusk that time of year—but then, when his neighbors came by the inn for a quiet ale before bed, he had to pick up tray and pitcher to serve. His only consolation was that no one had the strength to stay up late.

"You all know the legends, you know what is spoken." Grubby Hands seemed to have the attention of his own party, and a few locals clustered in around his table. "As winter is the Nethergrim—he comes forever back! Spring does not know of winter but as a memory, yet winter still comes. Summer plays and winter waits, and when autumn falters, winter comes. The Nethergrim is winter; he is war and tax and death in the crib. He is age and withering!"

"It's just a couple of dead pigs!" Martin gave up. He took his mug back from Edmund, and got foam in his beard from a distracted pull of ale. "Must be a fine thing to sit around in taverns all day making up stories instead of doing proper work."

"Merchants. Fah." Nicky Bird lay half across the table, using a rolled-up cloak for a pillow. "Here, Horsa, get your fiddle. Let's have us a song."

"Not a chance. I can hardly feel my arms."

Edmund poured himself dry and shuffled off through the tavern, dangling his pitcher in the crook of a finger. He did not need to look where he was going—he knew every warp and bend of the floor, and on that night he had no fear of bumping into dancers.

"And there they were, fast asleep in the bushes at the end of the field, like a pair of vagabonds!" Bella Cooper leaned close in counsel with Ida, matriarch of the Twintree clan. "It looks poorly on the Bales and the Overbournes, if you ask me. Lazy sons mean bad fathers."

Bella jumped when she noticed Edmund passing so near. "Not you, of course, Edmund. You've always been a good boy." She dropped to a whisper behind him. "Do you think he heard me?"

Edmund stumbled down the stairs into the cellar, keeping one hand to the old plaster wall. The only light came down from the tavern to make a halo from Geoffrey's red curls, showing him bent at the tap of the middle keg.

"—and if I catch you shirking one more time, just once more, you can pack up and walk, and I don't care where you go."

Edmund froze. Geoffrey crouched at the tap, but he was not pouring. Their father stood in shadow in the corner by the shelf of mugs.

"You think I'm joking, don't you." Harman Bale spoke low, too quiet to be heard up in the tavern. "You think you can just dawdle about, napping in the bushes on harvest day and making a laughingstock of this family? There's younger boys than you out begging on the roads. You just see how far you can push me, you just see how little it will take to get you thrown out of here. And don't think for a moment your mother can save you—I'll toss you out on your ear if I've a mind to, and she can moan all she likes about it."

Harman uncrossed his arms and stepped out from the wall. He seemed to notice Edmund only then.

"Father." Edmund nodded at him, then swallowed without wanting to. He stood aside to let him pass.

Harman stopped on Edmund's stair, far closer than Edmund would have liked. "It's up to you, son, but when you inherit this place one day, I'd think twice about keeping him around." He pushed past. By the time he reached the top, he had changed in face and voice. He called out to Horsa for a jolly song, just the one song to raise their spirits after such a long hard day.

Geoffrey turned the tap of the middle keg. "This one's almost done." His voice came out broken and weak.

"He doesn't mean it." Edmund stepped off the last stair. "He's just trying to scare you."

Geoffrey kept his face turned away. His skin shone pallid white between his freckles. A stream of ale dribbled out into his pitcher.

Edmund pressed his back against the cool plaster of the cellar wall. "I don't want to inherit this place, you know."

"Shut it. Just shut your stupid mouth."

"I wouldn't ever throw you out. I swear it."

Geoffrey stomped upstairs, holding his brimming pitcher cradled in both hands. Edmund replaced him at the tap, but the flow of ale sputtered out before his pitcher was half full. He set the tap in the last keg, then turned his face from the pungent burst of air it let forth before disgorging a stream of black ale. He wiped the thick yellow foam from the brim and brought it upstairs to find Grubby Hands still at it, louder than before.

"Gray he is, and where he steps, the cold lingers." Grubby Hands waved his fat arms all about, sloshing some of his ale onto the floor. "Tall he is, tall as houses, black of eye as deep as the end of the world! His fur is daggers, his teeth are knives, his hands blood red with a thousand crimes, and not time nor love nor bravery can stop their grasping. He cannot be slain, for he is the voice of the world when it says, 'I love you not.'"

Edmund made his rounds, avoiding the merchants' table— Grubby Hands had drunk quite enough for one night. As he passed the kitchen door, he caught the sounds of his parents in low argument, his mother pleading and weeping and his father growling, biting at the ends of her words.

"Did they ever tell you what it was?" Another stranger—the dusty tinker from the fair—leaned across from his table. "The Nethergrim, I mean. Did they ever tell you what they saw, what they did?"

"Three men only came back from the mountain." Horsa Blackcalf folded his hands on his belly. "Tristan nearly died of his wounds, Vithric was delirious for weeks, and John Marshal—if you could have seen the look on his face. John only said that it was done, that's all, and not another word about it since."

"No, no, he said Tristan ran it through!" Nicky reached out to grab up some of Martin's meager supper—a hunk of bread, and an onion that he bit into like an apple. "That's what he said—the Nethergrim died on Tristan's sword."

Horsa scratched his warty nose. "I don't see any gray in your beard, Nicholas Bird. I don't recall that you were yet born when they came back."

"Well, that's what my gran said." Nicky tossed the onion from one hand to the other. "Told me often, when I sat at her knee of an evening: 'Tristan slew the Nethergrim, aye he did. Ran it straight through the heart, and nearly drowned in its gore.'"

"Your gran was naught but an old—" Horsa stopped, glanced sidelong at Nicky, and contented himself with a dismissive shake of his head.

Edmund lingered at the table. "Did Tristan ever say himself what he'd done?"

"If he did, how are we to know about it?" Horsa placed his fiddle on his knee, gave it a few scrapes, then turned the pegs to tune it. "He left Elverain that same year, and he's not been back here since."

The dusty tinker made bold to hop across from his table and join them. "I'll tell you this, every bard and minstrel in every tavern from here to Anster sings it just the same, that Tristan stepped right up and struck the Nethergrim dead." He sat down next to Martin. "You've heard the songs, have you not? *And Tristan drove his sword into the jelly of its eye, the jelly of its eye, so praise you all good Tristan, for he—*"

Martin held up a meaty hand. "Tell you what, stranger, stop singing and the next round's on me."

"But maybe that's how it got about," said Edmund. "Maybe Tristan told the story, back in his own lands, or maybe Vithric did, before he died."

Horsa ran up and down the scales on his fiddle. "We've never pressed John Marshal for the whole of the story, though he's lived among us for nigh on thirty years. It wouldn't be right."

Martin nodded. "If keeping it in is what gets my uncle John through the days, then so be it."

"You younger folk, you strangers, you can't know what it was like back then." Horsa waved his fiddle bow around the room. "It was as though all the troubles from every old legend you'd ever heard came back all at once to threaten us with ruin. First it was livestock, then folk caught out alone, then farms and then whole villages—no message, no mercy, nothing sought but our deaths. It was like no sort of war made by men. We could not plead nor bargain—we could not even surrender. We were to be overrun, scattered out onto the roads and fields to be cut down one after the next, and our lords seemed able to do nothing. Then Tristan came, and Vithric, John and all the Ten. They fought for us, they died for us, they gave us hope. It's true, stranger, that we do not know what they faced in those mountains, nor even exactly where the bodies of our fathers and brothers may lie, but since the day those three came home, there has not been a single grute nor bolgug nor any such thing seen in settled lands. They earned our faith in them, and so we give it gladly."

"You there, the blond boy!" Grubby Hands thunked his mug. "Let's have another round over here!"

Edmund pretended not to hear him. He slid back into the dark, serving the tables farther from the fire. He passed around the back corner, then bumped into a goblet held right at the level of the pitcher.

"Ale, please."

A prickling chill shot up Edmund's neck. The man holding the goblet was younger than he sounded, with thick short hair just starting to go gray over a smooth-shaven chin. He wore dark clothes fit for a prosperous merchant but without a merchant's taste for loud color. He held up a parchment to read it by the light of a candle—it appeared to be the lineage of the royal family. Books and scrolls lay scattered all about on the table before him, beside a tray piled high with chicken bones.

A flood of memories struck Edmund dizzy. He had only just served the man—seen him, served him food and drink and then somehow forgotten he was there. Then he remembered that the man had been there for days, and then remembered that he had remembered this before and forgotten it, again and again. The rush-littered ground buckled below him. Not knowing what to do, he held out his pitcher to serve.

"On second thought, don't bother." The stranger shut his book. "Do these people ever stop drinking?"

"Do I—do I know you?"

The stranger favored Edmund with a chilly smile. "You do not." He rolled up his parchment and slid it into an ivory tube. "Prepare my horse."

Edmund looked down at the books again. "You . . . you're a wizard."

"And you are a peasant. My, what an enjoyable game. Now go prepare my—" The cough bubbled up from his throat. He bent and spat blood into a hand cloth.

Edmund looked up and around the tavern. No one paid the slightest notice to the stranger, despite the violence of his coughing, despite the handsome cut of his clothes and despite the tooled and decorated books on the table before him, each one of which was likely worth more than they could earn in a month.

"—my horse." The man shuffled his books into a pair of saddlebags and dropped them over Edmund's shoulder. "Now."

"Yes, my—lord?"

"You will address me as 'your eminence.'"

"Yes, your eminence." Edmund hurried outside. The din of talk and music swung shut behind the door. The sun set low behind the far peaks of the Girth, raising shadows off the roofs of his neighbors. The saddlebags weighed heavy on his shoulder, stuffed to bursting with thick, rectangular shapes.

Edmund ran his fingers down the worked leather strap of the bag, then in under the flap. He touched board-and-leather binding, a rough run of pages, the frill of a tasseled bookmark. He looked up at the waking stars, thinking he might take a moment to decide, but he knew that he already had.

His future stretched out a hand and beckoned. He weighed it all up in moments—he might be gone for years, but when he came back, when Katherine saw what he had become, she could not help but fall in love with him. He pictured himself grown tall and stern, dressed in dark finery and crowned with hard-won wisdom, slapping a bag of gold marks in the craggy hands of Tom's master and asking—no, commanding—that his friend be given his freedom. Yes, oh yes—and best of all, Geoffrey would have to inherit the inn. Father would have no choice.

The stranger emerged. Edmund turned to him, ready with the question that would raise him up, change his life and set him on a new course forever. "Your eminence—"

"No," said the stranger.

Edmund's mouth hung open. He stammered. "How . . . how?"

"You affect the posture of the supplicant." The stranger shouldered past onto the road. "I have seen my share."

"But, you don't even know what I'm asking." Edmund turned to follow. "Please!"

"Do I need to be told?" The stranger bent to cough again. "Your eyes tell me what I need to know. You want something from me and have nothing to offer in return."

"But I have read *The Seven Roads*! I know the keys and chords of the Five Wheels, the secret names of the Three Pillars! Test me, your eminence—test me, please! I know them all!"

The stranger looked Edmund up and down. "Well, I can't be right all the time. Here I thought you were begging to be taken as a servant, but no! You wish to become an apprentice. How old are you?"

"Fourteen, your eminence."

"Fourteen." The wizard spat a laugh, though the sound was too flat to be seriously taken as mirth. "By the time I was twelve, I had written a summation of commentaries upon each of the Seven Roads. By fourteen I could call and command forces that you could not even name, spoken words that you could not in a year perceive the meaning, pressed my mind through realms of thought whose merest shadow will be forever unknown to you. You aspire beyond your station. If you had come to me five years ago, I might have considered you, but now you are far too old."

He bent to cough again—it seemed to sharpen his anger. He stepped over Edmund and stretched out an arm toward the stables. "Now go get my horse before I discover that you have started to annoy me."

Edmund backed away. "Yes, your eminence. Please forgive me, your eminence." His voice came out just like Geoffrey's— a broken little squeak, the sound of someone who knows he cannot win.

The stables leaned up beside the inn, a newer and much flimsier construction set well back from the road beside the Twintrees' tall and ancient hedge. Edmund did not need to be told which horse. He set down the bags in the straw that lined the stall.

Anger flared in him, hotter than the shame he had swallowed. The flap of one of the saddlebags fell open to expose the silvered edging on the binding of a book. He stared down at it. His mouth went dry.

It was done in a heartbeat. Sweat broke on his palms—he wiped them on his breeches and felt along the wall for the bridle.

"Aren't you finished yet?" The stranger followed him in through the doorway of the stable.

"Almost, your eminence." Edmund threw the bags over the horse's back and covered them with the saddle. He bent down to fasten the girth, fumbled and tried again.

"Boy! Do you need light?"

"No, no—done, your eminence!" Edmund led the horse from his stall. He handed the reins to the stranger. He could not stop his fingers from shaking.

The stranger took the reins without looking. He gazed around him at the darkening village—the statue and hall up in the square, then back at the inn and then across the street at Jordan Dyer's workshop—all as though he expected to find something but did not.

"Hmm. Somewhat shabbier than I remembered it." He used Edmund's hands for a step into the saddle, then set his horse to a canter up into the square and onward into darkness.

Edmund breathed in through his nose, and out. He waited for the sound of hoofbeats to fade out of hearing, then raced back into the stable. He seized the book out of the straw and slipped behind the inn. His skin prickled—it was done. He would need to find a new hiding place.

Chapter 8

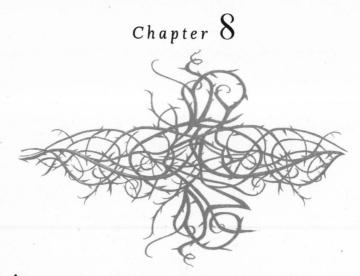

A raw wind raked the field. The sun rose behind clouds that stretched out to spin into wisps at the edge of the sky. Tom grasped the stilts of the plow. "Cush, now." The oxen strained in the yoke, and then the plow started moving through ground still heavy with damp.

"Your master should have had you go over this in spring." A hired man named Oswin followed just behind, smashing clods of earth left in Tom's wake with a mallet. Oswin wore a cap pulled tight over woolly dark curls. His face bore the marks of a childhood pox. His shirt was like Tom's, all stitch and mending.

Tom's floppy old shoes were little use against the seeping cold. The water got in and soaked him to the ankles, puddle after puddle in the furrows. "Cush. On we go." The oxen lowered their heads and pulled, blowing hard, battling their way toward the distant headland and a moment's rest at the end of the field.

"Aye, that's grand, how you do that," said Oswin. "Look at 'em go! Never seen that done without a whip."

The plow kicked and dragged in the hard-caked earth. Tom fought to hold it straight. The day promised work and nothing else, one furlong and the next until he dropped. The world was beautiful, the world was good—he said it to himself at the rise of every morning. Most days it was enough to get him through.

A blackbird took to singing in the trees beside him. She kept pace with him, flying from branch to branch along the field, then swooped in to perch on his shoulder. He felt her dig her talons in, just enough to keep herself from falling off. The wind swung in from the west, bringing news: tomorrow promised rain, by noon and not later. The blackbird ruffled and preened her feathers. The world was beautiful, the world was good.

"Hoy, Tom! There's a bird on your shoulder!"

Tom glanced behind him. He did not like the look on Oswin's face.

"Oh, ho, and she's a nice plump one." Oswin dropped his mallet. "Hold still, now. Blackbirds are good eating."

Tom shrugged up his shoulder. "Go." The blackbird sprang to flight just in time, flapping off an inch past Oswin's reach.

"Aw, curse it, what did you move for?" Oswin jumped and clapped the air, but had no hope of making the catch. "We could've had her in the stew!"

They reached the headland, a strip of treed and ragged ground between the fields. Tom steered the oxen through the long slow turn and set down the plow at the edge of the next furrow. He found himself wishing that he had not been sent to the fair. It seemed to make him want things that he knew he could not have. It was easier not to want them.

"Mother's grace, I'm hungry." Oswin leaned against the mossy boulder by the stream. "When's your master going to bring us something?"

"I'm trying not to think about it." Tom drew up his tunic against the cut of the wind. The sweat on his skin began to chill. The breath of the oxen steamed out—slower, slower. They looked at him. They were hungry, too.

"He doesn't pay me enough. He doesn't pay me half enough." Oswin knocked his mallet against the boulder. "So there, Tom, I've been wondering—why are you here?"

Tom could not guess what Oswin meant. When he could not guess what people meant when they talked, he just waited for them to try again.

"You're a bit slow, aren't you?" Oswin chuckled. "Why are you here, Tom, on this farm, a bonded slave to your master? What happened—your family all die on you?"

"Oh." Tom shook his head. "I don't know what happened. I was left on the step of an inn down in the city. My master bought me and brought me up here. I was just a baby; I don't remember it."

"Ah, right. That sort of thing." Oswin scratched his chin.

"Just as well you don't know your parents, then. Wouldn't be the sort you'd want to meet."

Tom shut his eyes. It was enough to make the day a bad one, all the way to night. It was enough to make him wish for sleep and the end of thinking. He took up the stilts and whistled. The oxen started down the field.

"Hey now, no harm meant, there." Oswin fell into step behind them. "I know who my mother is, and let me tell you, I wish I didn't."

Some people seemed to talk just to stop themselves from listening. That was what Tom had always guessed it must be. The words people spoke so often seemed to get in the way.

"So hungry I could eat that ox, and then the other one for afters." Oswin smashed a clump of earth with more effort than was needed. "I was at a feast once, you know, a great big feast up at the castle, just before your master hired me on. Did I ever tell you? It was one of those things the nobs do sometimes—throw a banquet for a few of us poor folk so they can sleep easy at nights. I was out begging by the gates one day, and they just pulled me in, sat me down and, oh, you should have seen it! Beef-and-onion stew, smoked herring on trenchers with peas and beans on the side. And they had things called figs, too, drenched in honey. Have you ever had a fig?"

The plow lurched sideways in the furrow. Tom set his weight against it and looked down. The ox on the left, a mottled dark creature twelve hands high at the shoulder, pulled up a hind leg and wobbled with every other step.

"Well, they're chewy and sweet," said Oswin. "I could eat them all day. And they have bowls full of salt at the table, did you know? Everyone gets one—you can just sprinkle it all over your food. And at the end they had baked apples with cloves and some white stuff that I thought was more salt, but it turned out to be pure sugar! You ever had sugar? Never had anything like it in my—hoy, what are we stopping for?"

Tom set down the plow. "Thunder's pulling lame."

"We can't stop now, we've got a whole acre to do." Oswin pointed all around him with his mallet. "We'll be at it till sundown as it is!"

"We won't be going anywhere if Thunder goes off his hooves." Tom knelt at Thunder's side. The ox rolled an eye at him, his face pinched in pain.

Tom touched his fingers down the injured haunch, felt the tremble and the heat. No good. "We should get the horses."

"Can't—your master rented them out to the Millers for the day. You're sure it's so bad?"

"It's bad, and it will get worse if we keep going. He needs rest."

Oswin snorted, then jutted his weak chin across the field. "Tell that to your master. Here he comes."

Tom stood and turned. His master, Athelstan Barnwell, stomped down the path from the farm—old, bent of back, his face a mask of sour lines. He held a whip in his hand.

"Morning, Athelstan." Oswin waved as he approached. "I don't suppose you've brought us some breakfast?"

"You're slow." Athelstan's voice was a salted field. "You're accursed slow. You make us miss good growing and you'll regret it."

Tom bowed his head. "Thunder's lame, Master."

Athelstan shouldered past and bent to examine the ox. "Which?"

"Back left, Master."

"Walk them."

Tom took up the stilts and murmured to the team. "Cush, now. On we go." They started off again.

The whip cracked down. Thunder gave a bellow and threw himself forward in the yoke. White fear blinded Tom—for a moment he could not tell where the whip had struck, could not tell panic from pain. He lost his grip on the stilts, then darted forward to seize them before the plow fell over. Athelstan watched their progress for a few paces, then held up a hand for them to stop.

"Pull him off," he rasped. "We'll slaughter him."

The oxen quaked, their heads curled to the earth. Blood seeped from the welt on Thunder's back. Tom reached out to touch his side.

"Master." He chose his words with care. Any hint of pleading would seal the ox's fate. "I can fix him, Master. He's a good worker. He just needs some rest."

Athelstan grunted. "I've no time for laggards and layabouts. Finish the acre today or that ox isn't worth his feed." He turned to Oswin. "You're off to Jarvis Miller's. You work to dusk. The pay's a penny—you keep a farthing."

Oswin raised his eyebrows to the brim of his cap. "A farthing?"

Athelstan thrust out his stubbled chin at Oswin's chest. "Get on with you, or you'll be back to begging your bread by nightfall."

Oswin muttered something ugly, then dropped the mallet and walked away across the field. Tom's stomach chose that moment to growl.

"Not a morsel, not a bite until you're done." Athelstan pointed down the field with the coils of his whip. "Get to work." He turned on his heel and slumped off.

Tom found his grip on the stilts and dug the share of the plow into the earth. He tried his best to shift the load from Thunder to his partner, Lightning, a somewhat smaller ox with a blaze of white around one eye. He spoke no more words—his urgings were hums and grunts, the push and pull of his hands on the plow. The sun reached its highest, then made for the west and fell. The sky turned orange-red, then dark blue. A flock of starlings ten thousand strong took possession of the trees. They were a kingdom, and talked of nothing but themselves.

Evening came to night. The cold returned. Tom's shoulder throbbed from the effort of making up for Thunder's limping gait. His stomach gnawed and churned. Weariness enfolded him. He sank until he saw nothing but the furrow dividing on the plowshare below him, dark waves cresting in a pattern that never quite repeated itself.

The plow stopped. Tom sagged against the stilts, letting himself breathe into the peace that came over him until he felt himself falling asleep. He jerked up his head. "Not far now. Come, now, onward. Not far."

The oxen did not move. Tom looked around him. They had turned the last furrow. An acre.

He stumbled forward to lay a hand on Thunder's heaving side. "You did it." He untied their harness and wound the leather straps over his shoulder. He grasped the plow by the stilts to drag it behind him. The oxen followed him home.

The door of the master's house hung wide. "You're accursed late." Athelstan leaned through the doorway and kept an eye on Thunder's shambling walk across the yard.

Tom dropped his head. "An acre, Master. All of it."

"To the pasture with you." The door slammed shut.

Tom dragged the plow into the byre. Heads rose from the straw all around him, most of them pink and woolly white with dark lobed slots for pupils, but among them a few whose eyes glimmered green in the moonlight that came in over his shoulder. Oswin snorted awake, then turned in the straw and put his arms over his face.

"Jumble." Tom whistled. "Jumble, come now!"

A laughing face thrust up from the straw, patches of black-and-white fur under a pair of half-cocked ears. Jumble woofed for joy and jumped from his bed in the corner of the byre. He leapt on Tom and licked his nose, beating his ragged plume feather of a tail on the hard earth floor.

"Good boy, Jumble. Good boy. Time for work." Tom reached down for the cloth bundle that lay on the tree stump he used for a table. "Bring them, Jumble. Get by, now."

Jumble raced to the back of the flock and barked. The cats *mrrfed* and scattered to the corners of the byre, leaping out of the way of the swelling mass of sheep. Tom picked up the shepherd's crook that leaned by the door and led the flock out into the yard. The oxen fell into step, dark shadows in a cloud of dirty white.

They marched north off the rise where stood farmhouse and byre, making for the pasture on a narrow path between the hedges. Jumble capered along at the back, darting left and right behind the stragglers. The bell that hung around the neck of the ram made the loudest sound in the world.

Tom found a place with good grazing where the land began to rise again. He sat down at the trunk of a lonely elm. Jumble pranced up and put a paw on his shin.

"Watch them, boy. Watch awhile."

Jumble padded away to the edge of the flock. The sheep got on with their evening meal, making slow circuits inside Jumble's guard, lambs following close to their mothers. The oxen lay themselves down to rest, too tired even to eat.

Tom opened the bundle. It contained a hunk of stale bread and a turnip. He wolfed them down, then sank back against the tree. The stars wheeled above him. The wind shook the grass at his feet. Peace came over him and sang him down. . . .

• • •

He startled up, not knowing where he was or what side of a dream he was on. The veil of sleep dropped away and left Tom sure he was awake and watching the sheep scatter wide across the pasture. Jumble backed away from the trees, growling with his tail dropped low.

The terror grew. Tom smelled, he heard, he felt something watching him, something sizing him up for a meal. The oxen stared about them white-eyed, ears perked, ready to bolt but unsure of which way to run. Jumble licked his chops—his growl broke into a whine.

"Calm." Tom got to his feet. "Calm now, all is well." Something made a noise, somewhere west down by the bend of the stream—a quick, hard clacking. He could not place the sound with any animal he knew.

"Round them, Jumble." Tom felt about him for his shepherd's crook. "Get by, round them, hurry!"

Jumble turned to dash. Tom was not sure if he was just running away, but when he reached the edge of the flock, he cut a hard left with a spate of frantic barking, rounding in the sheep before they scattered. More clacking came from a gap between the trees, and the sound of breath drawn hissing through teeth.

"Go on." Tom smacked the flanks of the oxen. "Run!" He sprang off through the clipped low grass, too fast in the dark to see a rock or clump of earth in his way and simply hoping for the best. The oxen followed at a charge. They could easily have trampled him, but kept an arm's length to either side.

Something flashed in the trees along the stream. Tom was nearly sure he saw a pair of eyes, bulbous and bright yellow, set too wide apart to match any creature he could name. "Jumble! Jumble, bring them!" He spared a look the other way.

Jumble had done his best, but could not force all the sheep to run in the right direction. A clump of ewes followed the ram away into the dark. The clacking sounded again, farther away but louder.

They reached the yard. The farmhouse door swung open. "What is all this?" Athelstan squinted out at Tom. "What are you doing back here?"

"There's something out there, Master. Out in the trees." Tom looked back north. Jumble raced up behind the last of the sheep, but they were missing four at least.

Athelstan flicked a look around at the flock in the yard. He glared at Tom. "Where are the rest?"

"They're in the pasture. I brought all I could, but—"

"You half-wit!" Athelstan reached for his whip. "Get out and find those sheep. Move!"

Tom hurried the flock into the byre, nearly bowling Oswin over in the doorway. He did not stop to explain what was happening. He turned and pelted back into the pasture, looking all about him for the missing sheep. He could hear nothing but the wind, no breathing, no clacking sounds—he could not even hear the ram's bell.

"Where are they, boy?" Athelstan stalked down off the rise, a bent shadow in the trampled grass. "If you lose them—"

Tom screwed up his courage and plunged into the trees, searching blind, following up under the eaves as far as he dared. It was no use—they were gone.

"Where?" Athelstan's face resolved in moonlight. The way he held the whip turned Tom's guts to water.

"Master, I swear to you, there's something in the trees." Tom cringed and sidled back. "There's something out there!"

Athelstan seized him by the collar and thrust him back toward the yard. "Get to the byre. Now."

"Please, Master. Please, I'm sorry. I would never have left—"

Athelstan cracked the whip at his heels. "Get yourself to the byre. You run there, boy, you kneel at the post and you wait for me. You think about what's coming when I get there."

Chapter 9

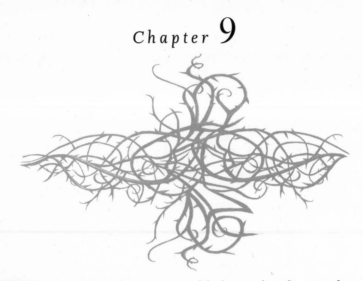

Edmund felt for a point of light in the sky. He drew it down. "Let the light of the stars descend."

He wavered. There was no point—there was a point. He looked up at the spin of stars and drew an axis. "Stars attend me. Let your light descend."

Nothing happened.

Edmund set the book on the log he used for a seat. He paced around his circle, and then back. What was wrong?

It had something to do with chords, or angles. Edmund lay back in the grass and tried to sort through what he had read before the sun went down. None of it made sense—not the ordinary sort of sense, anyway. He shut his eyes and fought to calm himself, taking each breath a little slower than the last.

The trouble was, whenever he shut his eyes he saw Katherine, and started thinking thoughts a long way away from the magical union of angles and Light.

He let his eyelids fall open. He watched the constellations wheel above.

"Let the light of the stars descend." He raised his hands, reaching for the rhythm. "Stars attend me. Surround me. Let your light descend."

Nothing.

Edmund glared at the sky. "Descend!"

The wind moaned and rattled through the trees. There was no point.

"Ugh." Edmund got up and took a seat on the log. He set the book in his lap and felt his finger down the pages, past the strange drawing of seven children on the rays of a star. He found lines of text a few pages before it, inked thick and firm enough that he could read them in the feeble light:

There are words that have never been spoken, words that cannot be spoken, words that, if spoken, would shake the earth.

"What does that mean?" Edmund wanted to throw the book into the weeds. "What can that possibly mean?"

These words trace thoughts too large for the mind to hold—they cannot be grasped, they can merely be touched in the tremble of a moment. This is the language of magic, the voice of all that is, the chatter of the growing grass, the command that holds the moon aloft in the sky.

Edmund rubbed at his temples. Maybe he was just too stupid. He bent to squint at the curling script:

Everything is connected to everything else. Everything is a symbol for something deeper. For the worker of the will, the symbol is a place to begin, the outline of a thought sublime beyond all—

"You'll go blind doing that, you know."

Edmund startled, and looked up. "Oh—Katherine. When did you get here?"

"Just now." She wore her hair loose over her embroidered shirt. Starlight touched her face from every side. "He's over here, Tom."

Tom stepped in silence from the darkness. A flock of sheep swarmed past him to surround the hillock in the middle of the pasture. Jumble rushed up barking and leapt on Edmund, licked his face and thumped his tail on the ground.

"No, Jumble—not on the book! Off the book!" Edmund grabbed for his forepaws. Jumble thought it a jolly game—he handed Edmund one paw and set the other down, once and again on the precious pages.

Katherine laughed. "Jumble—naughty boy!" She bent to ruffle him by the ears, and got a slobber on the end of her nose for her trouble.

"Here." Tom whistled. "Get by, boy. Round them, get by."

Jumble raced off to circle the stragglers. His barks came from down the hillock to the north, then west, then south. Tom leaned on his crook and turned with the sound, watching his flock gather in. "Why were you asking for light?"

"Never mind." Edmund reached down to retrieve the torn corner of a page. He shut the book.

"We won't want any light tonight." Katherine fussed at her belt, then laid something long and slender on her lap. "If we're to be Tom's bodyguard, we'll want to have our night eyes."

Edmund gazed down in wonder. "Is that a real sword?"

"It was my uncle William's. Papa brought it home from the wars." Katherine drew it halfway from its scabbard. "Want to see?"

She set it on the flat of Edmund's palms. He ran a thumb along the worn leather grip and then a finger on the simple disc pommel. The crossguard stuck out straight and unadorned, scored deep in one place where it must once have turned a very heavy blow.

"I'm glad you both could come." Tom sat down in the grass at Katherine's feet. "I didn't want to sit out alone tonight, especially not here."

Edmund followed the direction of Tom's nervous look, south over the trees at the shadowed mass of Wishing Hill. "Your master didn't believe you?"

"No." Tom shifted, leaning back. His face twisted in a grimace, then he sat up straight again.

"Here." Katherine held out a hand. "Let's have a look at you."

Tom rummaged in the threadbare bag at his side and drew out a stoppered wooden jar. He gave it to Katherine.

"Pull up your shirt." Katherine drew the stopper. Tom reached back and pulled up his ratty old tunic. Some of the threads got stuck in the wet, open wounds that crisscrossed on his back.

"Oh!" Edmund looked more closely despite himself. "Oh, ugh!"

Katherine dipped her finger in the salve. She touched it around the edge of a wound. Tom hissed in, then sighed out.

"I don't think I've ever hated anyone in the world—but, Tom, I hate your master." Katherine smoothed the salve along Tom's back, following the course of a hot red welt. "I really, truly hate him."

Edmund sat back, feeling ill. "But—did you find all the sheep?"

"No." Tom hissed again. Katherine traced his wounds one by one in salve. The wind pushed the ash trees, one into the next.

Edmund slid his fingers around to grip the hilt of the sword. He turned the blade point to the sky. "Listen—I've been thinking."

Katherine smirked at him. "Aren't you always?"

"I mean really thinking. Maybe we should run away."

His friends turned to look at him, brown eyes and green.

"All of us," said Edmund. "The three of us, together."

Tom let his shirt fall to his waist. Katherine replaced the stopper in the jar. "Where would we go?"

"I don't know, anywhere." Edmund raised his arms. "Free of here."

Tom plucked up a blade of grass. He chewed on it and looked around him, up at the far peaks of the Girth, then out over the pastures. "This is home. I belong here."

"That's the kind of thing you say to get from one day to the next." Edmund shook his head. "It isn't true. There's something better in this world, and if we have the courage, we can go find it."

"Seeking for something better means always seeking and never finding."

Edmund could not help but make a snort of disgust. "How long until those scars heal on your back? How long until your master finds another excuse to whip you raw?"

"Edmund, we're fourteen," said Katherine. "We can't just run away—we'd end up starving on the road, or worse."

"You don't know that for sure," said Edmund. "And what happens if we stay? We don't fit here, you know we don't. What's going to happen when we grow up? What's going to happen if we keep living the lives laid out for us? None of us, not one of us will ever be happy."

Katherine cradled up the cracked and weathered scabbard in her hands. Tom let Jumble onto his lap.

"I'm learning things in this book, in all the things I read." Edmund touched a hand to the binding. "There is a world out there, a great wide world. Seas of sand, cities of a thousand towers, courts of ebony and marble. We don't have to stay in this place."

"This is a good place," said Katherine. "A safe place. A lot of people died to make it that way. We should be grateful."

"How will we know if this place is good or bad if we never see another one? How will we know if our lives could be better if they never, ever change?" Edmund heard his voice echo back from the pasture and came to know that he had raised it too loud. "No one needs us here. If we stay, we'll all end up stuck in lives we don't want."

Katherine took her sword back. "Life is not all about getting what you want, Edmund. It's not just doing what you like and forgetting everyone who needs you. You're just being selfish."

"You used to want to be things, to do things!" Some part of Edmund told him to stop, but he ignored it. "You've changed!"

"Yes, Edmund, I'm growing up." Katherine snapped a look at him. "You should try it sometime."

"Oh, so you just want to sit around and wait until you get married off to some blacksmith? You think he'll let you practice with a sword whenever you like once you've popped out his babies? You think you'll ever touch a warhorse again? You think—" Edmund closed his mouth, but it was far too late.

Katherine turned away, blinking hard. "You are such a child."

"I'm sorry." Edmund wanted to bite off his tongue. "Please, I'm sorry."

Katherine kept her back to him. Jumble leapt from Tom's lap with his ears pricked up. Tom got to his feet and followed, around the log and down past the trees.

"I just hate it here." Edmund hunched down. "I don't want to stay at the inn, washing my father's mugs, pouring his ale and waiting for him to die. I hate it."

"I can't leave Papa. If I did, I think he'd just dry up and blow away." Katherine turned the sword over in her hands. She slid it back into the scabbard and set it down. "But I know what's coming. It makes me so scared, I can't sleep sometimes."

"I just wish something would happen." Edmund put his fists to his eyes to stop himself from crying. "I just wish—"

"Quiet."

Edmund turned on the log. Tom stood moonlit next to Jumble, gazing up toward the summit of Wishing Hill.

"What for?" Edmund got angry again. "Tom, this is important. We're talking about our lives, you know. Our futures. Aren't you even thinking about it?"

"No." Tom waved out a hand. "I heard something."

"Heard what?" Edmund paused for the briefest of moments. "I don't hear—"

A torn, hopeless scream drifted down from the summit of the hill. Edmund's heart bounced in his chest.

Tom whirled on Jumble. "Stay!" He sprang off toward the trailing echo of the scream. Katherine grabbed up her sword and leapt to follow.

"Wait! Are you sure we should—" Edmund crossed the old West Road just in time to see Tom slither into the trees ahead. He plunged in behind Katherine. Branches whipped and stung at his face. The darkness hid roots and twists of ground; he tripped and cursed and picked himself up again and again. He followed Katherine on a sharp turn left, then a rise and a switchback right. Another scream sounded from above, longer and more despairing than the first.

Edmund forced his way over a fallen trunk and took a scratch across his belly from the bark of a projecting limb. He caught sight of Tom on the slope above him, pelting through the trees like a hunted deer, then lost him again. He pushed himself as hard as he could go, crunching and cracking through the brush. He swung around a switchback at full tilt and nearly crashed into his friends.

"What—" He could not get his breath. He grabbed his side. "Why have—" Then he saw it.

On the trail before them lay the figure of a boy—facedown, arms hugged in under his chest and legs splayed out. They all stood still for one moment of horror, then rushed to his side.

The boy wore a ragged tunic under his cloak and oversized breeches crisscrossed with strips of old leather to make them fit. There were leaves in his hair where his head had hit the ground. Katherine knelt beside him and shook his shoulders, then turned him over.

"Oh, no," she said. "No."

She cradled Peter Overbourne in her arms. Peter's head lolled back. Tom searched down through his clothes and found a rip in his tunic. He drew his hand away, wet with blood. "A blade did this."

"That wasn't Peter we heard screaming." Katherine flashed him a look. "It was a girl."

"How did this happen?" Edmund could not keep his voice from quavering. "What's going on?"

Tom drew his hand across Peter's face to close his staring eyes.

"I don't know." Katherine lay Peter down in the leaves. "I don't know—look around, will you?"

Edmund stumbled off along the downhill side of the trail. He caught a glint in the undergrowth. "I found something." He reached down and closed his hand around the pommel of a knife, double-edged and sized for fighting. The blade caught the starlight as he turned it. "This is Geoffrey's!"

Katherine stood. "We'll go get help."

"Wait." Tom raised Peter's hand to the feeble light. It was spattered with a thick, dark liquid. So was the blade—Edmund touched some to his finger and held it up.

"What is this?" The liquid was blue, near to black.

Something crackled in the heavy undergrowth across the trail. Edmund had just enough time to let out a yell before he was thrown to the ground. A figure loomed in above him. It had a dark blue, noseless face, inhumanly round, with wide-set, bulbous eyes and a flat jaw that swung open to show a row of needle teeth.

Chapter 10

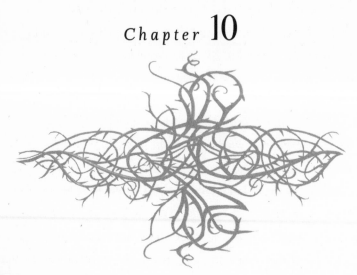

E dmund froze, his gaze held by the creature's liquid yellow eyes. It reached out to touch his face, the backs of its long fingers brushing his cheek—then it grasped him by the neck. He sucked in a gasp and tried to struggle free, but found himself helpless in its grip. With a push of its thumb against his chin it exposed his throat and pulled him closer. He flailed out with Geoffrey's knife, but struck the trunk of the tree beside him. The jaws swung wide—its teeth were arranged in two rows, one staggered behind the other. Its breath was sweet and sour, and very warm.

There was a rush of air above. Something landed on the creature, driving it to the ground and jerking Edmund forward. He smashed his shoulder into the trunk of a tree, then the creature loosed its hold and he sank down, choking for breath. Two figures rolled through the weeds before him. One of them gained the upper hand and pinned the other down—it was Katherine. She raised her sword, but the creature was as quick as it was strong. It lashed out from shadow and struck her across the jaw, then shifted its weight and dumped her on top of Edmund, squashing him down into the mulch. The sword tumbled end over end through the air and fell into the bushes by the lip of the trail.

The creature was wiry and muscular, curled and hunched but still tall as a man. It wore a vest made of slick, blackened skin from some unguessable source. Filthy cloth breeches clad its upper legs, ripped and ragged at the ends and held up by a belt made of dark rope. It held a hand clamped over a wound at its side—it drew a dagger in the other hand and advanced on them with a bouncing, bow-legged shuffle, spitting and gurgling in rage.

Tom rushed to stand over his friends, swinging his shepherd's crook in wild arcs. The creature wove and dodged, stabbing viciously at Tom, slicing into his improvised staff and driving him back. Katherine rolled off Edmund and aimed a kick at its belly right where it was wounded. The huge yellow eyes bulged wide—it let out a scream and stumbled back, giving Katherine a moment to scramble to her feet. Edmund tried to struggle up behind her, but his shoulder gave out beneath him.

The creature spun away from the swing of Tom's crook and leapt onto a boulder across the trail. The blood that seeped from the wound around its hand glistened blue near to black, a shade or two darker than its skin. It sprang at Katherine with its blade thrust out—she ducked out of the line of its charge and tripped it, slinging it over Edmund and off through the trees downhill. The creature flailed its limbs as it disappeared into the dark. There came a crunch, then the crackling slither of something falling through branches to the ground—then silence.

"Are you all right? Are you hurt?" Katherine dragged Edmund to his feet. Her hair fell in wild dark tangles around her face. There was an ugly, swelling bruise on her jaw.

"I'm fine." Edmund could not stop shaking. He rubbed at his shoulder. "I'm fine. Where is it?"

"Down there. It's not moving." Tom stood at the edge of the trail, looking down the steep slope of the hill.

Edmund grabbed for a branch and leaned out. The creature lay crumpled at the base of a tree far below. "I think you killed it."

"Let's get it into the light and see." Katherine pulled Geoffrey's knife from the tree trunk where it had stuck. She handed it to Edmund. "You cover us. If it twitches, stab it."

They descended the slope and approached the creature, casting wary glances all around. Katherine and Tom grabbed it by the ankles and dragged it back up onto the trail next to Peter. It was indeed dead—its mouth hung open and its yellow eyes stared at nothing, just as Peter's had.

"What is it?" said Katherine.

Edmund nudged it with his foot. "A bolgug, I think. I've seen drawings."

"A bolgug?" Katherine drew its long knife from the ground— it was as near a sword as a dagger, heavy bladed and made for thrusting. "That's not possible. The bolgugs served the Nether-grim, and the Nethergrim is dead."

Edmund did not know how such a thing could be possible, either—and yet there the creature was, lying sprawled at his feet. He knelt down next to it and gave it another tentative prod, and when it did not react, he turned its head to examine its face.

"Look at those teeth!" He ran his fingers along the bolgug's wiry blue torso and felt the wound at its side. The breeches it wore had been made for a boy, far too short but just wide enough for its sinewy thighs. The belt around its waist had been fashioned from a braid of long brown hair.

Katherine crouched over him. "Did you stab it?"

"No—Peter must have."

"Peter was running downhill." Tom spoke from a few yards up the path, bent low to examine the ground in the feeble light. "He must have been coming from the keep. This thing chased him down."

Edmund looked down at Geoffrey's knife. His guts gave a squeeze. "My brother must be up there!"

"And it was a girl who screamed, I'm sure of it." Katherine plunged about in the bushes for her sword. "Tom, you're the fastest. Go for help."

Tom glanced back at the corpse of the bolgug. "What if there are more of these things?"

"Then we will need the whole village in arms, and quickly. Go on."

Tom dropped his crook. "Be careful—both of you." He turned

to run back down the hill. Edmund followed Katherine the other way.

The trail wound upward to the summit, emerging at the blasted, broken gates of the old fortress. Light from within the courtyard crowned the ruined walls. Edmund dropped to a crouch next to Katherine in the last stand of trees. "That's a fire. A big one."

Katherine pushed her hair behind her ear. "Footsteps." She leaned out. "Two at least—maybe more."

"There, in the entrance." Edmund pointed. Another bolgug stepped out over the tumbled stones that choked the gates and peered around it, then made an awful clacking noise with its teeth. It bore a crude, broad-bladed spear in its hands.

Katherine sized up the bolgug, then gazed along the top of the wall. She chewed at the nail of her thumb.

"Geoffrey, you twit." Edmund muttered it under his breath. "What were you doing up here?"

"Playing and dreaming," said Katherine. "Same as us."

Edmund had a momentary vision of his mother holding him and weeping—oh, Edmund, don't blame yourself, there was nothing you could have done. Then his father put a hand to his shoulder—no sense throwing your life away, son. At least we still have you.

A new sound reached his ears—a frightened, very human whimpering. "Please, please don't. I don't know what you are, but please don't—"

"That sounds like Emma Russet." Katherine pulled up her sword.

Edmund started moving, and only then understood that he had chosen to risk his life. "There's a place around the back where the wall's crumbled down. Maybe we can sneak in."

They crept north through the trees, past the place where they had found the bones of Hugh Jocelyn's pigs. Katherine leaned out from cover, looking for any sign that they had been spotted by the guard. She waved Edmund on; he followed at a crouching run, along the side wall and around the tallest standing tower to the back.

"Here." He stopped at the place where the wall had collapsed until it was little more than twice the height of a man. Emma let out another wail from inside, a cry for her mother, someone, anyone. A bolgug cut her off with a grating squeal.

Katherine knelt and made a step with her hands. Edmund stepped in and Katherine hauled him up the face until he stood on her palms. He reached above him and felt for a handhold amongst the jagged stones that surmounted the wall. He found one and pulled—the stone came loose and rushed past his head, thudding into the grass below.

"Careful!" Katherine sucked in an alarmed, shuddering breath, but held him firm.

Edmund dug his fingers in and found a precarious foothold. He strained and dragged himself onto the broken top of the wall as quickly as he dared, then looked down into the courtyard.

A bonfire blazed beside the tall dark Wishing Stone. Miles Twintree lay beside it, bound hand and foot—he seemed to be making furtive struggles against his bonds. Emma Russet squirmed and sobbed, trying to crawl away from beneath a bolgug who seemed intent on shaking her into submission. The bolgug with the spear stood aside from the entrance to let four others pass by into the dark. These four walked in pairs, each pair carrying a child slung from a stick on their shoulders. One of the children had curly red hair.

Edmund's stomach dropped. He leaned out to whisper down to Katherine. "They're taking Geoffrey!"

"Not if I can help it." Katherine drew her sword and raced back around the fortress.

"No, Katherine, wait—there are too many!" Edmund flung out a hand, but by then she was gone from sight. He turned back to the courtyard, sick with fear. There was nothing he could do.

"Get—off!" Geoffrey kicked and squirmed. "Let go, let— somebody, help!" His captors dragged him away into the dark beyond the entrance.

Pages flicked in a blur through Edmund's thoughts. It was madness, utter madness—he had never cast a proper spell in his life, could not even coax a candle flame, and now he was going to try something that might set an untrained apprentice on fire. But Katherine, Geoffrey—he had to try.

"Hey!" He stood up on the wall. "Hey, you—ugly face, over here!"

The bolgug holding Emma dropped her to the ground and drew a knife. It opened its wide mouth to scream an alarm. The guard at the entrance turned and brought its spear up to its shoulder. A third leapt out from the shadow of the Wishing Stone with a nasty-looking spiked club in its hands.

Edmund watched the flame in the courtyard until he knew it, until its roving form was the face of an old friend. He made the sign for Fire—a red star ignited behind his eyes. He turned through the sign for Quickening, felt a rushing tingle on his skin, then smoothly on to Light, and this time felt it glow in unearthly harmony. There was no time to try the spell in any way but the most dangerous, no place to anchor it but within himself. Words came to him—they carved strange vibrations in the still night air:

"BY FIRE LIGHT IS BORN. IN LIGHT THE DARKNESS FLIES!"

Painful heat coursed up through his body. He felt as though a bellows had sucked all the air from him and replaced it with something dry and hot beyond words. He felt his heart give a lurch, then stop. He collapsed.

The fire exploded in utter silence, sending off a pulse of light that slapped the clouds.

Edmund heaved and gasped for breath. His heart started beating again—every thready pulse sent more pain through him. A gray tunnel formed at the edges of the world and drew inward. He struggled over onto his side. The nearer two bolgugs lay on their backs, clutching at their faces and squealing. The guard tottered, spear still raised, waving its dark blue hand before its face. It blinked its yellow eyes, squinted at Edmund and made ready to throw, but by then Katherine was upon it.

Katherine ripped the spear from its hands, turned it and

drove the point into its belly. She pulled it out, throwing the shrieking creature to the ground. The other two bolgugs regained their feet. They raised their weapons, but they passed their long fingers before their eyes and gibbered in confusion. Katherine hurled the spear at one, drew her sword and rushed the other.

The tunnel closed across Edmund's sight. He sank down. The pain left him. He knew he lay on stones but could not feel it. A scuffle reached his ears—then a squeal, or a scream. "Katherine? Katherine, I can't see."

Chapter 11

E dmund. Edmund!"

Edmund felt his bed shaking. He shifted, then groaned. "No. Don't feel well." His eyelids fluttered.

Someone touched his head, then gripped him by the shoulder. "Edmund!"

"Mum, no—let me sleep—" He opened his eyes. It was dark—he lay on dirt. His memory returned. They had taken his brother.

"Geoffrey!" He tried to sit up—everything went gray. He clutched at his head and sank back to the ground.

"I couldn't catch them." Katherine raised him to sitting. "I couldn't leave you here. I'm sorry."

Edmund blinked the motes from his sight. The fire was dying fast—it gave off rolls of a curiously thick and sodden smoke. Puffs of white ash rose in the plume, then broke and fell to dust the grass around the Wishing Stone.

As soon as Katherine let go, he slumped back down again. Nothing worked right. If he thought hard about one limb, he could move it, but then he forgot about the others. They twitched and shuddered on their own—they were cold. He was cold, so cold that he burned, but when he shut his eyes, it all went away.

"Please, Edmund."

Edmund. He spoke the name in his mind. He liked the sound of it, but did not know why it was his.

"Please. I need your help."

Edmund forced his eyes open. Katherine had a cut across the knuckles of her sword hand. The stars seemed to be vibrating. Miles Twintree sat ashen beside him, knees hugged in to his chest. Emma lay where she had been dropped next to the two dead bolgugs by the fire. She stared into the sky with blank, wide eyes.

"Up—I'm up." Edmund pushed himself onto one arm. He touched along his brow and drew his hand away to examine the blood. When had he hit his head?

Katherine propped him against the Wishing Stone. "What's the matter with you?"

"Spell. Don't know. I'm cold."

"How long until you can walk?"

Edmund shrugged—it nearly slid him sideways to the ground again.

Katherine caught him. "Tell me if you start to feel better." She stood and towed the bolgugs away from the fire. "Emma,

Miles—I want you both to think back. How many kids were up here with you?"

Miles buried his head in his arms. Tears streamed out along Emma's lashes and down the sides of her face, running back into her ears and her leaf-strewn hair.

"I can't see." Emma spoke in a very small voice. "I can't see anything."

"Please, you have to think." Katherine raised Emma's hands to cut her bonds. "How many bolgugs were here?"

Emma curled onto her side and wept without sound. Her feet were bare—a jagged splinter stuck out from one arch, broken off just above the skin. It looked like it went all the way through.

Edmund shut one hand in a fist, then the other, back and forth. Feeling returned in the form of a hot prickle, as though he had been sleeping on both his arms at once. He reached out, still trembling, and struck Miles on the shoulder. "Tell her."

Miles jumped. "There were—there were five of us. Me and Geoffrey, Peter, Tilly and Emma." He rubbed at the welts on his wrists where the bolgugs had bound him. "They came in all at once, couldn't count them."

Edmund curled forward to reach for the spiked club on the ground before him. It was covered in bluish gore. He nearly vomited.

"But I saw Peter get away." Miles raised his head. "I saw him get out through the front before they hit me. Maybe he's gone for help."

Katherine shot Edmund a warning look. "Let's hope so." She plucked out the spear from the side of one of the bolgugs. "Tom's gone for help, too. It won't be long."

The stars stopped shaking. Edmund tried again, and this time seized the club by the handle. He felt beside it and found Emma's shoes laid out by the fire, and then a jug that he knew had come from the inn.

Katherine walked over to Miles and held out the spear. Miles stared in horror at the glistening blood that dripped from its point.

"Take it," said Katherine.

Miles blinked and recoiled. Tears tracked through the dirt on his cheeks. He seemed much younger than twelve.

"Look at me." Katherine held him in her gaze. "I need you to be brave. Take it."

"What do you want me to do?"

She set the spear in his hands. "Guard us. Stand over there by the entrance and listen carefully for anyone coming. If you hear something, call for me—I'll be near."

Miles stood and limped to the gates. He turned around, holding the spear as though it were a snake about to twist in his hands.

Katherine twirled the air with her finger. "Other way, Miles. Point upward."

"Oh." Miles turned the spear.

Edmund sank back against the Wishing Stone. He shivered, and shut his eyes. The cold seeped in again.

Breath steamed warm across his face: "Edmund!"

He startled up. Katherine knelt over him. "Are you feeling any better?"

"Geoffrey." Edmund tried to struggle to his feet, braced between the club and the Wishing Stone. "We have to get after them."

"We will." Katherine caught him under his arm. "The light—that was you?"

Edmund barely had the strength to nod in reply. He staggered over next to Miles at the ruined gates. "Seen anything?"

"I'm sorry." Miles was crying, huffing in and crying. "We were just playing, just going to play chase-the-beggar. We shouldn't have come. I'm sorry, I'm sorry."

"Miles." Edmund felt out a space of stone to rest upon. "Have you seen anything?"

"Just a badger. How long do we have to stay here? I want to go home!"

Edmund peered out through the tumbled gap. He let his eyes open to the darkness until he could just make out the curve of the Tamber through the valley far below. No alarm from the village, no clamor, no shouts—no help.

Where was Tom?

"Emma?" Katherine spoke in gentle tones behind him. "Emma—can you see now? I'm going to have a look at your feet." Emma let out a painful hiss that sank into a sob.

"How bad is it?" Edmund looked back. "Can she walk?"

Katherine ripped a sleeve from her shirt and cut it into

strips with Geoffrey's knife. She raised Emma's foot and cradled it in her hands. "We will get out of here. I promise you." Emma turned bloodshot eyes on her.

Katherine placed a thumb and forefinger on the jagged end of the splinter. Emma sucked in a breath. Edmund thought of looking away a moment too late.

It did not come out easily. Edmund hunched down and plugged his ears until the screams died away.

Katherine splashed out the jug on Emma's foot, then wrapped it in the strips from her shirt. "That will have to do." She slipped a shoe on the other foot. "Here—up, now. We're going."

The pain seemed to rouse Emma from her stupor. "What was that light before?"

"We'll talk about it later. Come on, up."

Edmund pushed himself halfway to standing on the stones. He reached an arm. "Miles, can you help me?"

Miles did not answer. He stared out through the breach, eyes white and wide, mouth falling slack.

Edmund waved his hand. "Miles?"

Something rustled in the trees outside. Miles could scream even louder than Emma.

"Down!" Katherine moved before Edmund had time to think. She sprang across the courtyard and shoved Miles over in the grass along the foot of the wall. She peered out, then ducked again. She gripped her sword white.

Edmund crawled up, his heart pounding. "What's out there?"

"You tell me."

At the edge of the trees no more than ten yards distant stood something deep in shadow. It was far too tall and broad to be a man. It shifted forward—the faint light crossed its black, black eyes.

Edmund lost a breath to terror. Katherine pulled him back into cover. "Can you manage another spell?"

"The fire's out." Edmund raced through everything he had ever read, and found it all a heap of useless, fear-addled mush. "What are we going to do?"

Leaves crunched in the dark outside. Huge shoulders rolled in the gloom.

Miles let out a shriek and dropped his spear. "It's coming at us!"

The thing in the trees took a step forward—the shadows fell away from the contours of its face, revealing nothing but a mass of writhing thorns. Edmund heard another voice raised to a scream. He could not place it until he recognized it as his own.

"Up, up—out the back!" Katherine hauled Emma from the ground. "Miles, help Edmund—hurry!"

Miles pelted away into the dark. The tendrils at the ends of the creature's arms spread out across the mossy scatter of stones. Edmund heaved himself up and tried to run. He made it five paces before his legs gave out.

"Edmund!" Katherine turned at the Wishing Stone. "Miles, you left Edmund—Edmund, come on!"

As the quiggan serves the Nethergrim in fouled water, and

the stonewight in his mountainous lair—a page of the book teased at Edmund's memory—*so the thornbeast is his chief agent in vale and forest.* He remembered the rest. He looked behind him.

The thornbeast shoved what passed for a head into the breach. It was a writhen mass of vine and branch in the vague shape of a man, more than ten feet tall at its hunched shoulders. Its eyes were no more than two voids in the tangle, so absolutely dark that it was impossible to discern the substance from which they were made.

"Hurry. Hurry!" Katherine came back, dragging Emma over one shoulder. "Edmund, take my hand."

"Wait." Edmund struggled to his feet. "Don't run."

"Have you gone mad?" Katherine seized his arm. "We've got to—"

Edmund raised a hand. "I said wait!" Katherine kept a grip on him, but held still for the space of a terrified breath. The long, thorny filaments slithered toward them—but then they drew taut, scrabbling uselessly over the stones. It came no closer.

"I've read about this." Edmund looked at Katherine. "Thornbeasts can't walk over stone."

The creeping masses that made up the thornbeast's feet tried to touch down amongst the ruins of the entrance—then pulled up, again and again, unable to root themselves. It pulled back into the dark.

Katherine set Emma down against the Wishing Stone. "Miles, don't climb out! Stay inside." She thumped Edmund's shoulder. "I'd like to be there the next time your father says books aren't good for anything."

Edmund could only think that she had touched him more times in a single night than in all his life before. "If I remember it right, the book says that a thornbeast can move through the trees as fast as a horse can gallop on a road. I think it was trying to scare us into leaving so it could run us down."

Katherine nearly laughed. "Then we hold the gates and wait for help. Nothing else we can do."

Edmund glanced up at the stars.

"I know." Katherine breathed. "He should be back by now."

Miles sidled up beside them. "I didn't mean to run. I was scared. Is it gone?"

"It's just outside. Take your spear." Katherine picked up the club and Geoffrey's knife. She weighed them in her hands, then gave the knife to Edmund. "I'm going up onto the wall to watch it. When help comes, I'll need to give a warning."

"There are still bolgugs out there." Edmund sagged down into the grass. "If they come back, they'll have no trouble with the gates."

"They will if we give them some." She crossed the courtyard and scaled the wall, rolling onto her belly once she reached the top.

Edmund crept up to the gates and took another look outside. The thornbeast kept in shadow at the edge of the clearing, just shy of the mossy scatter of stones that choked the entrance.

"It's still there." He turned and sat against a clump of stones.

The rush of frightened action left him weary again, dizzy and terribly cold. He put his hands up his sleeves and tried to keep from shivering. He looked down at the straggled grass at his feet. The gray tunnel returned.

"How long have we been out here?"

Edmund blinked. He pinched his arm to rouse himself. "Not as long as it feels." He looked around him. Emma clung to Miles, huddled close by the foot of the wall.

"Stay awake, Edmund." Katherine crouched in shadow, half in view through a snaggled gap in the battlements above. She made a slow circuit along the top of the wall, from one edge of the ruined gates around to the other.

Edmund dragged himself to standing, and found some of his strength returned. He paced around the courtyard, swinging out his arms to get the feeling back. He tried not to look at the corpses of the bolgugs. The fire had crumbled to pure white ash—it no longer even smoked. A wedge of geese flew in overhead, but veered suddenly wide of the hilltop.

"That's the bell." Miles's voice broke high. "Hear it? That's the village bell!"

Edmund could have jumped into the air if his weary legs would have let him. The bell atop the village hall clanged out from the valley below—once, twice and thrice.

"There, you see?" He came back to the ruined gates. "It won't be long. Everyone's coming—I bet even Lord Aelfric's heard by now. All we have to do is wait a little longer, and—"

"On your guard, down there." Katherine hissed across his words. "Look outside."

Edmund crouched at the gates and peeked out. Tendrils writhed across the open ground before the gates, ripping and churning at the soil. Miles let out a whimper.

"What's happening?" Emma shivered on the ground.

"It's coming back," said Miles. "It's coming closer."

"Steady, both of you," said Edmund. "It can't get us in here."

The thornbeast took a step forward. Thorns twisted and writhed up and down the length of its foreleg. The shadows fell away, and the contours of its face grew into horrid suggestions.

"Don't look. It's just trying to make us afraid." Edmund glanced up at Katherine. "What's it doing?"

She looked as frightened as he felt. "I don't know."

A twig snapped in the grass some distance away—and then another, a distinct crunch of leaves.

Emma choked. "That came from behind us!"

"It's the monsters!" Miles wailed. "They're back! We're dead, we're all dead!"

Edmund turned. Footsteps sounded, a dozen strong, picking their way through the brush on either side of the castle.

"That's too many. Katherine, there's too many!" Edmund shot a wild look around him. There was nowhere to run. The village bell clanged out again from far below. Help might come, but it would come too late.

Katherine scrabbled down through the rubble, coming dangerously close to the reaching tips of the thorns. "We've got to hold them in the breach. It's our only chance. Miles—if they charge, come out into the entrance and brace the spear with both hands. Pick the first bolgug and let it run onto the point. Can you do that?"

"Y-yes."

"I'll be right beside you. You only need to hit it once. I'll do the rest. Edmund—help out however you can. If they break and run, don't follow."

Edmund raised his knife. The blade shuddered back and forth from the shaking of his hands. The footsteps grew louder, passing along the side walls and making their way around toward the entrance.

The thornbeast drew closer, coming full in view. It fixed its empty eyes on Edmund. He found it hard to breathe. He felt Emma lean on him—he thought she was trying to hug him, but then she slid past and fell over.

"Please." Emma curled tight on the ground. "Please, I want it to be quick."

Miles sat down beside her. "My mama said I was too small when I was born." He sounded calmer than he had all night. "They weren't even sure if I would live. I always knew it, inside—I wasn't supposed to get to grow up."

"Miles, stand up. We have to fight." Katherine somehow advanced, step after step toward the gates. Edmund took up the spear and followed. If there was one thing he was going to do before he died, it was stand beside her.

The rustling stopped. The thornbeast seemed to hesitate. It looked to one side.

A light burst the dark, a torch tumbling end over end across the entrance. It nearly went out on the descent, but it landed true. The thornbeast turned to regard something Edmund could not see. Its back began to smolder, giving off curls of smoke.

"Torches forward!" A familiar voice sounded from outside. "Stay together—all together, everyone. If you waver, it will kill us all. Forward!"

The surge of hope nearly knocked Edmund flat.

"Papa." Katherine let her sword fall to her side. "Papa, we're in the keep!"

More cries came: "Miles?" "Matilda—Tilly!" "Miles!" "Emma—Emma, where are you?"

"Father!" Miles leapt to his feet. "I'm here, Father!"

John Marshal stepped into view through the entrance. He raised a torch and advanced on the thornbeast. "Look over here. That's right, over here. I am dangerous. I will burn you."

The thornbeast heaved up its shoulders and pressed the flames deep within its body. It released, leaving a few scorched branches and a spent torch that tumbled to the ground. It reared up.

"Papa!" Katherine rushed to the breach. Edmund found himself coming with her, though he had no idea what injury a spear might do to a ten-foot heap of thorns.

"Follow John!" He heard his own father's voice raised to a bark from the other side of the keep. "Curse you all, forward!"

Two files of torches appeared at either side of the ruined entrance. The thornbeast looked even worse in better light. It advanced on John Marshal, but found a dozen torches in its path. It turned the other way—Harman's party wavered, but held. It drew back, sinking down the slope into shadow.

"Ha!" A lone figure broke from the crowd and stepped to the edge of the slope. "That'll teach you!"

"Hurry, everyone! There is still danger!" John Marshal pointed inside with his sword. "Gilbert Wainwright, Harman Bale, go in and get the children—pick them up if they cannot walk. Move, I say! Nicky Bird, you twit—get away from those trees! It is not beaten!"

Harman and Gilbert rushed into the courtyard. The rest of the men milled about in the entrance. Some carried spears of widely varying lengths and states of repair, others held long-bows with arrows at the string and a few had nothing but their torches held aloft against the night.

John stepped into the gap. "Grip your spears, turn and face the trees! Keep those torches up—they are the only things keeping us alive!" The men jumped and spun about, pointing their weapons out into the gloom.

Harman shot a look around at the dead fire, the scattered weapons and the bodies of the bolgugs. He gripped Edmund by the shoulders. "Where's your brother?"

Edmund felt his legs begin to buckle. "They took him, Father."

"It's all right, son. I've got you." Harman grabbed him around the middle and heaved him up. He stumbled back over the rubble, nearly tripping on the rough, uneven stones. Martin Upfield reached out to help them down. The ground in front of the keep had been raked bare to dirt.

"John, I see it." Jordan Dyer kept an arrow at full draw. "A dozen yards down, off north. It's moving away."

"Just what's going on here?" Edmund's father got his footing on the ground. "Where did those blue things come from?"

"Make a circle," said John. "Keep those torches high— spread them out, make sure there are some in every quarter. Fire is the only thing it fears. There is no time to question. Do it now."

The farmers and tradesmen of the village did their best to obey. They pushed Katherine and Edmund in with the children and surrounded them in rough ranks. Edmund found Tom there, shivering pale beneath the moon.

"Tom!" Katherine hugged him, then held him out to look him up and down. "Oh, I was afraid you'd died—here, help me with Edmund."

Tom put an arm under Edmund to bear him up. Edmund turned to accuse him, to hiss "Where were you?" in his ear, but the words died when he got a good look at the cuts running up under the sleeves of his ratty shirt and the scratch that ran from his eye to his jaw.

John Marshal stepped out before the men. "Point your weapons outward and watch your quarter. Keep your eyes to your direction, and if you see something, the first thing you do is shout a warning. Do you all understand?"

"Aye, John," said Henry Twintree. "We hear you."

"We will take stock of things when we're down safe in the village." John turned on his heel. "Now, march!"

They descended the hill with spears and torches held

out on all sides. John Marshal sped them to a jog once they reached the West Road, almost too fast for Edmund, even with his friends to help. Dark cottages passed by, fallow fields and livestock pacing back and forth at the rails of their pens. The stone roof of the hall rose to view, its watchlight ablaze, then the mill, the inn and the houses of the village.

A cry went up as they reached the square. Men clustered in council beneath the broken statue of the knight. Mothers held their children close, braced on the steps of their houses as though a slammed front door could ward off all evils. John's party broke ranks and dispersed into the crowd—their neighbors demanded and exclaimed, milled and embraced in the glow of the watchlight, their long shadows shifting and moving across one another. The bell atop the manor rang out loud and long. Voices rose to a clamor as every man who had been up to the hill started the same breathless story as his fellows.

Tom let Edmund down against the base of the statue. Katherine set her sword to the earth, then curled over her knees.

Edmund leaned back and looked up at Tom. "We should find a place to talk."

A wizened hand grabbed Tom from behind and spun him around. Tom went rigid, then dropped his head. "Master."

"Did I give you leave to go back up that hillside?" Athelstan clenched a fist in Tom's face. "Did I, boy?"

"Hey!" Katherine sprang up to come between them, but Athelstan's icy croak cut across her words: "You hold your tongue. I will stand no more of you. It was I who took this boy in as an orphan, I who bought and paid for him, and he is my chattel—mine! He is my property, do you hear? The sons and daughters of free men should have no business with him. You may go jump on a spear for all I care, but when this one dies, it will be at the stilts of my plow!"

Katherine balled her fists, but Tom met her gaze and shook his head. The crowd parted to allow Athelstan to shove him away toward the road—only to find John Marshal standing in their path.

Athelstan wagged his stick at John. "Move aside!"

John's face was cut stone. He raised his sword. Athelstan flinched and backed away.

John turned his blade and dropped it into its sheath. He stepped close and spoke private words in Athelstan's ear. The old man grunted and shook his head. John held out a hand. Silver glinted as it clinked into Athelstan's palm.

Athelstan stared down at the coins. He closed a fist around them and pointed a finger at Tom. "One night." He stalked away.

John took Tom by the arm and led him back to Katherine. He pressed another coin into her hand. "Take out a room at the inn. Get some food and rest. I will find you there."

He pulled Katherine close and kissed her forehead, then gripped Edmund's shoulder. "I am very proud of all of you."

Katherine led them away through the throng, arm in arm toward the inn. Edmund could not remember ever feeling joy at the sight of the sheltered wooden steps, but his heart skipped up high as they drew near.

Then it sank into his feet. Geoffrey.

His father stood in the doorway, speaking slow and quiet. His mother held her apron to her face.

"It's done with now. No one's going back out there tonight." Harman reached out for his wife, then saw Edmund coming with his friends. He turned away and stepped inside. Sarra quivered on the step. She let her apron drop and blinked up at the stars.

"I tried," said Katherine. "I'm sorry. I wasn't fast enough."

Edmund came up on the step. "Mum." He did not know what to do or say next.

"My son." His mother seized him close, but her tears were for grief. "Oh, my son. My son."

Chapter 12

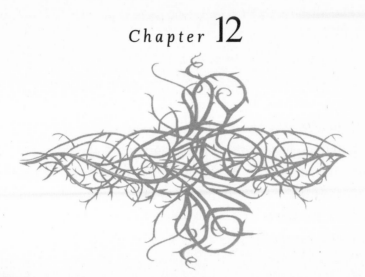

Edmund slumped at the table in the corner of the tavern, head down on his crossed arms. He felt as though he must be spinning, turning round and round on the tabletop, but knew that he could not be, that he was lying still. Tom sat beside him, and Katherine across, their long legs touching at the knees. Two bowls of mutton stew lay between them, Katherine's nearly full and Tom's nearly empty. The hearth fire blazed with the brief light of kindling, already dying down by shades.

"Our daughter is in those woods!" Jarvis Miller stood at furious odds with Henry Twintree by the door. He pointed at Edmund's father. "So is his son—you cannot tell me that we are to do nothing!"

Henry Twintree threw his arms wide. "And what would you have us do, Jarvis—charge about through the forest in the thick of night with that *thing* out there, and who knows how many bolgugs besides?"

"Oh, it's all fine for you, isn't it? Your son is home safe and sound!" Alice Miller's voice broke up worse with every word. "You'd sing a different tune if it was your child out there, your own child gone and you don't even know—"

Edmund plugged his ears. He stared up hard at the ceiling, then over at the fire. Writhen thorns moved through every shadow in the room. He turned to the wall, but he could not stay that way—too dark, too alone.

"I saw your light," said Tom. "It lit up the whole sky."

"It just about killed me, too." Edmund tried to pick at his bowl of stew, but it tasted dull and flat.

"Is that why you're tired?" said Katherine. "Do spells hurt the wizard?"

Edmund propped himself on his arms. "There's not really any such thing as a spell the way most folk think about it, one that you can just say over and over. If there was, then wizards would already rule everything, wouldn't they? If you could make a spell that kills someone from far away, what's to stop you from doing it again and again, killing anyone who opposes you until you're the king of all the earth?"

"Oh," said Katherine. "I'd never thought of it like that."

"Every spell is something special, fit for the moment when it's done." Edmund pushed his bowl across to Tom. "It's not just the words you say, but the way they make you feel, the meaning and the rhythm, the connection you make with them.

It's not just the things you think, but how the place and time you're in can change them."

Tom picked up the bowl and started slurping. "That sounds hard."

"It is hard. It's like making up a song on the spot—I could teach you how one note sounds against another, but if you don't have the music inside you, then you won't know what sort of song might be best right when you sing it. It depends on where you are, what you're feeling, and even who's listening." Edmund paused to yawn into his hands. "A good spell keeps a balance. There's a famous old wizard who wrote that nothing can truly be created or destroyed, just changed and moved around. That means a spell works best if the wizard finds a way to pay for the change he wants to make with another change. You might cast a spell that keeps a town safe from harm, but the cost is that no one can feel happy there."

"There doesn't seem much use in that," said Katherine. "Why be safe and unhappy?"

"That's just the way it works," said Edmund. "If you can't think of a way to balance out the good and the bad, though, then the cost will fall on you. That's what I did tonight—it's called drawing through the center. You can try to force the spell, but to do it you have to give of yourself. Sometimes it just hurts, or makes you tired, but it can even turn back on you like a curse."

"Well, however you did it, it was brilliant," said Katherine. "Those bolgugs were blind as bats."

The glow that spread over Edmund only made him feel worse when he remembered—Geoffrey, kicking and struggling, disappearing into the dark.

"We can't just sit and do nothing." He turned on the bench he shared with Tom. Almost everyone he knew stood, sat, or leaned in every available space in the tavern, all of them afraid, none of them looking like they knew what to do. Mothers held their children on their laps and on the tops of the tables before them. The old folk hunched by the fire, their craggy faces cast up red in shadow.

Tom spooned up Edmund's stew in great hungry gulps. Katherine reached across the table and took hold of his bony wrist. She pushed back his sleeve to examine the cuts that ran up past his elbow.

"What happened to you, anyway?" said Edmund. "It took you ages to get back to us."

Tom raised the bowl to his lips and drained it to the dregs. "I'm not much good with stories."

"Please, Tom, tell us." Katherine let go of his arm. "What happened?"

Tom set the bowl on the table. "I was coming down the hill as fast as I could." He looked at his scabbed and bloodied hands. "It was dark—I tripped and fell down the slope, but fell tumbling. I guess that got me to the bottom faster than I could have run."

Edmund sucked a breath through his teeth. "That explains the bruises."

"Some of them. I ended up in the brush by Swanborne stream,

so I pushed through, trying to make for the path to the village. I remember feeling the hairs stand up on the back of my neck, and then a badger came out of cover and rushed by the other way. There were no birds—it was so quiet." Tom shook his head. "I should have stopped. There was a smell, like brambles in winter, and then it was right in front of me."

Edmund blinked. "It?"

"You saw it. It was all thorns apart from the eyes."

"What happened?" said Katherine. "Did it hurt you?"

Tom raised his arm to reveal a set of jagged rips down the side of his tunic. "Almost."

Fearful memories swam in his eyes. "It doesn't breathe. All I could hear were thorns scraping on the branches behind me. I ran and dodged, I tried every trick I could think of, but I couldn't shake it off."

"You couldn't have been that far from the village," said Edmund. "Why didn't you call for help?"

"I couldn't afford to waste the breath. It pushed me back the way I came, up the switchbacks to the top of the hill. Every time I tried to break away and turn for home, it cut me off. After a while I figured out that it wasn't even going full speed—it was just herding me up the hill, letting me run ahead so long as I ran where it wanted me to go. I was getting tired, but it wasn't—I knew I couldn't go on much longer, so I stopped trying to turn against it and went straight down the hillside. I put everything I had left into it. I felt like my heart was going to come right out of my chest. I ran to the edge of Swanborne gorge, and I jumped."

Edmund gaped. "You jumped the Swanborne?"

"It hurt. I thought I'd broken my leg when I landed, but it was just twisted. I saw the thorn-thing come to the edge, then turn back into the trees, going uphill. I guessed that it must be going after you, so as soon as I got my breath, I ran straight down the banks and onto the village green." Tom nodded to Katherine. "Your cousin Martin heard me shouting from the road. He started calling people together. Some folk wanted to wait for Lord Aelfric, but your father lit a torch and—well, you know the rest."

Katherine placed her bowl of stew in front of Tom. "You were very brave."

"Why? All I did was run for my life."

"Quiet. Eat the stew."

Tom did not need to be told twice. Edmund looked out across the crowd of his neighbors clumped in fearful, whispering knots throughout the tavern. "You know, you'd think someone would have thanked us by now."

"They're too scared to think of it," said Katherine.

Jarvis shouted at Henry, calling him a coward. They sprang at each other—tables fell over, folk swarmed out of the way, and if the front door of the tavern had not opened between them, they might have come to blows.

"I am not your lord." John Marshal stepped in amid a blast of cold night air, one thumb hooked in his belt, fingers cradled around the hilt of his sword. "I am not your leader. I am just a man of this village, but I have knowledge that might aid us. If you will have me, I will organize a watch and see that we are as well defended as can be tonight."

"Anyone against that?" Edmund's father looked around the room. "Thought not. We're all yours, John."

"Then by your leave, and in your name, I summon the levy of Moorvale," said John. "Those of you who serve in it, take up your weapons and assemble in the square. Bring torches if you have them. Let us move quickly and secure the bounds."

"Wait—all of you, wait!" Jarvis Miller jumped up on the step. "What about my daughter? We cannot leave her out there!"

John shook his head. "I am sorry, Jarvis—Alice, Harman. We have little hope of finding your children tonight, and should we stray into the forest, we risk more loss than we have already seen."

"You cannot tell me you're going to just leave my little girl out there! You cannot—"

"I have seen a thornbeast rip a dozen armed men to shreds!" John stared Jarvis down, then softened again. "I will lead a party to search the woods as soon as I judge it safe enough. Now come, all the levy. Everyone else remain here—you will be much easier to guard if you stay together."

Katherine jumped up to cross the room ahead of the levy men. Edmund tried to follow—Tom grabbed him and helped him over to the door.

"I can come too, Papa." Katherine buckled her uncle's sword at her waist. "I feel much better now."

"No, child, you've done enough. You too, Edmund. Rest here, and we will try to make some sense of all this in the morning."

"But, Papa—"

"I said no." John Marshal left with the men.

Edmund's father remained by the door after the last of the levy passed outside. He cast a long look around at the huddled groups of mothers, children, travelers and old folk left behind. He rounded on Edmund. "Where's your mother?"

"Upstairs."

"Well, you watch that nothing gets taken. Perfect chance for it."

"Yes, Father."

Harman narrowed his eyes at Tom. He jabbed a finger at the bowl of stew in his hands. "Did you pay for that?"

"John Marshal did, Father." Edmund said it like a sigh. Tom sidled back into the shadows.

"So." Edmund's father looked him up and down. "What was your brother doing on top of a hill in the middle of the night? Any guesses?"

Edmund looked at his feet. He shrugged. "I don't know."

"The two of you share a room." Harman dropped his voice, though not so low as to stop half the tavern from hearing. "If he's been sneaking out at night, why didn't you tell us about it?"

Edmund bit his lip hard.

"I'll tell you why—because you didn't know, because you've been doing the same thing." His father loomed in close. "Slipping out to read your books again, were you? I guess we must have missed a few."

Edmund faced up to him. "I didn't know you cared what happened to Geoffrey. I thought you wanted to just shove him out onto the road if he caused you any more trouble."

A spasm passed across Harman's face, remorse chasing anger so quickly, they could hardly be told apart. He shook a finger at Edmund. "You listen to me. Your brother looks up to you. He wants to be like you—even I can see that. He went to play in the woods because you do, and now look what's happened."

He turned his back and stalked out.

Edmund shut his fists. He could feel the eyes of his neighbors on him from every side. His father slammed the door.

"He didn't mean that." Tom took his arm and led him back to their table. "He's just afraid, that's all."

Edmund let bitter silence answer for him. He set his jaw against his fist and nursed a mug of goat's milk someone had left on the table. A dim tumble of voices filtered in through the door, then shouted orders, then the dwindling tramp of boots marching off down road and lane. Katherine made rounds of the room, checking on everyone, making sure no one was hurt, that no one needed help. Tom stood and steered her by the shoulder to an empty chair. She sat in it, then buried her face in her hands.

Robert Windlee shook his wispy white head. "When the old die, I can bear it, we've lived out our spans, but when it's a child, just a child—" He clenched fingers gnarled to oak roots by a long life of labor. "It's a curse to see such times in old age, when you're past helping it."

Mercy Wainwright's baby started fussing, then wailing, and then other children joined in a piercing chorus from every corner of the tavern. Alice Miller rocked over herself, hunched and shuddering, not even seeming to notice the comfort others tried to give her. Emma Russet lay curled atop a table, wrapped in the blankets from Edmund's own bed, her bandaged foot sticking out at an awkward angle.

Edmund turned his mug round and round, working at the hole in his thoughts. Why did he want to look at the far corner table? There was no one there.

"You're thinking something." Tom sat in beside him. "I can always tell."

"I'm trying to make myself think." Edmund pressed at his temples. "Not much is happening, though."

"Do you want me to go away?"

"No—here, I'm not thirsty." Edmund held out the mug. Tom took it, and drank down the milk in one gulp.

Edmund drummed his fingers on the rough wood. "The feeling comes, over and over, that there's something I need to remember." He sighed. "But everything's spinning. Nothing makes sense."

"Maybe when you rest, you'll remember," said Tom.

Edmund put his head to the table. Sleep rose in silver waves, tipped with the poisoned spikes of his dreams.

• • •

He woke. Scattered bowls and mugs ranged along the tabletop before him. The side of his face felt damp.

A braid of honey hair swung down across his view. "What book?"

Edmund sat up. He rubbed at his eyes. "Did I say something?"

"You said a few things." Missa Dyer sat across from Luilda Twintree, a half-finished game of hopsnakes between them. "You were sleeping—you just mumbled something about a book."

"Ah. Oh." Edmund pushed his bangs from his forehead. The fire burned low. His neighbors surrounded him on the benches, chairs and floor—some sleeping, others hunched in silent worry. Katherine lay curled by the fire, draped in her cloak. From the look on her face she was having a nightmare.

"Sorry. Must have been a dream." He ran a hand along his cheek. The wetness was spilled ale. He glanced down at the game. "You've already lost, you know."

Luilda sighed. "I know." She moved a snake. "Just trying to pass the time."

"We brought some food around." Missa moved a hound in to block. "We didn't want to wake you."

"Thanks. Not hungry." Edmund tried to stand, and found that most of his strength had returned. "Just want to go—check on the horses. In the stable. Be right back."

He slipped out through the back of the tavern. Torches flickered down by the mill—men's voices melded into the murmur of the river. He crept past the inn's store of empty kegs, through Knocky's garden and in between the Coopers' and the

Millers'. He poked his head around the corner. The old statue of the knight stood alone in the square, lit along one side by the watchlight on the steps of the hall.

He took his chance and rushed into the open, then west down the road. The fields of Moorvale stretched off into the darkness low and earthy black, striped with the chaff of the harvest. He drew level with the old ruined keep, its snaggled outline reaching dark against the stars.

"Keep up back there!" John Marshal's voice carried far across the silence. Edmund spied a clump of torches approaching from the west. He leapt the fence and hurried north into the pasture. The patrol passed by on the road, their tread slapping echoes off the side of Wishing Hill.

The book lay where he had dropped it, though by luck it had fallen closed in the leaves beside the log. He picked it up, then felt in the undergrowth and found his leather bag. He opened the drawstring and slid the book inside, then retraced his steps to the road. Excuses for what he was doing out alone came to him as he ran, but he found no need for them. The patrol he had seen had passed on up toward Dorham, while another moved off onto the moors across the river, their position clear from the barking of their dogs.

Edmund stole back across the square and around the back of the inn. He slipped inside and ducked through the doorway of the best private room, the only one with a hearth of its own. He drew out the book and set it on the table, then lit the lantern hanging by the door and moved it close. The light

MATTHEW JOBIN

fell crossways over the rounded, sweeping script on the open pages before him, kindling burnished glints on the leafwork around the elaborate capital letters. He turned through page after page until he found what he was looking for.

"It's the Nethergrim. He's come back."

Chapter 13

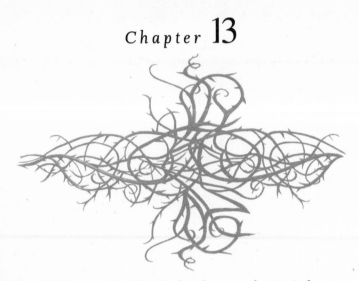

n here." Tom pushed back the door to the inn's best room, letting in the sound of someone murmuring a lullaby from the hallway beyond. "He said it was important."

Katherine followed him in. She wore a blanket around her shoulders and her hair in a messy braid. "Edmund, I told you—you'll go stone blind doing that."

"I didn't want to wait for morning." Edmund held up his quill to the feeble light of the lantern. He trimmed the tip sharp with his knife.

Katherine bent to stoke the fire. "Tom says you found something."

"Many things." Edmund dipped the quill into the inkhorn. He blotted at the upper corner of the only scrap of parchment he still owned, and made a note: *Seven children on the star. Blocky Hand and Curled Hand agree. Seven inside eight, repeated twice.* He scattered a trace of dust across the words to dry the ink.

Tom hovered over the table. "Is that a man on that wheel?"

"You're in my light." Edmund flipped the page.

"Sorry." Tom moved. "Is this about what happened tonight?"

"Sit down and I'll tell you." Edmund stretched back his neck with a grimace.

Katherine took the chair across from him. Tom pulled up a log from the stack of firewood. From outside the shuttered window came the scuffle and tramp of a patrol going by on the road.

"All is well," spoke a voice, though not so loud as to wake any who had found sleep that night. "Midnight—or there-abouts—and all is well."

Edmund flicked backward through the parchment pages of the book, turning past a succession of diagrams and passages of writing in all manner of hands and hues. Some of them ran left to right, but others up and down, and still others twisted back and forth across the parchment like oxen plowing a field. "I'll start here."

Firm black lettering ran in two columns down the pages under his hands. He traced his finger along the close lines of text and read aloud:

"'Also numbered amongst the servants of the Nethergrim are the bolgugs, who are said to be the hounds in his hunt for the flesh of the young. They are the height and figure of a man, but of a dark blue hue, like unto the skin of a blueberry. They walk bowed and bent, but are yet hale and quick, and fear no hurt. Their heads are round and their eyes bright yellow.'"

Katherine raised a hand to the bruise on her jaw.

"'Hunger rules the bolgug—it has no thought save for the ceaseless gnawing in its belly, wherein lies a'"—Edmund skipped over a hole in the text, a place where the parchment had rotted and crumbled through. "'A'—let's see—'a bolgug can gorge itself forever and forever and yet feel that it starves unto death. A pack of bolgugs, on their own, will ravage the land without pause, feasting on the flesh of man and beast until they are destroyed. Only in the presence of a mastering will can they do anything but rend and devour.'"

Katherine pondered awhile. "The bolgugs we saw on the hill could easily have eaten the children, but they didn't. Instead they bound them up and took them away—and we still don't know why there was a fire up there."

"What about the other thing we saw—the thing made of thorns." Tom leaned from his makeshift seat to stare down at the script. "Does your book say anything about that?"

Edmund turned the page. There was a drawing of the creature they had seen atop the hill, rendered in meticulous detail, its tendrils twined around the gilded first letter. "'As the quiggan serves the Nethergrim in fouled water, and the stonewight in his mountainous lair, so the thornbeast does his will in vale and forest—thorn-handed, black of eye.'"

Katherine exchanged a horrified glance with Tom. The lantern between them guttered and failed.

"But this can't be." Katherine reached out to trim the wick. "The Nethergrim is dead. He died on Tristan's sword."

Edmund fiddled with his quill, fearing to say what he must. "That's what we've always been told."

Katherine's features dropped into a frown. The flame awoke, fizzing and smoking until it found the oil.

"Sixty men went up the mountain, but only three came down again." Edmund plunged on before he lost his nerve. "Vithric died before we were born, and Tristan's not been back to Elverain in years. Your father is the only person who could have told people what really happened, but so far as I know, he never has. After they returned, there were no more attacks, so everyone just took it for granted that Tristan killed the Nethergrim, that the bad old days were gone for good, but—how can we be sure?"

Katherine crossed her arms. "What are you trying to say? What are you saying about my papa?"

Edmund stared down at the book, unable to meet Katherine's gaze. "I'm only asking—are there things he's told you that he hasn't told anyone else?"

Katherine turned away. She drew a breath, and let it out. "Sometimes, in the evenings, after we've eaten, Papa will sit by the fire with a cup of wine. I mend his clothes and watch his face as he goes up that mountain, up to the Nethergrim again and again. He's never told me what happened there—and I don't think it's something I would want to hear."

Tom let his chin rest on his fists. He flicked a look at each of his friends. "Maybe Tristan did stick a sword in the Nethergrim. Maybe it wasn't enough."

"We don't even know what sort of creature it was." Edmund felt through the bits of twine he used for bookmarks. "Not even wizards can agree on it—some seem to think he's just a very large and nasty bolgug, while others say he's an urgebeast, which is a 'fiend made flesh by evil thoughts.' This one here, some southerner, he argues that the Nethergrim must be a thornbeast, for all tales of his deeds arise from villages in the eaves of the great woods of the north. He adds to this the account of Eudo the Bald, wherein—well, he just goes on for a while about all the creatures in his service and the ways they can rip people to bits. And then, back here, I found this."

He ran his finger to the top, following a script inked thick in red: "'There in the Girth, at the marriage of the rivers, the men who served the Nethergrim did make their hallowed havens, their grand, forbidden halls in the shadow of the mountain. From that fastness they reigned in fearful might, and bid all men bow and give offerings. In those days the bolgugs were said to roam the streets by night, choosing victims to sate their master's hunger.'"

Tom swallowed. Katherine shivered, and drew up the blanket around her shoulders.

"If I've read this right, there was once a race of men in the north who came under the sway of the Nethergrim." Edmund tapped the feather of his quill on the page. "These men had lords that ruled over them—they had a name that I think would come out in our speech as 'Goodly Folk' or 'The Fitting,' 'the Suitable Men' or maybe even 'Gatherers.' So far as I can tell, these Gatherers served the Nethergrim of their own free will, and built a kingdom with its help."

"What kingdom?" said Tom. "Our kingdom?"

"No, another kingdom, long before." Edmund felt a twinge of pride at the looks of stunned awe on the faces of his friends. "Haven't you ever wondered who built all the old things you see around you—the village hall, maybe, or the old keep on Wishing Hill, or the bridge? No one knows how to make a bridge like that anymore. Haven't you wondered why the West Road is so straight and wide when it just goes through a few villages and then off into the wilderness? The world wasn't always the way it is now."

He drew a slip of vellum from the book. "There's a note stuck in between these pages, here. It's a list. Mithlin, 515. Longsettle, 498. Rushmeet, 476. Byhill and a scribble, then Quail, 447 to 455. Dorseford, 428, Chessmill, 409, then Longsettle again, 384 to 390."

Tom scratched his temple. "What are those numbers?"

"They're dates," said Edmund. "The numbering of years."

"I've never heard of that," said Katherine. "What year is it now, then?"

Edmund shrugged.

"Places and dates." Katherine stroked her chin, then winced when she touched the bruise. "Every twenty years or so, and villages all through the north."

"It sounds like the wizard who wrote all this was trying to trace the Nethergrim's steps," said Tom.

"He wasn't a wizard when he wrote it." Edmund shuffled the book in front of his friends. "Look very closely at the inks."

Katherine moved the lantern near the page. "The writing along the sides is a deeper black."

"It's much newer," said Edmund. "The main text is long-winded and comes at things from a number of different points of view, but the notes are all just corrections and additions added many years later. This isn't a wizard's book, you see—it's an apprentice's book."

"A child wrote all this?"

"Well, no one wrote the whole thing. This book is very old—at least two dozen people have written in it, three of them in languages for which I don't even know the letters. Each apprentice studies what's there, then binds in some more pages to copy down what his master teaches him. In some places you can even see where a master corrects a student—this last one's master had the long, scribbly writing you can see a few pages back here. And as you go farther back—see? That scribbly writing becomes the main text, and is corrected by this strange blocky hand. Master to student, one after the next, for centuries."

"I guess that would make the last one your master, in a way," said Tom.

A shudder seized at Edmund. His gut clenched in—a memory wisped from his grasp, leaving him with nothing but the sense of being watched by a pair of hard, cruel eyes.

"I've been wondering about that," said Katherine. "You said your father burned all your books, so how did you get this one?"

A guilty start nearly made Edmund drop his quill—then he wondered where the feeling came from. "I can't remember. I really can't. Father must have missed it, I think."

"I doubt he could miss this one." Katherine raised one side of the book to look at the cover. "You could buy a horse with this thing—a good horse. How many hiding places do you have, anyway?"

"Only the two." Edmund stared at the wall. "You're right, this does not make sense. My father did find all my books, burned every single one, I'm sure of it. I can feel it, there's something wrong with my memory."

"Maybe it's because you hit your head," said Tom.

Edmund shut his eyes and strained, and for a moment—no. Nothing.

Katherine turned a page. "Ugh!" She let it drop open. "What is that?"

There between them lay the drawing of seven children arrayed upon the star. Symbols turned and twisted all about the design, seeming to coil in around the little bodies.

"That is what the Nethergrim does to children." Edmund smoothed the page flat. "It's a spell."

"But I thought it just ate them," said Katherine. "That's what all the legends say."

"When legends get old, they twist in the telling," said Edmund. "This is what really happens. I'll try to read a bit: 'Bring a blade for He-That-Speaks-From-The-Mountain in the—the large exalted hollow household,' I think that says. 'Bring then seven children from the villages of the wheat slaves and clean them,' or maybe 'purify them in the marriage of the rivers, and'—I just can't get this next part, something about a pact, a sealing of words."

"I don't see how you can read that at all." Katherine squinted down at the page. "Those aren't even letters!"

"They are—they're just not the letters of our language." Edmund stared hard at an elaborate symbol, flipping its meaning over and back. "There is a bargain struck, a spell cast by a man but grounded in the power of the Nethergrim. Each of them takes something from the children, something different."

Tom looked at Edmund. "What happens to the children?"

"They die." Edmund traced the diagram. "One by one, they die, and as they do—" He scanned along through the text, trying to draw sense from a thicket of curled and interlocking glyphs. Was the join mark supposed to descend like that, or had the scribe made a mistake? It could as well mean "Youth in a Thousand Seasons under the Seventh Path through Death" as it could mean "Seven Youths Turn Death into a Thousand Seasons."

"A bargain." Katherine knit her brows. "What does it mean?"

"I don't know yet, but the wizard who drew this made some notes on the next page." Edmund pointed. "See there, at the bottom? 'Seven children on the star.' And down there—'Seven inside eight'—when he gets excited, he tends to use too much ink. In two different places he writes that there must be seven, and that if there's not enough—let's see—'the circle will break, and the Form will not form.' It sounds as though if there aren't seven children, the whole thing's ruined."

"But there were only five children up on the hill," said Tom. "And three down in Roughy."

"But we rescued Miles and Emma—and Peter's dead." Katherine's dark eyes lit. "The Nethergrim needs seven, and he doesn't have it!"

"My brother is alive, and he'll stay alive until the Nethergrim collects seven children." Edmund stabbed a finger at the parchment. "Geoffrey is alive, and if we can find where those bolgugs took him in time, we can save him. Here, there's one more entry."

He flipped back to the middle of the book and placed his finger amongst close lines of ink faded green with the years. The words seemed to crawl under the wavering light of the lantern as he read along:

"'And there, in those chambers, did I see with mine own eyes his works in all their dread and decaying splendor, for rotting there in that cold sanctuary lay the hoarded wealth of centuries, taken by force and fear and left to ruin in a lightless grotto. Upon the star lay seven children. The people wept for fury and for shame as the light of their torches did fall upon the crypt where stood the little graves set row upon row upon row.'"

The fire crackled alone for a while.

Katherine shook herself. "But it can't be the Nethergrim. Tristan killed him—he's dead. My father was there."

Edmund looked up at her across the parchment expanse of the book.

She sighed. "I'll talk to him."

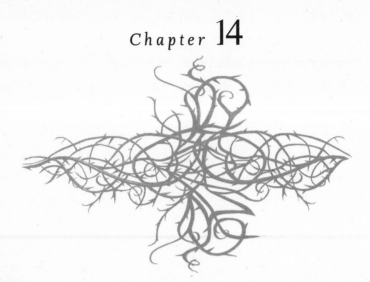

Chapter 14

Dew lay on the grass and mist rolled above it as Katherine walked home in the gray-black quiet of the hour before dawn. She crept across the yard just as the first traces of coming light touched the distant edges of the moors. She stopped to listen at the door of her house—no sound from within, no smoke from the chimney, but the window had been left unshuttered. She leaned in and pressed the door open with the greatest care, only to find her father seated in shadow at the table, still in his cloak and riding boots.

"Katherine," he said. "You should have waited for the sun."

"Tom came with me on the road." Katherine stepped in and shut the door. Chill had taken hold of the house after a day and a night without fire. She reached for the flint and tinder by the hearth.

"I spoke to Edmund last night." She sparked the lantern to

life and set it on the table between them. "He thinks the Nethergrim has returned."

Her father looked away, out through the open window. The light found him old, drew in the lines around his eyes, found the gray in his hair and hid the brown.

"He has a book, Papa. I don't know where he got it. He found some things in this book, about the bolgugs, and the other thing we saw—the thornbeast. They're the Nethergrim's servants, the ones who help him take children away. Edmund read about all the horrible things that he's done, and—Papa, what happened on that mountain?"

Her father put his head in his hands.

"Papa?" She reached out for him. "Papa, please . . . what's wrong?"

Dawn broke across the stubble on his jaw. "Have I ever told you how I first met Tristan?"

"No, Papa."

He turned to her. "My daughter. I owe you as much truth as I can bear to give. When I am finished, I will tell you what you must do, and you will obey me. Do you understand me, Katherine?"

A void opened in the pit of Katherine's stomach. She sat down. Her father breathed in, then out.

"I come from the Burrs, a long line of hills through the downlands on the southern border of the kingdom. My father—your grandfather—was a stable groom, a man who had spent his whole life caring for horses. That is the trade my brother William and I spurned for the adventure of war. We hired on as men-at-arms in the garrison of our lord, and it was there that I met Tristan for the first time. You might not believe that your papa was ever young, but I was—very young, not much older than you are now."

He looked down at his scarred and calloused hands, and clenched them in. "I was there the night our lord tried to storm the home castle of the Duke of Westry. I was one of the men who scaled the gatehouse and let down the bridge for Tristan and the other knights. Your uncle William died there, on the ladder next to mine. I wish he could have seen you."

Katherine recoiled. It felt for one disorienting moment as though she was seeing her dear old papa for the very first time. She saw through what he had worked to become, to what he had been before—a lonely, frightened man who had lost too much, too young.

"After the war," he said, "I was very much adrift. My brother was dead, as was my liege lord. Tristan, my captain and my hero, had fled the battlefield. I was not yet twenty, yet I felt I had made such disastrous errors that my life now stretched before me without joy or purpose. I had followed a greedy fool, and in my desire for glory made myself imagine we had a cause beyond his greed. Now we that remained of his army splintered and made for home, and tried to forget all that we had seen and done.

"William was the younger brother, the apple of our mother's eye. I had promised to look after him. They never forgave me when I came home to tell them he was dead. They did not curse me, but they would not stop grieving, and after a while I could no longer stand the sting of it. I left them to be alone with my thoughts, promising I would return one day to set everything right. I never did.

"I won't say much of the time that followed. I don't care to remember it. I made my living as a groom, wandering farther and farther north, sleeping in grange and byre and keeping myself to myself. There were places I could have stopped, folk I would have liked well enough to make my friends, but I would not, and as I lay awake in yet another haystack, I would wonder why I could not stop roving, until I realized one night that I was searching for Tristan.

"I did not at first know why I was looking for him. I thought I hated him. If you ever go to my homeland, you will find many folk there have a very different opinion of Tristan than they do here. He was a deserter, a false hero, never mind the fact that the battle was already lost when he left it. If he was such a hero, they said, why did he abandon us at our greatest need? I thought for a while that I wanted to kill him, or at least drag a confession from him, an apology, an explanation for all that had happened. I dreamed of finding him one day and hurling my grief at him, shouting, 'Why did you not stay? I believed in you. I thought we could not be doing so wrongly if you were there to lead us. It had to mean something if you were there, but then you ran, and I was left alone with my doubt.'

"As the miles and faces slid past me, though, I came to know that I wished to find him for a different reason. I wanted only to know if he felt as sorry as I did for what we had done, and whether he knew if there was a way to make the night-mares stop.

"Quite by chance, I came into the north not long after Tristan, though I did not know it at the time. I found work as a groom and stablehand in the town of Bale, where your friend Edmund was born, just down in Quentara over the hills. I remember the winter morning when a fellow groom rushed into the stables where I was mucking out the stalls and gave me the news that was racing through the town. A hamlet newly founded on the old West Road into the Girth had been sacked by fiendish creatures and its people driven out. The Nether-grim was rising, and that was news enough, for Quentara's north and west borders are hard against the mountains, and they had as much to fear from the Nethergrim as anyone. But what made me drop my shovel was not the fear of bolgugs. The groom told me of the desperate defense of the village hall, and the three-day flight to Elverain afterward. This tale had a hero, a knight from the south who had rallied the people, fight-ing trog and mound-boggan single-handed, driving back their host again and again as he led the villagers to safety. Without this man, it was said, not a soul would have reached Northend alive. They even had a name for him.

"I had found Tristan at last. I left Bale that same day, and walked through the new year's snow to Rushmeet and then north, and so crossed the borders of Elverain for the first time in my life.

"It was the simplest thing, when I arrived. I was expecting to have to look for him, to wheedle an audience somehow, but when I walked across the drawbridge of the castle, there he was in the ward, standing upon a cart and exhorting the folk of the castle to rally with him, asking for men to follow him against the Nethergrim. He knew me when he saw me, though we had spoken only once or twice before. I must have seemed like a ghost from his past, but his eyes lit up in welcome as I approached. I knew then that I did not need to ask him anything. I pledged to follow Tristan, then and there, and though there was death and darkness and fear in our future, it was the saving of me.

"Soon enough, as you know, we had gotten quite a band together—the Ten Men of Elverain, as they called us. Tristan and Vithric, of course, and Sir Unwin, who was there when I arrived. He was the eldest; he must have been forty-five or so. A local man from Roughy, but a veteran of the wars from away south. Lord Aelfric is a friend to the Duke of Westry, and so had sent a small force under Unwin to fight against our old lord in the wars. Tristan and I could easily have met Unwin in battle a few years before we came north, and let me tell you, I'm glad we didn't. Then of course the Twins, Owain and Bram, the finest archers I have ever known. Bram was the better shot, by the way, just to settle that argument—but only by a little. Owain did not really mind, since he was a better shot than everyone else, and quicker with a sword. A better singer, too, and fancied himself the more handsome of the pair, hard as it was to tell them apart.

"Then there was Bill Piper, the spearmaster, Thoderic, sword-and-hatchet man, and Quicksilver Jack from Tumble Bridge—

what a terror he was! You couldn't ask for a quicker hand when he was sober, but the trouble always lay in keeping him sober. And then of course your uncle Hubert Upfield. A great ox of a man—your cousin Martin is his very image, head to toe. Once we taught Hubert how to fight with that mattock, he was like a walking siege tower.

"Good men, all." He said it near to a sigh. "Good friends. How I miss them sometimes."

He shook himself. "Well—we had come together at the right moment, that was certain. Even as Tristan and Vithric assembled our band, foul creatures of all sorts started to harass the edges of Elverain and Quentara as they had not done in many years. We rode all about the borders, hunting and being hunted, sometimes with levies of local men but as often as not alone. During those early months we stayed near settled lands and played our part in the events of the day."

"The Siege of Mithlin Mill," said Katherine. "The Battle of the Potter's Field."

"Yes, that sort of thing—and all the while Vithric was watching, recording, thinking. I had few thoughts beyond the next campaign, the next urgent message from harried peasants, but Vithric was in the opening moves of a great game against the Nethergrim. I cannot possibly rate his intellect too highly. Our enemies were monstrous things, striking out of cover, out of shadow and mist without warning. We should have been ten steps behind them always, but Vithric found patterns, traces of the mind of our enemy in every maneuver. There seemed no depth he could not sound. He and Tristan would confer together at our lodgings long into the night, and the rest of us began to find ourselves in the right place when trouble struck more often than not. The attacks diminished. The people were glad, and so were we, but Vithric told us that our enemy was not in retreat. The Nethergrim's forces had been pulled back in preparation for a more determined strike, one that Vithric said might overrun all of the north. We thus resolved to take the fight into the mountains as soon as we could.

"The following spring, when the passes were clear, we made our first sorties into the Girth. It is a vast and lovely place, though teeming with danger. I would like to have seen it in more peaceful times. I won't say too much of it, only that we found bolgugs there, and boggans, quiggans and things for which I had no names. We found ruins there as well, which was a surprise to everyone save for Vithric. They were quite a sight, even in their decay. There were great blockish manses and squat towers crumbled almost to the foundations, with narrow cellar stairs that led down to places I'd rather not describe. We found and searched as many of them as we could, routing the awful things that had taken up residence there.

"As the months went by, we came to understand that we were involved in a game of cat and mouse. We would probe the defenses, searching the ruins we found for some clue that would lead us to the lair of the Nethergrim, and all the while its creatures would be on the hunt for us. We had to choose our battles very carefully, and still our explorations were not without loss. Thoderic was slain in battle on one of those journeys, and none of us escaped without wounds, but we gave our enemies enough to worry about that the attacks back in settled country slowed to a trickle. We found great stone tablets carved with very strange writing, and after a while Vithric seemed to learn how to read them. By autumn he must have learned enough, for he and Tristan assembled us in secret council at the castle.

"We met in Lord Aelfric's chambers late one autumn evening. I remember it was windy that night—the shutters moaned and rattled, but it was far too cold outside to open them. The Twins, being youngest, had to stand since there were not enough chairs. Vithric lit a single candle, and we all leaned forward to listen to him. I can still see those faces, just as they were. 'The Nethergrim is asleep' was the first thing he told us."

"Asleep?" said Katherine.

Her father chuckled. "Not quite what we had expected to hear, either. Vithric told us that the Nethergrim had arisen before, in long-ago days out of all record save for the tablets we had found. It had been placed into a deathless slumber by a mighty spell—we had the great misfortune of living in a time when that spell was about to end. Our only chance was to find the Nethergrim before it awoke. Aelfric considered awhile—I could see he wasn't quite convinced—but at last he said he would send a levy of fifty men to serve under Tristan.

"Three days later the levy assembled in the castle yard and Tristan rose to address them in the presence of Lord Aelfric and all the court. He told us that this journey would be so perilous that he would think no less of any man who chose not to go. I remember the look on Aelfric's face when he said that; he wasn't used to the idea of volunteers. It did not matter, though—by then we all would have followed Tristan off a cliff. The men gave a great shout and we marched from the castle and then down through Northend—Bill Piper on one side of me with his great boar spear on his shoulder, your uncle Hubert on the other, hefting that tree-trunk mattock like it was kindling and singing in rounds with the Twins in that great boom of a voice. It was a fine day for a parade, and all the folk of the town turned out to see us off. There is nothing like a cheering crowd to speed you on your way, but soon enough we had gone beyond hearing, and the silence was all the worse for it. We marched into the mountains by nightfall, each man sunk deep in his thoughts of what was to come."

Katherine's father seemed to come back from far away, and the look of fond reminiscence died upon his face. "And now, child, we reach the part of the story that no one knows, none save the three who survived it. What I am about to tell you is an oathbound secret. Here I break that oath."

Chapter 15

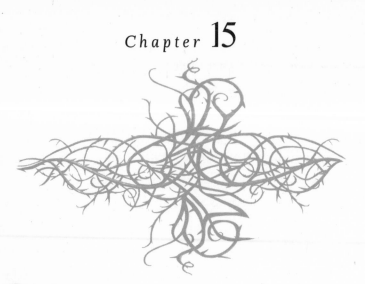

*S*he has a Voice.

Edmund shivered. He had burned through the last of his family's store of oil, and charred up the wick of the lantern to a crisp. The window of his bedroom stood open for light, but it let in a hard blue draft.

It is beautiful beyond expression. Firm Hand, author of the last of the pages in the book, scribbled in the margins around a twist of ancient symbol: *It is the first time I have ever felt what other men describe as love.*

"Who are you?" Edmund leaned low on his arm. "Who is She?" He stared at the script, but it gave no answer.

She cannot die. She cannot ever die. Fool that I was to think it. The script lost its firmness, turning spidery and crowding to the edges of the page: *She is the fount and source of all thought, all power, all that is hidden to men. Those who served Her long ago rose to a dominion beyond the dreams of kings. I will do as they once did, I will serve Her as they once served Her. She has called, and I have answered. I am to be Hers forever.*

Edmund sat back and rubbed at his eyes. Geoffrey's spare tunic hung over the edge of the trunk beside him—a hand-me-down, like all of his clothes. Toys lay piled in the corner: a few knights carved from bits of wood, a sword made of sticks bound with twine, a top that never spun right.

"I will find you." Edmund pinched across the bridge of his nose, half to wake himself and half to stop himself from blubbing. "I swear I will." He searched again through all the places in the book where he had found some hint, some guess at a direction in the mountains.

Two centers, one a city, the other a forbidden stronghold for the Gatherers. A place where rivers join in a valley. A list came next, the names of all the rivers Edmund knew and one he did not: The Tamber, the Rushing, the Mara, the Swift. Do they all drain south? Ask Aelfric if he has a copy of Plegmund.

"Plegmund." Edmund beat at his weary mind. The same Plegmund who wrote *Journey Beyond the White Sea*? Aelfric—Lord Aelfric?

A rap at the door: "Edmund? Son?"

Edmund jammed the book behind his bolster just in time. His mother opened the door. "Oh, son—you didn't sleep."

"Mum, we can save him." Edmund sat on his quill. "We can save Geoffrey, I know it."

His mother lowered herself down at his side. "My boy." She

touched his hair. "My good boy." She had not slept either—he had heard her weeping through the walls for the whole of the night.

"Oh, my son." She dragged a kerchief across her face, then blew her nose. "You loved your brother, didn't you? You did."

Edmund grabbed her sleeve. "Don't talk like he's dead— Mum, he's not dead!"

"You tried." She squeezed his hand. "I'll never forget that you tried."

"Please don't give up. Mum, don't."

His mother balled up the kerchief, then stretched it out. "You had a sister. Did your father ever tell you?"

Edmund reeled. A sister? "No—when?"

"The year before you. She came out blue. She—" His mother could not finish. She hunched down, and Edmund found himself with his arm around her, holding her through shudders that shook the bed.

"Oh. Oh." She kissed his cheek, got tears on him. "My sweet boy. You are my only now. My only."

Edmund opened his mouth to tell her that he would not give up, that he would follow every trace he could—and understood just in time that it was the last thing he should say.

His mother got up slowly, every breath a sigh. "We should go down now. Lord Aelfric's here. He wants everyone in the square."

"Yes, Mum." Edmund reached for his boots. Maybe Lord Aelfric knew something that could help. It was worth a try, at least.

"Make sure you get some breakfast." Edmund's mother gathered up her hair on her way downstairs, braiding without looking. "I put your clod-shoes on the step. We're harvesting on Redfurlong this morning."

Edmund stood stupid in his doorway. "Today?" He came down into the tavern and opened the front door. His neighbors shuffled past on the Longsettle road, gathering up toward the square in a bleary clump. His father stood with a dozen local men by the stone steps of the hall, all of them wearing the dingy green tabards of the village levy. Some leaned upon spears, and the rest carried longbows and clubs or axes. A half-dozen dogs curled in among them, shaggy collies and sheepdogs wagging their tails in anticipation of the hunt.

"I must ask you once again, everyone, for silence." Harry stood a step above the men, in polished mail and bright surcoat, an ornate longsword kept in a silver-chased scabbard at his belt. "My noble father is well aware of the events of last night and what they may portend. That is why we have come here today, to beat the bounds of the village and search for any sign of your missing children. My father has graciously chosen to release these dozen of your men from their labors to aid in the effort, and asks no extra tax from your village in recompense, so much does the sorrow of this day fill his heart. You must place your trust in him, as is his due from you, his people."

Edmund stepped out into the empty sunshine. Morning lit the mountains cold and cheerless in the west. He pressed into the swelling crowd.

"There he is!" Hob Hollows slapped Edmund's shoulder as he passed. "There's our man—the Wizard of Moorvale, you are!" His brother Bob grunted and nudged Edmund's other side—as close to talking as Bob ever got.

"Story's getting around." Wat Cooper leaned in to grin over Edmund. "Thought I saw that light up on the hill last night. Whole village is talking about it!"

"Ha, and here we thought you'd be serving us our ale all your life!" Hob burped out a laugh. "And now think, lads— who's to inherit the inn once Edmund here's run off to apprentice himself to some great fancy wizard somewhere, now that—"

Hob stopped—both his brother and Wat Cooper glared at him. Edmund bit his lip, willing himself not to burst into tears right in front of them.

"Oh—hey now, Edmund." Hob scratched his straggled beard. "Don't take that wrong. There's hope for Geoffrey yet, I'm sure."

Edmund thrust onward without answering, slipping in between his nervous, chattering neighbors until he reached the front of the crowd.

"Would that we all could search the hills and wastes for this missing boy and girl." Harry bore a bright helm under his arm. He raised his other hand, palm extended up in a gesture of studied oratory Edmund had once seen sketched in a manual on courtly grace. "I do not think I need remind you that no fear of foul creatures in the woods should make you forget the winter soon to come. It falls to you all to work the fields, so that you may reap the grain you have sown and store enough to last your families through to spring."

"It's not our fields we're working today." Someone muttered it just quietly enough. "It's yours."

"Now those of you assigned to the search will march up to the keep as one force." Harry turned to address the levy men—most of them double his age. "There we will inspect the ground for signs of these creatures and have the dogs track their scents if they can. If we must follow more than one trail from there, we will divide into companies of no fewer than five. I want everyone to keep close—no straying off on your own. Be on your guard at all times; an attack may come from any quarter."

Edmund kicked at a pebble. "Waste of time." He stood on his toes and looked around for Lord Aelfric.

"Good squire, if I may." Martin Upfield raised a hand. "What are we looking for, exactly?"

Hugh Jocelyn waved his cap from the back of the crowd. "Yes, does this mean there are more of them bolgugs about?"

"Don't be stupid." Jordan Dyer flicked his fingers. "Bolgugs don't come out in the day."

Hugh shook his head. "Shows what you know, you young fool."

"We do not know anything for certain." Harry raised his voice over the argument. "We will use the greatest caution until we are more sure. Now—"

Loud ringing sounds drowned the rest of his words—Aydon Smith mending a levy spear in his shop across the square. By the time Harry caught Aydon's eye and signaled him to stop, the villagers had turned his ordered plan into anarchy.

"I saw one this morning, you know." Gilbert Wainwright carried the oddest weapon present—an antique battle-axe whose thick oaken haft and double head seemed far too heavy for his wiry arms.

"What, a bolgug?" Half the village turned around. "Where?"

"Out by Longfurlong, just after dawn," said Gilbert. "I was on my way to mend the far fence and saw big yellow eyes over by the rocks near the creek."

"Are you sure?"

"Well, it wasn't a squirrel!"

Harry raised a hand. "Wait, now, wait—let's not jump to conclusions."

"That's right next to my father's house!" Lefric Green had a voice only a mother could love—and Luilda Twintree, for some reason. "You might have warned us."

Gilbert looked indignant. "Well, I haven't seen you since last night, have I?"

"You could have come by this morning! My old mother—"

"Will you all please just listen for a moment?" A note of frustration crept into Harry's voice.

"Sir?" Jordan Dyer cupped a hand to shout. "Maybe we should start down at Longfurlong, sir."

"No, it won't be there anymore." How Nicky Bird had gotten himself chosen for the search party was anyone's guess. "We should head right into the woods."

"And then what, just blunder around all day and hope we run into them?"

Nicky jerked a thumb. "Harry's got a plan!"

"Yes, in fact I do have a plan, and if you would all just—"

The grand double doors of the village hall swung open, forcing Harry to step aside before he was knocked off the stairs. Lord Aelfric of Elverain stood the same height as his son, though he would have been taller in his youth. The silver thread in his belt glinted the same shade as his hair and the many rings that adorned his liver-spotted hands. A half-dozen castle guards followed him out onto the steps. They wore long green tabards like the village men, though theirs looked in much less need of a wash.

"My people." Lord Aelfric spoke in a voice gone thin and airy with the years. "I grieve with you on this dark day. You may lay trust that we will do all we can to secure this village. We have brought a generous boon of food and drink for the harvest. My son will lead a troop of guards to ensure that your work goes on without hindrance. Return you all to the fields, for the frost will not be delayed by your sorrow, nor your fear."

Edmund, like everyone, expected him to say more, but he simply waited in silence, looking past them at something down the road. Edmund turned—four men approached the square from the west, bearing a shrouded corpse between them. All talk ceased as the procession drew near, and a way was made for the passage of the dead.

Peter's mother stepped out of the crowd. She caught sight of her husband walking behind the men. Their gazes met. When the body had come within five paces, she fell to her knees, and then, reaching her hands over her head, she curled down to the earth.

Telbert Overbourne knelt beside his wife. He put his arms in hers. For a moment they shuddered together, then they staggered up and followed the body of their son as it was borne up the steps of the hall and into the darkness beyond.

Lord Aelfric waited for the corpse to pass, then strode down off the steps toward the stable. The villagers looked at each other, shifted and murmured, then dispersed.

"My lord?" Edmund elbowed through his neighbors to the edge of the crowd. He found Lord Aelfric stretching out his back beside his horse and sizing up the leap into the saddle.

"Here, Father, let me." Harry stepped up beside Lord Aelfric and knelt with his hands laced together.

Aelfric glared at him. "I can still gain my saddle alone."

"Yes, Father." Harry stood away. "You are not still angry?"

"This is a fool's errand, boy. There are greater things at stake than the lives of a few—" Lord Aelfric cast a sidelong glance at Edmund, and fell silent. He climbed up stiff into the saddle.

Edmund did not know how to begin, but Lord Aelfric had already taken his reins. "My lord—wait, my lord! Has anyone ever asked to borrow a book from you written by Plegmund of Sparrock?"

Aelfric stopped his horse. He narrowed his eyes. "And who might you be?"

"Edmund." He remembered to bow. "Edmund Bale, my lord."

"Oh—Father, this must be the boy who cast that spell last night." Harry held out an arm, though he did not quite touch Edmund's shoulder. "Wait—I recognize you—from the fair! Better with a spell than a longbow, I must say!"

Edmund stepped around Harry and in front of Lord Aelfric's horse. "My lord, please—if you search only around Wishing Hill, you won't find my brother, or Tilly Miller. There's something else going on, I know it, and—"

"Heed some advice." Lord Aelfric folded gloved hands on his pommel. "From all I have learned in a long life, the secrets of magic are most assiduously guarded by the men who make use of them. Were I you, I would find a way to lose my growing reputation as—what are folk saying?—the Wizard of Moorvale, before too many real wizards hear tell of it."

Edmund felt a cold hand on his heart. "I just want to find my brother."

"Do not hope much." Lord Aelfric spurred his horse around Edmund and off down the road.

Chapter 16

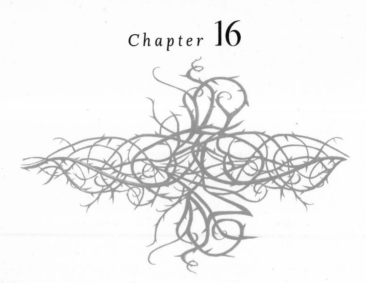

John Marshal sat some time in silence, seeming to sink as the sun rose outside. He went so long without speaking that when he started again, Katherine was halfway through making their breakfast. She turned to listen, still swirling a spoon through what was shaping up to be a rather bad pot of porridge. The look on his face tore at her, worked the void in the pit of her stomach yet wider.

"Vithric seemed to know which way to go, more or less, though it was still more than a week before we reached our goal." John ran his fingers across his brow. "It grew cold and began to snow on us as we went on, far deeper into the Girth than we ever had gone before. We took a few wrong turns, which gave us some days of low spirits and argument. The mountains were quiet, very quiet. There was no sign of bolgug or shrike, no ambushes at our camps. There were precious few animals of any sort up there—all eaten or driven off, I would think—so what struck me most on those days of travel was the emptiness and silence of the land. It seemed to come down on us, somehow, and smother all talk, all the merriment and jest that soldiers use to keep up their spirits on the march. I would be eating the evening meal and suddenly realize I had not spoken a word all day, and neither had anyone else. Silence turns your thoughts down strange roads. A shadow fell over us all, and it began to guide our thoughts and deeds though none spoke of it. We were in the heartland of our enemy, and we knew we would not pass unchallenged, yet nothing happened, day after day. We marched longer, slept less, and guarded ourselves with ever greater vigilance without saying why. The lack of hindrance seemed to make Vithric all the more worried, and though he was no mountaineer himself, he tried to urge us on to even greater haste. I didn't want to ask what he feared, and I doubt he would have told me. He wouldn't have wanted it to get out to the men.

"At last, late one afternoon, we came up through a shallow pass to find a great half-crumbled tower of the same fashion as the others we had seen. We found more glyphs and symbols carved upon its walls. Vithric grew excited when he saw them—he told us we must be very close to the lair.

"We climbed the pass toward the tower as the sun set before us, and looked out into the valley on the other side. There we saw the host of the Nethergrim, and many of the men cast themselves to the ground in terror."

Katherine's father looked around the room as though he saw something other than the furnishings of his house. "In the gray of twilight great shadows moved, some seeming to grow and shrink with the moment. If I told you that we saw a valley filled with nightmares, I would not be far wrong. Shapes both ponderous and lithe moved below us, each with its own gait, all terrible to behold. We came to know that we had until then met but skirmishers, the lowest orders of the forces arrayed against us. Here stood the core. None were arrayed as soldiers, for these were not men. The skin of a stonewight makes a crumbling, scraping noise as it moves about. It is an awful sound, like a fortress falling to pieces, stones cracking and sliding from the thing only to be absorbed back into its feet and remade by the moment. We could smell the swamp stench of dozens of boggans, see the flitting flash of a score of shrikes, hear the dry cracks of a swarm of thornbeasts writhing as one mass. The glare of the firesprites lit the ground red in places. Never have I seen a piece of land so accursed; the grass was torn and burnt, and the river that ran south out of the valley hissed and steamed. I do not know if such creatures need food or rest, but though they seemed to have been in that valley long enough to ruin it utterly, they did not seem to be encamped. No, they were merely gathered before the mountain at the valley's head, circling its foothills, waiting. Their master was about to rise. No one needed Vithric to say it.

"Tristan pulled us back from the edge and behind the wall of the tower. We knew that our deaths lay in that valley—I freely admit my only thoughts at that moment were of escaping before we were detected by what we had seen below. Strange it may seem to you, but as I stumbled into cover and looked

MATTHEW JOBIN

at my panicking comrades, I had the sudden wish for a leg of mutton in verjuice and mustard. I don't know why: perhaps I thought I'd never had quite enough of them, and thought that now I never would. I suppose I was trying to convince myself of all the things it was worth running for.

"Tristan addressed us there, beside the ruins of the tower. I don't remember exactly what he said—the words were not as important as the way he said them. He told us that what we saw in that valley would soon run riot over all we held dear if we faltered. He said there was no time left to prepare, for the Nethergrim would soon rise, and then it would be too late to fight or to run. Everyone, everything we loved was on the hazard that night, but still he gave a choice. He would not fight beside the unwilling; he let those men who could not stomach what was to come go free. Five turned and left us then."

"I didn't know that." Katherine brought her porridge to the table. "I would have thought I'd have heard of them."

Her father shrugged. "They didn't make it home. The rest of us waited for full dark, then crept over the pass. The Twins led us on a high, difficult cut across the side of the peak, up and away from where we had seen the creatures, taking cover wherever we could. We hoped to reach the entrance of the lair and slip inside unseen. It was a long, slow trek, every step of it made in fear. We could no longer see the creatures in the valley, save for the firesprites, who seemed to flit and twist about below us in some eerie dance. Even at that distance the sight of them filled us with dread, but so long as they stayed where they were and showed no sign of noticing our passage, we were able to press on. We crept along, each of us doing his utmost to stay silent. Until the night your mother died, those were the longest hours of my life.

"We had gone well over halfway, and had reached the slope before the entrance with no sign of trouble. I began to think our ruse would work—then one of our wide scouts must have run smack into a thornbeast. There came screams and a whipping sound. The firesprites in the valley below turned at once and came our way, along with, I could only guess, every other horrible thing we had seen. Panic very nearly scattered us, but Tristan pulled us back together. He ordered Unwin and the Twins to lead the men at a run up to the lair as he rushed back with Bill and Hubert to hold the flank. We fought a running battle up the slope, with bolgugs and shrikes, the quickest of our enemies, rushing to cut us off from the entrance that we could see looming dark as pitch on the slope before us. By then I had been in a good number of fights, but never had I felt such terror. We were overmatched and we knew it. Men were being picked off left and right as we ran, bowled over and shredded by shrikes or falling with crude spears hurled into their sides. Those of us that remained staggered up into the entrance. I remember one man who had made it up with us looked down to see the wound in his belly and collapsed right there. We knew the slowest of the creatures coming for us would be the worst—the boggans, the thornbeasts and stonewights. And then. And then."

He looked out across the spreading dawn. The porridge sat untouched. A rooster crowed twice before he spoke again.

MATTHEW JOBIN

"I remember Tristan's face, the notches on his sword. It was Vithric who reminded us of why we had come. He told us that the Nethergrim was still asleep, that if we could reach its chamber in time, it would take only one man to kill it. He asked for Tristan to come with him, and decided to take one more, just to be sure. He chose me. The rest of the men turned to stand against the horde of creatures coming up the slope, to try to buy us enough time to do what we had come to do. It was a mournful and terrible thing, to leave your dearest friends behind to die for you."

Katherine reached out for her father's hand, but he pulled it away.

"I can still see them," he said. "I see them shadowed against the night sky, the outline of their spears held ready, the Twins perched high upon the rocks, bows drawn side by side upon a field of stars. But the three of us descended into darkness. The central tunnel was very large, and would have led directly to the lair, but a great wall of masonry had been constructed to block it up. The dim sounds of battle began behind us as Tristan and I looked about wildly for a way through. There seemed no way forward, but Vithric rushed to the side wall, spoke one word of command and opened a passage that led into a complex of rooms and tunnels that could have easily housed a hundred men or more. They were built as though tunneling through solid mountain rock was nothing, and I marveled even in my fear as we raced onward. All that was not stone within was rotted to ruin, yet still it was a majestic place, and by the glow of our torches I glimpsed the fullness of the art of those who had built the towers in the mountains. By then the echoes of the battle had died away, though we did not know if that meant it had ended or that we had gone too far down to hear it.

"At every turn Vithric scanned the walls, pausing sometimes for a few moments to collect his thoughts and read what was carved into the stones around him. At last, at one junction, he stopped, turned and pressed his torch into my hand. 'The Nethergrim is just down these steps and on to the right at the end of the great hall,' he said to me. 'There is another way that must be secured. You two go on to the lair and I will meet you. If you reach it ahead of me, do not fear! It is still asleep. Kill it—whatever it is that you see, kill it. Strike for the heart!'

"As he spoke, we felt a thump and a rumble from the direction we had come, and then the sound of pursuit, the long echoes of the caverns drawing all motion into one muddled rush. 'They've broken through,' I said—I might have screamed it. Vithric ducked into a narrow side passage just big enough for a man to pass through, and disappeared. I ran with Tristan down the stairs, leaping over piles of rusted armor and littered bones, and all the while the echoes of the chase grew louder.

"We emerged into a great empty chamber that ran flat and carven to our right, but ascended sharply up to our left as a rough-hewn tunnel to meet the masonry wall somewhere in the darkness far above. It was clear that the wall was no more, though, for we saw the glow of firesprites descending the passage, and felt the rumble of stonewights following. Tristan and I rushed out into the open. I imagine that the chamber we ran through would have made me stop and gasp in awe at any other time. All I can recall are great vaulted ceilings and pillars shaped into the likenesses of grim and mighty creatures—a boggan, a coiled serpent, a giant with its face inside its belly. At the end of it stood a pair of stone doors as high as a castle wall, carved with designs I could not place. It seemed a hopeless thing, but we put our shoulders to the doors and shoved with all our strength while our doom thundered ever closer behind us. Those hinges must have been very cunningly built, for despite their great size and weight, the doors began to give way, and we slipped between them into the lair."

John swallowed, and licked dry lips. "And there, laid out upon the bier—there, the Nethergrim."

"What was it, Papa?" Katherine could not keep the question in. "What did it look like?"

"A beautiful young woman," he said. "Fast asleep, her belly swollen big with child."

Katherine would have guessed almost anything before that. "I don't understand."

"Neither did I," said her father. "I have never understood."

He wept then—the tears sprang out, as though they had been pressed within him for years. "I did not know what to do. I stood dumb—I had steeled myself for anything, any sort of horror from a nightmare, but not for this. The woman—hardly more than a girl—she lay with her hands across her middle, as though to feel or to caress the child within her. Perhaps, had I time to think longer on what to do, I might have stopped, but there was no time to think, for the enemy was upon us.

A rumble sounded from the passage behind, the servants of the Nethergrim racing in to kill us before we could kill their master. But then, was their master truly what lay in beauty on the star in the chamber before us? I looked at Tristan—all this passed between us in a moment—and he decided.

"He pushed me into the chamber. 'Go,' he said. 'Heed Vithric—it is asleep! He said to kill whatever we saw!' So I stumbled forward. Tristan turned to defend the doorway, to buy with his life enough time for me to do what we had come to do. I think if I had looked back, I would have seen the full measure of his skill in that moment, but it did not matter. He faced a host, an army, and even his vantage in the doorway would not hold as the stonewights came to batter it open. Just as I reached the dais, I heard the clang of Tristan's sword as it fell to the floor. I felt despair, for I knew nothing now stood between me and the Nethergrim's servants. I would not have time to strike before I was cut down.

"Then Vithric came, and at last I knew what a great wizard can do when pushed to the final gasp of desperation. The whole chamber shook, the statues outside shattered and fell, yet still I stood as though I was a statue myself. The sleeping girl before me bore a smile of undying love, a mother's love. I have never forgotten that smile. Some nights it is all I see."

Katherine bit her lip—if she had not, she would have begged her father to stop. The rooster crowed again outside.

"I raised my blade, there in that place beneath the earth." John moved his trembling hands in echo of his words. "I stood above her, I took a hard grip upon my hilt—then she opened her eyes. She looked up at me in pure and innocent confusion. She asked me who I was, where she was, then said she had been stolen, taken from her village by the bolgugs. She asked me if I was there to save her."

"Papa—"

"And I did it." He spoke almost too low to hear. "I brought my blade down upon her."

"Then—*you* killed the Nethergrim." Katherine clutched to the thought, the hope of it. "Not Tristan. You did."

He would not let her keep it. "I don't know what I did. I have never known."

He looked outside again. "Even as I struck, Vithric's spell began to shake every chamber of the mountain. The creatures turned to flee—I think most were crushed as the pillars gave way in the passage before us. Tristan had taken wounds in the leg and side, and Vithric was out cold, but I tried to drag them up and make a run for it. I found the door through which Vithric had entered, and between Tristan and myself we managed to pull him along and heave our way up through the shaking passages. It must have been luck that brought us back the way we came. We emerged at the mouth of the opening and saw the scattered bodies of our friends and comrades, just as we had feared. We staggered out into the night and rolled down the snowy slope, and for a while we knew not whether we were alive or dead."

Katherine tried and tried but could not think of what to say. The truth was much more horrible than anything she had dreamed, and she had dreamed many horrible things.

"And that was it," said her father. "We all three swore never to speak of what had happened under the mountain—how could we explain what we had truly done? Folk wanted to hear that we had slain a beast, a thing that looked like what they feared. If we had told them what we had truly seen, and truly done, then the world might be left in as much doubt as we were—or worse, make trips into the Girth to see for themselves. I begged Tristan to let the poets make what stories they would, to let fond legend cover over the truth. We drifted apart soon after—we could no longer stand the sight of one another; it made us remember too much. Tristan was granted lordship over all the lands in the Girth he could claim, and rode off with a few hundred folk to settle in a long-abandoned valley. Vithric went south and rose to great renown before he passed away far too young. I lived alone in the hills for a while until your mother found me and brought me down into the world again. After a few years of peace I started to think that perhaps I truly had killed the Nethergrim, that what I had seen was a trick to make me falter at the last. I awoke to life again, lived in love for a time, and raised my beautiful daughter."

He breathed out a long, slow sigh. "And then this." He snuffed the wick. "Come outside, child."

Katherine rose, heartsick and bewildered. She followed him out, down the path between the turned trestles of the garden.

"I have made arrangements, for you and for the horses." He drew on his gloves. "Lord Aelfric will be here with his men before dusk." He raised the leather loop and pulled back the door of the stable.

"Arrangements? Papa, please, wait—" The stable was old and close, lovely and warm with the heat of horses. A few heads rose along the fieldstone passage—a snort, a whicker here and there, all calm.

John stopped at the stall that held his own riding horse—a chestnut stallion of middle years with three white stockings and a long, glum face, still in saddle and bridle and chewing on his morning hay. He reached into the sack by the stall and fed him a handful of oats. "Whatever may happen, whatever else you may one day learn of me, you must know that I have always loved you, that you were the whole of my life. I did all that I could. I truly did."

Katherine hugged herself behind his back. It was not supposed to be this way. She had held Peter Overbourne's body in her arms—she had nearly died herself. She thought she had scrubbed everywhere, bent over the Bales' washtub with a rag in the dark, but Tom had told her there were still spatters of black-blue blood behind her ears. She wanted breakfast, a day to sit and let the memories shudder through her, and for Papa to tell her—

"I am sorry, child." John opened the door to his stall. The void rose to claim her.

Behind the door lay his sword, his shield, and two saddle-bags packed full. She leaned against the wall to hold herself up.

"Katherine." Her father touched her arm. "I must go away for a while."

"You're going back." She could hardly see him for the tears. "You're going back to the mountain."

He bent to take up his sword belt and buckled it to his waist. "Lord Aelfric will keep you safe until I return. This farm is too remote, too near the Girth. Do you understand?"

She drew back from his offered hand. "Oh, no, no, you cannot do this. You can't do this—you can't just tell me a story like that and expect me to just—Papa, let me come with you!"

He reached down for his shield and strapped it across his back. "Please don't make this harder than it already is." He heaved the saddlebags over his horse's withers. "Will you give me your hand before I go?"

Tears stung at her eyes, but she held out her hand. He took it, and she threw her other arm around his back. "Is it dangerous, where you are going?"

"Yes."

"Then why?"

"Because the danger will grow worse if I do not. I must find the Nethergrim—whatever it truly is—and destroy it, once and for all."

She stepped back. "I can do things, Papa. I can help. Let me help!"

"No, child. I never meant for you to take on the troubles of the world. My road will be hard enough—I need to know you will be safe."

"You raised me, you trained me to fight. Why?"

"You seemed to like it. Now promise me you'll stay out of trouble. Please, child."

She trembled a moment, and gave in. "I promise."

He pressed her hands once more and took the reins. She

stood aside as he led his horse from its stall and down the passage. He opened the door and the dawn came through to frame them dark before her.

She followed to the threshold. "If I had been your son, would you have taken me with you?"

He stopped and half turned. "Be safe. I will come back soon."

She sat down in the open doorway and watched him go. Horse and rider disappeared around the curve in the Dorham road.

"You can't know that," she said.

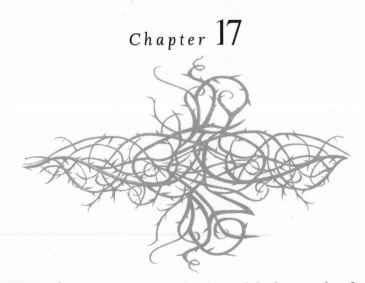

Chapter 17

Tom slumped through the door of the byre and in from the blustery chill. The oxen staggered in behind him and laid themselves down side by side in the straw. Oswin sat at their tree-stump table, slurping at his meal of frumenty porridge. He leaned over to push the door closed behind them. "East furlong done?"

"Most of it." Tom dropped down by the dent in the earth that served as their hearth. Jumble raced over barking and licked at his face.

Oswin ladled out the rest of the porridge into the bowl they shared. "Cold one today. Who'd have thought it so early?"

Tom sat up and took the bowl in his lap. He leaned some kindling in the hearth and blew the fire back up to a blaze. Jumble lay down at his side and put both front paws across his knee.

"Heard about what happened," said Oswin. "Get any sleep last night?"

Tom yawned, wide and long, curled down over his hand.

"Thought not." Oswin shook his head. "That's the thanks you get."

Tom scraped out the last of the porridge from the pot and filled it with water from the leather skin that leaned by the trunk. He felt behind him in the straw, pulled out a sack and rummaged through it with one hand while spooning up his porridge with the other. He drew forth a few bunches of herbs from the sack, a mass of roots and a handful of willow bark.

"I was down in the village this morning for drill and practice." Oswin laughed short and hard. "That's right, they think I'm Moorvale enough now to draft me into the levy. Guess those bolgugs have them worried."

Tom set down the bowl for Jumble to lick clean. He ripped the bark and scattered the pieces in the water.

Oswin dug around by the hearth and pulled up his cracked clay mug. "I'll tell you what else." He filled the mug from the waterskin, then settled back in the straw. "That friend of yours—what's his name, the blond kid—he's the worst shot with a longbow I've ever seen."

Tom smiled. "So they say." He pulped roots of bruisewort and tansy and mashed them between two stones, then scraped off the paste he had made into the bowl. He dipped his finger into the pot—warm enough. He ground some mallow leaves into the paste with the broken end of an axe haft, then searched around him on his hands and knees for a cup.

Oswin scratched at his pockmarked chin. "Can't help but wonder how you know what to do."

"Plants talk to me sometimes."

Oswin snorted.

Tom picked up the cup and poured out a careful measure from the pot. He brought cup and poultice to the oxen.

"Drink." He raised the cup to Thunder's lips. Thunder sniffed at the mixture and balked.

"Your master's made his fortune on your back, you know," said Oswin. "Never seen livestock driven so hard do so well."

Tom reached down and gripped under Thunder's chin. "Drink." Thunder opened his mouth and let Tom pour the pungent mixture down his throat.

"There. Not so bad." Tom tied the poultice around Thunder's leg, smoothing the cooling paste around the injured flesh so it would set and harden all along the strain. He touched a hand to the ox's forehead. "Rest."

Thunder gave out a long, grateful breath. His eyelids began to droop. Tom returned to the hearth and poured himself some water from the skin.

"Listen, Tom." Oswin leaned across the fire. "I'm going to give you some advice. You've got to leave this place. You're a fool if you stay here."

Tom looked up. There was something oddly eager in the way Oswin spoke, but he could not work out why.

"I'm only telling you this because I've come to like you,"

said Oswin. "I've been about, seen folk who have it rough, but you're about the limit."

"Where would I go?"

"Anywhere. Hardly matters. Get clear of Elverain and you'll be too far gone for your master to find you. A year and a day in town air and you can start again. You could be an apothecary if someone taught you to read, get paid good silver to make those potions of yours. You know how well they do? Velvet cloaks, Tom, velvet cloaks and wine."

Tom shook his head. "I can't leave. I'm needed here."

"By who? The oxen? You'd heal more oxen off this farm than on it, if that's what you care about."

"My friends need me."

"Spoken like a boy. No one needs his friends, not for long. Family, sure, a wife maybe, but the friends of your childhood are like the clothes—you grow out of them. Those two friends of yours are bound down different roads than you are. There'll come a day when the distance gets too wide, and then they'll find ways to be rid of you."

Tom looked into the fire. He saw Katherine, married and happy. He saw Edmund, busy and important. He could not see himself at all.

"You know what I'm going to do?" said Oswin. "I'll tell you. I've been saving since the day I got here. I'm no more than a penny short of enough to get me back to Tambridge and buy into some land. I've got a cousin or two down that way who've done well enough for themselves—should be no trouble talking them into a bargain. As soon as I've got enough, off I go. I doubt I'll even tell your master goodbye. He doesn't deserve it."

Tom heaved himself up. He reached for the shepherd's crook. Jumble followed him to the door.

Oswin drained his mug. "Nothing to hold me here." He reached a hand for Tom to help him to his feet. "Same goes for you, Tom. You remember what I said."

. . .

Blackbirds sang over the Marshal's farm. The wind ripped at the lone red oak on the pasture hill, pulling off one leaf and then another.

Katherine crossed the yard from house to stable with a jug of water in her arms. The warm, safe feeling that had always greeted her when she stepped within made its depth known by its absence. She worked past noon, alone, grooming and feeding, cleaning stalls and bringing in fresh straw. She left Indigo to the last. When she had brushed him down, mucked his stall and given him a carrot, she found at last that there was nothing more to do but wait. She sat down in the straw beside him.

Indigo slurped at the water in his trough, then munched through the last of his grain. He stepped near and put his nose to Katherine's hand.

"He'll come back soon, with Geoffrey and all the children." Katherine ran her fingers down Indigo's long, straight face. "Everything will be put to rights. You'll see."

There rose from outside the meterless clamor of many hoof-beats. Katherine stepped from the stables to see a company of riders approaching on the Dorham road. Sunlight caught glints on shirts of burnished mail—Lord Aelfric led, followed by Harry and surrounded by the knights of his household.

"My lord." Katherine kept her head inclined. "All is ready."

Lord Aelfric looked about him, and waved his men down from the saddle. "Each of you, take one horse with you on a lead. If there are too many, we will come back for the rest. We must have them all safe within the castle by nightfall." The men spread out through the paddocks, hopping the fences and reaching for the mares.

Harry dismounted at Katherine's side. "They hurt you." He reached up, almost touched the bruise on her chin. "Has someone seen to it?"

"Tom did," said Katherine, and when the name did nothing: "My friend. He was also up on the hill last night."

"I meant a proper healer." Harry had shaved off his sparse and silly fuzz of a beard. "We have two at the castle, of different schools. Please let them see to you." The chin beneath bore a cleft, though very faint.

"There is a girl from my village who is hurt much worse than me," said Katherine. "She got a splinter through her foot. We fear that the wound might fester."

"Yes. Yes, of course." Harry turned. "Father, may we take the peasants injured last night to be tended at the castle?"

"You may not." Lord Aelfric walked his horse away toward the paddock. "If we do it for one of them, we'll soon enough have our best healers tending every runny nose from here to Dorseford."

Harry looked to Katherine. "Send her. I will pay the cost myself."

"Thank you." Katherine remembered to curtsy. "You are very good."

"Am I?" He fixed her in his gaze—wheatfield eyes set in just proportions on a face that looked too solemn for his years. "I think I am in danger of turning out rather badly."

Katherine did not know how to reply, not with so many knights walking to and fro through the farm around her. She let Harry's horse nuzzle at her side. She had named him Sparrow as a foal—he still remembered the first pair of hands ever to touch him.

Lord Aelfric spurred his mount. "And while you are here, boy, pick out one of the older colts for your next steed." He rode off along the fence line. "The one you have is not fit for someone of your rank. You'll make a fool of yourself, riding to court on such a rouncy."

Harry shot his father a wounded look, and stroked his horse's mane. Katherine watched boy and horse together— Sparrow waited on Harry's moods, felt his distress but did not fear him.

"You there, man—what are you about?" Lord Aelfric raised his creaky voice at one of the knights. "Curse you for a fool— have you never handled a mare and foal before?"

Harry waited for Lord Aelfric to move beyond hearing, then glanced at Katherine and dropped his voice. "Your father is a brave man. Brave enough to speak rough words to his lord when he must remind him of what is right."

Worry seized at Katherine. She shot a glance at Lord Aelfric's stiff, distant back. "Is your father angry?"

"I fear he is. John Marshal came to the castle last night— early morning, really." Harry sighed, and half smiled. "My noble father does not like being roused so late."

"What happened? What did Papa say to him?"

"The defense of our people is a sacred trust that may not be thrown aside when it becomes an inconvenience. There are no excuses that remove us from the protection of the innocent. The mantle of guardian, once donned, may be removed only to become a funeral shroud." Harry let himself laugh a little. "I think I have his words exactly. Oh, Katherine—you should have been there. You should have seen my father's face when John Marshal spoke to him so. I wish—I wish I'd gone with him."

"So do I."

"No." He reached out—then glanced at the men all about him and dropped his hand. "Please, no more of this. When I thought you—it made me think—"

"Boy!" Lord Aelfric turned his horse at the edge of the pastures. "Did you not hear me? Go in and choose yourself a steed. We must get these horses secured."

Harry shut his fists. It took him awhile to work himself up to the words, but when he spoke, they had fire: "So, my lord and father, we are to protect our horses, and leave our people to cower in their hovels? Do I have your instructions perfectly?"

Every knight and man-at-arms in hearing fell silent, all

at once. Lord Aelfric glowered from the paddocks—Harry dropped his head and stepped into the stables.

"Katherine Marshal." Lord Aelfric rode her way. "Collect your possessions. I am bound, by my word of honor to your father, to bring you safe within the walls of my castle. You will remain there for the nonce, safe from whatever harm might further befall these villages. When this crisis is past, I will have my seneschal give some thought to your future, should John Marshal fail to return."

Katherine curtsied. "Thank you, my lord." She waited for Lord Aelfric to dismiss her, then retreated up through the garden.

She stepped into her house, the little daub-and-wattle cottage she had shared with her father all her life. The fire lay dead, the floor swept, and everything set in its place. She looked outside to see Harry leading Indigo from the stables. He waved at her, and beckoned.

She stood at the threshold, to savor for a moment the path that she knew she could not take. Oh, how it would be good— to step from farm to castle just at the moment when the farm seemed a less than certain home for the first time in her life. How sweet, how good it would be to turn from her father's protection to Harry's, to cross from one happy dream to another without a gap. How easy it would be to forget her frightened neighbors and sleep safe behind a castle wall. How easy it would be to let Edmund weep for his brother alone.

She picked up her pack and shouldered it, cast one last look within, then shut the door behind her.

The knights had assembled two dozen mares and colts be-tween house and stable. Harry walked Indigo out into the yard just as Katherine drew near. He turned her way, but Sir Ranulf cut between them.

"Come then, girl." Ranulf reached down a hand. "You may ride pillion with me."

"Sir knight, I will not." Katherine nodded down her head to Lord Aelfric as she passed. "I thank you, my lord, for your generous offer, but I am going to my village."

"Katherine?" Harry stepped out behind Ranulf's horse. "But, wait—it's not safe there!"

"That is why I am going." Katherine pushed back the gate. "My friend lost his brother last night. My village trembles, fearing for the lives of their children. I will be an aid to them if I can, and suffer with them if I cannot."

She stepped out onto the Dorham road. She looked back at her home, the cottage and stables, the paddocks and pastures, all she had ever known. It felt like someone was ripping her guts out, over and over again. She sped her walk—she would not give Lord Aelfric the pleasure of her tears if she could help it.

"Boy!" Lord Aelfric's voice rose to a shout, but faltered. "Where are you going? There is much to be done before dark!"

Katherine looked back to find Harry following her—jogging, for it was in truth Indigo leading their way.

"Harold—Harold! Leave off this nonsense at once!" Lord Aelfric rode to the edge of the fence. The knights exchanged knowing sneers, and not a few of them shook their heads.

"You told me that one of these horses is mine to take, did

you not?" Harry shot the words over his shoulder. "I choose this one."

"Then where are you taking him?"

"To his trainer." Harry drew level with Katherine. He held out the reins.

She took them—their hands curled together for as long as they dared with so many watching. "If you want my opinion, Harry, I think you are turning out very well."

"I will come by the village as soon as I am able—tomorrow at the latest." He knelt before her. They both knew she did not need the help, but she stepped into his hands and gained the saddle. She felt Lord Aelfric's glare, but kept her back to him.

Harry stepped back. "Trust in your father, as I do. He is the finest man I have ever known." He cast a bitter look back toward the farm. "I wish he was my own father."

"I wish I was his son."

His smile broke wide. "No. Every day I thank the stars that he had a daughter instead."

Chapter 18

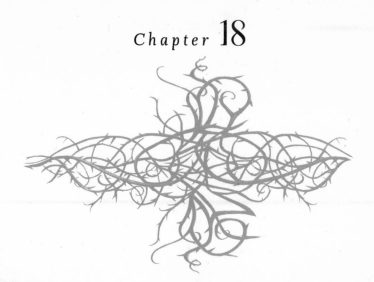

E dmund sat on the step of the inn, mending a threshing flail in the thin light of a day when all the warmth in the world seemed to drain into the blank blue sky. The village had reverted to what looked like normal business—the only obvious change in the frantic rush of the harvest were the castle guards who roved the fields in pairs. Missa Dyer swept dust through the doorway of her brother's workshop across the street while Henry Twintree marshaled a drove of oxen onto the road with the help of his eldest son. Nicky Bird perched on Baldwin Tailor's roof to mend a hole while Baldwin harangued him from the square below, loudly accusing him of shoddy workmanship and the use of bad thatching. Even Telbert Overbourne shuffled past, looking pale and crumpled but carrying his sickle for some day work.

"Hard at it, there, Edmund?" Two of the castle guards made their way up the road, their tread slow and heavy from a long patrol in armor. The taller and younger of the two made a sweeping bow. "Or should I say, your wizardliness."

"If I'm a wizard, why am I untying this knot with my fingers?" Edmund tried yet again to tease apart the frayed leather cord that bound the beater end of the flail to the handstaff. "Did you see anything out there?"

"I am happy to say that there is nothing to report." The guard's voice grew muffled as he bent to shrug off his armor. "Save that I now know every path and stream in this village as though I was born here and had never set foot outside it, and have counted all the leaves on all the trees and found them in good health and order, and have taken the liberty of naming all the frogs down by the creek, placing them into clans by the markings on their backs and taking for myself the title King and Overlord of all Frog-Kind. If only a man could grow rich upon a tax of flies."

Edmund grimaced as his nails found hard purchase on the knot and worked it loose. The guard's chain armor slid clinking to the ground along with the arming coat he wore beneath it. Missa Dyer stopped sweeping and leaned on her broom to watch.

The other guard, a sallow-cheeked man somewhat older than his companion, stood watching the cloudless sky with an air of distrust. "It'll go hard for us if this keeps up. Too many days like this mean trouble later."

"That's not how it goes," said the taller guard. "Cold early means it lets up by the solstice."

"That's an old wives' tale, that's all that is." The older guard stomped up past Edmund and into the inn.

"I think he's getting bored with me." The taller guard threw armor and coat over his shoulders. He sniffed at the air. "Mmm—smells like stew's on."

"Not even a trail, then?" Edmund turned as he passed. "No tracks?"

"If my mother cooked as well as yours does, I'd never have left home." The taller guard followed his companion inside.

Edmund tried to work his fingers into the knot on the other side of the flail. He bent his fingernail, cursed, and flicked the smarting nail against his thumb. He put his finger in his mouth and sucked on it, then looked up, his attention caught by an urgent wave from across the street.

"What?" He put a hand to his ear. "I can't hear you."

"*I said.*" Missa shot an apprehensive glance at the open front windows of the inn. "*Is he married?*"

"Is who married?"

Missa waved her hand above her head. "*The tall one!*"

Like it was market day. "How should I know?" Like nothing had happened.

"*Ask him!*"

Edmund set his teeth. "Can't you see I'm busy?"

"*Ask him later! Please!*"

"Yes, yes, fine, all right. Later." Edmund prevailed at last over the second knot. He blew on his chilled fingers and used a new length of cord to bind the ends of the flail back together.

He stood up and gave the mended flail a few experimental swings, then threw it over his shoulder and went through the front door of the inn.

A guard thunked his mug. "Boy—hey, over there."

Edmund hurried on, pretending not to see the hands raised from the table by the fire.

Thunk, thunk. "Hey!"

"What's that boy's name again? The blond one."

"I think it's Richard."

"Richard! Get us another round, will you?"

Edmund stopped by the kitchen door and looked back. The five guards watched him expectantly for a moment, then one waved his mug back and forth.

Edmund stomped down the cellar stairs.

"That's three farthings," he said when he returned with the ale pitcher.

The sallow-cheeked guard threw back his coif to show a narrow, balding head. "The castle's paying." Edmund shrugged and poured out the ale.

"You're that one, aren't you?" said another guard, more lately arrived from Northend. "The wizard."

"No."

"Oh."

A guard raised his full mug. "To Lord Aelfric, for picking up the tab."

"I'll drink to that," said another, and did.

"Speaking of which." The newer guard turned back to

Edmund. "I didn't get my fill of this fish. Have you got some more back there?"

"I'll go look."

"Leave the jug, will you? There's a lad."

Edmund set down the pitcher and pushed back the kitchen door. "They want more fish."

His mother sat next to a bubbling pot of stew. She held the ladle in her lap—she looked up slow and late.

"Mum." Edmund leaned by the door. "Mum?"

Sarra heaved herself up and smoothed down her dress. "They can't have more fish, unless they'd like to go catch some themselves." She sniffed her mixture, then dipped in a finger and tasted it. "Hand me those bones on the table, will you, dear?"

Edmund turned back inside the tavern. "There's no more fish. We've got bread and cheese, frumenty, leek soup, some turnips. That's it."

The guards looked disappointed. "You don't have any mutton?"

"You ate it all this morning."

They shrugged at each other. "Sounds all right, I suppose."

Edmund could not bear the thought of seeing his mother again. He went out the front and around the side of the house. The grain shed stood at the highest point between the inn and the river, above a handsome sweep of yardland leading down to the banks. The slope dropped off to the right, through the wide croft that spread back from Henry Twintree's house all the way to the riverside, dotted with nearly enough apple trees to earn it the name orchard. One tree stood above all, the great double trunk that gave the family its name. Miles Twintree dangled halfway up its branches, a basket in the crook of his arm. "Edmund!" He waved with an apple in hand. "Edmund! Want one?"

Edmund held out his hands to catch the apple, bobbled it, then seized it in. He nodded up at Miles. "Thanks." For the briefest of moments he felt better. He pushed back the door to find his father hard at work on a sheaf of barley on the threshing floor.

"Edmund." Harman did not miss a beat. He raised his flail and brought it down, knocking ears of grain from the stalks and collecting them in the wide, flat winnowing basket.

"Father—" Edmund brought himself to the edge of speaking, but could not force himself across it. He joined in; father and son tensed and released in turn, one swinging down as the other drew back.

They filled the basket and brought it outside. Edmund took up the winnowing fan to blow air across the lip of the basket while his father tossed the grain. He caught his father watching him—a strange, intent look as hard-fixed as anger. Bits of chaff puffed out in a wide sweep onto the path.

Edmund brought the winnowed grain inside and hauled out another sheaf. He worked himself up to speaking again, then lost his nerve. He dropped the bushel on the threshing floor and knelt down to cut the twine around the stalks. His father started hammering at the barley the moment he got up and out of the way.

The sun reddened down past the door. Edmund got a splinter from the handle of his flail. He stopped to pick at it, felt the long slide of pain when he drew it from his hand. His father stopped threshing, and held him in that strange look—then turned abruptly away.

"The light's starting to go." Harman set his flail by the wall. "We'll finish up tomorrow."

Edmund could hold it in no longer. "Father, he's alive. Geoffrey is alive."

His father stopped at the doorway. "Don't go raising false hopes, son. Your mother's had it hard enough—you'll kill her."

"They're not false!" Edmund willed himself to speak before his father could leave. "Father—Father, wait—I have a book!"

His father bowed his head and seemed to buckle. "Don't grow up like me, Edmund." His voice husked and quavered. "Say you won't." He stepped outside.

"Father!" Edmund grabbed for his shirt. "You don't understand—I'm not saying Geoffrey is alive because I believe it. I'm saying it because I have reasons to think it's true."

His father turned, in shadow from the dying sun.

"I have a book." Edmund let it all out in a babble. "I don't think I'm supposed to have it, but I do, and I've read things in it about the bolgugs, and the Nethergrim—I've found things, I think I know what it wants, what it's trying to do. I'm putting it all together, and I think it means those bolgugs were taking Geoffrey alive, taking him away into the mountains.

The Nethergrim needs seven children, that's why the kids went missing down in Roughy. He has to have seven children, but he only has five. Please, Father, you must listen."

"I am listening." His father knelt close, searched his face. "Edmund, where? Where are they taking him?"

"Into the Girth, to a valley where rivers meet. I don't know which rivers yet, but there's only four it could be—Katherine's gone to ask John Marshal for help, and—we can save him. Father, we can save Geoffrey. We can."

His father gripped his shoulders. "Go back to the start, son, and go slow. Tell me what you've learned, and I promise you—"

"Edmund?" His mother's voice rang out across the yard. "Edmund, come inside now!"

Harman stepped to the door. "We're talking, Sarra!"

"Please come now, dear." She sounded shrill—her words echoed to the river and back. "It's time for supper!"

"Supper can wait!"

"Now, Harman!"

"Curse it all, woman, I told you—bah." Harman grabbed for the door. "Come on, son. We'll talk it over inside."

Edmund felt a weight lift from him. He followed his father down the shadowed path and in through the yard. They found the kitchen door hanging wide and a pot of stew boiling to the brim.

"This is going to burn!" Harman pulled the pot from the fire. "Sarra, where are you?" Edmund stepped past into the tavern. The feeling that something was terribly wrong came a moment too late.

MATTHEW JOBIN

The castle guards sat slack at their table, staring into space and babbling sounds that did not add up to words. A single rushlight cast them in wavering shadow—from above, near the ceiling. Edmund looked up—his mother hung suspended in the air, held there by nothing he could see, but whatever it was, it pinched her hard, making dents along her arms, in her belly and on the side of her neck. She held the rushlight in one dangling hand.

"No alarms, if you please." The faltering light cast a face in sharp relief behind her. "Not a sound, not a shout. Do just as I say and she lives."

"Who's that? Edmund, is your mother in there?" Harman thumped through the kitchen door. He gasped and rushed forward, but Edmund held out his hand and shook his head.

"Edmund, is it?" The stranger twisted his features into a vicious smile. "And this is your father? I can only think that these two failed to raise you as they should. Did they never tell you that it is wrong to steal?"

Edmund stared, unable to think or move, locked in the stranger's narrow gaze. Beads of sweat rolled down the man's brow. He coughed, his body shook—Sarra wobbled in the air and nearly fell. The rushlight dropped from her hand and guttered in the trampled straw. It nearly went out—then it caught the straw ablaze. Orange light swelled the room.

Edmund's father put up his hands and spoke as slowly and as calmly as he could. "I don't know what this is all about, but I promise you that you may have anything you want from me, anything at all, if you just let her go."

"I'll let her go when I please," said the stranger. "Put down that flail."

Beneath his terror, Edmund felt something moving in his mind—and with a start he came to know it for what it was. It felt like the moment when he first learned to read, the first time the shapes and squiggles on the page had resolved into thoughts. It was at once strange and familiar, a tune he knew though he knew he had never heard it before.

He could sense the stranger's magic.

He could feel its flow around him. He heard the subtle chord of the spell, recognized its design from the pages of the book. He could even see its flaws.

The stranger wavered, seeming to grow older with every breath he took.

"You're drawing through the center." Edmund advanced, staring hard into the stranger's bloodshot eyes. "You don't have the strength to keep that up for long."

The stranger flicked a finger. Edmund's mother let out a moan—a trickle of blood ran down her neck. The side of her dress ripped open and a welt formed beneath.

Harman stepped up close at Edmund's side. "Son, the flail."

Edmund looked down. He had forgotten that he was holding it. He set it on the floor.

"All right, then," said Harman. "We're unarmed. What now?"

The stranger glared at Edmund, his face drawn skull white. "You know what I want."

Edmund took the cellar steps all in a bound. He knocked

aside the piece of plaster behind the last keg, pulled out the book and bolted back into the tavern.

"Put it there, on the table, then get back." The stranger's voice came strangled. "Stay out of my way. If anyone comes too close or makes a sudden move, I will snap her in half. Don't think for a moment that I won't."

Edmund came forward, ducking past his mother's dangling feet. He set the book on the table and retreated. The balding guard slumped out of his chair and pitched over onto the floor.

"So this is all your doing." His father curled his fists. "I never believed all that stuff about the Nethergrim."

"Oh, you should believe," said the stranger. "Though, really, what you believe or think is of no consequence."

"What have you done with Geoffrey? What have you done with my boy?"

"You'll hold your tongue, peasant, if you want to keep what you still have." The stranger edged over to the book, so busy watching for a twitch from either Edmund or his father that he failed to mark where he placed his feet. He brushed his leg through the straw that had smoldered to life next to the dropped rushlight. The trailing ends of the fabric strips wrapped around his breeches caught fire.

Everything happened at once. The stranger yelped in pain and reached down. Sarra dropped, struck a table and rolled to the floor. Edmund sprang for the book. The stranger snarled and produced a long, thin knife.

"Edmund, back!" Harman rounded the tables and charged,

knocking Edmund aside over a bench. Edmund tripped, struck the floor and saw stars.

"Run, Edmund!" His mother tried to pull him up and flee with him. He shrugged her off and gained his feet—and found his father swaying over the burning straw with the stranger's knife stuck in his gut.

The stranger staggered over to the table, grabbed up the book and turned to run. Edmund's father toppled down into the rushes. Sarra shrieked out his name.

"Father!" Edmund leapt over the growing blaze to kneel at his side.

"Oh, no." Sarra stumbled near, already weeping. "Oh, no, no, no."

Edmund rolled his father over onto his back and leaned in to inspect the wound. Harman gasped and choked, his hand clamped over a dark stain on his shirt.

"Help!" Edmund leapt out onto the road. "Please, someone help!"

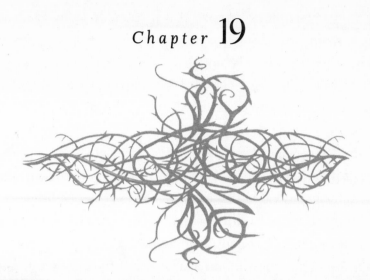

Chapter 19

The village bell clanged out, loud enough to be heard for miles. Troops of castle guards tramped the roads outside—they shouted to each other to mark the time, to announce and report that they could find nothing. The neighbors were gone, home to worry and wonder for themselves. They had gripped Edmund's shoulder, told him to be brave, told him that his mother needed him. Someone had even called him master of the house—he could no longer remember who it was, only that he had nearly punched the man.

He took a stick and poked at the embers, stirring them up hot again. The fire gave him something to do. Moans sounded from upstairs, his mother speaking low and soft amidst the mutter of the healers. Lamplight shifted through the gaps in the floorboards above.

The bloodstains were far too much to bear. They ran in spatters up the stairs where they had carried Edmund's father, up to his bedroom to survive or not. Edmund stood over the place where his father had fallen, offering silent bargains—*spare him, spare him, let him live and I swear that I will be a good son.* He reeled back across the empty tavern and sat down before the fire. He tilted his head into his hands. *Spare him.*

The door opened. Edmund covered his face. "We're closed."

Someone stepped inside.

Edmund turned. "I said—"

Katherine stood in the doorway. She wore her embroidered shirt, breeches and riding boots. The light of the fire made a halo from the careless wisps of her hair. She carried a leather pack over one shoulder and saddlebags over the other. Ropes bound a round shield tightly to the pack, crossed by her uncle's sword.

She set down her things. "How is he?"

"They don't know yet."

Katherine touched her foot to the burned, sodden circle on the floor. "Papa's gone."

"Gone?" Edmund wiped at his eyes with his sleeve. "Gone where?"

"Up into the Girth. Hunting for the Nethergrim." She seemed to tremble. "I need a place to stay."

Edmund stepped around the turned tables and the mess of discarded blankets from the night before. He reached down for Katherine's pack and hauled it over by the wall.

She held out a tarnished coin on the flat of her palm. "Is this enough for a few nights?"

Edmund just stared at it until she put it away.

They sat together by the hearth without speaking for a time. The noises around them grew in the silence. The fire licked and hissed; a log groaned, then split with a loud crack. The wind sang droning, and above them, rolling upward with every breath, moans and gasps grew in volume and pain until they became wails.

"Come on," said Katherine. "Let's get some air."

If the village hall of Moorvale seemed uncommonly old, the bridge that arched over the river at the eastern edge of the square was ancient beyond reckoning. It was massive out of all proportion with the modest wood-and-thatch houses that surrounded it—even Jarvis's handsome new mill seemed flimsy and ephemeral by comparison. The river ran deep and fast beneath its span, lulling and rushing by the banks in an endless half-musical drone, one note that changed with the moment and yet never changed at all.

Edmund hunched at the river's edge, watching eddies curl black below. "Have you ever felt as though the ground won't hold you up, no matter where you stand? Like you're sinking everywhere?"

"Yes." Katherine sat with her arms on her knees, her hair hanging loose across her face.

"I'm sick of waiting for the world to hurt me some more." Edmund felt about him on the bank. He found a smooth, flat stone and turned it over in his hands. "I want to do something."

"I made a promise," said Katherine. "I told my papa I would stay out of trouble. Even if I broke it, what would we do? We don't even know where to go, let alone what to do if we got there."

"He's my brother." Edmund flipped the stone into the water. It skipped once and plummeted.

"We're only fourteen."

"But we know things. We can do things."

"I made a promise." Katherine skipped a rock of her own. It skittered again and again across the water and disappeared into the dark.

Edmund sank over his arms. He could not cudgel what he remembered from the book into any sort of shape. "I can't. I just can't think anymore."

He sprawled back in the grass. Katherine lay down beside him. The wind blew cold along the riverbank. They moved closer so slowly, they did not know it until they touched shoulders.

Katherine turned her head. "You were very brave last night."

Edmund dug his fingers in the grass, and through it to the mud. The names of the constellations rose before him, then melted away, leaving stars.

"Papa will save them." Katherine sounded far away, and not very sure of herself. "He will."

• • •

Tom tensed, took his grip and hauled the axe over. The head caught and drove into the wood, running a split down to the end. He set his foot and pulled loose, turned and swung again, breathing heavy, round and even. The sound of every chop came back to him in echo, once and twice across the barren field.

The sun fled. The flapping sleeves of his overlarge shirt got in the way on the downswing, but it had gotten too cold to take it off. He made a pile by the stand of birch above the banks, dragging each limb down by the stream before he chopped it and then setting up the pieces by the charcoal pit for Aydon Smith to find. He took no pauses in between, for that would make his hunger worse.

Tom made his progress down into the dark, hauling by the place where the Dorham road crossed the stream. A magpie alighted in the branches of the alder nearest by. She watched him work—the last glimmers of the sun caught in her quick dark eyes. He raised the axe and brought it down, turned and set and did it all again, one breath into the next. The tensing was a part of him, the release, the pause and the hunger. Black spread from gray, quicker down where the growth was older, among the trees last lopped before he was born.

The magpie cackled and fled. Tom listened, then looked. He set down the axe. "Who's there?"

Hoofbeats sounded on the footbridge over the stream. A shape moved past on the Dorham road.

Tom leapt down to the banks. The horse stopped to drink on the far side of the stream. Even in the dying light the outline of an empty saddle stood out plain along its back—his back, a gelding or a stallion. Saddlebags hung from under the cantle, one closed, the other slashed and dangling open.

Cold dread seized Tom. He stepped onto the bridge. The horse raised his head to look at him.

"Oh, no." Tom reached out for the reins. "No."

Chapter 20

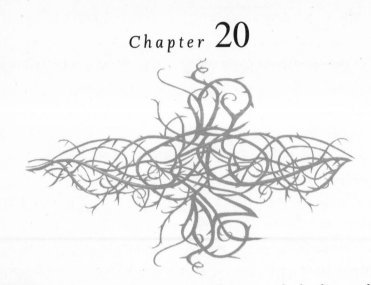

Tom raced down the Dorham road, leading John Marshal's wayworn horse as fast as he could go. He sprinted by the turn for his master's farm without the least precaution, hurrying past thick cover with no thought spared to the curious quiet. The horse gave a whinny of alarm too late—hands snaked out from the undergrowth to seize his shoulders, and then his master's face loomed from the darkness in hateful, hard-glittering triumph.

"You've done it now, boy." Athelstan croaked the words. "You've done it now."

Tom twisted to look behind him. Oswin held him fast by the arms.

"Stole a horse, did you?" Athelstan stepped out onto the road. He nodded to Oswin. "That's good work. If we hadn't caught him here, he'd be in Quentara by tomorrow."

"I'm not running away!" Tom twitched in belated struggle. "It's John Marshal's horse—Master, please, he's in trouble—"

"Leave the horse. Let John Marshal go a-hunting for him." Athelstan held out a hand to take Tom by the shirt.

Oswin jerked Tom back from Athelstan's reach. "That'll be a penny."

Athelstan scowled.

"A penny, or I let him go," said Oswin.

Athelstan reached into his belt and drew forth a coin. "Half a penny now, half when I'm done with him."

"Fair enough." Oswin shoved Tom forward with one hand and plucked up the coin with the other. He kept his face averted from Tom, his features set and grim.

The two men pressed in tight at Tom's sides and frogmarched him up to the farm. A lone candle burned in the window of the master's house. Moon-white faces peered out in its light.

Athelstan glowered, then glanced at Oswin. "Bring coals from the fire, and tell the women if I catch a light or a sound from that house when I am done, they will regret it."

"Coals? What for?" Oswin got no answer. He shrugged, let go of Tom's arm and strode over to the house. The candle snuffed and the window drew shut.

Athelstan took hold of Tom and shoved him through the door of the byre. Tom stumbled in the doorway and fell to his knees in the straw. A thick braided whip lay coiled around his tree-stump table. The sheep and oxen milled about at the back, bleating and mooing at the late disturbance, while the cats prowled belly-low in the corners, looking for a way out. Jumble rushed up to Tom, then past him, barking in fright at Athelstan's feet with his paws splayed out to beg.

"Please." The last of Tom's shock gave way to terror. "Master, please, I'm sorry. I won't do it again."

"Oh, that you won't." Athelstan picked up the whip and stretched the coils in his hands. "I'll make sure of it."

He dragged Tom over to one of the two rough posts that braced up the ceiling. A peg had long ago been driven into its side, high enough that a man could hang by his hands from it with his knees bent.

"It's been a while since you were kissing that post." Athelstan gave the whip a few experimental cracks. "I would have thought I taught you well enough then to mind your place. Mark me, boy—you'll learn this time."

Jumble could stand no more. He advanced in a storm of growling barks, jaws open wide in angry display.

"Shut your noise, you cur!" Athelstan cracked the whip across Jumble's muzzle. Jumble sprang whining to the back of the byre, scattering the ewes and lambs to all corners. Oswin stepped inside with a bowl of glowing coals in his hands and stood gaping at the mayhem before him. The cats seized their chance to bolt through the open door.

"Put down that bowl, you addle-pated jack-in-the-dirt!" Athelstan jabbed a finger into Oswin's gut. "Get the rope and let's get to it!"

Oswin set the bowl on the stump next to Tom. A look of regret spread on his pock-scarred features, but then it hardened into stony resolve. Athelstan stripped Tom's shirt from his shoulders, hauled him up and shoved him face-first against the post.

"Master, I was coming back," said Tom. "I was coming right back. I swear I won't do it again. I won't run, I promise."

The grating rasp Athelstan made bore only the most passing resemblance to laughter. "No, you won't be running again. But your promise is of no account." He placed something in the coals, something that rang when it struck against the side of the bowl.

Oswin grabbed hold of Tom's wrist and drew it up to the peg. Tom writhed and tried to slither away, but Athelstan seized him firm and squashed him against the post until he lost his breath.

"You ungrateful pile of filth." Athelstan's breath hissed warm across Tom's neck. "I took you in when you were nothing at all, just an orphan babe half dead of fever, covered in muck and wasting away in the reek of an alley. I clothed you, I fed you and raised you, and this is how you thank me."

"Please, Master. I'm sorry. I'm sorry! Please don't hurt me."

Athelstan grabbed Tom by the hair and jerked back his head. "I should have left you to die! Do you think I bought you out of kindness? Eh? Do you? Do you think when I picked you out of all the stinking brats for sale that day that I did it because of the way you looked at me? Eh? No, I picked you because all the other children for sale in the alley that day were girls. I needed someone to work in my fields, to learn from me, to gain by me, but every time my wife would swell in the belly, out would pop another girl, another milkmaid, another dowry to pay, so instead of a son I had to settle for you. That's why I chose you, boy—because I have no sons."

Tom stared upside down into his master's hard blue eyes. "I could have been your son."

"You are no blood of mine." Athelstan slammed Tom's head against the post. "You are property. You have no purpose in this world but to serve me and mine until you die."

He reached for what he had placed in the bowl. "I'm going to whip you, boy, you know that. But that's not all, not this time."

He held it in front of Tom's face—it glowed a dull red. "I'm going to brand you, like the stupid animal you are." He thrust it back into the coals. "You'll wear my mark for the rest of your days, and no matter where you run, the world will always know that you are mine."

Tom let out a hissing moan that sank into a sob. He felt Oswin's fingers move to tie the knot.

A growl rose to a snarl, and then a black-and-white shape slashed across the byre. Jumble leapt at the men, and this time sank his teeth deep into Oswin's arm. Oswin let out a yelp and staggered away from the post, waving his arms all about to try to shake off his attacker. He stumbled back amongst the sheep, startling them and sending them in a panicked surge for the open door.

"Back!" Athelstan struck at Jumble's muzzle, opening the cut he had made with his whip. Jumble cried out, dropped his tail and backed away. Oswin made a similar noise, clutching at his bleeding arm.

Athelstan jabbed a finger into Oswin's belly. "Get those sheep back in here, you twit, and kill that dog!"

"No!" Tom twisted around to look, to beg—and froze, hardly daring to twitch. The ropes that bound his hands had begun to give under his weight. He groped upward with his fingers—the top of the knot fell loose in his hands. Oswin had left it half done.

Oswin picked up a shovel from the corner and swung it like an axe. Jumble fought back with all his might, but was over-matched. After a few swings and dodges he retreated through the doorway with Oswin in pursuit.

Tom worked his thumb under the knot and pulled it open, then held his hands over the loosened ends of rope. He bowed his head against the post and drew in a long, slow breath.

"Now, boy." Athelstan came up close again. He let the coils of his whip trace down Tom's naked back—it was impossible to mistake the hungry quaver in his voice. "This time I swear to you that you will learn your lesson at last."

"I already have, Master."

Tom spun from the post and struck his master hard on the jaw, sending him sprawling back across the byre.

He raced outside to find Jumble at bay, cornered against the wall of the master's house with Oswin rearing up above him, shovel raised for one last crushing strike. He had never truly known rage before.

"Oswin!" His shout distracted his target for just long enough. He charged and leapt, throwing all his weight into a flying tackle. He slammed Oswin into the wall, seized the shovel and flung it far across the yard. There was no need to tell Jumble to follow. They streaked out onto the road together, leaping the footbridge before Athelstan could come out to start the hue and cry.

• • •

The hearth fire in the tavern spat and groaned. Edmund curled forward to shift the logs and sat back again.

"Have you slept?" Katherine sat beside him, still dressed, slumped in the other of the tavern's two proper chairs with her sword laid sheathed along her legs and her booted feet crossed at the ankles. She hardly moved, save for two fingers that tapped without rhythm on the hilt of the sword.

"No." Edmund crossed his arms, but he could not stop shivering. Every now and again his mind would grip on to something—a man serves the Nethergrim, a living man, a wizard—but then his thoughts would dislodge once again into the melting rush.

Katherine set down her sword and drew up a blanket on her shoulders. "They stopped the bleeding. He's got a chance. A good chance."

Edmund worked his hands together. He could not keep the question down. "Did you love your mother?"

Katherine stared at him. "Of course I did."

"Did you get to tell her, before— Were you there, at the end?"

Katherine turned to the fire. The roaring flicker danced in her eyes and tossed her shadow about the walls in looming triples. "I remember her just as I saw her last. Her hair, her eyes, her mouth. She tried to take my hand, but she was cold and sweaty, so I pulled away. 'I'll see you again, very soon,' she said, 'and when I do, all the world will be brighter.' Then they closed the door, she tried to give birth to my brother, and she died."

"I'm sorry," said Edmund. "I shouldn't have asked."

Katherine leaned over on her arm. "And whenever I hope, whenever I despair, there she is."

Edmund churned his hands in his hair. "What sort of world is this?"

Katherine opened her mouth to answer him—and closed it again. The flames found a seam of wet wood, seized upon it and brought it whining to ashes.

There came a frantic knocking at the door. Edmund crossed the room, pulled up the bar and opened it. Tom stood on the step, half naked and half broken, the cut on his forehead leaking blood into his eye.

"Tom!" Katherine threw off her blanket and rushed to the door. "Tom, what's happened?" She put her hands on his shoulders. "What has he done to you?"

"I've run away."

"I'll kill him." Katherine balled up her fists. "I will kill him!"

"Quiet." Edmund joined her at the door. "How far behind you are they?"

"I'm not here for me." Tom stepped aside. Behind him on the street stood a saddled horse with a long glum face, chestnut save for three white stockings. Katherine made a noise like she had been punched.

"I found him by the footbridge on the Dorham road," said Tom. "He was trying to get home."

Edmund slid past onto the step. It did not take a great horseman to see that John Marshal's stallion had been running all day.

"Papa." Katherine put her hands to her face. "Oh, no, no."

Edmund started moving before he knew what he had decided. He dove down to his hiding spot and dug out the last scrap of parchment he still owned. He seized his quill and inkhorn and brought the parchment back upstairs to the light of the fire. He set it on the table and started scribbling: *Dear Father—*

Tom looked down at the parchment, then up at Edmund. "What are you doing?"

Edmund reached for Katherine's sword and held it out by the scabbard. "I want you both to understand that I don't really know where I'm going—but I'm going. I'm going into the Girth to try to save Geoffrey, and the other kids, and John Marshal, if I can. It might be stupid, it might get me killed, but I am going, and you can come with me if you like."

Katherine stared at him, then seemed to come awake. She took the sword.

"Go to the kitchen and grab what you can find, but keep it

quiet." Edmund padded up the rickety stairs to his bedroom. He fumbled over to the trunk and pulled out a thick woolen tunic his mother had made for him the winter before. He slung his quiver onto his back and grabbed his longbow from the corner. He turned at the door, remembering his knife—then changed his mind and brought Geoffrey's.

He slipped back down to the tavern. "Got enough?"

"All we can carry." Katherine turned a pot of water over on the fire, then picked up her pack from the corner of the room. She pawed through it, dumping out belts, sets of hose and the blue dress she had worn to the fair, then started stuffing it with hasty bundles of food.

"Edmund?" His mother's voice came weak and weary down the stairs. "Edmund, what is going on down there?"

"Nothing, Mum." Edmund held the door open for his friends, then whispered as he shut it: "Goodbye."

• • •

The shadow of the statue in the Moorvale square stretched out long and faint down the road. The moon that cast it was a cat's-eye edging over a bank of high cloud, miserly with its light, cautious and sly. Another row of clouds crowded the opposite horizon, and between them, a funnel of air led up their raked walls to the great and lonely theater of the stars.

Edmund shoved the woolen tunic into Tom's hands. He grabbed the reins of the horse. "What's his name?"

"Berry," said Katherine.

"Tom can ride him." Edmund led Berry around to the door of the stables. He found Jumble waiting there, cut and bleeding across his muzzle but still wagging his tail.

"He's coming, too," said Tom. "He's got nowhere else to go."

Indigo stamped a hoof and snorted from the first stall past the door. Edmund had to duck under his head to pass by. He felt his way along in the dark to the stall at the end—Rosie's stall, a horse the color of dead blood, bought cheap at market by his father the year before to serve as the family riding mare.

Tom stood slack and shivering in the faint cut of moonlight by the door. "Where are we going?"

"Put that shirt on." Katherine grabbed her saddle and threw it over Indigo's broad back. "We'll get you clear of the village and then we'll work things out." Tom put his head through the neck of Edmund's shirt and shrugged it on. It fit well across the shoulders but was far too short in the arms.

"We should take the long way out of Elverain." Edmund pulled Rosie's dusty saddle off the rail. "Down the Longsettle road and over the cutoff by Woody End, then up the banks of the Swift. That might take us straight there."

"Papa took the West Road." Katherine reached down to fasten the girth under Indigo. "If he's trying to come back on foot, I don't want to miss him."

Edmund rummaged in the dark for Rosie's tack. "If we go that way, Tom's master might hear us going by and come after us."

Katherine slid her sword through the loops by the pommel. "He can follow us right up into the Girth if he likes."

Indigo lowered his head to let Katherine slip the bridle on. He stamped a hoof, impatient to leave. Jumble barked in reply.

"Then what?" Tom bent to quiet Jumble with a pat behind the ears. "Do we know where to look?"

"We have some guesses." Edmund fussed with Rosie's girth—every time he thought he got it straight, he found that he had twisted it on the other side. "We're looking for a high mountain valley with ruins in it, at a place where two rivers meet. There's more I can tell you on the road." Rosie turned her head and shrank from the bridle. She was easily three times Indigo's age, and looked much less eager at the prospect of a sudden departure in the middle of the night.

Katherine poked her head into the stall. "Edmund, are you ready?"

"Er—almost."

"Ride with it like that and you'll be riding under her soon enough." Katherine stepped in and bent to fix the mess he had made of Rosie's tack. "Come on, girl. Come." She clicked her tongue and coaxed Rosie from her stall. Indigo came out on his own. He ducked under the door and led them out to the road, then stopped, facing up into the square. He cocked an eye at Katherine and stamped. Jumble walked out in front and looked back at them, waiting with his odd-colored ears pricked up.

"Indigo says the West Road, too. That decides it." Katherine leapt into the saddle. Edmund dragged himself up onto Rosie's back on the second try. Tom had no more skill than Edmund did, but was so tall that his ungainly jump could hardly fail.

Clouds came in to claim the moon, leaving the village deep in darkness. Edmund looked to each of his friends, then up at the shuttered window of his parents' bedroom. There was nothing to be said. Indigo started at an eager walk, and the other horses fell into step—up the Longsettle road to the square, then around the old statue of the knight, and away.

Chapter 21

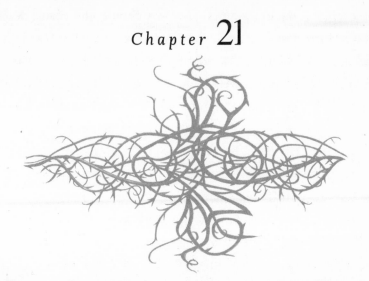

Katherine let Indigo pick their pace up the rising crests of the foothills. Neither Rosie nor Berry looked happy to keep up, but neither would they let themselves be left behind. Jumble seemed to find their progress rather too slow, for he raced up ahead, turned and scampered back to them again and again, traveling two miles for every one trod by the horses.

Trees drew in, oak and elm around the tiny hamlet of Thicket. The grange smelled of hay and threshing, the woodlot of hewed hardwood. Edmund expected a challenge, at least a call from Thicket manor, but all lay mute around them. No one stirred in the houses, no one came out to ask who passed in the dark.

"We're really going." It was Tom who said it.

They rode on through the Widows, past the rotted cottages and thrown fields and by the place where stood the battle marker and lay the long graves. The clouds had blown wide and left the moon alone in the sky. The dead commons of the old abandoned village lay to the left, straggled grass chased in silver light. Curled weeds and hardwoods ran the opposite edge of the road. Edmund drew out Geoffrey's long knife and looped it in his belt. Every shadowed stand of trees might hold an ambush. His heart beat for the thrill and the fear.

He drew level with Tom. "Have you ever been up here?"

"Never. What's that stone thing?"

"That's the cairn. This is the Widows—folk used to call it Byhill." Edmund swept a hand. "This is as far down as the Nethergrim came—last time."

"Oh—the Battle of the Potter's Field. That was here?"

Katherine pointed. "Just over there, behind the oaks."

"I like the song they made about it, even if it's sad." Tom looked out across the graves. "It's different, though, when you see it as a place."

The black line of the West Road rose on the foothills, driving its course up turns in the land as though its builders had thought it easier to move earth than to change direction. Oak gave way to pine, elm to spruce, crowding in around the bramble-choked tofts of cottages collapsing with the years beneath the twisting weeds. The last of the fields on either side of the road had been left unplowed for so long that it was hard to tell if they had ever been farmed.

"That's it," said Edmund. "We're clear of Elverain."

Tom breathed out. "I've run away." He looked behind him.

Katherine dropped back to ride abreast. "I'm glad you came."

"So am I." Edmund said it, and then felt how much he meant it. "You know, I should have thought—we could have brought him a weapon."

Tom shrugged his bony shoulders. "I wouldn't know what to do with it."

"We'll want to get far from settled country before we rest." Katherine reached out to touch Berry's neck. "How is he bearing up?"

"He's tired," said Tom. "He must have come a long way before I found him."

Katherine's features contracted in worry. "Papa." She twitched in her heels—Indigo needed little prompting to speed them to a trot again.

The clouds slid from the distant peaks of the Girth, opening the deeps of night. Jumble gave up his gambols and kept pace at Tom's side. Edmund fell back into his thoughts. Ahead lay his brother, somewhere amongst the black and jagged teeth of the mountains. Behind lay his father, in agony or already dead. His breath steamed out into a chill that deepened as he rose.

"Maybe we should try to plan things out." Tom drew level with his friends. "In those stories you like to tell, the heroes always seem to have some sort of plan."

Katherine sat up straight in her saddle. "We should. I'm forgetting everything Papa ever told me."

"We are on a perilous journey, after all," said Edmund. "What do you think your father would do in our place?"

"He'd say to keep a watch as we go." Katherine steered Indigo off to one side. "I'll take left and upward. Tom takes right, and Edmund, look and listen behind us as much as you can. And from now on ride with your longbow strung. A pack of bolgugs aren't going to sit by and wait for you to get ready."

"Yes, my captain." Edmund turned a smirk on Tom.

Katherine drew up the bind on her scabbard, putting her sword within easy reach. "We should make Upenough before dawn. From what I've heard, it's thirty miles on past Thicket, give or take."

"Oh." Tom peered up ahead. "I didn't know there were more villages up this way."

"There aren't anymore." Edmund craned around to watch behind him down the road. "Upenough marked the farthest border of the kingdom before the Nethergrim came. You've heard the story—it's where Tristan and Vithric first met."

"I always get the stories mixed together," said Tom. "I can never remember what happened where or when."

Katherine gave Rosie's head a gentle push to keep her from wheeling right around. "You don't need to sit backward, Edmund. Just look and listen over your shoulder."

"Oh—right." Edmund turned forward again, and after a reluctant moment so did Rosie. "After that we start searching for a valley where two rivers meet. There should be ruins there, too—some sort of grand fortress. Did your father ever tell you of a place like that?"

Katherine paced along in silence for a while. "I don't remember—from what he told me, there are dozens of ruins up here."

"Maybe if we look, we can figure out the same things Vithric did."

Her smile came weak, but it came. "If anyone ever could, Edmund, it's you."

"With the help of my bold companions, of course." Edmund turned to include Tom—and found him staring up ahead with his brows dropped low. Jumble bristled and let out a throaty growl.

"He smells something," said Tom. "So do I. A death smell."

Katherine drew her sword. Edmund did the same with Geoffrey's knife, then put it away again—what good was a knife from horseback? He gripped his reins. "What do we do?"

"Forward, slow." Katherine reached around to pull her shield off her back. "Watch every side, and don't say a word unless you need to. If I make a move, follow it."

Indigo blew out a snort, stepping high with his head arched forward. Edmund dug his heels into Rosie's flanks to keep pace. They followed the road up out of the trees and onto a ridge of barren ground, every breath taken sharp between their teeth.

Katherine nudged Indigo in between the other horses and half a length in front. Moonlight glinted off the boss of her shield. They rose through a meadow to find a new fold of mountainside, cut by a pass of a length that could not be guessed at in the dark. The farther they climbed, the farther away the peaks seemed to get.

"It's ahead." Katherine turned with the road, and as Edmund followed, the shapes of houses stuck out in shadow against the sky. The village of Upenough clung dead to a ridge over the last remove of useful land up the pass into the mountains, no more than a ragged run of hovels left to fall apart in silence.

The air hung thin beneath a sky dusted wide with stars. The land around them lay so still that the careful walking tread of the horses came back in dull echoes.

"This must be how Tristan felt." Edmund shot fearful glances left and right, expecting the glow of yellow eyes behind every tumbledown byre.

"Stop, everyone." Tom leapt from Berry's back, nearly tripping from the stirrups. He scrabbled into the weeds beside the road. Jumble followed him off into the dark.

Edmund hissed in fright. "What is it?" He tried to nudge Rosie over to look, but she cowered, ears flat along her head. Indigo shoved past, carrying Katherine to the large dark object next to Tom at the roadside. There rose a smell that made everyone retch.

"It's stiff." Tom rolled it onto its back—a bolgug. "Dead for a day or so."

Edmund kept his sleeve across his mouth. "What killed it?"

"A sword." Tom let its arm drop. "From above."

"From above?"

"From horseback." Katherine turned Indigo forward again. "If I remember the story, there was an inn somewhere. It's likely the only shelter left."

Tom scrabbled up and they pressed on, past weeded-over cow paths that would once have served as cross lanes, up toward a clump of huts bald of thatching and falling to bits under the shadow of a burned-out village hall.

"That one." Edmund pointed. "It's got a wooden roof, and I think that's a stable around back."

"Everyone down." Katherine brought them to a halt. "Tom, take the horses."

Edmund slid out of his saddle behind her. He drew Geoffrey's knife—the skin arched and prickled up his arms.

Katherine beckoned him over to the doorway. "Smell that?"

Edmund nodded—sick and sweet. More rot, more dead things.

Katherine pulled off her glove with her teeth, then took her sword in a fighting grip. "Ready? Here we go, then." She kicked the door—it came off its cracked leather hinges and fell inward. She went through with her shield up and her sword over its edge. Edmund followed at her back—and trod on something soft.

"What is that?" Katherine's voice rose and quavered from the dark. "Is it—?"

Edmund forced himself to kneel over the corpse. "No— another bolgug." He leaned out the door to catch a breath of good air. "Tom? Get a torch lit."

They fumbled farther in, feeling out against a haphazard row of trestle tables. "Seems like a tavern—can't see a thing." Edmund got a mouthful of cobweb. "Augh!" He spluttered and bent, hoping with all he had that he had not swallowed a spider.

"If anything wanted to ambush us in here, I suppose it would have by now." Katherine moved off across the room. "I found the hearth."

"I put the horses out back." Tom bent low to get under the sagging lintel. He stood up inside with a torch sputtering in his hand.

Katherine let out a cry.

Edmund turned, his stomach sinking. Katherine knelt over a sword lying on the hard-packed earth of the floor—plain and martial with a wide iron guard and a hilt wrapped in hide.

"Oh, no." Katherine picked it up—a piece in both hands. The blade had snapped a few inches past the guard. Edmund did not need to be told whose it was.

"That doesn't mean he's dead." He crouched at her side. "It doesn't." He caught sight of something small and blood-specked next to Katherine's foot and sucked in a breath. She read his face and looked down before he had decided how to tell her.

Katherine screamed and jumped away from the severed finger on the floor, a man's finger cut off at the first knuckle. Edmund bent low and looked around. He found no others, but amongst the stains of bluish black on the floor were some that were rusty red.

"Katherine." Tom grabbed her shoulder. "Katherine, look at me! The bolgug in the doorway was bludgeoned. Do you understand what that means?"

Katherine looked up at Tom.

"Your father survived—he got out." Tom paced around the floor. "He didn't bleed much in here. He got out right after he was wounded—he probably killed that bolgug on the way."

"But—why didn't he come home?" Katherine sat back on her haunches. "He was hurt."

"He wasn't finished," said Edmund. "Whatever he came up here to do, he was still going to do it."

Katherine heaved herself up onto a bench, still shaking. Edmund looked to Tom. "We stay here."

"Until dawn. We'll need to set a watch." Tom slid the torch into a sconce on the wall. "I'll go fix the door." He grabbed the dead bolgug by the feet and dragged it outside.

· · ·

The fire threw flickers on the steep-angled ceiling—faint ones, muted mottles cast by embers whose failing heat did little to ward off the draft from the door. Edmund rolled onto one side, then the other.

"Can't sleep?" Tom sat up in his bedding, faced out from the fire with one long arm stretched over his knee. Whipping scars crossed his naked back—some old, healed to white, others red and new.

"I guess not." Edmund propped himself on his elbows. Chill swept into the space between his chest and the bedroll beneath. They had encamped as close to the hearth as they could get. Katherine curled away on Tom's other side, sleeping on a pillow of her hair. She had put her bedroll down last, crushing Edmund's hopes that he might feel the warmth of her breath. Instead he got Jumble's breath—the dog had wormed himself in between him and Tom, and seemed to be having a dream where he was chasing something, for his paws paddled and scratched through the bedding. A dusty old hat lay discarded on the tavern floor—a shank of bone, an upended mug. Their shadows fell long behind them.

"It's strange to sleep in a different place." Tom reached to the nearest table. He felt around in his sack and pulled down a crust of bread. "I'm not used to it."

Edmund sat up. He nudged the unburnt edge of a log onto the embers. It did not catch.

"And no one's been back here?" Tom kept his voice to a murmur. "Not in all these years?"

"Not that I know about, not since the Nethergrim came. See these chairs?" Edmund nudged the closest one. "I'll bet Tristan and Vithric sat right here the night they met. The folk who made it with them down to Elverain never came back—never felt safe enough, I suppose. It looks like some of them left right in the middle of supper."

Tom gathered a handful of kindling that had fallen half burnt off the fire. He poked them one by one onto the flames. "I wish I had a brother like you."

Edmund looked at Tom. He did not know how to reply, so he rummaged through his bags and drew out an apple. "These are from the Twintrees. Always the best."

"If Katherine's father went on, he went on without a horse." Tom took the apple and bit in. "If we go the same way he did, we might catch up."

"I hope so." Edmund found himself repeating the words under his breath. He reached out and stroked Jumble's belly.

"He likes that," said Tom.

"Do you?" Edmund scratched some more. "Hey, boy?" Jumble opened his eyes and lolled his tongue.

Tom finished his apple—flesh and ends. He dropped the

MATTHEW JOBIN

seeds on the fire. "My master rented John Marshal's east field when I was five, for the price of one day's work from me every month. I counted out the weeks by the days that Master would send me over—I'd wait for them, dream about them. I'd gather chaff and John would thank me for it. I'd chop firewood and Katherine would come by with a mug of water. No one cursed me. No one hit me. Before they sent me home, they would feed me supper. It's the only time I ever ate at a table."

The fire died back. Tom fell into red shadow. "I can't bear to think he's dead."

Katherine turned in her sleep. Edmund forced himself to look away before Tom caught him staring. "I forgot to tell you on the way. The Nethergrim might still be alive."

"I'd guessed that much."

Edmund felt his fears loom up around him in the dark. "We don't know where we're going."

"I believe in you," said Tom. "You're the smartest person I know."

It almost made Edmund feel better. "You should get some sleep. I'll take a turn watching."

Tom lay back in the bedding. "I'll try."

Chapter 22

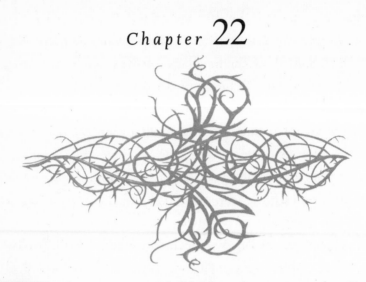

The last stars twinkled high and west over the Girth, giving way with each passing moment to the widening of dawn. Edmund turned at the side of the inn, and stopped. The whole of his world lay beneath him, lit to cold burning by the sunrise. The Dorwood stretched in endless, deathless green across the north; the West Road wound through the foothills and down through a patchwork of pasture and field. Past that, the sun sat red upon the moors, flooding the world in new light. The sight took his breath away—but the wind dug deep beneath his collar. He hurried around behind the inn and shouldered back the door of the stable.

"Breakfast." He held out the wooden bowl.

Katherine unbent from the stall farthest down with the currycomb in her hand. Her breath steamed out white in the cold. "You cooked?"

"There was a hearth, and dry wood, so why not?" Edmund

picked his way over broken tools, bits of wood and piles of hay dropped all about on the hard dirt floor. He found Rosie saddled and brushed, her saddlebags slung under the cantle.

"Oh, it's warm." Katherine cupped the bowl in her hands. Curls of wind found their way through the many cracks in the walls—they moaned in haunted harmony and set the flame of her lantern to wavering.

Edmund rummaged back through the stall for Rosie's bridle. "Brrr—drafty in here."

"It's draftier outside. I'm enjoying this while I can." Katherine spooned up the porridge. "This is delicious! How did you do it?"

"It helps that you brought my mother's whole store of herbs with you." Edmund dug a finger under Rosie's halter, but she did not want to leave.

"Oh—did I?" Katherine spoke with her mouth full. "It was dark."

There came a kick from the door of the next stall. "My lord calls for his carrot." Katherine reached into her bags. "Here, one for Rosie."

Edmund broke his carrot in half and held the pieces in his palm. Rosie twitched up her ears. He stepped back—she stepped out, looking at the carrot, then the door.

"I was just thinking when you came in." Katherine jingled the harness in her stall. "Tristan must have stabled Juniper right here, all those years back."

Edmund looked about him. He had never imagined the stables from that story as a grand place, but neither had he expected them to be quite so shabby. He felt a whiskered muzzle at his hand—Rosie nearly got her carrot for free.

"Papa always said that in the days that followed, Juniper did as much to save the folk of this village as anyone," said Katherine. "They say he trampled down dozens of bolgugs, that he charged at foul creatures when men lost their nerve—the second-finest horse ever born."

"Second?"

Katherine stepped out into the passage. "Second." Indigo walked after her, crunching on his carrot.

Edmund kept the carrot in his hands just out of Rosie's reach, using it to lead her outside. The stable door opened west onto a view of the peaks, their caps of snow going pink with the dawn. "How far is that?"

Katherine looked. "It's hard to say—I'm not used to land like this. Forty miles, maybe."

"Ugh." Edmund rubbed at his legs. "I'm still sore from yesterday."

They found Tom standing on a broken-down cart, looking east over the long descent behind them, back toward their home. He held Berry loose by the reins, letting him pick at the meager grass by the roadside.

Edmund opened his palm—Rosie dove for the carrot. "Saying goodbye?"

"Making sure no one's following us." Tom turned and swung his leg from the cart—he looked like a stork, but he got himself up into the saddle without trouble.

"Did you have some of this porridge?" Katherine dug out another spoonful from the bowl.

"It was very good." Tom turned Berry around to face the rising road. "I liked the thyme and the parsley."

"Edmund's got his mother's touch." Katherine looked around her, then set the empty bowl on the cart. Jumble took that as his cue to swoop in for the dregs.

"We'll have to keep our eyes open for any place the road might split." Edmund put a foot in the stirrup and sized up the leap into the saddle. "Or a river, any one of them might—hold still, Rosie. Rosie! Hold still!"

Rosie rolled a look at him and pinned her ears back. Edmund hopped on one foot, following her shuffle to the side. "Stop that!" He put a hand on her withers to try to hold her in place. "She always does this."

"You can use the cart, Edmund." Katherine got Indigo's bridle on. "Tom did."

"No, no. I know how." Edmund tensed his back leg. This time he would get it right, out in the daylight where Katherine could see it. He lowered down and sprang for the saddle.

Rosie shifted in the middle of his leap, leaving Edmund to waggle his leg in the air and crash back to the ground. "Ow!" He yanked his foot from the stirrup. "You stupid old affer!" Rosie dropped her head and danced away.

Katherine reached down to help him up. "Don't worry, it takes time to learn." It could not have felt worse if she had laughed and kicked him. Her touch meant nothing if she thought him a runt, good for making porridge, a weedy little boy who was just like his mother.

"I don't know what I'm doing wrong." Edmund crossed his arms. "She just hates me."

"Move slower around her." Katherine caught the reins and looped them back over Rosie's head. "Speak soft as you come near, and always keep a hand on her side when you move past her rump."

"You don't do any of that with Indigo."

"Rosie's not Indigo."

"She's afraid of you," said Tom as he walked Berry nearby. "She's had a hard life. When you get angry, she thinks you're going to hit her."

Edmund felt heartily sick of Tom and his bumpkin wisdom. "Oh, how do you know that? We only bought her last year!"

"It's in her walk," said Tom. "It's in her face. She flinches when men raise their voices. Whoever owned her before your father treated her very hard."

Edmund looked back at Rosie. "Oh. Well—I didn't mean to hurt her." Rosie regarded him in tense suspicion, then let him run his hand along her broken-down withers. After a while she turned to push her nose into his palm, something he could not remember her ever doing before.

"I'll make a horseman of you yet." Katherine knelt with her fingers laced. "Step in."

Edmund could not think of how to refuse. He put a foot in Katherine's hands and let her raise him onto Rosie's back.

Katherine made the leap into Indigo's saddle look so easy

that a child could do it—even though Indigo was three hands taller than Rosie. She started them off at a walk, through what would once have passed for the center of the village. Rosie made up her mind to follow close at Indigo's flank, while Tom let Berry amble behind. They passed the burned-out husk of the village hall in silence, then ascended into the arms of the pass.

"I can see why they called this place Upenough." Katherine glanced back over her shoulder. "Look at that!"

Her voice echoed back, once and again—and again. Edmund turned to look just as they crested the rise. He caught one last glimpse of his home—he thought of his father, made a silent wish—then Rosie paced on for another stride and it was gone.

The valley they entered dropped before them for a hundred yards, then rose on a southwest curve—a long scar up the side of the Girth with walls of spruce and fir folded into slopes that split and ran and split again as they descended to meet the road. Trees thinned to copses and then stands, dotted out to lone adventurers and then gave way to open green that ran to gray and then to white. Edmund breathed in air sharp with chill and the resin of trees, empty of all else save the scents of rock and dry dirt.

"If it weren't for the road, I'd think we were the only people ever to have come here," said Katherine. "The only people in the world."

The sun rose at their backs, glinting with sudden fire off the far snow on the summits. Sweat broke along the shoulders of the horses. Pine and spruce crowded in along the road, hanging their branches so that the riders had to duck from time to time to avoid a face full of needles. The action of their roots had conspired with the work of long years to shift the ground beneath, laying bare the broken edges of tight-laid stonework under grass and earth. The top of the pass came into view far above, a bare saddlebow of rocky ground between a pair of white peaks.

Tom drew in a long breath through his nose. "I could live up here."

They found their guard of spruce trees falling back as they climbed, defeated by the chill and the height. The road ran lonely through a whispering sweep of bristle grass. The sun passed its zenith and began its fall.

"We should have seen him by now." Edmund waited until Katherine had gotten a few lengths ahead before he whispered it to Tom, but the wind chose that moment to fall off to nothing.

Katherine shot them a glance over her shoulder. She pressed the pace, craning up at every rise and then slumping down again, lower each time.

They ate in the saddle, unwilling to rest while their horses could still carry on. Even Indigo started to tire—he breathed loud and hard, his head swaying down with every stride. Edmund could not find a way to sit that could ward off the worsening sores from his saddle. After a while it was all he could think about, that and the cold.

"What is it?" said Tom.

"It's my legs." Edmund reached down to rub a hand on the

inside of his thighs. "It's—everything. Everything hurts." He would say no more of it with Katherine so near, but he wondered to himself why riding horses was not the exclusive domain of women.

"No." Tom pointed ahead. "What is *that?*"

Edmund looked up. Katherine had stopped a few lengths up the road. Some distance past her—it looked close, but was as likely as not still a mile off—was something made of stone, something taller than a house.

"Everyone off." Katherine jumped to the ground. "The horses can't help us up here."

Edmund slid from his saddle. He drew out his longbow and slung his quiver on his shoulder. He could not quite catch his breath, though it might just have been the mountain air. Tom took the reins of all the horses. It seemed to take a year to reach the stone structure, for it was in truth quite far away—and much taller than a house, easily as tall as a castle tower. The road approached on a long loose curve, turning to run straight up to one side—and through. It was an arch.

Katherine strapped her shield to her arm. "Edmund, nock an arrow."

The arch stood out alone on a shoulder of slope, near to nothing and a gate to nothing. Edmund found himself ducking under it though the blue-gray lintels were three times his height above. He looked up under the passing expanse—it was not one arch, but four, a building supported by great corner columns that held up a vaulting roof. Carvings remained on the ceiling, sheltered from the worst of the weather. A row of men posed in a line that wrapped the borders—one wore the horns of an elk, another perhaps the skin of a bear. They presented themselves one by one before another man. This man held a star and a dagger, the star out, the dagger up. The point of the blade pierced a cloud between two disembodied hands. Around and below danced other forms. They were not men.

"I don't like it." Tom would not come in—neither would Jumble or the horses. "I don't like those carvings, or the men who carved them."

Katherine passed by Edmund. "Oh, no." She peered out each entrance of the arch. "Which way?"

Edmund turned all about him. North, west, south—one guess to make from three. Each road led off into wild nothing, westward over a snowy pass and the other two directions through scraggy mountain meadow. Nothing he could see outside the arch told him anything of use. In all the stories of all the great heroes he had ever heard, the hero never fails simply because he cannot find the villain. It was intolerable.

What would Vithric have done? Edmund let his mind go still. From all that he had ever read, Vithric was not the sort to let his feelings get in the way of his thoughts. Vithric would have stopped shaking his fist in frustration and started sorting through what he knew, pondering the facts before him until he found a solution.

"If we want to figure this out, we have to work out what these folk were thinking when they made this place." Edmund returned to the center of the arch and looked at the carvings above him. "We have to try to think like they did."

Katherine followed at his side. "We have to think like a bunch of scary old dead people who served a horrible monster?"

"We do." Edmund lay on his back. "This was once a crossroads, a place people might have passed through every day. This was made for them, not us."

"That's horrible to think." Katherine sat down against one of the posts. "What must it have been like, living your whole life under the Nethergrim? Do you think they all wanted to live that way—that they were evil themselves?"

"I don't think they were," said Edmund. "Even when a whole kingdom goes bad, some people will still try to be good—and many more will just get used to things, try to live their lives without getting into trouble."

Katherine grabbed for a fluttering wisp of her hair and worked it back into her braid. "I hope I wouldn't give in."

"I don't think you would." Edmund smiled. "Katherine the Outlaw."

"Katherine the strung-up-by-her-toes, I'd bet." She gazed up. "We have to choose right, or we might never find Papa and the kids in time."

Edmund squinted at the carvings on the ceiling, trying to tease out the meaning of the symbols wound all around the lintel blocks, but there were far too many—more than he had ever seen, even in the book. He could hardly read one out of ten.

"Those four, one to each direction, they're much bigger than the rest." Katherine pointed with her sword. "If this is a crossroads, maybe they say where to go."

Edmund looked. "They might."

"So—north. What's that one?"

"I can only say what I think it means," said Edmund. "I don't know how it's supposed to sound."

"How it sounds doesn't matter. What it means might."

"That one says Brown-Harm-of-Bees."

Katherine looked at him. "Brown-Harm-of-Bees?"

"A bear." Tom's voice floated from outside.

"Right—right!" Edmund clapped his hands together. "Tom, that was clever!"

"Thank you." Tom tossed a stick for Jumble to fetch.

"So that's how they do things." Katherine crossed her arms. "They make symbols that don't quite say what things are."

"Maybe that way was wilderness," said Edmund.

Katherine looked north. "It certainly is now. What's the symbol for east, the way we came?"

Edmund turned. "Village-Slaves-Wheat."

"So where we live was the best farmland. West?"

"I'm not sure I've got it right—Center-Exalted-Thousand-Men."

"That sounds promising." Katherine sat up to look. "And it does go over the pass. What about south?"

Edmund looked. "That-of-Goodness."

"That-of-Goodness?" Katherine looked at it. "Well, that can't be it. I'd say west, then. Looks like we have some more climbing to do."

"Wait." Edmund stared at the southern symbol. He looked back at the picture of the procession coming before the big man. "I remember from the book, the wizard wrote about two centers, two places. One was their great city, the other was some special place, reserved to the highest men, the Gatherers."

"But wouldn't the Nethergrim be at the center, if they built a kingdom around it?"

Edmund pointed. "Look at the picture—see the big man? That is He-That-Speaks-From-The-Mountain. Now, see how he's looking up? The Nethergrim's the pair of hands." He felt a surge of certainty. "The great king of the kingdom took his tribute from the little men in the procession, but he got his power from something else."

Katherine stood up. "Why wouldn't they show the Nethergrim, if it was the source of all their power?"

"I don't think most of these folk even knew what the Nethergrim looked like. There were orders of men who ruled above the rest, who learned the hidden truth. He-That-Speaks-From-The-Mountain is a king, but he is also a servant, a sort of emissary of the Nethergrim. The Nethergrim's secret is part of his power, known only to the mighty few."

"Hunters, farmers, warriors, mothers and craftsmen." Katherine turned with the procession above her. "All bringing gifts to the big man—who's probably not really a giant, he's just drawn like that because he's important. I'll bet in real life he was short."

"If you're the big man, then you owe the Nethergrim your place in life." Edmund stepped south into the open and took Rosie's reins. "If you're one of the little men, then the Nethergrim is a hidden force, the unseen power behind the throne.

It could be anywhere, anything. It could be listening when you curse it under your breath. You don't dare to speak the truth."

Katherine hesitated, looking out the western arch. "Edmund, are you sure?"

"I'm sure." Edmund put one foot in the stirrup. Rosie gave him no trouble at all.

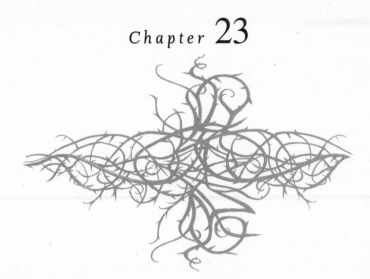

Chapter 23

The road was a ghost, a trick of the eyes. There was not so much as a wagon rut to mark its course, no breadth of flattened earth. It seemed no more than a lucky run of turns over broad and rippled ground—but at each bend, each place where it became a question of which line of land to follow next, there stood another stone that looked just like the Wishing Stone back home, worn smooth by endless wind and unnumbered rains. Katherine rode watchful, her back up and tight, one hand on the reins and the other bearing her shield at the ready.

Edmund looked back. They had come down crossways to the falling sun, from the heights of the pass into a long vale that dipped low enough to allow a run of trees along its bottom. The wind blew sharp and westerly, tossing crumpled clouds across the sky and hissing down between the summits to rip along his cheek.

"Look." Tom leaned from his saddle to point. Through a gap in the trees far below, Edmund caught sight of water, a band of twinkled silver winding through the green.

Edmund lost sight of it in the trees again. "It's a bit small for a river, isn't it?"

"It will turn into a river if we keep following it," said Tom.

"But is it the right river?" Katherine could not answer her own question. Neither could the others.

They passed another arch—Edmund beneath, his friends around. Men came in a cringing procession before an empty throne. A pair of hands hung above it, carved as though they floated in the air—long, thin hands holding star and dagger. The big man stood on the other side of the throne, dressed in might. He held a symbol—a letter, a crooked loop with spines. Edmund squinted at it—Death-Craft-Provide-Thousand-Seasons. The meaning teased at him, almost resolved into a thought.

"Are those bolgugs?" Katherine steered Indigo in beside the arch. "Right there, in front of the throne."

"They are—and other things. I think that's a stonewight." Edmund examined the scene awhile longer. "And they're in front of the throne, faced away, toward the little men. They don't bear gifts, either."

"They're guards," said Katherine. "His army."

"Men serve the Nethergrim, and so the Nethergrim's creatures serve the men." Edmund reined Rosie back—she seemed to hate the arches as much as Tom did. "That gives them the power to rule over other men, many others, and to destroy anyone who opposes them. Look at all those dead men off to the side."

"And those ones, over there—they're having their hands cut off, and those ones—ugh!" Katherine turned away.

"I can read some of this." Edmund followed the symbols carved farthest in and away from the wind. He read along, skipping over the parts he could not make out: "'Their men I took captive . . . of some I cut off their feet and hands, others their noses and lips, still others I blinded. I made a trophy of their chieftains' heads, in tribute to That-of-Goodness . . . their women I took to make my wives . . . their city I leveled to the ground, their fields I sowed with salt, in service to That-of-Goodness . . .'"

Edmund stopped reading. A shiver worked its way up his back. "They carved this into stone." He shared a look of horror with Katherine. "They were proud of it."

"We should find shelter soon." Tom had let Berry pace on ahead. "It's going to get very cold tonight."

"It doesn't feel that bad." Edmund lingered at the edge of the shelter. "These pictures might help us figure out if we're going the right way."

Katherine nudged Indigo back into the open. "I'm listening to Tom. He's the one who sleeps outside half the year."

A valley folded out beyond the arch. Spurs of mountain crossed to end it, but the road did not climb them. It led down and down to the floor of the land, down from bare mountain into folds thick with trees, down over roots twined in roots and farther down through a gully and into a gawping mouth.

The river—for it had gathered enough rivulets and streams to earn itself the name—flowed in at a foaming rush. The road ran beside it, a hard stone path bounded on one side by water and the other by a wall.

"Look at this place! It must have been shaped, somehow." Edmund peered inside the tunnel, and then around him. More symbols marked the stones that braced the entrance—Suitable-Gatherers-Goodly, and Household-Exalted. He twitched in his knees—Rosie would not go in until Indigo led.

The light of evening spilled in across the carvings on the tunnel wall beside him, another line of men bearing gifts. The men wore feathers, wolves' heads, death masks. They raised their arms in groveling salute.

"There's a bit of color left on these." Edmund reached out to touch, then drew back from the coating of muck and slime.

"Edmund, watch about you!" The river drowned the echoes of Katherine's voice. "Keep on your guard."

Rosie crunched something underfoot. She let out a snort and leapt aside, nearly throwing Edmund from the saddle. "Steady, girl!" He put his arms around her neck. "Steady!" He peered down.

Bones. Many bones.

Katherine struck a light and set tinder to torch. She held it up in her sword hand, then sucked in a gasp. Indigo crushed a skull beneath his hoof. The faces in the walls loomed and leered.

"Please, girl." Edmund felt the panicked arch in Rosie's back.

"Steady." He swung out a leg and dropped to the ground. Bones clacked and scattered across the floor.

"Is this place a grave?" He knelt to pick one up—it flaked and crumbled in his hand. "Remember what the book said—the graves of the children, the victims laid all in rows."

Katherine dismounted and felt around at her feet. "None of these are children, and they're not laid in graves." She held up a leg bone. "The bones of grown men—and other things, all jumbled up."

"The tunnel ends ahead." Tom reached the edge of their torchlight. "There's wind."

"There was a battle here. Long ago." Katherine picked up something round—a helm with a spike on top. A piece of it broke off and clattered to the floor. "This is bronze."

Edmund reached into his pack for a torch. He lit it from Katherine's and looked about him. The light found other shapes amongst the bones—a spearhead, a buckle, a shield shaped like no shield he had ever seen before. Green tarnish clung like moss to all of it, and almost nothing could survive being picked up or touched. Even the shield, a massive curved rectangle that was almost Edmund's height, crumbled in half when he tried to move it. The skull beneath it rolled away, its jaw came off—two rows of needle teeth.

"This is ancient, all of it." Edmund sat back on his haunches. "This kingdom came to an end—maybe it was overthrown."

"And good riddance." Katherine stepped back along the tunnel. "Look how this lies—where we stand it's all a muddle, but on our way in it's mostly the bones of men. Then farther on it's more bolgugs. They must have been the first line of defense. Then—I don't know what sort of thing has bones like that, and I never want to know. Most of them fell faced the way we're going, as though they were in retreat. That means the men won, the monsters lost, and then—Edmund! Look at this."

Edmund followed with his torch. The bones grew in number, piled over themselves in heaps, until he reached a place where they lay shored up against a pair of enormous, fallen plates of bronze.

"Doors." Edmund brought his torch up close. They had been thrown from their hinges to lie atop a mass of crushed bones and armor.

"It's all right, Jumble." Tom slid from his saddle in the darkness behind them. "I'm here, don't be scared." The horses whinnied, first Rosie and then Berry.

"This was a gatehouse." Katherine looked around her. "If you were trying to go south, this would be the only way. Whatever's on the other side would be very well guarded, at least from the north."

"We're following a river," said Edmund. "The book said that the Nethergrim can be found in a valley where two rivers meet."

"I think you steered us right." Even in the belly of the tunnel Katherine's smile made Edmund sing inside. She moved off across the bone-strewn tunnel and handed her torch to Tom. "Let's keep going. I don't think I could rest in this place."

"Just a moment." Edmund turned back to the wall and held his torch close enough to see the carvings. The shelter of the tunnel had preserved even more color there than near the entrance, giving them clear and sickening detail. They looked to be scenes of praise for He-That-Speaks-From-The-Mountain. In one picture he held an axe in one hand and the head of a man in the other. His army had been carved small about him—the hands of the Nethergrim floated above, opened wide as though to bless the event.

Edmund stepped along the wall, fascinated and repulsed all at once. He-That-Speaks-From-The-Mountain took tribute, dispensed hard justice, commanded and was obeyed. He led armies, both man and monster, and stood above them all, lightning-handed, seeming to slay whole nations from afar. He held out an arm at granaries full to bursting. He made signs and rain fell, others and the sun shone. The people rejoiced and fell in worship at his feet. The hands of the Nethergrim framed every scene, sheltering allies and pointing at enemies.

"Who were you?" Edmund held the torch up close—the slant of its light caught and changed the carven faces, making them seem to leer down at Edmund from the corners of their eyes. For a moment he recoiled, unable to shake the fear that He-That-Speaks-From-The-Mountain was about to peel himself from the wall and come for him.

The next scene along took his breath.

"The star, with the children on it." Edmund was not sure his friends had heard him over the noise of the river, so he said it louder. "The star, it's here!" He turned, and found that he had come far along the tunnel—the flame of Katherine's torch looked like a candle, and all between was dark.

"We should leave." Tom's voice barely rose above the rush. "This place—I don't like it."

"I'll bet you anything the places beyond it are worse." Katherine took the reins of the horses. "Edmund, let's go!"

"Come see this!" Edmund raised his torch. The carving of He-That-Speaks-From-The-Mountain shifted in its aspect, seeming once again to gaze up at the Nethergrim in feral and expectant joy.

"I feel like someone's watching us." Tom came first, leading Berry and holding Katherine's torch. Jumble followed, winding in between Tom's feet with his tail dropped low.

"It's just the carvings." Edmund tried to make his voice sound braver than he felt. "A trick of the light, you know."

"What did you find?" Katherine brought Rosie and Indigo, one lead in each hand and her shield slung on her shoulder.

"This." Edmund turned back to the wall. "Look."

"That's the picture from your book! The children on the star."

"The same picture exactly—it's as though someone drew it while looking at this." Edmund's torch spat and guttered low. Rosie whinnied and pawed at the floor, knocking a bone sliding along it. Jumble started growling, but it broke into a whine.

Tom turned back and forth behind his friends. "Someone is watching us. I'm sure of it."

"Hold that steady!" Edmund peered up closer to the wall. "See that symbol, there in his hands?"

           MATTHEW JOBIN

Katherine followed him. "I thought that was a weapon."

"It's a word." Edmund traced it with his finger. "*Death-Craft-Provide-Thousand-Seasons*. And look, it's there on the star. See how he's looking up to the Nethergrim with his arms raised? It gives him the power to do something to the children." The answer teased at him and danced away.

"It certainly doesn't look like he's about to eat them for dinner." Katherine took the torch from Tom's hand. "What are those, over there?"

Edmund looked. "Numbers, next to symbols I can't read—place-names, I think."

"Which numbers?" Katherine moved her torch from right to left.

Edmund had no choice but to follow—his own torch had fallen to the strength of a rushlight. He looked closer. "The top one says 515."

"And this one?"

"498." Edmund blinked. "Oh."

He read on down with the flame. "Then 476, 453, 428—the numbers from the book. These must be village names beside them! It's all part of the same scene—I think these are the years when the spell was done. Yes! See? There's space for more entries."

Jumble started barking—the terrified noise of it came back again and again across the channel of the river. The horses were no better—even Indigo snorted and stamped.

"They're afraid." Tom looked left and right. "They think something's coming. So do I."

"We should go," said Katherine.

"Wait—wait, I've almost got it!" Edmund traced his fingers on the wall: "He-That-Speaks-From-The-Mountain serves the Nethergrim and builds a kingdom with its help. Every twenty years he takes seven children before it and casts a spell that kills them, a spell marked *Death-Craft-Provide-Thousand-Seasons—*"

Understanding came like cold water down his neck.

"Life." He turned to Katherine. "Endless life."

"Oh. Of course." Katherine gazed up in horror at the carvings. "Twenty years—long enough for a young man to start growing old and want to be young again."

"The greatest gift of all," said Edmund. "What better reward for the Nethergrim's most faithful servant?"

"Good! Very good—well done, indeed. I was only a little quicker to grasp it myself."

Edmund dropped the torch. The voice spoke from an arm's reach beside him, and in a sickening rush he came to know that he had heard it before.

"It was Edmund, was it not?" The man sounded older than he looked—a strong chin shaven smooth, and a pair of hard, cruel eyes that drank the torchlight. "And how very thoughtful! You brought me just what I needed."

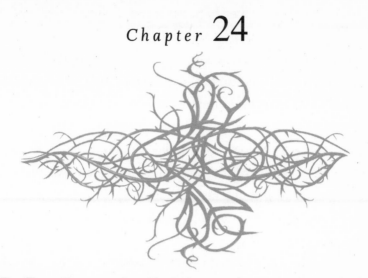

Chapter 24

"What a stroke of luck this is." The stranger's teeth were rather bad. "I had been preparing to mount a whole new expedition to get my seven—but here you are."

Katherine drew her sword. "Tom, Edmund, run!"

"Run? From me?" The stranger raised his hand—the world began to rend, the top and bottom halves of Edmund's vision sheared apart. Then it stopped, and Edmund found himself swaying where he stood. The stranger crouched before him, bent to retch out blood onto the cavern floor.

"You—!" Fury woke in Edmund. He raised his torch to bash it over the stranger's head—but something massive knocked him aside before he had a chance to bring it down. Rosie let out a squeal as she bolted past, shoving Edmund to the wall and nearly trampling the stranger. Flapping footsteps approached before and behind—bolgugs armed with clubs and spears, gnashing their long needle teeth.

The stranger staggered back out of reach. "Bring them down!" The bolgugs brayed as one and charged.

"Edmund, if you know any more spells, now is the time!" Katherine stabbed out and slashed across the first of the bolgugs, driving them back and giving Tom a moment to snatch up a piece of one of the old, broken shields from the ground. Indigo let out a bellow and reared. Edmund looked around him at the river, heard the turning point of its rush. Pages of the book flashed through his memory, a spell he had read only once and never even thought to try. Words formed—he raised his hands—

He felt the force of a strike to his shoulder, then a weight dragging on his back—then the pain. He stumbled to his knees.

"Edmund!" Katherine's voice was half shout, half scream. "Tom, Edmund's down!"

She darted to the flank, coming in over the brandished sword of a bolgug to jam her blade into its mouth.

"No! Hold—do not kill!" The stranger's voice came torn. "Leave them alive!"

Edmund gasped, collapsed amongst the bones. His right arm would not move. He turned—he had never heard of anything like what he saw. It loomed up red, a hundred jointed legs without a head or a face. Spiky barbs projected everywhere, each tip seeming to bear dozens of smaller ones, all waving and grasping from a middle that seemed made of reflections of itself that fell forever down. Another barb shot forth—it struck Berry in the flank and sent him in a galloping panic down the tunnel.

"HOLD, I SAY!" Light flared purple-dark. The red thing

MATTHEW JOBIN

scuttered back from sight. The stranger fell to a seizure of retching, and sagged against the wall.

Edmund reached back. He tried to jerk the barb free and nearly passed out from the pain. He dragged himself up—he could not breathe all the way in.

"Take them—alive."

The bolgugs pulled back and circled, spears over swords, narrowing in around Edmund and his friends.

Jumble bared his fangs and growled. Indigo kicked out and smashed a bolgug into the wall. For a moment it seemed they had a chance—then Tom took a hard chop across the piece of shield he held and pitched down to the floor. The torch went out—the world around Edmund exploded in clangs and snarls. Something stepped on him, then kicked him.

The worst, the very worst of all was the sound Katherine made as she fell.

"NIGHT IS DAY." A pair of eyes glowed white. The stranger advanced, the rest of his form in shadow. "Gather them up, and kill that horse."

Edmund backed away, trying his best to stay silent. The river roared ever louder in his ears, running to foam beneath the bank just behind him. He felt something bubbling in his throat. A thunderous whinny sounded in the passage, then the grating calls of the bolgugs.

"Where's the last one?" The stranger's eyes roved—then fixed on Edmund. "Ah."

Edmund drew in all the air he could. He turned and threw himself into the river.

• • •

"You are fifteen, perhaps?"

Katherine did not answer. She felt the change in slope, then the widening of echoes. Light shone down the grade, the red sunlight of day's end.

"Or possibly younger." The wizard angled in beside her. "I have never been much of a judge of such things."

Katherine tried to raise her head enough to look at him. The bolgugs had bound her hand and foot and slung her over Berry's back. Her shield arm was almost numb—where it was not numb, it burned and throbbed. She felt a grinding when she tried to bend the elbow.

She let herself fall limp. "Where is Edmund?"

"The little blond boy?" The wizard rode a shaggy, shy little mare. "Dead in the river by now, I'll wager. No matter either way. I have my seven."

He reached down and brushed back her hair from her face. "Not yet a woman. Young enough for my purposes."

Katherine tried to squirm from his touch—a bolgug seized her by the leg and held her firm. Another loped along with Berry's reins in its claws, keeping pace with ease. They rode out under the waking stars, high up the side of somewhere dark and vast, somewhere that made voices come back as though another group of people just happened to be saying the same things far away. Berry walked on tired but afraid, carrying both Tom and Katherine over his back with the high step of a horse unsure if he should try to bolt.

"Let me go or my papa will make you sorry." Katherine could have laughed at herself for saying it.

"Oh, ho, are we indeed to start all that?" The wizard let her head drop against Berry's sweaty flank. "Very well—it is a long ride. No, little girl, whoever your papa might be, there is nothing left for him to do but weep and mourn."

Katherine tried and tried to think of brave things to say. Tom shifted his bound hands and took one of her fingers between two of his.

"How touching," said the wizard. "Was this boy your promised one? Your betrothed, perhaps?"

"I am her friend," said Tom. "And there's no need to ask how old I am, because I don't know."

"You are not finished growing, that is all I care about. What are you looking at?"

"The trees."

The wizard laughed—coughed, then spat on the road. "Holding on to something?"

"You cannot take my thoughts away."

"Oh, I can take everything away."

Katherine did not want to say it. She thought she had won out against herself, but then she heard herself softly speaking the words: "Does it hurt?"

"The spell?" The wizard angled his mare in close. "I imagine that being drawn and quartered is worse, but not much else. All the pain of growing old—all the little aches of body and heart, pressed into moments. Your body will wrinkle and sag

before it has had a chance to flower. Your hair will lose its lus-
ter, coarsen to white and thin out. You'll feel yourself shrivel
up and fall apart, sixty years in the space of a few breaths. I am
sure it is agony beyond telling."

Katherine held on hard to Tom's fingers. "Why? Why are
you doing this?"

"Because I will live, and so you must die." The wizard retched,
and banged his chest. "There is nothing else, no other cause."

"What you are doing is wrong. It is evil."

The wizard seemed to give this thought. "Simple as it is, there
were days when such a plea might have made me pause and
consider." He waved a hand, as though dismissing the notion.
"That was long ago. I have learned much since then—suffice it
to say that life will teach you the truth of things if you survive
to see enough of it."

The sun shot the last of its fire off the mountains. Color
drained from the world.

"I tested good and evil both," said the wizard. "I found them
to be nothing more than words. There is nothing but life—life
here, life now—and no matter how long it is, you are bound to
want more of it. All other thoughts, all other sentiments curl
and wisp away in time, leaving only the need to live on, live
longer, live more."

Tom raised his head. "You are a pitiful man. Your end will
be a bad one."

The wizard curled his mouth into a sneer. "I should expect
no better from an unlettered peasant. Understand, boy, that

because of what I will soon do to you, and to others like you, I will *have* no end."

"You will, just like those men carved on the wall. You know it, you will always know it, so every moment of your life will be lived in fear." Tom held the wizard in his gaze. "For a man like you, all the time in the world will not be enough, no matter how many years you steal, they will all still slip like dust through your hands, and you will face your end in terror, because you do not know what life is."

The wizard placed a hand on Tom's neck. He spoke a word that seemed to buzz from all sides. Tom screamed. He kicked and bucked, nearly knocking Katherine off Berry's back. One bolgug seized Tom and held him in place, the other yanked hard on the reins.

"Mind your tongue." The wizard let go. "I need you alive— not whole." He spurred his mare and pulled ahead.

"Oh." Tom shuddered and moaned. He lay limp.

Katherine buried her face in Berry's side. She could find nowhere to hide from the fear, not for the briefest moment. The autumn air was her last, the stars her last, the smell of horses. With a sword in her hand, on her feet she could be brave— but they had swarmed her, pulled her down even as she tore and slashed. Indigo had fought and kicked, but the bolgugs had driven him off with fire. She had breathed in relief when she found Tom alive, bundled beside her on Berry's back—but then again, it might have been better if one of the bolgugs had driven its knife home and robbed the wizard of his prize.

Tom found her fingers again. He squeezed hard and whispered, "Don't give up."

Katherine turned, her cheek pressed against the moving front of Berry's leg. Tom's green eyes had gone glassy. His ill-cut hair hung down in clumps from the top of his head.

Something in the way he spoke, and in the way his eyes flicked past her, made her feel more hope than any words he could have said. She let her head drop again, then turned it slow, trying to pretend that she was looking at nothing in particular. She caught the sight for just a moment—a ragged outline on a ridge against the stars. It might not mean a thing, it did not really make much sense, but it was enough.

Jumble was following them.

. . .

Edmund could no longer feel the cold. The piece of log he had found could only bear him a few inches under the water. There had been a time when he had still looked about him, guessed and gauged the wind, hoped for a run of current to help him to shore. He had tried to kick for a while, to push, but the river bore him where it went.

It had gone dark, an empty sky with raking clouds, and all the world sinking ever and forever down—

With a start he came to know that he had fallen asleep and fallen under. He drew up his head and spit water. Some had gotten down his lungs—he hacked it up, felt the action shiver his dangling feet so far away. He just please did not want it to hurt when he let go.

MATTHEW JOBIN

Thoughts rose unbidden to his mind, all that he had ever wanted and would never have. They were not happy thoughts, but he could not stop them. He had loved a girl—he really had loved Katherine—but she did not love him and never would, so maybe it was all just as well. Maybe she would survive, somehow, find a husband one day and some happiness. He wished it, wished her life, and said goodbye.

A nightingale sang from the river's edge and he decided to call that the moment. He let go—the log rose at once and breached the surface beside him, and just as quick he reached for it again. The log sank beneath him, holding him up for as long as he could hold on, and with a sense of horror he came to know that he would hold on for as long as he could, that he would suffer until he could suffer no more.

With every drop into the water he would find some way to rise a bit, take some note of the world and make some try at living. His body loved life, loved and wanted to be alive, but love, he thought, like life, always fails. He just please did not want it to hurt.

He remembered other joys. When he saw the words in a book, when he pressed in against them and found the places where each thought was bound to all others—

He went under. He spat, seized up, and coughed. The dark water slid from his eyes and he breathed.

And he had loved to sing. He had loved his family, he truly had. He had wanted his parents to understand who he was, but he had failed.

He had been proud that he could swim—the thought made him want to laugh.

It felt as though if he just turned around, he could see this boy, somewhere below or above.

He let go again, but did not mean to this time. The trunk rose to the surface, bumping at his back as he passed. He flailed out, despairing, and hooked a finger on the stump of a branch before it could spin away. He turned it, lying with his arm twisted up over his shoulder, nothing but his face above the water. The motion had given his body a spin. For a little while he stared at the clouds above. He wondered if he could just love the silent motion and let that last him the rest of the time.

Something dug and pain came—the point of the barb scraped in against the blade of his shoulder. He had not thought about that arm in some time, for it no longer did anything and did not much complain.

The pain gave way in time, and then all was numb.

He watched the stars. He saw his life for what it was, his self for what it was. He wept, but not for Edmund Bale.

"I would have given all." He did not know if he was speaking or just thinking. "I would have given all, for her, for them."

He did not even know he had let go. He only knew that he could not feel either hand. He held air, knew that his heart could not stop trying to beat, even then, even then under the water. But the air would end, and then the water would come in.

It was going to hurt and hurt, but then it would stop.

Chapter 25

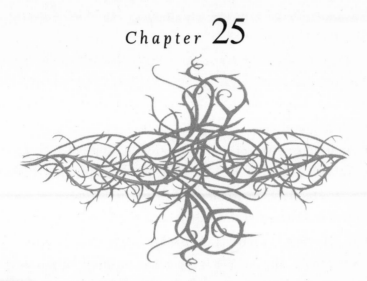

Edmund woke to the feeling of something holding his arms. He remembered drowning, dying—but he was not dead. He struggled and fought, trying to free himself.

"Edmund." Someone touched him. "Edmund, rest. Lie still."

Edmund opened his eyes. The first thing he saw was a fire.

"You are safe, but you must be quiet." A hand drew away— a hand bound in rags soaked through with blood.

John Marshal sat back on his haunches. "Do you remember what happened to you?"

Edmund stared up at John, then past him. Night had come full and starry above. The folds that wrapped his arms were the blankets of his bedroll. He lay on a space of cleared ground in a thick bank of spruce. The wind blew and blustered, howling through the tops of the trees—when it gusted, the branches rocked and shivered, but down beneath it hung slack.

Edmund tried to move—his shoulder reminded him that it was there. The pain made him gasp, almost gag.

"It's just as well that you were out cold when I found you." John Marshal's voice moved over his head and behind him. "That barb would have been harder to dig out if you could have felt me doing it."

Edmund tried to roll himself so that his shoulder hurt less. "I was drowning." But he had dreamed—just the tiniest bit of it came back. He had dreamed of flying.

He set his face in the grass and made a hollow for his cheek. The fire had been built small, hardly more than twigs and tinder. His shirt, cloak and boots hung suspended over the flames on a makeshift frame of sticks. Something moved in the dark beyond. The light glinted on the metal buckles of tack and harness—Indigo.

"We have no time for long explanations." John Marshal brought him a bowl of something warm. "I fell into an ambush just past the mouth of the tunnel and was forced to make a retreat up into high cover. When I came back down to press onward, I found some bolgugs trying to corner Indigo in a gully. We gave a good account of ourselves—I don't think any escaped to bring a warning. After that I got hold of Rosie, there, and was just starting to wonder what it meant when I found you on the riverbank."

Edmund turned his head. Rosie cocked a look at him, twitching her ears from the edge of the fire. Somewhere in her flight she had stepped on her dangling reins and snapped them.

"I searched inside the tunnel, and found this." John Marshal held Katherine's sword across his palms. "Edmund—I know that you are injured, I would never press you in such a state, but I must know. Did Katherine come with you?"

"We found your horse," said Edmund. "We thought you needed help."

John Marshal looked ready for grief. "Did she—was she also in the water?"

"No—no, Master Marshal!" Edmund reached from his bedroll with his good arm. "He took them—they're alive, they have to be. He needs them alive."

"He? Who do you mean?"

"The stranger. The wizard." Edmund stared at him. "You don't know?"

"I'm starting to think that I don't know nearly enough." John pushed the bowl under Edmund's nose. "Have some of this, and tell me what you've learned, as quick as you can tell it."

The smell made Edmund retch. He shoved the bowl aside. "There's a wizard behind this—he's the one who stole the children. He's taking them to the Nethergrim, to cast a spell that will steal their lives away."

John opened the saddlebags and started moving things from Indigo to Rosie. "Where? Where is it done?"

"In the mountain, in its chamber." Edmund winced as he drew back the bedroll. The cold seized him hard. "We've got to hurry. The spell needs seven children, and now he has them. They won't be kept alive for long."

"The closest thing to safety I can give you is to leave you

here in hiding." John slipped the bridle over Indigo's head. "If I don't return within a day, you must try to make it back on your own."

"No." Edmund heaved himself to his feet—and nearly staggered onto the fire. "I'm coming with you."

John shook his head. "I will not place you in more danger."

"That wizard stole my brother and my friends. He hurt my father." Edmund reached for his shirt, and tried to slip it on his good arm first. He got tangled in the folds. John helped him put it on.

Edmund found that his bad arm hurt when he moved it— but it moved. "I'll be in danger anywhere in these mountains." He reached down for his boots. "If you go without me, I'll just follow you."

John nodded—and smiled, just a little. "It seems I never judged you fairly." He pulled up Edmund's cloak and held it out. "There is much more to you than I had guessed."

Indigo snorted and champed at his bit. Rosie backed away from Edmund's approach, swiveling her ears in all directions.

"I wish I could say the same for your horse." John shut his saddlebags. "She's a sweet old girl, but no campaigner. There's nothing for it, though—we must press on as quick as we can."

Edmund let Rosie have her distance. "There are apples in your saddlebag. Right there on your back. I could get some."

Rosie turned her head to regard him. She twitched her meager tail. Edmund held out his hand, down at the level of his belt, palm up.

"That's my girl." Edmund let her approach, hesitate, then

snuffle. "Who wants an apple?" He reached for his saddlebags and found his longbow and quiver, still strapped alongside.

John took up the dangling ends of Rosie's reins and made a knot in them. "It's hardly fair giving Rosie an apple and leaving Indigo to go hungry." He reached in for another and held it out flat on his palm. Indigo did not let it stay there long.

They walked the horses down the slope, John first and Edmund following, stopping to listen at intervals. They could hear nothing but the howl of the wind against the trees—no creature of any sort made noise above it anywhere. They reached open ground, and then the road.

"We've one more pass to climb." John helped Edmund up into the saddle. "The river flows through a gorge up ahead, no way through at the waterside. We must use the greatest caution, especially—" His words ended in a hiss of pained breath.

Edmund looked down. "Does your hand hurt, Master Marshal?"

John climbed up onto Indigo, using his left hand where he should use his right. "Tristan always said, whenever we came home—every great adventure leaves you more than you were, and yet less."

• • •

Black lines under stars. The world an empty floor. Edmund put his hands in his sleeves, a loop of rein between them.

He turned in his saddle. The land behind was all a shadow. He rode west, up the walls of the Girth on a path that often came perilously close to the river gorge it followed. It rose through oak and alder, up past spruce and fir and still on up to harder ground. The river cut farther and farther down below him, its noise a distant and unceasing thunder.

Rosie heaved and puffed, sweating cold down her flanks. She picked her weary way in the dim, a long tumble down to death on either side. Edmund kept his knees in close and tried to move in the sway of her walk, no matter how much it chafed at his sores or pulled at the half-healed cut on his shoulder. John rode Indigo some distance ahead. The dull glint of the sword in his belt was the brightest thing on the mountainside.

They turned with the road, hard against the edge of the gorge, then over a spur of rock so chancing and exposed that Edmund forgot to breathe until they had come down again. He had to peer at the shapes he found on the other side for ten long paces to know what they were—broken teeth blue in the moonlight, works of stone grand beyond anything he knew, all thrown down in ruins on the keel of a farther, higher spur. The trail twisted in to run beneath them and then up over the last pull into a pass. Rosie kept as far from the edge as she could, feeling out her steps with nervous care.

Edmund followed to the turn and passed under the shadow of the ruins. Rosie did not want to walk so near to them—Edmund did not want to look at them, but he could not help himself. The ruins made toys out of castles—each stone its own monument, columns and lintels lying sundered in the avenues, dead houses for giant men. Moonlight came into angle for a moment and shone through a wide passage, onto a row

MATTHEW JOBIN

of faces carved along a wall in terror and judgment and bitter majesty. Empty eyes. Mouths open to shout forever. Edmund looked away.

"What was this place?" He shrank from the sound of his own voice—the mountains ate it and spit back an echo that was little more than wind.

"I remember asking Vithric that." John's voice came down from somewhere in the gloom. "I was sure that this must be the great stronghold of the Nethergrim—what could possibly be worse than a place like this?" His laughter came soft, and without real mirth.

Rosie placed a hoof wrong on the trail, scraped over a rock and stumbled. Edmund grabbed for the saddle and hunched down. They lurched toward the precipice, Edmund's stomach gripped in—they were falling—then Rosie caught herself and braced on a hind hoof. With the slow strength of terror she gained her feet and stood upright. They quaked together, Edmund down across Rosie's back, both of them breathing rough and loud.

"Edmund, are you all right?" John raised his question to a shout. "Edmund!"

Edmund found his voice. "We almost fell."

"Come down from the saddle, then. We'll walk them from here."

Edmund dismounted. He stepped around to pull off the saddlebags, never once turning his back on the ruins. He dug through the bags for the last of the apples. "Come, girl. Just some walking now. It'll be easy."

Rosie had her ears back. Her eyes rolled—she wanted to run but could not. Too steep. Too tired.

"I know. It's a bad place." Edmund held out the apple. "I'm afraid of it, too. Let's go on past it."

Rosie put her head in his hand. She snuffled, then ate. He touched the whorl of russet hair in the center of her forehead. "Good girl." He put the saddlebags over his shoulder, took the reins in one hand and started up the trail. The reins drew taut, then Rosie followed.

John waited with Indigo where the trail reached its steepest. He stretched out a hand to pat Rosie's broken-down flank, then turned to lead them on. Edmund kept watch on his feet, testing every step before placing his weight. Sweat broke through on the back of his shirt. After a time he no longer felt the cold.

The stars turned in slow procession through the bottom of night. The saddlebags dug at Edmund's shoulder. Weariness drew in. At last the trail dropped to a gentle grade and followed in between two peaks.

"Watch closely, now." John kept in step beside. "We're coming to a place that would be very easy to defend. If there is anything set to guard, they'll be able to see us coming from a good way off, even at night."

A ruined tower stuck out dark against the stars. The wall that projected from it would once have run all the way to the gorge, but it lay long shattered, its massive blocks weathered and sunk across the broad saddlebow of the pass. John kept his sword out and ready. Wind burst sharp up the slope, howling in the crevices.

"Sit a moment." John paced out amongst the broken foundations of the wall. "There are only a few ways through this rubble—I might learn something of our quarry here."

Edmund let the reins slip from his fingers, not fearing for a moment that Rosie would go anywhere. He found space under the shelter of the tower where the wind did not bite so hard. Cramps seized and shuddered his exhausted legs. He thought of Geoffrey, then Katherine, then his father—then tried his best not to think of anything.

Indigo grazed in a circle by the tower, picking through the wispy grass without seeming to find much. Rosie let her head droop to the ground, dead asleep on her feet. Edmund drew his cloak around his shoulders. He lay back and looked up. The carvings of long thin hands, of Gatherers and their victims ran under the lintel of the doorway behind. What little he could read upon it spoke of the turn of seasons in the stars, the might of king and army, an ordered harmony above and below.

"They were so sure, so fierce and proud," he said. "They thought their kingdom was going to last forever."

"Nothing does, not in this world." John's voice came back from amongst the blocks of wall.

"They conquered and ordered things, tried to make their world in the image of their thoughts—and now it's rubble, bits of pictures and words that no one really understands." Edmund gave up trying to read them. "Doesn't it sometimes make you think that building things is no use?"

"What I think is that I love my daughter, and I will save her if I can. What I think is that things like love and hope are the substance of life, and that what gets carved on the side of a tower amounts to very little of importance. Come, I will show you something that means more to me than every word in every language ever written."

Edmund got up. He reached for Rosie's knotted reins and led her in amongst the blocks. He did not have much of a guess at what John had found, but even still he had expected something a bit more grand than a splat of horse dung.

"I am no great tracker, but I've been looking at what horses leave behind all my life. This was dropped tonight." John reached for Indigo's reins. "We're close behind them. Come, onward. We can ride from here."

Indigo started at an eager trot as soon as John gained the saddle. Rosie puffed and pushed to keep up. Grass gave way to dirt, then dirt thinned out over rock. The angle of the rise before them diminished, rolling Edmund's view down through star and cloud as they approached level ground at the top of the pass.

They emerged over a vale so wide and deep that it made Edmund spin to look into it, a needled and unbroken darkness—fir, spruce and pine like grass in a gully. He stared down and did not know how far it was, how tall he was, but the bottom of the land was not the greater marvel. Around him, rising up on every side, were faces all of snow and folds of gray, summits tall enough to pierce the moon. Awe moved in him, both wonder and dread.

"In the dark hours of my life, I knew I would come back here." John pressed in his heels to start them down the long, narrow drop from the pass. A shift of cloud revealed another ruin on the floor of the valley. The cast of light and frame of mountain gave Edmund little clue to its size, but it had walls and avenues and another snaggled nest of broken towers.

He heard the music of the river long before he saw it. It wound at a rush down the eastern wall of the valley, passing under a bridge that resembled the old stone bridge at Moorvale in every detail. Rosie did not trust it, and had to be led across the span.

"Let's have them drink." John dismounted and led Indigo down the banks. "We'll want to consider our course. Eat something if you can."

Edmund pulled a cloth bundle from his pack. A scent rose to him—flour and eggs cooked thick with a hint of spice. It brought thoughts of home, but no hunger. He put it away again.

"Which mountain?" He joined John Marshal at the edge of the road. They had come down switchbacks on ridgelines halfway to the bottom, and all the peaks around him looked more or less the same.

"There." John stretched his good hand out to point. "We have a choice before us. We can look for the ascending trail the Twins found on our first approach, or we can follow the road down to the floor of the valley."

Edmund came to understand that he was being asked to give counsel. "What is good or bad about either way?"

"The risk of the first is that I might not find our way quickly enough. The Twins were better guides than anyone I have ever known—they found that trail and led us along it, on a path so steep and treacherous that we would have no hope of bringing the horses. The second way carries a different sort of danger. We'll be taking the shortest and most direct path to the entrance in the mountain, but through heavy cover, through a place that thirty years ago swarmed with every kind of horrible thing you could imagine. I have no idea what might dwell down in that valley these days—but if I was this wizard you spoke of, that's the place where I would lay an ambush against anyone following me."

Edmund stepped back to look about him. The valley floor was vast and dark, but the folds of mountain northward looked like a fine place to die of a broken neck. "I say downward, on the road. We can't lose any time."

"I think the same, but I wanted you to know what you hazard." John raised a hand. "But stop a moment. You are sure you are resolved on this? Edmund, you are young, you have the chance of a long life before you—you may be the only child your parents have left. I do not say this because I think little of you, I say it because I think much of you, and would have you grow to manhood and live happy if you can."

Edmund felt grateful to be asked. "I don't think I could live happy if I turned back now."

John nodded. "Very well, then." He put a foot into the stirrup. "Sling your quiver onto your back from here on, and keep that knife close to hand."

MATTHEW JOBIN

Chapter 26

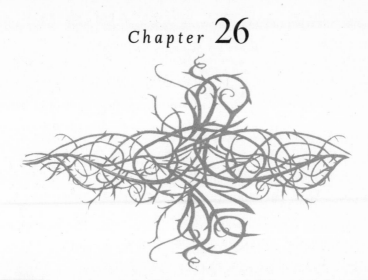

The road turned off the ridges and descended through a very odd sort of forest, thick with needled saplings to the shoulders of the horses but dead bare above. The air lost the blustery sting it had carried on the heights. Leafless branches passed overhead, thin shadows against the sky.

"It looks so strange." Edmund heard no echo of his voice for the first time since entering the Girth.

"Last time I was here, the firesprites were busy setting the whole of this valley alight. I think it all must have burned before the end." John reined Indigo back to come alongside. He leaned off the saddle to look at Rosie's legs.

"What's wrong?" said Edmund.

"You don't feel it? She's starting to limp."

"Oh. I thought it was the bumpy road."

John sat up straight. "She is old, Edmund. She's been driven very hard—she won't be able to carry you much farther."

Edmund stroked a hand on Rosie's mane. "When we get back, folk will scarcely believe all the things she's done."

The closer they got to the floor of the valley, the closer in the undergrowth grew on either side—then it blurred across the verge and forced them to ride single file. The land buckled up and ran flat. The mulch turned muddy thick between the brambles. Rosie snapped a twig underfoot—she startled and staggered, too weary to jump. The road would have been no better than any wild stumble through the woods, save that everywhere else, looming up through weed and sapling, lay broken, weathered hunks of mossy stone.

Edmund hugged down and shoved past a lace of reaching branches. "What was this place?"

"I had hoped that you might tell me." John held out his sword to push and slash along. The rush of the river grew louder again—though deeper, more water but on a slower run over flat, old earth. Edmund shoved onward to find John Marshal waiting in the open. Their road met another in the shadow of a mammoth stone, like the Wishing Stone at home but three times the height.

"From here we turn north." By some trick of the land John's voice seemed to come from all directions. "Just south, beyond that stone, this river joins another, and from there downstream you might as well call it the Swift. It leaves this valley through a cleft I could find no way to pass, but I traced up the banks with Tristan in our younger days."

"The marriage of the rivers. Just like in the book." Edmund let Rosie come to the junction at any pace she liked, which turned out to be an exhausted, wobbling amble. He touched her withers. "Rest soon. I promise." He found himself wishing for another apple to give her.

John took the turn northward at the stone. Edmund stopped at the junction to listen and to look. He could hear the violent joining of the rivers, caught glimpses of the water churning white beneath the moon. Carvings on the great stone told him what he already knew, that he was in the hallowed fastness of the Nethergrim, and that if he was a good and faithful servant, he should already be on his knees.

"Onward." John gave him no time to sit and gape. The road northward ran on a rising course up the shoulder of a shadowed mountain, a grand, dead avenue fringed with the remnants of tower and wall and mansion, all built from massive blocks of blue-gray stone. Walls and columns stood amongst the burned skeletons of trees, poking through the younger growth in places and retaining just enough of their former shape to let Edmund guess the rest. There lingered a feeling of ceremony, of show, a message to any who trod upon the road—seek you the favor of That-Which-Dwells-Within-the-Mountain, or despair.

"The halls of the Gatherers . . ." Edmund turned to John. "What do you think it was like back then, living so close to—"

"Quiet." John gripped his shoulder hard. He spoke in a tense whisper. "Hear it?"

Edmund froze, his heart in his mouth. Rosie raised her head with her ears flat back. John wheeled Indigo sharply aside. Edmund turned in the saddle—he saw nothing, but into the hush that fell broke a rapid series of noises from somewhere behind him. They began as an innocuous rustle, but grew quickly louder and closer, shaping into the sound of something very large approaching at a rush through the trees.

"Gallop!" John drew his sword. "To high ground, Edmund—go!" There came a burst of splintering wood to the west. Rosie bellowed in terror and sprang to a run without being asked.

Edmund grabbed at the reins and hunched down over the saddle. The arrows bounced in his quiver, threatening to slide out over his back. He dared a look aside and caught sight of something very tall looming around the corner of a broken stone house.

"Thornbeast!" Edmund looked around for John, and found him following on Indigo. The thornbeast came on with the gait and speed of a charging bear, thrashing up through the undergrowth along the road.

"Get ready to dodge," shouted John. "Now! Pull up!"

Edmund hauled on the reins—Rosie's back arched hard, nearly throwing him. The thornbeast dove in across the road, sweeping its tendrils through the place where they would have been if they had kept their pace, and crashed onward into the trees on the other side.

"Gallop again!" John passed him. "Hurry—it runs faster in the trees!"

Edmund jammed his heels into Rosie's flank, though she had started her gallop a heartbeat before. He looked ahead—two furlongs more and the broad street ran up onto hard stone, out of the trees to safety.

"Another!" John's warning came just in time. Tendrils

MATTHEW JOBIN

whipped past Edmund's face. Something snapped loose from the saddle—he reached down to grab his longbow before it fell to the road. Indigo drove himself between Rosie and the thornbeast, giving John the space to slash his sword across the flailing, twisting thorns.

Edmund could do nothing but hunch down on Rosie's back and try to move with her run. He could feel the weakness in her hind leg as though it were his own, could feel how close she came to tumbling every time she came down on it.

"One more furlong, Edmund, one more and we're clear." John pulled up alongside. Trees ripped and toppled, and the thornbeast came again. Both horses lowered their heads and brought out the last of their speed. A tendril strained to its farthest limit and caught Rosie in the leg—she squealed but kept her pace, leaping over fallen stones before Edmund had time to see them. The ground rose, the trees thinned . . .

They were away, they were free.

The next thing Edmund knew he was tumbling through the air. He lost hold of the longbow—he had time to look back and see Rosie falling, her back hoof caught and twisted in a hollow. Her head tossed back and she crashed down hard. John shouted his name—then he struck the ground and saw white.

"Edmund!" Something thundered the ground, and something else scrabbled from another direction. Edmund could not draw a breath, could not make his chest heave in and out. He rolled over, snapping one of the arrows that had spilled from his quiver. His injured shoulder screamed and grated. Rosie lay sprawled a few yards back of him, her hind leg sticking out at a frightful angle. The thornbeast knocked a tree aside and came out onto the road. Its roots clawed and sewed through the earth. Its lightless eyes drank everything.

Rosie turned her head to look at the thornbeast. She groaned and tried to drag herself away, raising herself on her forelegs but unable to stand. Edmund managed to roll onto his side. Everything hurt—but not for long. The thornbeast reared up high overhead.

"Edmund! Your hand!" The thunder grew louder. Edmund turned to look—Indigo was charging straight for him, on a barreling course right under the reach of the thornbeast. John leaned from the saddle and held out a hand. Edmund raised his own up to meet it, and felt his arm nearly jerk from his shoulder. The stars spun, then the ground, and he was moving.

"I've got you." John pushed down on his back to hold him across the front of the saddle. The pommel dug hard into his stomach. Rosie's screams filled the valley.

"Don't look!" John put a hand across Edmund's eyes. Indigo galloped smooth and hard up to high, rocky ground. By the time John reined him to a halt, the screams had died away.

"Is anything broken?" John held him by the back of his shirt. "Can you move everything?"

Edmund tried his arms, then his legs. John lowered him off the saddle to slither in a lump on the rocks.

Indigo's flanks heaved in and out like a bellows. John knelt over Edmund and checked his bones. "Nothing broken—except ribs, maybe. Come on. Up."

Edmund wobbled to his feet with John's help. He looked

back over his shoulder before he thought to stop himself. The thornbeast crouched in the middle of the road, a quivering, writhing blot—then it moved off into the trees, leaving scattered bones in a dull red squelch on the road.

"Never forget her." John turned him forward again. "So long as you live, never forget her."

Chapter 27

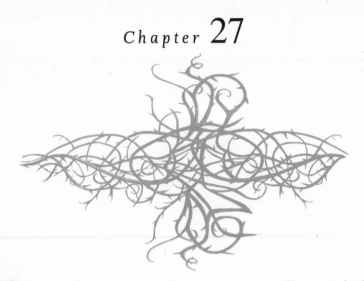

John led them on a treacherous ascent, walking with the
reins in one hand and his other arm bearing Edmund up.
They rose onto rock, out of all danger of the thornbeast, on
a path that broke off like a cliff to the left and was but a little
less deadly to the right. There could be no mistaking where
the path led—it served as a long tongue for the mouth of the
mountain.

"Rest here." John took a torch and felt his way through the
entrance of the cave. Up close the gaping maw looked to have
taken a punch, smashed in along one side to spill rocks onto
the path. Edmund sank to his knees—he could not draw his
breaths in all the way, not without feeling stabbed between the
ribs.

"Rosie." He had hardly spared her a thought in all the time
his family had owned her, save to devise ways to make sure it

was always Geoffrey who had to muck out her stall. She had died trying to save them both; he curled down and cried the way he used to cry when he was little.

After a time he gave some thought to where he was. He stood and limped to the cliffside. A set of carvings ringed the edge, but he could not bring himself to look at any more of He-That-Speaks-From-The-Mountain and his endless, vicious vanity, nor so much as glance at the open hands of the Nethergrim. The drop beyond would give anyone who fell over it a good space of time to think on death before he met it. The wind moaned loud across the mouth of the tunnel, a haunted chord that made mockery of hope.

John emerged, looking pale as parchment. He walked past—bent of back, grown older before Edmund's eyes.

Edmund turned. "What's wrong?"

"I don't understand it." John sat down on a rock. "It's blocked. There's no way through."

Edmund peered through the entrance. "There's nothing in there?"

"Nothing but a fall of rocks and the bones of my old friends." John took a panicked look about him, up and down the dark slopes of the mountain. "Edmund, I am sorry. I don't know what to do."

The chord in the wind grew louder, and rose in pitch. Edmund tried to stop up his ears. The thought of Katherine and Geoffrey, Tom and the others, about to meet their deaths inside—it was too much to be borne.

"It cannot be—it cannot be!" John got up. He grabbed the last torch from Indigo's pack and rushed back into the entrance.

Edmund thought that, perhaps, it could well be—but he was not going to give up while he had breath in him. He slithered back down the way they had come, hunting left and right for another path. He found the road ahead of him littered with the arrows that had spilled from his quiver—it looked as though a rather talentless company of archers had just shot a volley. He gathered up what he could find, and found his longbow stuck through the branches of a bush. He was about to dare going back into the trees—back in reach of the thornbeast—when a noise made his heart leap.

"Woof."

It was not loud, but it was distinct, clear enough for him to know just who had made it.

"Jumble?" Edmund looked over the rocks. "Jumble!"

A black-and-white shape slinked its way below, up a path so narrow that it would not have looked like a path from above at all, save for the fact that the shape managed somehow to cross it.

"Woof." Jumble wagged his tail.

"Master Marshal!" Edmund turned to wave. "Master Marshal, over here!"

The torchlight swelled to the entrance. "Edmund?" John Marshal scrabbled down the mountainside, leading Indigo as close to a run as they could go.

"Down there." Edmund crouched over the rocks. Jumble sat on his haunches, waiting.

"Call that luck if you like." John unburdened himself of his torch and all else he carried save the sword. He felt out over the drop beyond the edge of the trail. "We were in something of a hurry last time I was here. If we'd known about this way, some of my friends might have survived."

Edmund looked over the side. He swallowed hard. "I can't imagine that wizard climbing over this. He's sick half to death."

"You're assuming he walked." John reached over Indigo's back to pull off saddle and blanket. "I'll wager the bolgugs carried him—and the children. You'd hardly believe how strong they are."

He shot a grim smile at Edmund. "Then again, I suppose you would believe, wouldn't you?"

"But how are we going to bring Indigo?"

"We're not." John put his arms up around Indigo's head, and drew away with the bridle in his hands. "A horse his size could never make this traverse. We'll have to trust that he can find his own way home." Indigo let the bit fall from his mouth and shook out his glossy mane.

John stepped around in view of one of Indigo's large brown eyes. "Now, don't you dare try to follow us." He unfastened the girth and set the saddle on a rock. "You run home, you run home fast, do you hear?"

Indigo twitched his ears and stamped.

John sighed. "We'll just have to hope." He felt his leg over the side, scrabbled past the edge and trod a few feet along. In the poor light it looked as though his next step would be over the side of a cliff. He held out a hand behind him. "On we go. Don't think."

Edmund grabbed his hand—the bad hand. He felt the stump of the missing finger, and heard John hiss in pain. "I'm sorry!"

"Hold tight, you fool! Onward."

Jumble waited until they reached his vantage, then turned without a noise and slipped around the cliffside. The wind laced over the edge of the pass, keening past the rocks and freezing Edmund's fingers numb. The moon dropped down behind the peaks, pulling its light from the world just when he needed it most.

"Master Marshal." He worked his grip through scree and rubble until he seized on rock. "Can I tell you something?"

"There is no possible way I could stop you." John felt out ahead of him. "That bit there's no good. Don't put your weight on it, just step over, stretch and step—there."

"What I mean to say is—" Edmund felt sure that his handhold was going to come right out of the mountainside, but it held firm. He got his breath. "I like your daughter."

John hummed a laugh. "I know."

"I mean to say that I really, truly like her." Any one and single step could be the very last he would ever take. He could not see the bottom, even if he had wanted to risk another look down. "Very much."

"I know what it is you are trying to say." John helped him around a large loose rock on the trail.

"I am in love, though. I am."

John spared a glance at him. "It may indeed be that you are. Stranger things have proven true."

Jumble nearly fell off ahead of them—his frightened yip bounced back many times—but then he seemed to find his way along to somewhere safe, for he turned and poked his head from behind a hook of rock. Edmund followed John around it, and beyond found himself on what felt like a king's highway by comparison to what had gone before—a winding path up a sickening drop, but one on which he could place both his feet astride. He looked back at the way he had come; a burst of belated fear seized at him.

The upward trail grew more tiring than dangerous—a wrong step more likely meant a twisted ankle than certain death. Edmund's breaths came easier after a time, and though there was no part of him that was not bruised in some way or other, he began to hope that he had not broken his ribs after all. Jumble ran before them and then back, sniffing at the trail with his tail stuck high. He darted abruptly aside, scrabbling up through bare ground into the dark.

"Get your knife out." John paced off their trail. Edmund drew his brother's knife and followed up the slope. He could just make out the square of exposed earth around the edge of a thick wooden board.

"A board in the ground? Out here?" Edmund looked about him. They had risen through a jagged pass—even at night it seemed plain that the mountain of the Nethergrim would be all but unassailable save for the entrance down at the end of the road. A handful of men could have held off an army on the trail he had followed with John, and everywhere else was fissure and abyss.

"This board was recently laid—as though we needed more proof." John worked his fingers under the edge.

"If we see the wizard, what do we do?"

"Stab him to death. I didn't think that needed saying." John gripped and heaved the board over, exposing the top of a worked stone shaft.

"Someone's talking down there." Edmund crouched at the opening. "Loud, but far away—and there's a funny smell." He knelt and reached down. "There's a ladder."

John turned and slid a foot over the edge. "It holds." Jumble nosed up to the entrance, then tried to put a paw over.

"No." John ruffled Jumble between the ears. "Good boy. Stay."

He descended a rung, then looked at Edmund. "I'll say it once more. From here on, the danger will grow much worse. You can stay up here—no one would think the worse of you."

Edmund felt a wish to go home so bright, it hurt. He fought it down. "I'm going."

"All right, then." John climbed down out of view. "Quiet as we can from here on."

Edmund turned to feel out the ladder once John was out of view. He set his foot on a rung, and then another, and descended past the level of the ground.

He touched down on a stone floor covered with untold

years of fallen dust and the detritus of insect life. Something tiny and many-legged skittered away.

"Grab hold of my shirt." John breathed in Edmund's ear. "We'll have to crawl." The square of starlight above seemed like a bright summer's day compared to the void into which they had stepped. The tunnel that led from the shaft could be sensed by the faint drift of air and by the echoes trailing down its long, narrow gullet. It smelled of old earth and rotting stone, clammy and sepulchral.

John bent down and felt out the low ceiling of the tunnel before him. Edmund followed as quietly as he could. They advanced in a crouch, dropping to their knees every few yards to pass under a hang of rock. The walls pressed close at Edmund's shoulders. Cobwebs broke off in his hair. The husks of insects crunched underfoot. There was not the faintest hint of light. The slightest sounds took firm shape against the silence—the scuff and shuffle of their awkward march, John's breath, his own breath, and beneath all, disconcerting in its sudden clarity, the tense beating of his heart.

Edmund.

The voice jerked him up, made him listen in fright for its source. "Who's that?"

Edmund Bale. Why are you crawling to your death?

Edmund turned all about—but he was in a tunnel, with blank walls on every side. The voice came without an echo—it was not a sound he heard with his ears.

Do not throw your corpse onto the pile. The voice

sounded—it felt—like both his mother's and Katherine's at once—soft and feminine, the trail of a lullaby. **You are worth much more than that.**

Edmund stopped to whisper. "Who are you?"

Whom do you think?

Edmund crouched, his face almost touching the fouled stone of the tunnel floor. He knew.

I was here when the first tree burst from its seed. I will be here when the last one withers and dies. Use any name for me you wish.

"Why are you talking to me?" Edmund felt John silence him with a hard grip of his hand.

I speak only to those I deem worthy to hear me. The minds of most men are painfully constricted.

John turned back down the tunnel. Edmund followed. The moments crawled past without apparent effect. The floor descended at a faint but noticeable slope for a while, then leveled out and ran flat. They crept on and on, making not a sound, for what began to seem like eternity.

You have such promise, Edmund Bale. You truly can be all the things you dream—but not if you persist in this.

John stopped, then pulled Edmund's hand down to touch the floor. Edmund felt his fingers around a hole that stretched across the width of the tunnel. The smell vented up through it, choking and sweet, a sort of rotten chamomile overlaid with the stink of bloated corpse.

John spoke at Edmund's ear. "Broken chimney."

Edmund lay flat by the edge of the hole, his hands over his head, though it was no use. There was nowhere to hide from the Voice.

How do I know what is to come? Child, how am I speaking inside your thoughts? How do I restore old men to youth? Did you imagine, after all that you have learned, that I would still be some slobber-jawed monster, some dumb beast that needed a good stabbing? I am not mortal, Edmund, nor am I bound by much else that constrains a creature such as you. I can see the paths before you, and what will come of each.

"Another ladder." John shuffled over the edge. "Down from here."

Edmund felt out with his fingers and gripped the rung. He descended, favoring his injured arm as much as he could, and touched down in a long-dead hearth—right into an empty, rusted iron pot. Where John led him from there, or what the rooms and passages they stumbled through might once have been, would not have mattered much by then even if he could see them, for the Voice came again to blot out all things.

With every step you approach your end—a hard death, too, as deaths go. I am curious, at least, to know why you rush toward it.

Edmund formed an image of Geoffrey, tried to draw it in as much detail as he could, the snub nose and the freckles. For some reason it was easier if he thought of Geoffrey angry, Geoffrey jealous, that sour look that crossed his face when he thought he was being ignored.

Do you indeed love your brother? If you do, is it only because you spring from the same womb? Think on that awhile, and then perhaps we can discuss this thing you call love.

He gave up and tried Katherine—Katherine, her eyes and lips, the long spill of her hair—

No. You would not long have loved the girl. See her old, see her sagging and gray, and try to love that.

Edmund reached for rage. He balled it up inside him, tried to harden his purpose.

Is that why you are here? To stop me? You might as well seek to stop the wind from blowing. I am not evil—child, there is no such thing as evil. There is only life, then death, only thrashing and struggle, then stillness.

"Edmund!"

Everything shook. He shook—John was shaking him.

"What is wrong with you?" John let go.

"Nothing. I'm fine." Edmund turned away. "Where from here?" He felt around him, stumbling over debris whose shape and former use he could not guess. He stood at the corner of one passage with another, one running flat, the other descending at a sharp angle.

"I am not sure." John spoke little more than breath. "But we are being sought. Do you hear it?"

Edmund fell still again and heard the sound of slapping footsteps, seeming to come from every direction at once—then a shriek, and the clacking of teeth.

I have waited long ages to meet you, Edmund. I touched the thread of your coming centuries before you were born. Heed me, hear me, and be master of your fate as much as any mortal man can ever be.

Edmund bit his lip. "Go away."

For me, Edmund, there is no such thing as away.

Edmund put a hand to the wall. He felt chill stone laid without mortar, each block locked in perfect smoothness with the next, all of them covered in carvings from the height of his knee to his shoulder. He traced across the stone hands of That-of-Goodness. It felt as though they moved to touch him back.

He tugged John's sleeve. "This way. Down."

Their path descended steep, over rubble so thick that he thought more than once there was no way through. The air hung still and stale—the hard wind on the slope far above seemed like the memory of another world. The passage ended in a vast cold chamber, for their footfalls came back to them once and again, from far beyond, beside and above.

"Listen for an ambush." John started off at a wary shuffle. Edmund gripped the back of his shirt and followed, fumbling in the utter dark. He flailed out and touched stone, a pillar— no, a vault, a long run in the direction of their walk.

"I passed this way last time I was here." John whispered by his shoulder. "This is the path Vithric took to reach the chamber. We dragged him through on our escape—I remember he cried out in his delirium and tried to seize at something."

Edmund traced with his fingers, feeling out the slots recessed along its length. Most held smooth stone tablets laid on their ends, marked by symbols incised beneath. "It's a library." Another set of shelves stood an arm's length across.

These are my thoughts, Edmund, the secret knowledge I gave to my servants over centuries—more wisdom, more power than all that could be collected from every city in your little kingdom. Edmund, it can be yours.

Edmund let go of John's shirt. He drew a sharp breath in.

You have in you the seeds of greatness. Have you not felt it? There is much that we could do together, if only you would heed me.

Edmund touched tablet after tablet—book after book, hundreds and hundreds in their rows and piles.

Understand what it is that I offer. You lose a brother, but you never really needed him. You lose the girl—Edmund, you are fourteen. There will be others. Many others.

The Voice seemed to get closer, somehow, so close that Edmund thought he could feel warm breath across his neck. *Eternal life, Edmund. Power beyond the dreams of kings. Mine is the only love you will ever need.*

"Edmund?" John Marshal hissed out from the darkness ahead. "Edmund, where are you? We must hurry!"

Edmund stood statue still. The Voice seemed to caress him, to enfold him in its whispers.

Serve me, Edmund. Join with me. Set yourself upon the rising path. There are no good and evil choices, only wise and foolish ones. Search inside yourself—my words are truth, the only truth. You hold the future in your hands. Do not let it slip from your grasp.

Edmund did search inside himself, alone in the silent dark. For a moment it felt as though he was back underwater, drowning again in the freezing river.

He found the truth—or it found him. He wanted to laugh, at himself more than anyone.

"You're afraid of me." He pulled his hand back from the shelves. "That's why you're talking to me. Maybe you can see the future, and you're afraid of what I will do."

This much is certain, Edmund Bale. The Voice lost much of its sweetness. **If you carry on against me, I will be your death. It is written in the stars, graven in the earth. The rivers mutter it when no mortal is listening. The choice is yours.**

"You are lying to me. You are lying to get me to give up."

Are you willing to gamble your life on that?

Edmund felt his way onward, out past the end of the shelves.

How disappointing.

"Up ahead." John grabbed at Edmund's sleeve. "See it?"

Edmund peered, and to his surprise found that he did see—just a little, a glow so faint that he was not quite sure it was there at first. It cast the outline of the shelves in purple-black, showing that they ran for a hundred yards, but ended. The sounds of speech rose to hearing from ahead, taking on a distinct character—solitary and male, airy and sharp—and coming close to intelligible despite the warping echoes of the chamber around them.

"That voice." Shock dawned on John Marshal's face—then fury. "I know that voice." He plunged on toward the source of the light, ducking into the mouth of a level passage beyond.

"Master Marshal—wait!" Edmund loped along into the passage as quickly as he could. Somewhere ahead the stranger chanted and coughed, his words piled over each other in echo. He found John Marshal halted at a bend, pressed tight against the inside wall. The corner made something less than a right angle; flickering light from ahead spilled out long against the opposite wall, projecting a shadow onto the crumbling stonework. The shadow was too faint and distorted to resolve into a recognizable shape, but every few moments it moved, shifting about with an appearance of restlessness. From one side of it projected a point that looked just like the head of a spear.

"As this Fire burns, so you are consumed." The stranger's voice resounded from beyond the end of the tunnel. "By smoke you are consumed. As Fire becomes earth, you are made dust. You are taken by That which waits to topple the scales of the world. You are taken and made dust, and I take here my surfeit. We drink you, we drain you, your life becomes ours. Your life becomes my life. Your life becomes mine."

Edmund rolled forward, putting his hands to the foul, dirty floor. The tunnel grew wider and taller around the bend; firelight flooded down its length, casting the shadow of a bolgug standing ten paces away.

"YOUR LIFE BECOMES MY LIFE." The voice gained in strength. The bolgug shuddered its bulbous head and clacked its long teeth together. John turned to lock eyes with Edmund, then stepped around the corner and charged.

At five paces' distance the bolgug shrieked and raised its spear. John dodged under the point and cut its alarm short with a thrust of his sword. He shouldered the twitching bolgug aside and bolted down the last few yards of the tunnel, black blood arcing in droplets from his blade. Edmund grabbed for his longbow, nocked an arrow and started after him. There was no time left to be afraid. An entrance widened before him—a square of light, fire and smoke.

The braced ceiling of the chamber into which they sprang arched high and cavernous above. Smooth walls fashioned of large, mortarless blocks of blue-gray stone formed a chamber of eight sides around him, marked all about with the soot of some ancient fire. A disintegrating jumble of objects lay smashed under bits of fallen ceiling—flanged metal vessels tarnished to green, tapestries rotted half to dust. Seven other exits led from the room, each a squat, deeply recessed door made of ancient and desiccated oak save for one large entrance choked with rubble. A platform rose one foot high in the center of the chamber, clear of all debris—a seven-pointed star chased with carvings filled with grout and ants' nests and yet still sugges- tive of a crawling fear. Even its shape, seven points in a room of eight sides, was strangely sickening in its odd-angled aspect, but none of this was what made Edmund start in horror.

At the center of the star was a roaring fire, the only source of light in the room, above which hung an iron cauldron that roiled and bubbled, giving off an awful stench and a stream of thick black smoke. The smoke did not rise to the ceiling as smoke should—it rolled and twisted, splicing itself out into ropy strands. Seven figures of various sizes lay on their backs along each of the points of the star. Tom was closest, his bony arms draped to the floor. Katherine looked like she had died in the middle of a nightmare, hands crossed on her breast as though to ward off a blow. Geoffrey curled on his side the way he always slept—he seemed younger than he was, the little pest Edmund had protected and tormented at turns throughout their lives. The smoke snaked into the mouth of one victim after the next, spilling out through their noses to form a shape at the center of the star that grew more solid by the moment.

Would you like me to appear as a dragon, perhaps? The voice of the Nethergrim was no longer like Edmund's mother's, or like Katherine's. It felt like a hungry worm burrowing into the side of his head. The smoke pulsed in time with its cadence. I could, if you like. There were folk who once gave me tribute in that shape—it is how I got the name you use for me.

Edmund clutched at his ears. "What are you?"

Or perhaps a lovely young woman, as before? The Nethergrim formed from coils inside coils, snaking mouths with too many tongues, the constant knowing that something was poised to reach out and seize you from behind—that there was nowhere to turn, nowhere to run and be safe. I did enjoy that, for a while—but this time I feel more inclined to rend and to shatter. Shapes appeared within the smoke—monstrous faces, claws and bristled limbs, a boiling profusion of eyes.

"AS THIS FIRE BURNS, SO YOU ARE CONSUMED." The stranger stood over the brazier, with his arms splayed out at angles and signs of awful power in his hands. "BY SMOKE YOU ARE CONSUMED. AS FIRE BECOMES EARTH, YOU ARE MADE DUST." The book lay open on a lectern beside him, its pages weighted down by a jagged bronze knife. A half-dozen bolgugs stood about the chamber—they snarled and whined, and reached for their weapons.

John Marshal stood dumb for a moment, rooted to the spot by what he saw before him. "Vithric." He raised his sword—his voice rose to thunder. "*Vithric!*"

Edmund stared at the stranger. Vithric?

The spell had already done some of its work. Vithric's voice no longer faltered in the chant. The wrinkles on his face had smoothed, and his hair had turned a rich full brown. His skin flushed with blood, his lips had gained flesh—they were set in a rictus of lewd and terrifying bliss.

"Vithric!" John chopped a bolgug aside. He lunged for the star, for the place where his daughter lay—but more bolgugs raced in from all sides, too many. Vithric smirked and resumed his chant.

Edmund drew back and loosed his arrow—terror seized his fingers, and the shot came closer to hitting Katherine than

Vithric. In the time it would take to breathe twice more, John Marshal would be outflanked by three of the bolgugs. The other two stood guard in front of Vithric, swords held at the ready.

You once turned a bonfire into light and it nearly stopped your heart. The Nethergrim rose and roiled, as though to stare Edmund down. **Work against me and your death is sealed. Bow down before me and your death will never come.**

A moan sounded. A diminutive figure twitched on a ray of the star—white hair, a wrinkled face contorted in agony. The figure collapsed—a child, aged to his death in mere moments. The smoke grew more solid, a tail flopped forth, the multitude of eyes became two, slitted and orange-bright.

Edmund heard, saw, and felt the awful draw of youth passing from the child into Vithric, and something else into the Nethergrim. The meaning of the spell came clear at last—Vithric was stealing their lives away, and the Nethergrim was feeding on the agony of their dying minds, growing more powerful with every tortured moan.

"You are taken by That which waits to topple the scales of the world. You are taken and made dust, and I take here my surfeit. We drink you, we drain you, your life becomes ours."

All at once Edmund knew. He knew how to stop what was happening, and the terrible cost of it.

He threw down his longbow. "Master Marshal, clear me a path!" He dropped his head and charged, though a pair of bolgugs raised heavy-bladed swords to bar his way. John Marshal parried, wove and ducked. His sword flashed and wove—he shouldered one bolgug aside, but the other seized at the quiver slung over Edmund's back. Edmund shrugged it off, spilling arrows all around, then dodged through the gap.

There is nothing you can do, Edmund. All is lost. Save yourself.

Vithric's spell was cleverly done, supremely clever—the cost of the spell, the agonies of the victims, were being absorbed by the Nethergrim. To block it directly would be beyond any wizard ever born, so Edmund chose to join it instead. The bolgugs guarding Vithric screamed and gnashed their teeth. If the spell did not kill him, the bolgugs would.

Edmund took one last look at Katherine's sleeping face.

"I TAKE THIS COST AND PLACE IT ON MYSELF." He matched the cadence of Vithric's chant. "I HOLD THEIR PAIN TO ME, I HEAR THEIR THOUGHTS IN MINE. I HOLD THEIR PAIN." He inverted Vithric's signs, traced out the signs of Life and Making. "I TAKE THIS COST AND PLACE IT ON MYSELF."

It worked. It hurt, it hurt, but it worked.

Edmund buckled, flooded with the dying torment of Tilly Miller. He felt her trying to hold on to one happy image, her mother smiling down on her as a baby, felt her trying to make peace with the life she would never get to have. He heard her shrieks in his own wailing voice. Somewhere underneath it was the awareness of the pain in his own body. He tasted something salty and metallic in his mouth.

Vithric's smile broke. His eyes went wide in alarm.

Edmund held the pain, denying the Nethergrim her feast. He stumbled up toward the star and reached for Tilly's withered hand. He held it tight as she died.

Vithric's spell lost its power.

Everything stopped.

The orange eyes fixed on Edmund, and a mouth formed in the smoke beneath, as if by chance. **So be it, Edmund Bale.**

Vithric let out a scream of frustration and rage. The eyes dissolved. The tendrils shivered and broke apart, and rose toward the ceiling, like smoke should.

Chapter 28

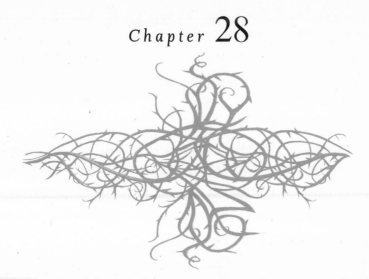

Edmund breathed. His heart beat—fast, but steady and strong. Vithric crouched, huddled and shaking behind the cauldron. The Nethergrim rose as a formless wisp of smoke between them. Her Voice spoke no more inside Edmund's mind.

Edmund spent a dizzy moment wondering why he was still alive. His spell had worked. It had not killed him, but it had cost him—a little blood, a flood of tears and nightmares enough to last a lifetime.

He looked around him. John Marshal lay sprawled atop the corpses of the last two bolgugs, the sword spilled from his injured hand.

Vithric moaned and struggled to his feet. Edmund met eyes with him. He should have seized the moment to attack, but only words came: "You were a hero."

Vithric snarled and leapt across the star. Edmund drew his knife—but Vithric was faster. A punch to the gut doubled Edmund over and sent him staggering back, knocking cauldron, book and lectern down in a heap. His knife skittered out across the floor. Before he had a chance to retrieve it, he felt Vithric's hands around his neck.

"A lesson on the subject of heroes." As a man in his healthy prime, Vithric was of good girth and strength, brimming with a fierce energy. "Heroes often die rather young." Edmund struggled and kicked, but could not get free, could not breathe. An explosion of red blotted his vision—the curses Vithric hissed at him seemed to come from farther and farther away.

Then there came a huff of wind, a thud and a gasp of pain. Edmund felt the grip around his neck go slack. He staggered back and fell, heaving for air. Vithric stood above him, swaying, clutching at the arrow driven deep into his shoulder.

"Get away from my brother."

Edmund twisted to look behind him. Geoffrey advanced, another arrow held at full draw.

Vithric curled his lip. His fingers twitched—then he turned and bolted into the gloom through the door behind him.

Geoffrey rushed to Edmund's side. "Did he hurt you? Are you hurt?"

"No—not hurt. Not bad, at least." The agony of the spell shuddered through Edmund, a wound that only he could see and feel. He sat up with Geoffrey's help and looked about him—children waking to scream on the rays of the star, the rotting, broken treasures crawling with vermin, the thick smoke rising from a red-orange coal fire that made monstrous sport of their shadows. The fire brightened—some of the coals had fallen on the book and set it alight. Shrieks and flapping footfalls resounded from the many passages that led into the chamber, getting louder by the moment.

"Hurry, pick them up." Edmund shoved Geoffrey across the star and lurched the other way. It was as he had hoped—and feared. Five of the seven children had been spared, but two had been taken by the spell and lay dead of old age. A toothless, ancient man lay next to Tilly Miller, his face a mass of wrinkles. He had twisted almost double in his final pains.

Katherine was already moving, rolling over to reach for her fallen sword, so Edmund leapt across to the next ray of the star and found a girl his own age. He helped her to stand; Geoffrey did the same for a boy who was perhaps a year younger.

The girl fell weeping beside the body of the toothless old man. "Elwy!" She seized his wrinkled arm. "He's seven, he's only seven!"

Edmund looked at the children who had survived the spell, then back at the two who had died. A boy of seven, and Tilly Miller, youngest of Geoffrey's friends.

Understanding broke upon him—the spell took the youngest first.

"Up!" He dragged the girl away from the corpse. "Cry later—we've got to run!"

"Someone get my papa." Katherine turned through all

directions with her blade held out, watching each of the entrances. Tom sat up on his own and pried a spear from the grip of a fallen bolgug. The sounds of approaching footsteps grew louder, seeming to converge from every side.

Edmund reached down for John Marshal and found him alive but groggy, blood running free through his grizzled hair. He got a shoulder under John's arm and helped him to stand, but before they had taken a step, a door beside them burst wide and more bolgugs rushed through with their spears thrust out before them. There was nowhere to run—even if he let John drop, he could not dodge away in time. He stood frozen in a hopeless stare at the point of the spear rushing in for his belly.

A blade flashed out, knocking the spear point down to strike the floor. The bolgug had just enough time to look aside before the blade swept up and cut its throat.

It was Katherine—she stepped between Edmund and the next bolgug, and drove her heel at the outside of its knee. There was a sickening snap, and the bolgug stumbled forward into the thrust of her sword. She gripped the dying creature by the shoulder and turned it, using its body as a momentary shield so that she could spare Edmund a glance. "Which way out?"

Edmund got his bearings. "This way!" He hauled John toward the door through which they had entered. Tom took up a position at Katherine's side, holding back the bolgugs that tumbled in over the corpses of their leaders. Edmund had never seen such a look of fury on Tom's face, nor dreamed he ever would. It saddened him, somehow.

"Just hold that spear out, Tom. Keep them under threat." Katherine edged sideways, circling the bolgugs with a fierce light in her eyes. "The rest of you, go with Edmund." The girl and the boy—two of the kids from Roughy, Edmund could only guess—followed him toward the doorway through which he had come.

The remaining bolgugs formed up across the chamber— two with spears and two with short, heavy thrusting swords. One fell with Geoffrey's arrow in its bulging yellow eye, but the rest came on at a rush, leading with their snapping, gnashing jaws.

"Everyone behind me!" Katherine rocked onto the balls of her feet. She feinted a lunge with the point of her sword, halting the charge of the first two bolgugs and acting as though she did not see the third coming in on her flank until she reversed and slammed its spear aside. It spun away—and dropped with an arrow in its throat.

"That's my last." Geoffrey ducked back behind the guard of Tom's spear. The two remaining bolgugs pressed a fierce attack, stabbing and ducking, looking for a gap. One of them screeched and dove forward, swinging with hungry abandon. Katherine pulled in her blade to twist its thrust, using its uncalculated force to draw it close and then reversing to give it a vicious crack on the mouth with the pommel of her sword. It staggered away, clutching at its broken teeth and howling in pain.

Tom pedaled backward, jabbing out his spear to keep the

bolgug on his flank at bay. Geoffrey raced through the doorway ahead. Edmund felt less of John's weight on his shoulder—he seemed to be coming awake and regaining his strength. A few more steps and they were free of the chamber of the Nethergrim.

A scream drew Edmund's glance aside. The bolgug on their flank had turned from Tom and gotten hold of the girl from Roughy by her waist-length braid. It jerked in its arm and snapped her to the ground, then opened its mouth to take her throat.

Katherine wheeled and flew into a sprint, ignoring the broken-toothed bolgug though it had recovered and pressed at her flank. It gave her a slash to the thigh; she cried out but finished her strike, leaping off with her other leg in a flying lunge to bring the girl's attacker down.

Before Edmund knew what he was doing, he had dumped John Marshal through the doorway and turned to charge barehanded through the chamber. Katherine drove her sword into her target's back and crashed to the floor on top of it, then twisted and tried to draw out her blade in time to block another swing from the last bolgug. Too late—the bolgug raised its sword to skewer her down to the floor. Edmund could only cry out her name.

The blow never landed. A spear whiffed past and took the bolgug smack in the chest. It coughed, waved its arms and pitched over backward.

"Pick her up!" John Marshal slumped, his arm still extended

from the action of the throw, and then Tom pulled him back inside the passage. A chittering, scraping noise sounded from somewhere past the dying fire, shrieks and more footsteps approaching at a charge.

"Katherine." Edmund got his shoulder under hers. The wound looked bad, too much bright running blood. She bit her lip, her face twisted in a grimace.

She put her sword in his hands. "Let's go." She pushed herself standing on her good leg. Tom grabbed hold of her other side, and they all staggered out in one battered huddle.

The grating calls of the bolgugs seemed to come from everywhere, resounding up and down the passages, sometimes seeming to approach but never reaching the tunnel through which they scrabbled and ran. The darkness was total—Edmund kicked something hard and heavy that he could not see. He hopped in pain for a moment, then set down his foot before Katherine's weight brought him to the floor.

"Where from here?" Geoffrey's voice bounced wide in the library ahead. "I can't see anything!"

"Straight on, between the shelves!" Edmund coughed—the hard grip of Katherine's arm around his chest sent arcs of pain through his ribs, though at the same time it was the best thing he had ever felt in his life. "Everyone hold hands. Follow me." There was no time to doubt his memory—he dodged up through stair and doorway, clanging the sword on the walls as he pumped his arms to gain speed. The children clasped tight to his shirt, moving as one with arms over shoulders and hands at hems and sleeves. Katherine hopped along with almost all of her weight on her good leg, puffing from the effort of their long ascent. By the time they reached the ladder in the hearth, the cries of the bolgugs had died away to wailing echoes.

"It's up here." Edmund steered them over to the ladder and felt out for the rungs. "Geoffrey, you're first. Turn right at the top and keep crawling. Go, all of you."

He felt them shuffle past, one by one, until only John Marshal remained with him below. They could not see each other—they did not need to see each other.

"Well done, Edmund." John squeezed his hand, then turned to climb.

Edmund held out the sword to guard their escape, though he could see nothing of the passage behind him and had heard no sounds of pursuit. He grabbed hold of a rung, and could not resist casting a defiant look behind him at the darkness. "You're a liar. You didn't kill me!"

Not yet.

The answer stole his triumph, and propelled him up the ladder as fast as he could go. Tom helped him into the tunnel at the top. The children slithered and shuffled along in a dark silent line before him, and though they did not need to hold hands anymore, they still did.

Geoffrey laughed for joy. "Daylight!" They gripped each other hard—elation passed between them like a shock. The glimmer ahead rose from mirage to formless glow to the shine of morning.

Edmund came out last, helped by Tom. They all staggered about for a moment like a pack of drunks, then fell heaped on each other in the chilly light of an autumn dawn. When Jumble came barking up the slope, they did not even have the strength to seem surprised.

The girl from Roughy cradled her brother close—it was impossible to tell if she wept for relief or for loss. "How did you find us?"

"Tell you later." Edmund sank on his haunches. He let the sword fall from his hands. The strength of panic left him; he had very nearly died. Pins and needles shot up from his fingers and toes, then a chill and a wave of sickness. The tortured memories born of absorbing the spell circled at the edges of his thoughts, gathering in whenever he closed his eyes. Jumble came up to greet him, to lick his face and shake paws, but succeeded instead in toppling him over.

"It's not that bad." Katherine tried to shove Tom away from her leg. "Help the others first! Help Papa!"

"Stop it." Tom knocked her hand aside and felt around the edges of the wound. Katherine gasped.

"It's not that bad," said Tom.

"That's what I just said!"

"You'll be fine if we stop the bleeding." Tom looked about him. The girl from Roughy pulled off the kerchief that covered her hair and held it out.

"Thank you." Tom took it and bound the wound. Katherine winced, then sank down on her stomach. "Papa, are you hurt?"

"I think I'll survive, child." John struggled to his feet. He took hold of the board and slammed it down over the hole.

Edmund slumped back on the broken scree. The wind blew hard—clouds ripped and raced across the sky toward the sun. He looked over at his brother, then at the whippy bowshaft in his hands. "Is that my longbow?"

Geoffrey snorted. "Not anymore."

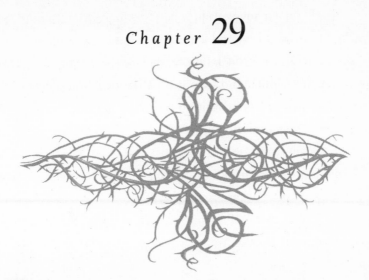

Chapter 29

There was still much to be managed. Neither triumph over Vithric nor escape from the Nethergrim would make the sides of the mountain any less steep, nor secure a safe passage through the valley below. Edmund waited with his brother at the end of the trail, at the place where they had taken off Indigo's saddle and tack. He did not even dare to shout his encouragement at the figures making the perilous traverse toward him, lest he startle them and send them tumbling down the mountainside. He learned the names of the kids from Roughy as he helped them up onto the road—Sedmey and her brother Harbert. He found himself saying that he was sorry he had not come sooner; Sedmey silenced him with a kiss on the cheek.

The sun had risen full by the time Katherine came into view, helped by her father as much as he could but still forced to make it through the worst on her own injured legs. Edmund clutched a twig and wrung it until it snapped.

She made it across in safety, though when Edmund reached down for her hand, he found her ashen gray about the face. Her father came up last, looking little better. Edmund let them lie and find their breath, but drew Tom and Geoffrey aside with a look.

"How long a march home, do you think?" He walked them to the edge of the rocks. "Three days?"

"Five at the least." Tom took a considering glance behind him at their party. "We'll need water soon. I remember seeing a river down there."

"I remember seeing a few other things when they dragged us through." Geoffrey had somewhere scrounged another arrow. "Are you sure it's safe?"

Edmund turned back to the mountain. He could hear, when he listened closely, the whisper of the Nethergrim. It seemed not so loud as before, but it was everywhere.

"A horse!" Harbert cried out from the edge of the rocks. "There's a horse coming!"

Geoffrey nocked his arrow. Tom pulled Harbert down into cover. Edmund had not the faintest idea if any spell he tried would work, so he reached for a rock. The horse sprang from the trees at a trot—riderless, pacing up through open country without the slightest show of fear.

Edmund picked his way over to the road. "Indigo!"

John Marshal's laughter made him sound almost young. "I

won't say I'm surprised." He helped his daughter to her feet. "That horse never listens to me."

Edmund knew enough to stand out of Indigo's path. There could be only one place the horse was going.

"Indigo." Katherine wrapped her arms around his neck. He put his great gray head over her shoulder, looking almost tame.

"That solves some of our marching problems." Edmund turned back to Tom and Geoffrey. "And if Indigo survived down there, so can we."

Geoffrey twirled the arrow in his fingers. "If we go soon, we might get through by sundown." He held it out to point across the valley. "We could make camp at the foot of the pass, there."

"It's a one-day trip over that on foot, give or take." Edmund tried to locate the source of the thrill he felt. "We'd be well set for the day after."

"Clear weather tomorrow." Tom glanced up at the sky, then around him. "Past that there's no telling. The sooner we're off high ground, the better."

Edmund weighed it up. "I can't see us risking less by waiting. Thornbeasts don't need to eat the way we do. If it's down there now, there's no reason to think it will be gone tomorrow."

He looked from Tom to Geoffrey, and found them nodding their assent. He knew the thrill for what it was. They had endured—they had prevailed. He knew that he should be afraid of the journey still to come, but could not bring himself to feel it.

"Master Marshal?" He stepped around Indigo's flank, giving

space for Katherine to hop past with the saddle in her arms. "Master Marshal, we've been making plans."

"I know. I heard you." John Marshal stood away from the children, turned toward the mouth of the mountain.

"Oh." Edmund waited. "Then—what do you think of them?"

John clapped a hand on his back. "I think you sound like some old friends of mine. Lead on."

They descended on the road through the first weed and scrub and then on through the scatter of bones. Edmund told the others of Rosie's last run. It did not surprise him that Katherine cried for her, or even that Tom did—but Geoffrey truly wept, long and open.

"She was a good horse, she really was." Geoffrey dried his eyes in the elbow of his sleeve. "Me and Miles used to feed her apples sometimes."

They dug out what remained of the provisions from the saddlebags, and did not halt to debate their course any longer. No matter what might lie in the valley below, be it bolgugs, the thornbeast, or Vithric himself, to linger by the mountain was to starve or die of thirst. Katherine took up each of the kids from Roughy in turn to sit in front of her and rest awhile on Indigo's broad back. She then offered to Tom, but he said he was happy to walk, while her father protested that he was too heavy to ride double with anyone. Geoffrey declined in his turn, saying he could not possibly shoot his longbow straight from horseback, after which Edmund felt he had no choice but to pass on his chance as well. It seemed terribly unfair—after all he had suffered and done, he thought he had more than earned a lazy mile in the saddle with Katherine's arms around him, even if her arms were only there to hold the reins.

Their first camp was blustery and cold. There, closer to safety than any of them had been in days or ever thought to be again, they felt in full all that they had saved and lost.

"Why Tilly?" Geoffrey hunched by the fire. He looked up at the kids from Roughy. "Why their little brother? Why them first?"

"They were the youngest; they had the most growing left to do." Edmund did something he had never done before. He put an arm around his brother's shoulders. "Geoffrey, there's something I must tell you."

He watched his brother's face crumple as he spoke—they might find their father in his grave when they came home. Geoffrey put his head in his hands, Sedmey and Harbert gave themselves up to sobbing for little Elwy, and even Katherine seemed bowed down in sorrow. It might have turned much worse from there had not John Marshal raised his hand and begun a tale that Edmund would not have believed, save that it was mostly about Edmund's own deeds. It made him blush— he could hardly hear the words by the end of it, so much did he feel Katherine's gaze on him. He took his turn to fill in the gaps, making much of John's steady guidance, and avowing that without Jumble he and John would have been too late to save anyone. Jumble got everyone's attention for a while after that, so much that he seemed to get confused and retreated to sleep in Tom's lap.

Edmund proposed they set a watch, just as he imagined the

Ten had always done. He volunteered to be first, and sat up to tend the fire wrapped in Indigo's saddle blanket. He thought for a while that everyone else had fallen asleep, but then John Marshal got to his feet and strode off to sit on a boulder.

"Master Marshal?" Edmund got the feeling he was wanted. He shrugged off the blanket and approached.

John turned half around and nodded. "Sit awhile."

Edmund sat beside him. "Aren't you tired?"

The lines crinkled in around John's eyes. "When you reach my age, you may find sleep a less-than-constant friend."

Edmund waited. John watched the mountain. Seasons came and went on his face. At last he spoke: "You are only fourteen."

"Fifteen next summer, Master Marshal."

John looked back at his sleeping daughter. "Will you guard her? Will you swear to watch over her?"

Edmund found himself expecting it. "You're not coming home with us."

"You know as well as I do this has only just begun," said John. "Vithric's spell seemed to feed the Nethergrim, somehow, to give it strength and form. I don't know how it works, but I do know that I cannot allow it to happen again."

The mountain of the Nethergrim sat silent across the valley. It would have been a blessing to drift awhile in triumph. It would have been a blessing to imagine the world restored.

Edmund tried to make some sense of all that he had learned. "Vithric must have already done the spell once before. He should be over sixty by now, but he didn't look nearly that old."

"I was told Vithric died of a wasting disease." John shifted, then winced, and bound the bandage tight around his injured hand. "He must have faked his death years ago, the first time he started to fall ill. The spell bought him a decade or two of life, and then the sickness started to consume him afresh. As I'm sure it will again, once he has lived through the years of youth he stole from Tilly and the other boy."

Edmund felt despair eating away at his victory. "Why is the world like this?" He shivered. "Why does it feel so cold, so hard?"

A smile flickered on John's face, one that was neither happy nor sad. "What would be the worth of goodness, in a world that always rewarded it?"

Edmund turned John's words over and over in his mind. He wondered for a moment if he would still feel so utterly grown up when he got back home.

"Know what I ask before you agree," said John. "I charge you to protect my daughter, to stand her friend whether or not she ever returns what you feel. Do not swear unless you understand."

"I swear it." Edmund held out his hand. John gripped it in his.

Edmund glanced back at Katherine. "When will you tell her?"

"I'll let things go as long as I can, let her feel some ease for a while. I'll try to keep it secret until I have you all down safe in Elverain."

Edmund could not help but smile. "With respect, Master

Marshal, you don't know your own daughter. She'll work out what you're thinking long before that."

He proved right, though for the next four days John Marshal would not answer Katherine's ever more worried looks. A fall of sleet came just as they reached the tunnel in the valley beyond, and frightening as the place still was, they felt tempted to stay in its shelter for a while. Tom would not allow it, though—he stepped out to test the wind and returned looking far too grim to be challenged on the subject. The sleet turned to snow by the time they reached the second arch, then to freezing rain on the long descent. They nibbled through the last of the salted meat before they came in view of Upenough, with two days' march still to go. Tom scrounged some roots, but they tasted so bad that Edmund thought starving the lesser evil. They found John's severed finger on the floor of the inn. No one knew what to do with it, so they buried it at the side of the road.

The rain let up at the edge of Thicket. They were all wet through, footsore and bedraggled, but the children skipped into the air at the sight of curling smoke from the hearths of the hamlet ahead. There was no trace of food on the wind, but the smell of hay and home fire was enough to set Edmund's stomach growling.

"Look!" Sedmey fairly shrieked it. "There's people!"

Folk came out of their houses to stare. Others turned to look in from the pastures—some of them even waved. Edmund felt certain he had never known happiness so pure. The slowly falling fear and rising hope had not prepared him for the moment—field and pasture, hedgerows and cows—home.

"Papa. Papa, don't you dare."

Edmund turned to find John Marshal walking over at the verge—bent low, as though the wind blew before him, not behind. Half a furlong ahead a trail branched south just before the road reached the first of the fields.

"Papa, you come home." Katherine's voice tore at Edmund. "Don't you dare turn off this road!"

John raised his head. "I am sorry. Child, I am."

The children stopped their march to stare at Katherine, then at John, though their first good meal in a week was a matter of yards away.

Geoffrey looked to Edmund. "He's not coming back?"

"I have been asleep too long," said John. "I have lived in that dream a man can have, where he thinks if he lives quiet and raises his children well, that the world owes him peace. Now that I better understand what the Nethergrim truly is, I must find the roots of its evil and pull them out while I can."

Katherine crossed her arms. "Then I go with you."

"I cannot allow it."

"Who says you can stop me? I've got the horse."

The children dropped their mouths wide in shock. Katherine and her father stared each other down, looking more alike than Edmund had ever seen them.

John Marshal broke first. "I was wrong to leave you the way I did back in Elverain. If I tell you where I am bound this time, will you be content to wait for me?"

"If you are marching off to some mountain somewhere, then no."

"I am not. I am going to Tristan. His lands are not so far, Katherine—king's roads all the way. Do not worry for me."

Katherine bit her lip. She blinked fast and looked away.

Her father wavered, then seemed to make an effort to master himself. "I will send word, I promise you."

Katherine scrabbled to the ground. "Then take Indigo." She offered the reins. "Please, Papa."

"He is not mine to take." John gripped her hand. "You are in Lord Aelfric's care while I am gone. He will not forsake you, whatever happens—he owes me far too much. Look to him, and to your friends, and before you know it, I'll be home again."

Katherine bowed her head. Her father embraced her, then turned to Tom. "Come. We have miles to go before we rest tonight."

Tom stepped out from the children and came to stand by John. Jumble followed at his heel. Edmund felt a moment of shock—then relief and gratitude.

Katherine's face showed none of those feelings. "You're sending me home, but you're taking Tom?"

"You have a home to which you may return," said her father. "Tom does not. If I let him go back to his master, I would be maiming him as surely as if I held the whip myself. I am taking him on to a new chance at life—I am bringing him to Tristan, in hopes he can find him a place among his household. Perhaps I should have done this long ago, but now is much better than never."

"Goodbye." Tom looked more sad than eager at the prospect. "I will miss you."

"I'll miss you, too." Edmund clasped him by the arm. "Safe journey."

Katherine seized Tom around his bony shoulders. She tried to speak, to bless him for the road, but could not seem to find words, so she held him close once more and let him go.

Tom followed John to the head of the trail. There they stood for one moment more, and then, as there was nothing left to say that would do more than prolong the ache of parting, they turned and strode away.

Geoffrey and the kids from Roughy ran onward to the houses, shouting that they needed dinner very badly and that their parents would surely pay for it. Edmund stayed with Katherine, watching her father and their friend diminish until they passed on over the farthest of the hills.

They left Sedmey and Harbert to sleep at Thicket grange, promising to send word down to their parents in the morning. The shadows grew long by the bend of Wishing Hill, throwing a shroud over cottage and tree. Katherine walked Indigo a few lengths ahead, leaving the brothers to themselves.

"Mum'll need a lot of help, if—" Geoffrey could not finish. Edmund watched night come sweeping from the east. He hoped, hoped hard, and spent a while thinking on what hope really was. He wondered whether things were fated to be, or if it only sometimes seemed that way. He wondered it all the way home.

The inn sat quiet—quiet enough that his heart misgave him. There was no one on the steps, no babble of talk through the shutters. Geoffrey crossed his arms on the road, looking very small. Katherine came down from the saddle and took his hand. Edmund drew in a breath and pushed back the door.

He found the place quiet, but not empty. A few of his neighbors sat with ales by the fire. They all stood up, like he was Lord Aelfric himself come in for an evening ale. One look at their faces told him what he had been waiting and hoping to hear. Nicky Bird started to say something, but Martin Upfield clapped a hand over his mouth and pointed upstairs.

Edmund climbed up to the bedrooms. He turned toward his parents' room first, then spied the light coming from under his own door. He pushed it back to find it made into a sickroom, his father laid out, swaddled on his pallet, and his mother bending down to tuck him in.

"If you want an ale, ask Martin—and if you want dinner, forget it." Edmund's mother had her back to him, so his father saw him first. Harman stared, one long look that said more than any words could say, then squeezed his wife's hand.

Edmund's mother turned, and nearly kicked over the lantern. Edmund had to grab her so she did not faint and fall on top of his father.

Edmund's father reached out trembling from the bed. "Going to build some shelves in here. Been thinking about it, there's some space over there. Any books you like, son. Any books."

"Mum—Mum, ow!" Edmund wriggled—her grip was almost as tight as Vithric's. "My ribs. I hurt my ribs."

MATTHEW JOBIN

"Oh, oh, my son—oh, Katherine!" Sarra met her at the door and kissed her hands. "We thought—we were so afraid."

Edmund knelt at his father's side. Harman looked pale and drawn—but whole, breathing even, the bandages wrapped around his middle clean of blood. The letter Edmund had written him lay on the pallet at his side.

"Had time to think, think hard on things, what I meant to say if—when you came home." Harman tried to prop himself up, then grimaced, and sank back. "Had time to think on it."

Edmund nodded to the door. "Tell us both."

Harman peered past him in confusion at Katherine. She stepped aside to let Geoffrey through.

Chapter 30

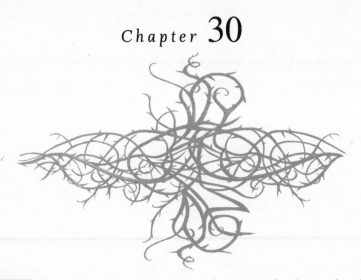

Edmund set down the jug. "That's two farthings for the table."

"Sure you won't have a sit with us awhile?" Nicky Bird slapped his back—right on the healing cut on his shoulder. "Come on, Edmund, give us the story again!"

"I told it last night—and the night before." Edmund set out the mugs around the table.

"We want to hear it good and proper, before the minstrels get wind of it and mangle it up." Martin Upfield knelt to stoke the fire. Someone proposed a brave song, a glad song, and soon after, Horsa Blackcalf started up a jig on his fiddle.

"Quit that noise, curse you!" Edmund's mother shouted from the kitchen. "My husband is sleeping up there!"

Edmund made his rounds, dodging more requests for a story or a song. He stepped out the door for a breath of air, and

found his brother sitting alone on the step, staring up at Wishing Hill and past it to the Girth.

He sat down. "What are you thinking about?"

"Home, I guess." Geoffrey looked around him. "Doesn't
seem so bad anymore."

Edmund leaned back to rest on the step. From the inn behind him came a rising roll of talk—he heard his own name
spoken once and again.

"You're going to be a wizard," said Geoffrey. "A real one."

"Of course I am." Edmund looked across at him. "It's what
I've always wanted."

Geoffrey shook his head. "It's not a question of what you
want anymore. You're going to be a wizard because that's what
we need of you."

Edmund snorted. "When did you get so grown up?" As soon
as he said it, he felt sorry—but Geoffrey only smiled.

Edmund breathed in the scent of home—turned fields and
haystacks, wood and earth. "I used to wish and dream for
something to happen, something to make me feel that my life
was a grand adventure."

Geoffrey punched his arm. "Wish granted, you twit."

"I said it to Katherine and Tom, the night Vithric stole
you and Tilly." Edmund looked up to the Girth. "I told them I
wanted to run away, to someplace with excitement and danger."
The mountains seemed to loom in, to menace and wait.

"I'm going to make you study," said Geoffrey. "You'll wish
you'd never learned to read before I'm done with you."

"And I'm going to make you practice with that bow," said Edmund. "Next time, you've got to hit him in the heart."

Horsa prevailed upon their mother to at least play one, a quiet one—and it really was good, the sort of song that stirs sad with happy and seems to hint that they are halves of a whole. The moon rose over the last fine night of the year. The warm spell that had come to bless their return was about to end—autumn would soon make its first stumble with winter ever closer on its heels. Edmund closed his eyes. The wind rushed up the lanes of the village and through the tops of the trees all around, one note of joy, of gift, of hard things done. It would have been as near to perfect as anyone could ask, were it not for the whisper he heard beneath.

THE JOURNEY CONTINUES . . .

BOOK 2, COMING
SOON!